STATE
SCARLET

———

STATE SCARLET

DAVID AARON

G. P. PUTNAM'S SONS
New York

G. P. Putnam's Sons
Publishers Since 1838
200 Madison Avenue
New York, NY 10016

Typeset by Fisher Composition, Inc.

Library of Congress Cataloging-in-Publication Data

Aaron, David.
State scarlet.

I. Title.
PS3551.A6S7   1987   813'.54   86-25391
ISBN 0-399-13243-0

To my Mother,
who taught me to write,
and to
Chloe and Tim,
who made it possible.

2.1.4: There are four stages of strategic alert: Condition Blue, Condition Yellow, State Orange, and State Scarlet . . . State Scarlet is declared by the National Security Council when a nuclear attack upon the United States or its Allies is considered imminent. The President's authority to initiate the use of nuclear weapons is thereby predelegated to the Unified and Specified Commanders. . . .

—JSOP/81-N *Nuclear Employment Policy and Procedures*

I. SATURDAY

I

After a sleepless night, Terence Culver placed two calls. The first went to the White House, the second to Horst Bauer. He dialed direct from a small booth in the Bundespost office across from the railway station in Hamburg.

The receipt from the stout woman at the cashier's counter stated that the call to Washington, D.C., had taken one minute and 49.17 seconds, and the subsequent one to Munich only 14.87 seconds. The tall, red-haired young man folded the receipt carefully into his American passport and stepped outside onto the walkway that arched over the street to the train station.

It was just after six o'clock on a hard, gray Saturday morning. The station was empty except for a group of Turks huddled around an alcohol burner making their morning coffee. Culver walked briskly to the first of three yellow telephone booths next to a shuttered wurst stand. He picked up the phone as soon as it rang.

"Horst?"

"Yes."

"It's done."

"Finally. When?" Bauer's voice was still thick with sleep.

"Just now. But I'm not sure they believed me."

"It doesn't matter, just so long as you've made up your mind." He suppressed a yawn. "If they don't respond, we simply set it off. That will accomplish our objective also."

Culver was silent.

"You have it with you?" Bauer asked.

"It's safe," Culver replied. "Listen, you have to find Graciela. They'll be turning the base upside down."

"I'll take care of her."

"And I want our part of the deal now."

"We meet as planned." Bauer hung up.

Culver put the receiver back slowly. He suddenly felt very tired. Above his head, the ARRIVALS and DEPARTURES whirred and clicked on a large, black board. The Mozart Express for Munich and Vienna was on Platform 10. Ticket in hand, he boarded a second-class compartment. By the time the train pulled out, at six-fifteen, he had already fallen into a heavy and troubled sleep.

2

Seven hours later, in Washington, D.C., the early morning sun flooded into the living room of the President's private quarters, an additional floor on top of the White House that is concealed by the balustrade that runs around the roof. The Assistant to the President for National Security Affairs, Dr. Karl Loggerman, was drinking coffee and eating a croissant while the President, still in his pajamas, skimmed the morning Intelligence folder.

The room had been furnished by the previous President like a modern California ranch home. Loggerman always winced inwardly at the incongruity of sitting in a room that belonged in Santa Barbara and looking through sliding glass doors at the Washington Monument. It was a civilization away from the stately, Federal-style rooms downstairs that the world knew as the White House.

The President chewed an unlit cigar and said little. A half-finished glass of orange juice was balanced precariously on the arm of his overstuffed chair. Other White House staff members wandered around the room talking and eating breakfast from a small buffet. In the four months since the new President had assumed office, Saturday morning breakfast had become a ritual. Some had driven an hour through the morning darkness, not for camaraderie, but to be there for the status and the presumed power. They waited on a word from the President, even a gesture, which might provide the upper hand in a battle with a Cabinet officer or a congressional leader. An anecdote from the President was a meal ticket that could be punched in Washington for months—or years, if need be.

Loggerman sat next to the President and carefully picked flakes of croissant off his vest. Unlike the others, he always dressed formally, that morning wearing narrow Italian pinstripes which he thought concealed his paunch and made him look taller than his five and a half feet.

"I see our grateful friends in Saudi Arabia are going to stick it in our ear again," the President said, stretching.

"Looks like it, Mr. President," said Loggerman.

The President put down the CIA daily briefing and leafed through the State Department overnight summary and the Defense Department situation reports. Loggerman shifted around in his hard, upright chair. He hated performing his morning national security briefing in front of the political hacks.

"What's this?"

"I thought you might be interested in that, Mr. President," said Loggerman, glancing around the room, "but I think we should discuss it only in private."

The murmur of acquiescence did not disguise the resentment of the other White House aides as they were herded out of the room. Loggerman overheard the Press Spokesman saying, "I know national security is an awesome responsibility, but sometimes I think Loggerman is just too big for the job." Only the Chief of the Secret Service Detail remained behind.

Loggerman was gratified. Access to secrets bestowed prerogatives that he enjoyed exercising. He often raised sensitive subjects, as he did that morning, merely to gain private time with the President. He knew that, despite the resentment of his colleagues, this strategy also increased his power and their respect for his authority.

The President read the transcript of a telephone call that had come into the White House the night before.

MISS MARCOT: Dr. Loggerman's office.
VOICE: Listen carefully. I am in possession of one of your nuclear weapons, and I want to talk to Dr. Log—
MISS MARCOT: Can you hold a sec?
VOICE: Wait—
SIT ROOM D.O.:   Duty Officer.
MISS MARCOT: Jack, I've got a weirdo on the line, and I'm up to my eyeballs.
D.O.:   Why don't you just put him on hold, as usual?
MISS MARCOT: I'm waiting for a call and Loggerman is [deleted] on the other line because he can't find his limo. Please, Jack.
D.O.:   I'll take care of it.
MISS MARCOT: You are a dear.
D.O.:   Hello?
VOICE: Who's this?
D.O.:   White House Situation Room, Senior Duty Officer.
VOICE: I want to talk to Dr. Loggerman personally.
D.O.:   It's practically midnight. Who's calling?
VOICE: Well, okay. I have a statement to make. I hope you will take it seriously. I am in possession of a nuclear weapon from the United States Atomic Stockpile. There is no PAPS associated with the weapon and I am in a position to fire it without a Release Hour Message, the Permissive Action Link Codes, or an Authenticator. If you don't know what I'm talking about, Dr. Loggerman will. I will contact him in twenty-four hours about the next step in this operation. If you have any doubts about the seriousness of this call, you can use that time to confirm that the weapon is missing.
   [end transcript]

"What the hell is this?" the President asked sharply. For the first time that morning he seemed fully awake.

"There's nothing to be alarmed about. We immediately checked with the Pentagon, and they assured us that there are no reported incidents or problems. In fact, I asked for a brief report on how we keep track of these weapons, and I thought you might find it interesting to look at . . ."

The President pulled a blue folder out of Loggerman's hand. As he went slowly through the three-page report, the lines around his eyes deepened. "Am I supposed to be comforted by this?" he finally asked. "Behind the soothing B.S., doesn't it basically say that no one really knows where *every* weapon is *all* the time?"

"No, no, of course not. I mean, of course we do." Loggerman tried to regain the initiative. "The report simply points out what it means to have tens of thousands of nuclear weapons, and to keep track of them all. And it's a matter of definition," Loggerman added, sliding into his professional lecturer's voice. "There are operational weapons, weapons in test, devices in development, weapons in various stages of maintenance, repair, assembly, disassembly; and of course there are spare parts. No one person could know where that many items are at all times, but we can assume they are all someplace in the system. A computer could keep track—and does—but of course it only knows what it's told. Like any large inventory—"

"You mean we're going to write off one of our atomic bombs as *inventory shrinkage?*"

"No, Mr. President, certainly not." Loggerman had stopped eating. The crumbs had collected in his lap. "This caller is undoubtedly a crank," he said slowly, trying to be reassuring. "There's no evidence whatsoever that any weapons are missing. He's obviously picked up some classified jargon about the Permissive Action and Authentication system, but anyone can get that from watching PBS. If he really had a weapon, he would've read us the serial number."

"Maybe." The President paused. "But what if he doesn't think like you, Dr. Loggerman? What if he doesn't want to make it too easy for us? What if he wants to buy time to get away? What if we're making a mistake in not taking this call seriously?"

"I didn't bring this up in order to create concern, Mr. President. Quite the reverse. I thought you would like to see how effectively things of this magnitude are handled. As you know, the Secret Service gets a hundred calls a week saying that someone's going to take a shot at you. For ten years they've just been empty threats."

The President turned to the Chief of his Secret Service Detail.

"Chuck, what would you do if you received an anonymous threat like that against me?"

"Dr. Loggerman's right. We do get such calls all the time, Mr. President, but we've got to treat every one of them seriously. It could mean your life."

Looking at Loggerman, the President said softly, "If this guy's not a crank, it could mean a lot more than my miserable life." He began ranging around the room, waving the soggy cigar, and running his fingers through his longish hair. Loggerman felt a speech about to come from the President. When that happened, he had learned to wait him out.

"The damnable thing is that we are going to have to live with these weapons until eternity, unless we do something foolish to end eternity. I wanted to be President so I could do something for this country and hopefully for the world. I want to turn back this nuclear madness. But the only power that's mine alone is to push the button and end the human race. And now, before I can even sit down and talk with the Russians, I find out that maybe there's some crank, or some terrorist, or some crazy person who's planning to push it first. What will happen then? A nuclear war?"

"I really don't think that's the situation here," Loggerman said simply. He recognized fragments of rhetoric from the recent campaign.

"I have repeatedly been told"—the President's voice kept rising—"that all these weapons are under control. But what does that really mean?"

"We have a system with double and triple guarantees that's worked for over four decades," Loggerman said evenly, concealing his impatience. "The briefing paper from the Pentagon spells that out pretty—"

"It doesn't reassure me. You say we can 'assume' that all the weapons are in the 'system,' but if you read between the lines," he tossed the folder back at Loggerman, "we really have no system to tell us whether this caller is bullshitting us or not.

"I've no doubt the military's been conscientious," the President suddenly conceded. "But there's nothing in the world that's foolproof. And I'm not saying that the threat is true. God forbid. It just seems to me that we ought to be able to prove that this person is wrong. We're dealing with the most fundamental responsibility of the presidency, and I want to be absolutely certain!"

"What would you like me to do?" Loggerman had decided to stop fighting. It also had dawned on him that the President's concern might even prove useful.

"I think we ought to do as our caller suggests. I want the Pentagon to go through the nuclear stockpile and make positively sure that not one weapon is missing. If it's a hoax, they waste some time and money. It wouldn't be the first time."

"This could take a while, Mr. President."

"Dr. Loggerman, our mysterious caller has given us twenty-four hours. Wouldn't it be nice to know if he's bluffing before he phones back? Don't let the Pentagon put us on hold."

3

As the small elevator sank from the President's private quarters to the White House basement, a sense of opportunity welled up in Karl Loggerman. He walked briskly down the heavily vaulted hallway past the row of portraits of first ladies and out onto the portico that led to the West Wing offices. The Rose Garden to his left was pregnant with spring buds of tulip, hyacinth, and flowering apple. Pulling open the glass door and climbing a ramp, he glanced into the empty White House Press Room where years before he had tried and failed to become an accredited correspondent.

Loggerman had floated on the fringes of power for almost three decades. He had been the archetype of a proliferating breed in Washington: the foreign policy experts, the strategic thinkers, the intelligence specialists—outriders of government who are not really scholars, not exactly journalists, not legally lobbyists, but self-made figments of each.

Prior to being named National Security Advisor, Karl Loggerman had been a senior fellow at the American Institute for Strategic Studies, which merely meant that he got an office, a desk, and unlimited local telephone calls. He kept his name before the public with doom-laden articles in publications ranging from journals like *Public Inter-*

est to newspapers such as *The Washington Times*. He was noted for pithy testimony before congressional committees, snappy, sound bites on the nightly TV news, and provocative lectures on the rubber-chicken circuit. But he stayed alive on consultancies from US government agencies and from large foreign and domestic corporations. An acolyte on the margins of the American and allied intelligence communities, he also occasionally accepted lucrative commissions from obscure research institutes for highly unspecific tasks.

Every three years or so, Dr. Loggerman would produce a book with the word "strategy," or "power," or "challenge" in the title. Because his doctorate was honorary, he keenly felt the need to constantly burnish his intellectual credentials. His thesis on "Bureaucratic Politics and the Bay of Pigs" had been rejected by his graduate advisor at Princeton as "a form of higher gossip."

An effort to recover academic legitimacy by joining the intellectually prestigious RAND Corporation foundered when he accepted an advance to write a novel. Already unhappy with Loggerman's tendency to "get creative" when he lacked the facts, his Director, Dr. James Thomson, announced in a memorandum to the staff that "Mr. Loggerman will now be devoting himself to the writing of fiction full-time."

Regardless of what his academic colleagues thought of him, Loggerman's political ambitions were not to be denied. He read the newspapers each morning less for news than to know who to call. On the Hill, in the agencies, and with the press, he traded his own insights for the inside story. He was a regular at foreign policy conferences from Bilderberg to Aspen, always swapping rumors about who was on top, who was emerging, and who fading on the political scene. For over twenty years, almost every potential presidential candidate in both political parties had been bombarded by his memos and position papers. He prided himself on having a sixth sense about politics, often spotting presidential timber long before the Washington press corps. And he now had a premonition that this incident, this lunatic phone call, could prove fateful to the President and to himself.

Loggerman passed the Cabinet Room and then the Oval Office on the way to his corner suite of rooms at the end of the corridor. Without greeting his secretary and staff assistants, he walked into his office and closed the door behind him. A blue light over the door blinked on to warn against disturbing him.

Inside, Loggerman suppressed the impulse to start pushing buttons and calling meetings. He believed that too many of his predecessors had failed because they merely reacted. This was an opportunity that had to be thought through. He sat in the heavy leather chair near the fireplace and rang for coffee from the White House Mess. His secretary had anticipated his needs; it was already on the way.

Loggerman leaned back. He closed his eyes against the bright light that poured through the tall windows of the office, making it hard for him to concentrate. He was reflecting on one of the cardinal rules he had developed years before in a monograph on White House leadership. After the first few months in office, the character of a presidency was essentially fixed unless there were an enormous upheaval or crisis. He had already concluded that the new Administration, his own, was a mess. No one was in charge. It needed a crisis to pull itself together.

A Filipino dressed in a blue blazer with the seal of the President on the breast pocket came in carrying a tray with Loggerman's special decaffeinated French roast coffee from Fortnum and Mason in London. The waiter struggled with the tray while trying to clear a space among the magazines. Lost in thought, the National Security Advisor paid no attention.

He was remembering how, like everyone else in Washington, he had been surprised when the President rocketed into the White House after only four years as a Senator, propelled by the public trust gained as a network news anchorman. Most of Washington assumed, wrongly, that Loggerman was often on television, he and the President were close, both somehow being in the media. It was an impression Loggerman fostered by being casually critical. Only the night before he had enjoyed shocking the guests at a dinner party in Georgetown by proclaiming that his friend, the President, had only two shortcomings—he had no political base, and he had no idea where the country should be heading. Loggerman admitted that, in domestic policy, a few obvious and urgent things had been done; but in foreign policy, he openly complained, there was paralysis.

He shook his head at how confident he had been that he would dominate the "clowns" on the National Security Council. On Inauguration Day, instead of attending the swearing-in ceremony, he had watched it on TV from the White House Situation Room while he prepared an ambush for the rest of the NSC members. When the new Secretaries-designate of State and Defense returned to their offices from the ceremony on the Capitol steps, they found a stack of directives on their desks that put Loggerman in control of the National Security Council machinery in the name of the President.

At first, his stratagems worked. He ordered studies of new policy options on everything from Arms Control to Zimbabwe to knock the bureaucrats off balance and bury them in paperwork. He broke up old bureaucratic alliances by arbitrarily changing standard operating procedures and naming himself to head key interagency committees. He instilled fear and uncertainty by pushing through personnel cuts in the State Department, the Arms Control Agency, and the CIA.

But now he was stymied. The President was extremely cautious in foreign affairs. Without his constant backing, the bureaucrats in State and Defense and the Intelligence Agencies could still tell Loggerman to go to hell, and often did. Increasingly, they did so even when he had the President's support.

He got up from his seat by the fireplace and poured a second cup of coffee. His eyes fixed vacantly on the gray-and-green geometry of the Josef Albers that hung over the mantel. The threat of a missing nuclear weapon would be the first major test of the Administration and his first opportunity to exert real control. Whether a nuclear weapon actually had been stolen was almost irrelevant.

This was his chance to put the Pentagon, his biggest headache, on a short leash. Managing the State Department was like nailing Jell-O to a wall. But trying to move Defense was like running into the wall itself. The President was pressing to start arms talks with the Soviet Union, and Loggerman could not even get Assistant Secretaries of Defense to come to meetings. If he could control Defense, he could then cope more easily with the aggressive young Secretary of State, who was constantly running off and trying to make foreign policy on his own.

Loggerman concluded that the Secretary of Defense must be his first target. As he reached for the phone on the coffee table, he glanced at his gold antique Girard Perregaux wristwatch. It was 8:32 A.M. Loggerman smiled at the possibility he might catch the Secretary of Defense still in bed.

4

Continuing scandals over three-hundred-dollar Allen wrenches and ten-thousand-dollar coffee pots had resulted, at last, in the appointment of a Secretary of Defense who knew something about the Pentagon's principal peacetime activity—purchasing. Formerly the CEO of a major discount department store conglomerate that provided one-stop shopping for everything from hide-a-beds to stock index futures, the Secretary's own personal taste was unashamedly upmarket: good brandy, good cigars, and what he called good talk. But the night before he had enjoyed too much of all three. He had smoked a Davidoff Château Margaux down to a stub while sitting until 2 A.M. on the French Ambassador's comfortable white sofa discussing the cultural values underlying the differences between European and American tax codes.

Now, blinded by the pain of running into the edge of the closet door, he was fumbling with the combination of the small safe that housed his secure phone.

The White House operator had hounded him out of a profound sleep to insist that it was urgent to call the National Security Advisor on the secure line. Unfortunately, the scrambler codes on his home phone had to be changed each day, and the Defense Secretary was totally inexpert at doing so. He had to get into the safe, open a rack of equipment, then locate and insert the correct new punch card. It was too much for the Secretary's brandy-swollen fingers and throbbing head. The cards fell all over the floor.

"Lieutenant! Lieutenant!" he yelled for his security detail. "For Christ's sake, come and fix the phone." His wife pulled the covers over her head.

Three minutes later, still standing in the closet in his underwear, he got through to Loggerman.

"Mr. Secretary, did I wake you up?"

"No, Karl, you didn't."

"Are you sitting down?"

"Yes, I am." He sat down on a small stool that he used for putting on his shoes.

"We've got something here that I would really appreciate your help on. The President might be a little off the deep end on this, but I think you can satisfy him. As you probably know, the National Military Command Center did that report on this threat that came into the White House last night and—"

"What report? What threat?"

"You haven't seen it? Well, someone called and claimed that they'd stolen a nuclear weapon. There're no reported incidents or problems. I think the whole thing's nonsense, and I told the President as much. But he's deeply disturbed by it, so much so that he wants you to double-check . . ."

"Oh God, Karl, there can't be any problem. That's the first thing I'd be notified about. If there's any suspicion of a glitch in the stockpile, I'm supposed to be told right away. So are you. So what does he want?"

"He wants to be reassured. I tried my best, but you're the only one who can really do that."

The implied compliment only made the Secretary more stubborn. "He's already got a report from the NMCC. You and I have discussed our command and control arrangements dozens of times. Some nut calls in and now—"

"Let me put it as simply as I can," Loggerman continued. "The President wants to know whether there's a weapon missing, and he isn't going to be satisfied if you tell him none's been reported AWOL. He wants you to go and find out what's going on."

"You mean he wants a two-man, on-site eyeball inspection of every damn nuclear weapon?"

"That's exactly what I think the President wants, and I don't believe he's going to accept anything less."

"That's a major military operation, and it's nuts. Our military readiness will drop to zero! You can't pull an inventory and conduct business at the same time. Believe me, I know. I was in retailing."

"Let me advise you he's pretty hot on this, and also about what he regards as a certain lack of responsiveness by your Department across the board."

"I'm not going to take military orders from the National Security Advisor, that's got to come from the Commander-in-Chief."

"Of course, you may talk to him directly. But keep in mind, I'm on your side."

"I'm calling the President."

As he hung up the phone, Loggerman checked the video monitor on his credenza that continually displayed the President's whereabouts. It indicated that he was in the small study off the Oval Office. Loggerman walked quickly down the hall to a door where a Secret Service agent stood with his arms folded. By stepping on an almost imperceptible lump in the carpet, Loggerman opened the door and passed through a pantry and into the study. The President was just about to pick up a blinking green phone.

"Excuse me, Mr. President, but if that's the Secretary of Defense, we should talk first."

"Tell him to hold on." The President put the receiver back in the cradle.

"I've just talked to him. It's the same old story of Pentagon footdragging. He hasn't even seen the NMCC report, but he refuses to check it out further. I think you need to yank his chain. He says he's not taking orders from anyone but you."

"I'll take care of this." He pushed a button, and the Defense Secretary's voice came over a small speaker on the desk.

"Mr. President, I've just spoken to Karl Loggerman and I want to assure you that there can be no problem of the sort he talked about."

"Karl tells me that you haven't even received the report on last night's incident." Loggerman winced.

"Well." The Secretary paused. "That's just my point. If there had been a problem, I'm sure I would have gotten a report."

It was the President's turn to pause. When he spoke, his voice was low and intense. "Maybe you and I have a different opinion as to whether this is a serious matter, but why don't we just regard it as an exercise. Let's pretend I'm the President of the United States and that, for whatever reason, I'd like positive assurance within twenty-four hours that none of our weapons is missing."

"It just won't work," the Secretary replied, ignoring the President's sarcasm. "First, it will cripple our military posture. Second, it will probably leak to the press. There'll be mass hysteria if people think a nuclear weapon is missing. We could have an enormous crisis over nothing."

"I'm not going to be pushed around by the threat of leaks," the President exploded. "Who is in charge of our nuclear stockpile?"

"The Director of the Defense Nuclear Agency. I'm sure he'll tell you the same—"

"Well, why don't the two of you meet me right here in an hour and a half, and we'll talk about it." The President clicked off.

The Secretary of Defense leaned back against the clothes hanging in his closet and shut his eyes.

5

Admiral Carstin "Chip" McCollough was pouring a second cup of fresh-brewed coffee in the galley of his forty-two-foot sloop, *Fusion*. It was one of those brilliant spring weekends in Washington, with the forsythia in bloom and the magnolias beginning to burst, when McCollough liked to slip away from the Defense Nuclear Agency to take a solitary weekend sail on the Chesapeake.

He was staring out the porthole at the neighboring boat that also had spent the night in Tuckerwill inlet on the Eastern shore of Maryland. It had just weighed anchor and was departing on the rising tide. McCollough was glad to see it go. The boat had arrived in the middle of the night and run aground, while the crew got drunk, played loud music, and carried on like they were having an orgy until past midnight. He was also happy they were leaving because he could then proceed with his morning ritual.

McCollough finished his coffee on deck. He stripped naked, then tied a rope to a bucket and tossed it overboard. Hauling it up, he held the bucket over his head and let the ice-cold water spill over his body. He dried himself with a huge terrycloth blanket. Still naked, he went to the stern and pushed the wooden seat out over the side. A converted racing boat, *Fusion* had no head. McCollough did not regard it a chore, but rather a refreshing act of nature to hike himself over the water to go to the toilet.

Suddenly, he heard the whomping sound of rotating helicopter blades. Frozen in place, he looked up to see a white-and-red-striped Coast Guard Sea Stallion rising over the spit of land between Tuckerwill inlet and the Chesapeake. A young ensign with a bullhorn leaned out of the open door. "If you are Admiral McCollough, you are to return immediately with us on the highest priority. Yes, Admiral, you can get dressed first."

As the helicopter approached a small asphalt landing pad discreetly located on the lawn between the Pentagon and Interstate 395, Mc-Collough was amazed to see a long black Cadillac limousine waiting for him. The pilot had told him nothing, except that he had orders directly from the Secretary of Defense to bring him back to the Pentagon. "Has the balloon gone up?" McCollough had asked. "What's our Defense Condition?"

"There's no military alert, Admiral, except for you," the pilot had replied.

McCollough zipped up his windbreaker and jumped down from the helicopter, instinctively crouching to avoid the blades whirling above his head. The left rear door of the limousine was held open by the driver. Climbing inside, he was surprised to find the Secretary of Defense.

"Hello, Chip, if I may call you that. Sorry to break up your weekend like this," the Secretary said in his most affable Chairman-of-the-Board manner, "but the President is concerned over something that I think you can help put him at ease about."

"What's happened? I haven't been in touch with my office—"

"I don't think your office would know anything about this, either." The car pulled smoothly onto the Interstate, quickly changed lanes through the light Saturday traffic in the mixing bowl, and headed for the 14th Street bridge. "Some crank called the White House last night claiming to have one of our nuclear weapons. There's absolutely no sign of any problem anywhere, but the President is exercised about it. I think it's important that he be reassured that the stockpile is fully under control and that we have all the necessary safeguards in place. I want you to brief him fully. We'll be at the White House in five minutes."

In his entire career, McCollough had never been to the White House or met a President. He looked down at his paint-stained pants and deck shoes. He had no socks.

"He's threatening," continued the Secretary, staring all the while out the window at the Potomac river, "actually, he's *insisting* that we pull a full-scale physical inventory of the whole stockpile." He turned to McCollough, "That's clearly excessive, isn't it?"

"Well, it would be one hell of a problem."

"That's what I told him!"

"How long would we have to do it? A month? Two would be better."

"He wants it in less than twenty-four hours."

"We've never done that before!"

"Don't tell the President that, Admiral."

6

After weaving through the concrete antiterrorist barricades at the southwest gate, the Secretary's car let them off at the basement entrance to the West Wing. The Secretary pushed through a cluster of young White House aides dressed in Saturday's unofficial uniform: blue blazers, dark gray slacks, and penny loafers. Their animated talk stopped as they stood inside to let McCollough through. Once inside the double doors, the Admiral followed the Secretary down a narrow corridor to the left and then back up a flight of stairs, passing a woman in a gray silk dress and Hermès scarf who paused to glance at Mc-Collough's bare ankles. He despised vanity, but he could not have felt more out of place if he were dressed like the American-Indian chiefs in the engraved portraits that lined the stairway walls.

They emerged on the main floor and walked down a short hallway with a row of small offices on the right. On the opposite side, Mc-Collough caught a glimpse of a large conference room hung with portraits of Theodore and Franklin Roosevelt. Where the hall curved to the left, they passed a Secret Service man standing on the right and entered the next door.

It was a tiny reception room, empty except for a desk and a couch. Through a wall of French doors, McCollough could see the Rose Garden. The President's Appointments Secretary materialized out of a small cubbyhole and led them into the Oval Office.

McCollough was struck by the President's rough and strong hand-shake, and impressed that he looked into his eyes and not at his clothes. He was waved into a brocaded wingback chair on one side of the fireplace. The President took the matching chair opposite, and the Secretary of Defense sat on the love seat between them.

Before the President could speak, a hidden door opened in the wall and a short, balding man carrying a red folder entered the room.

"Admiral, you know Dr. Loggerman," the President made the intro-duction. The National Security Advisor looked at McCollough as if he should give up his seat, but after an awkward moment he drew over another chair.

"I expect you've been briefed," the President began, "but let me tell you my side of the story. I'm deeply concerned about the possibility of a missing nuclear weapon. I've listened to my other advisors," he gestured toward Loggerman and the Defense Secretary, "and they are all very reassuring.

"I realize the odds are that this caller is nothing but a crank. Lord knows there are enough lunatics in the world. But that's my worry. Karl tells me there are now more than fifty thousand nuclear weapons on both sides. How long before the odds catch up to us? I can't shake the feeling that we might not know if a weapon had been stolen."

McCollough searched the President's face. He detected no hidden agenda. "It's something I've always worried about, too," he said quietly.

The Secretary of Defense just stared.

"We always have to assume," McCollough continued, "that something could go wrong, that somehow our security could be breached. Otherwise, we might fail to take every conceivable precaution. I agree with you that the absence of any reported incident may be meaningless. This leaves us with two choices: We can find out if an atomic weapon is missing by holding an inventory as you have ordered, or we can rely on the fact that our safeguards make the claim implausible, if not impossible. Even so, an inventory would make sense if it were cost-free."

"Money's not important here."

"Of course," McCollough agreed. "But as I'm sure the Secretary has explained, it's an enormous undertaking. We've got nuclear weapons at more than a thousand places all over the world from Greenland to Guam. We've got weapons scattered all over Europe and the States. We've got them aboard ships in every corner of the globe. It would be almost impossible to keep a crash inventory secret, and you know better than I the political costs if the story gets out. Let me also add that one of the immeasurable risks is that such an effort could be so disruptive that it might, by itself, jeopardize the security of the weapons stockpile.

"So, when you weigh all that against the remote possibility that a weapon could be stolen secretly, a rush inspection doesn't seem warranted. That's the case I think the Secretary is trying to make," McCollough concluded.

The President opened a humidor on the coffee table in front of him and took out a large cigar. "Shirley MacLaine carried a big box of these Cohibas back from Cuba as a gift from Fidel Castro. I was very grateful to her until I found out from the CIA that Castro had sent *two* boxes." Everyone but Loggerman laughed.

The President chewed on the cigar without lighting it. "I've been briefed at great length on how to start a nuclear war, but never about a situation like this. You say, Admiral, that the chance of a weapon being stolen secretly is remote." His tone turned suddenly tough. "Well, persuade me." He stood up. "We'll walk while you talk. Don't be afraid to identify places where there might be slippage. Then I want to show you something."

As the President and the Admiral stepped out onto the terrace of the Rose Garden, Loggerman and the Defense Secretary were caught off guard, not knowing whether they were invited on the walk or not. Then they both sprang from their chairs—Loggerman, ever sensitive to protocol, giving way to avoid a collision at the door. On the steps they passed a Secret Service agent talking into his shirt cuff—"We have a movement, we have a movement"—and caught up to the President and McCollough on the path down to the main driveway. The Secretary fell in behind them while Loggerman took to the grass to be next to the President.

"There are two major aspects," McCollough was saying, "physical security and personnel security. They're tied together by the two-man rule, which is the foundation of our entire program.

"No single individual is ever left alone with a nuclear weapon, even for a moment. All of the weapons are constantly under some form of custody by at least two officers. They watch the weapons and they watch each other. They're armed and they're authorized to shoot to kill to prevent anyone, including their partners, from taking any unauthorized action with a weapon."

"This still puts a premium on quality people."

"Yes, sir. We use the most extensive, exhaustive, and state-of-the-art psychological tests to weed out potential unreliables. And we keep on testing all the time to make sure that undesirable personality changes don't develop. All of our people are required to report on one another as a basic principle of security."

"How many of these people turn out to be security risks?" The President stopped on a small rise overlooking the South Lawn and the Ellipse. Tourists waiting to visit the White House were lined up along the tall wrought-iron fence. The Washington Monument stood crisply against the bright blue morning sky. Loggerman and the Secretary clustered around. Four Secret Service agents stood guard from a discreet distance away.

"I wouldn't call them security risks exactly," McCollough replied, "but approximately one thousand custodial personnel each year are transferred or otherwise relieved of duty because of infractions of the rules, emotional or other behavioral problems."

"How many is that again?" Loggerman broke in.

"About a thousand," the Defense Secretary repeated. "But that's because the program's so strict. These aren't crazy people or criminals. Virtually all of them continue to serve honorably in the Armed Forces."

"But they're already handling our bombs," the President countered. "They've passed all your tests, and then you still find something wrong."

"Mr. President, guarding nuclear weapons three-hundred sixty-five days a year is very stressful business," the Secretary said.

"I'll bet it is. I'm beginning to feel it myself. Karl, how many people a year have their top-secret clearances pulled?"

"I don't know the exact number, but it's not more than a handful."

"That's quite a difference." The President gazed thoughtfully at the Potomac river gleaming on the horizon. Then he waved his cigar at McCollough to continue as he set off across the grass, his advisors spread out on either side. Loggerman could feel the wetness from the lawn beginning to seep through the glove-leather of his Italian loafers.

"Physical security has two parts"—McCollough was trying to keep his presentation organized—"the protection of our Special Ammunition Storage sites, SAS sites as we call them, and then there are the safety systems for the individual weapons.

"The SAS sites are strongly fortified compounds surrounded by double electrified fences, mine fields, bunkers with heavy automatic weapons, and so on. They are equipped with a variety of sophisticated sensors—infrared, millimeter-wave, acoustic—that can detect any attempt at intrusion. We've even got seismic devices that warn of anyone trying to dig a tunnel into the compound. The SAS sites can hold off a battalion-sized attack, by themselves, for at least four hours."

"That won't stop the Russians."

"No, but it'll handle any likely terrorists until help can arrive. Actually, most of our biggest stockpile sites are even more secure, because they're located inside other major military installations.

"Then there are the systems that protect the weapons from unauthorized use. I assume you're aware of the Permissive Action Link system?" McCollough glanced over at Loggerman.

"Those are the codes that are carried around by your military aide in the doomsday 'football,'" Loggerman explained. The President nodded.

"Unfortunately," McCollough continued, "these PALs sometimes are nothing more than combination locks. On some of our older weapons, the PALs are just padlocks."

"So after all this mumbo jumbo about Codes, and Release Messages, and Authenticators"—the President stopped again and turned on the Secretary of Defense—"in the end it comes down to some guy spinning the dial on a padlock he could pry off with a crowbar?"

"That's very uncommon," the Secretary responded. "Isn't it, Admiral?" It was not a question.

"Yes, but this *is* one of the slippery areas. In fact, most of the weapons deployed with our troops don't have PALs, PAPs, or any kind of physical locks. We just rely on the two-man rule."

"Why's that?" The President's voice sounded incredulous, but he smiled and waved at the tourists who had begun snapping pictures. The Secret Service started moving toward the fence.

Loggerman broke in. "Originally, these PALs and PAPs were invented for the weapons we deploy with our allies, to make sure they can't use them without US authorization. Our military considers it an affront to their loyalty and discipline to have locks on their own weapons."

"There's a practical reason, too," the Secretary added. "They figure that in a real war, none of this complicated rigmarole will work. By the time all these coded PAPs and PALs and Authenticators are sent back and forth and unscrambled, they say the Russians will overrun our weapons."

"Knowing how the Pentagon operates, they've got a point," the President said, with a final wave to the crowd. "So, that's the type of weapon our mystery caller claims he's got?" The President gestured to Loggerman to give McCollough the red folder he still carried. "Admiral, tell me, what d'you think?"

McCollough read the transcript of the call as they started walking again toward a stand of trees near the southeast gate.

"Well, he knows what he's talking about," McCollough said uneasily.

"How many other people would be as knowledgeable?" Loggerman asked.

"For starters, just about every one of the thousand people we wash out of the program each year."

"That must be what it is," the Secretary pushed forward. "Some malcontent, upset because he's been drummed out of the corps. Simple as that."

"Simple if he doesn't have a nuclear weapon," the President added.

"Mr. President, can I tell you a story about the original atom bomb program, the Manhattan Project?"

The President nodded. The Defense Secretary fell back in behind them.

"It may have been the largest single effort in the history of mankind, and a security man's nightmare. Thousands of scientists; twenty-five thousand engineers; one hundred twenty thousand construction workers; five universities across the United States; a half dozen laboratories in the US, England, and Canada; thirty major corporations; two new cities, Los Alamos, New Mexico, and Oak Ridge, Tennessee; almost half the electric output of the Tennessee Valley Authority; a billion dollars a year; and all top secret.

"Only four members of the Congress knew. General MacArthur was kept in the dark. Vice President Truman was never told. But the scale of the project, not to mention the rush, meant that security would inevitably be compromised. In the end, the Germans knew, the Russians knew, even the Japanese and the French knew. The atom bomb came as a surprise only to the American people.

"We're up against the same kind of problem," McCollough concluded, "and you've put your finger on it—it's the law of large numbers. We've got so many weapons and so many people handling them that the laws of probability say that someday, somehow, something could go wrong."

They had arrived at the foot of a huge, old oak tree. A network of steel cables helped support its ancient limbs. Only a few new leaves struggled forth from its farthest branches. It swayed majestically in the soft spring breeze.

"Now let me tell you a story," the President said, his voice taking on the color of a network anchorman. "This old oak is from the original hardwood forest that covered the whole Atlantic seaboard when the colonists first came to America. The tree was already big when the White House was built, and survived when the British burned it down in 1813. It was here when Andrew Jackson threw his famous inauguration party, and when the States went to war against one another, and when Lincoln was assassinated. It shaded Woodrow Wilson and Franklin Roosevelt as they were dying, and witnessed Richard Nixon's humiliating farewell.

"Every President has come to hold this tree in trust, as he does the nation. Someday both may die. But I intend to pass them on to my successor alive."

Without waiting for a reaction, the President set off alone toward the White House. At the Diplomatic entrance, he stopped and checked his watch. Catching up to him, McCollough could hear the sound of excited young voices and looked over to see the Rose Garden filling up with children in wheelchairs.

"Well, gentlemen, what are your recommendations?" The President bit off the soggy end of the cigar and put the dry stub in his mouth.

The Secretary of Defense was eager to speak. His words came in short gasps from the effort of the walk. "I remain convinced . . . that this crank call doesn't warrant disrupting . . . our entire nuclear security program . . . I'd be happy to have a full-scale examination . . . of our procedures by the National Security Council . . . Karl, I think you should chair the study." He smiled, hoping to gain Loggerman's support. "But I don't think . . . an inventory is called for."

"Karl?" the President turned to his National Security Advisor.

"The idea of a study is a good one," Loggerman said. The Secretary looked relieved. "But I'd like to hear what the Admiral thinks."

"Mr. President, I can brag that our past record in protecting the stockpile is perfect, but I can't say the same for the future, or even the present. The Secretary is probably right, the risk is extremely low, but it's not zero.

"At the same time, we don't have to be completely passive. We can do a computer screen to compare our master inventory at Headquarters with the local inventory lists at each SAS site, weapons depot, and so forth. That should take only a few hours. It would at least give us a base line," McCollough concluded, "and might even show whether we have any anomalies or other things to look at more closely."

"That's a reasonable compromise, Mr. President," Loggerman said quickly, trying to keep the issue alive but under control.

The President did not look satisfied. He checked his watch again and then shrugged. "All right. But if there is even one of your 'anomalies,'" he said the word slowly, pointing his cigar for emphasis, "you're going to count 'em like beans—every single one of them."

7

By the time the helicopter carrying Admiral McCollough settled down behind the huge white satellite dishes at Ft. Belvoir, the initial responses were pouring into a makeshift operations center set up in a third-floor conference room at the Defense Nuclear Agency Headquarters. Copies of inventory lists from each nuclear weapons storage site were taped on the walls next to Xeroxes of the corresponding portion of the master inventory. Discrepancies were marked in red.

"It looks like we've got the plague," McCollough said in disgust. "How can the field reports be so widely different from the master inventory?"

"Well, it *is* very misleading," said Sandy Warren, the Admiral's special assistant. "If you look closely, you can see that a lot of the anomalies are obviously accounting errors."

Warren was a short, intense civilian with dark curly hair and thick glasses. He walked over and tapped on the reports from Korea. "We've had a buildup here in the last twelve months. The principal depot for nuclear artillery shells in Pusan lists twenty fewer weapons than our master computer. But if you look over here"—he tapped the lists for the Special Ammunition Storage sites near the armistice line at the

38th parallel—"you see that they collectively have twenty *more* than they are supposed to have."

"So it all evens out?"

"We don't know yet, and we may not be able to tell for a while. They're being moved around a lot, and with the weekend, the paperwork's not up to date. There are cross-depot movements that complicate it even more. Some of the weapons also change category if you send one to a rear echelon for servicing or repair, for example."

McCollough ran both hands over his crew-cut gray hair. "When will we know, net-net, what the story is?"

"In about thirty minutes. We told the field that this was a time-sensitive exercise and all reports had to be in by 11:30 EST, 16:30 Zulu. They've been doing a good job so far. We are also inputting the reports into our Cyber 70, so we can manipulate the data with some regression analysis and eliminate likely accounting errors. You'll have a pretty clear readout by 11:45."

"Fine," said the Admiral. "That, I'm afraid, is when our work will really begin."

McCollough avoided elevators. He climbed the three flights to his office and went directly into his private bathroom, where he shaved and changed. For sailing and fighting he wanted loose clothing, but for the bureaucratic wars he preferred the discipline of a crisply ironed shirt and a freshly pressed uniform.

He had no desk. Instead, he stood at a large lecturn near the window. On a legal-sized sheet of yellow paper, he outlined the basic tasks that would have to be accomplished in the next twelve hours if the President ordered a crash inventory. He made a list starting with nuclear weapons stationed on US territory:

- Peacekeeper and Minuteman III ICBM Fields
- Midgetman Dispersal Bases
- Continental US (CONUS) Air Defense Sites
- CONUS Strategic Defense Sites
- CONUS Zone of Interior (ZI) Depots
- Alaskan Command (Army) Storage Sites
- Alaskan Command (Air Force) Air Defense Sites
- Strategic Air Command Bomber Bases

- US Navy Special Ammunition Storage Sites (Ashore)
- Department of Energy (DOE) Nuclear Weapons Laboratories
- DOE Nuclear Weapon Production Facilities
- DOE Nuclear Test Site

He then drew up a list of categories of overseas US nuclear commands:

- US Army Europe (USAREUR)
- US Air Force Europe (USAFE)
- Supreme Allied Commander Europe (SHAPE)—NATO Nuclear Weapons Support Program sites
- US/UK Channel Command
- Atlantic Command (SACLANT)—Azores, Greenland, Bahamas
- South West Asia (Persian Gulf/Indian Ocean) Command (SWACOM)
- Pacific Command (PACOM)
- United Nations Emergency Forces (UNEF)—South Korea
- Southern Command (SOUTHCOM)—Panama (Also Check Roosevelt Roads Puerto Rico and Guantánamo)

McCullough stared at the task in dismay. Each of the commands had scores of nuclear installations—in the case of Europe, hundreds. In addition, he knew that weapons were stored in countries who denied their presence. For contingency purposes, weapons were secretly deployed in North Africa and the Middle East. They came under no formal command but were linked directly to his office through a special State Department liaison office in the Bureau of Political/Military Affairs. And there were weapons afloat with the Navy. They were deployed in hundreds of ships at sea. As they steamed from one part of the world to another, they were chopped from one command to another. McCollough held his head in his hands.

Sandy Warren came in, with a ream of computer printouts trailing after him.

"Well, what are the damages?" McCollough asked.

"Really, it's not that bad. The good news is that we can get the hardcore question marks down to thirty-two."

"You mean thirty-two nuclear weapons we can't account for?"

Sandy nodded.

"And the bad news?"

"Sir, the computer tells us that the anomalies don't necessarily correlate with actual inventory variances."

"You mean if we can't account for one, it may not be missing?"

"Right. Of course, that would be good news. But by the same token, if we register one as *not* missing, it may or may not *be* there. That, sir, is the bad news. Given how much we move these weapons around, a quick snapshot like this only gives us a blur. The inventory lists just can't tell us what's really going on out there minute by minute."

"Then take a look at this list." Admiral McCollough handed Warren the several sheets of yellow paper he had been working on. "Add any of the nooks and crannies I've missed. I have a feeling we're going to need it." McCollough waved Sandy Warren out of the room as he picked up the green phone and asked for the Secretary of Defense. Sitting down on the window ledge, he prepared himself for a long and unhappy conversation.

8

The tennis ball sailed out of the court and onto the South Lawn of the White House. Karl Loggerman's frustration was growing. Not only were the baseline volleys of his military aide running him ragged, but it dawned on him that the Secretary of Defense had escaped his net. While he lost the argument with the President, the Secretary still managed to shift most of the responsibility onto McCollough. Loggerman feared that the Admiral would defuse the crisis prematurely. He banged into the back fence in a futile effort to retrieve a lob.

It was love–40, triple match point. Loggerman's first serve was long. As he tossed the ball up again, aiming for a lucky spot in the trees, the phone in the metal box beside the court clanged sharply. His second serve was wide.

"I'll get the phone," his aide called out.

"I get that serve over," Loggerman called back.

"It's for you, sir, an Admiral McCollough."

"Yes?" Loggerman wiped his face with a towel. "What?" He broke into a smile and then frowned. "Wait a minute, the Secretary wants me to pass this news to the President? Please remind him that only a few hours ago he told me that this was a military matter. He'd better report to his Commander-in-Chief personally." He hung up and slapped his aide on the back. "I'll let you off easy. If you can find my ball, I'll call it a draw."

The President listened to the Secretary of Defense on the secure phone, while standing at the heavy green bulletproof windows of the Oval Office. He watched his National Security Advisor directing an aide and several White House guards in a search through the bushes.

"We went through all that this morning," the President finally interrupted. "In about twelve hours, we're supposed to get another call and probably some kind of threat. Your computer check has only increased my concern." He stopped as the Defense Secretary pursued his argument.

"Mr. Secretary"—his voice became hard and formal—"I was sworn in as President of the United States about a hundred days ago, but nobody in the Pentagon seems to have noticed. Well, now I'm going to prove it. I'm putting you personally in charge. You know what I want, a physical inventory of every single weapon. Plan to be here at eleven-thirty tonight to report to the National Security Council.

"And one more thing, no leaks. You tell your troops that there's a court-martial for everyone involved if the story gets out!"

He slammed down the phone. He could see that out on the lawn Loggerman had found his tennis ball. He pushed the button on his intercom. "Get me Sean Gordon."

9

His first conscious sensations in the morning were always of her warmth—her arm across his chest or her leg entwined with his.

He ran his hand up her back, amazed and stimulated by the smoothness of her skin. She murmured into his shoulder.

From the sound of the Pacific pounding on the rocks below, he knew it was high tide. Laura would sleep late. Sean Gordon's Saturday routine would be to run on the beach, then return to the cliffside cottage and make a big breakfast for the two of them. He would squeeze a half dozen oranges and fry four eggs over-easy with hash brown potatoes and fresh sand dabs. That evening, they were to attend a student production of Chekhov's *Three Sisters,* but for the rest of the day they were free to lounge about on the large, down-filled pillows that filled the tiny living area. They would read. They would listen to music and to the surf. They would make love. Sean Gordon had never thought such a life was possible.

Slipping out of bed, he pulled on his running shorts and laced up his battered yellow Nike Tailwinds. He went to the large counterpane window and pushed it open. The fragrance of sea and sage filled the room. The morning was cool and foggy; he would need a sweatshirt. As he tried to quietly slide open a drawer, the phone rang.

Laura rolled over, reached out blindly, and the phone fell on the floor. She crawled half off the bed and picked up the receiver.

"Hello," she said thickly. "No, I'm not Mrs. Gordon . . . Yes, he's here," she said, burying herself under the comforter and holding the phone up in the air.

"Yes, this is Sean Gordon."

"This is the White House operator. I have a call for you."

The skin on Gordon's chest and arms prickled. He swung the window shut.

Another voice came on the line. He recognized Peter Andretti, the President's Appointments Secretary. "Stand by, would you, Sean, the President wants to talk to you."

Gordon could feel the excitement and the sense of helplessness coming over him. He sat down on the bed.

It had been a long time since he had talked to the President. He was one of the few in Washington who had stuck by Gordon, despite the bad publicity and worse rumors that had followed his last mission. The President was then only a freshman Senator, but he managed to help quell demands for a congressional investigation into Gordon's actions.

And when he soon became a serious candidate for President, Gordon briefly allowed himself to hope his own career might revive. But Peter Andretti, then the candidate's campaign manager, set him straight.

"The candidate loves you. He'll probably call you every day for advice. But if he wins, don't expect anything. You're too hot ever to get confirmed by the Senate.

"And don't think it'll blow over, Sean. Each time your name comes up, when a journalist, or congressional staffer, or lobbyist wants to know about you, they'll push a button on their computer and Lexis/Nexus will generate your file. You're stuck with the label the press put on you. It's permanent. You know how it works in this town."

He did indeed. Washington, D.C., was a place that dealt in symbols, not substance; appearances, not reality; where truth was a function of power, and facts just stones on a pile. Gordon had been effective and successful, but he never really fit in. His independence and disregard for procedure had been considered a plus by the CIA when he had been spotted as a young Peace Corps volunteer in Zambia. The Agency had then spent the next fifteen years trying to extinguish those qualities. Gordon took no offense. He simply ignored the bureaucrats. His Catholic upbringing taught him that civilization would not endure without bureaucracy, but could not be created by it, either.

Fiercely loyal, he tended to be a loner who would do anything for his friends except just call to chat. His dedication to accomplishment, rather than the mere acquisition of power, made him unpredictable and dangerous in the eyes of his colleagues. Never a recipient of awards or even regular promotions, Gordon had advanced only because higher rank was required for the missions he was assigned. On the Georgetown social circuit, Gordon had been dismissed by a ruling hostess, Mary Ellen Suslip, as "brilliant, mysterious—but no ego."

Those were precisely the qualities that had appealed to a bipartisan succession of CIA Directors, National Security Advisors, and Presidents. He had received a series of difficult, dangerous, and increasingly thankless assignments. Even before his last mission, Gordon had begun to wonder where his life was headed.

His career in the Clandestine Service extracted a heavy price from his family. Often abandoned for long stretches, his wife developed a successful Washington lobbying firm. They led hectic lives, coming together too infrequently, making love too urgently in an effort to break down the growing barriers between them. Lying together afterward, they would often exchange intimate little "hellos," as if recognizing the strangers they had become.

To try to hold on to each other, they had a son and then found that the idea of "quality time" was a cruel hoax. All three would joke that they needed a wife. When the boy was eight, he went to boarding school. A year later, Gordon and his wife split up, each hoping that there might be someone else who could fill the growing emptiness in the lives they were leading. By the time they found out otherwise, too much blood had passed under the bridge for them to continue as husband and wife. But she had given him comfort and support when the going got rough in the aftermath of his last assignment.

After Andretti's warning, Gordon had finally admitted to himself that he had been burned, used up. He did not bother to wait for early retirement, he simply resigned from the CIA. After giving a few lectures at his alma mater, the University of California at La Jolla, he agreed to stay on in the Visiting Professionals program. When his friend was elected President, his calls from Washington became less frequent. After his inauguration, they stopped altogether. Until now.

"Yes, Mr. President." Gordon stood up. Laura clutched the comforter around her face, her eyes wide. "Fine . . . yes, the teaching is going well . . . You're right, it's not Washington, but La Jolla has its compensations. . . ." He looked over at Laura. "No, no, I'm staying in shape. That's more important than being able to read and write in this part of the country."

Gordon was silent for a long time as the President spoke. The smile faded and the tiny lines across Gordon's forehead and around his mouth grew into furrows.

"I respect that, Mr. President, and I'm honored, but . . . no, I have never bullshitted you, and I assume that's why you're calling me."

Gordon was silent again for a long period. "Certainly, if it's that important, I can be there tonight. I'll get to El Toro Air Base by myself, but I have to ask a favor. I don't have a tuxedo anymore. Could you have somebody call Sam Scozna over on L Street? He's got my measurements. Thanks. See you this evening."

Laura had curled up and turned away.

*   *   *

As the President put the phone down a continent away, he saw the disapproval in the face of his Appointments Secretary.

"What if this is just a lot of nonsense?" Andretti said.

"What if it's not?" the President retorted. "Do you think I'm going to put Loggerman in charge of World War III? Listen, if this is a real nuclear terrorist threat, Sean's the only one in that business I can really trust.

"Now get me the Soviet Ambassador."

10

"Sir, I don't mean to be impertinent, but I'll never get this job done if I keep getting pulled up by the roots to see if I'm growing." McCollough was talking to the Defense Secretary who had called for the fifth time in twenty minutes. "No, there's no code name for the inventory. I'm trying to avoid an overall project. It's too easy to leak the existence of a single operation.

"I've broken it down by region and subregion. In Europe, we're calling it a 'no-notice exercise.' For the Navy in the Far East, we call it a snap inspection. At the Research Labs, Los Alamos, Sandia Base, Livermore, we are simply saying it's an inventory. But we're sending the messages through different channels. To some of the unified commands, we're going through our agency housekeeping circuit; to certain European SAS sites, through EUCOM's cemetery network; to our ships, via the CNO's channel and so forth. All hell's breaking loose out in the field, but I'm trying to make sure no big thing's happening in Washington, because that's where all the press is focused. If you don't mind, I'm staying at Ft. Belvoir and away from the Pentagon. No reporters ever want to come down here.

"No, I don't yet know what to do about the ICBMs. They're not exactly easy to steal. Does the President really want us to unscrew the front end of every missile in order to count the weapons inside?"

McCollough shook his head at the Secretary's response. "I know he wants a *physical* inspection. But to do that in twelve hours will require swarms of men in the missile fields. Leaves will have to be canceled. The story's sure to leak. And the Strategic Air Command will scream that we're disarming ourselves; it doesn't help that I can't even explain why— Yes, I know what the orders are, Mr. Secretary. I'll try to come up with something."

McCollough stared at the phone. After a few minutes, he placed a call to Major General Andrew Hanson, Commander of the 14th Peace-keeper Missile Wing at Warren Air Force Base outside Cheyenne, Wyoming. A classmate of the Admiral at the National War College, Hanson was smart and, more important, McCollough knew he was reliable.

"Andy, Chip McCollough here. How are you? . . . Fine. Everyone is fine . . . Yes, the boat's in the water." He thought briefly of *Fusion* being towed back to Annapolis by the Coast Guard. He would have some explaining to do to his buddies at the Naval Academy Marina.

"Listen, I've got something a mite touchy, could you give a ring on secure? No, it's got to be right away. I'm in my office."

General Hanson called in fifteen minutes. "I'm sorry, Chip, but they still haven't approved a secure line at home. What's up?"

McCollough explained his problem. "So, you'll be getting an official message from SAC shortly. Don't fight it. Is there any way it can be done?"

Hanson paused and looked out his office window across the broad, empty country that rose into the Medicine Bow mountains. Dark shadows of patchy clouds raced over the landscape. "Well, sure, it's easy— depending on what you mean by a 'physical inventory.' We can simply interrogate the master computer on the status of all the deployed warheads. For redundancy, each missile launch control complex could do its standard computer maintenance checks on the warheads. Any anomalies would be obvious. That shouldn't take more than an hour."

"But is there any way to assure that someone hasn't screwed around with the computer?" McCollough asked.

"Well, that would be pretty tough."

"But not impossible?"

"I just don't know. But we could cross-check with the targeting computer. That's on a separate program in the Command Data Buffer, a different system. We could just ask every warhead where it's going, and if one doesn't answer, we know we've got a problem." When McCollough failed to respond, Hanson insisted, "The Command Data Buffer is our war plan. It's the family jewels. It's pretty goddamned secure!"

"But it's still indirect," McCollough sighed. He knew the President would not buy another computer exercise. "Isn't there any *physical* way . . . ?"

Hanson was growing impatient and irritated. He had planned a day of fishing in the mountains with his son and it was just about ruined. "Listen, I don't know what you are looking for. If you want something physical, how about the weight of each missile?"

"Yes, go on."

"We monitor the weight extremely carefully. The smallest variation and the weapon will land in Minsk instead of Pinsk. It's a way to cross-check that we have enough propellant in the MIRV bus and that the solid rocket motors haven't dried out. If somebody has run off with a Mark 21 warhead, which is what I guess you are concerned about, he would have to make a dummy accurate to within one-thousandth of a gram."

"Terrific!" McCollough exclaimed. "When you get the order from SAC, you tell them that's how you'll proceed. Meantime, I'll clear the decks back here. And Andy," the Admiral took a deep breath, "don't imagine what I'm concerned about. Don't think about it, and don't talk about it."

The Secretary of Defense was not certain the technique was terrific. He put McCollough on hold and called Loggerman.

"I'm sorry, Karl, but I have to talk to you about this ICBM inventory. If I have to open up every one of our missiles and count the weapons inside, I'm going to have a revolt from the Strategic Air Command. The whole ICBM force will be out of action for days while we put everything back together, test it, and so on. We're letting this caller carry out the equivalent of a first strike! He could be working for the Russians. This could be a plot!"

"I'm concerned about that, too, Mr. Secretary—what do you suggest?" Loggerman leaned back in his large green leather chair with his feet on the desk. He was chewing on a pencil and smiling. Across the desk, his military aide sat on the edge of a molded plywood chair. When the Defense Secretary finished explaining what McCollough wanted to do, Loggerman paused a long time before responding.

"Well, that's not really what the President ordered. I had better run it by him . . . I'll do my best." Loggerman hung up.

"Do you want the President now?" the aide asked Loggerman.

"Hell no! Just wait and watch how this works." Loggerman sat in silence a few minutes then called the Secretary of Defense. "Jesus, the President almost ate me alive. He's in one of those I'm-the-President moods . . . no, I wouldn't call him . . . he's still furious about your last conversation . . . well, he talked about getting a new Secretary of Defense. Have the Commander of SAC call me, and do the same with Admiral McCollough. I'll do my best."

Loggerman took the call from General Tinguely, the Commander of SAC. It was 50 percent profanity. When he refused to explain the reason for the inventory, the percentage went up to 80. In contrast, Admiral McCollough was calm and precise. Before hanging up, Loggerman said, "That's very helpful, thank you. And, Admiral, if you have any particular problems as this thing goes forward, always feel free to call me directly."

The National Security Advisor sat savoring the fact that the crisis was pushing him into a central role, just as he had hoped. He glanced at the monitor and saw that the President was having lunch with the editor of *Parade* magazine.

"Get me the President on secure. Say it's urgent," he called out to his secretary.

"I'm sorry to interrupt you, Mr. President, but the Secretary of Defense insisted that I raise this issue with you immediately . . . Yes, it's the inventory. He's trying to relitigate your decision by saying he'll have to dismantle all our ICBMs. I talked to SAC and Admiral McCollough and found out they've got a way to monitor each missile physically without opening up every silo. Unless you want to talk to him, I'll just tell him to do it their way . . . No, it's not just computers checking computers . . . Fine . . . One last thing, I think he'd just as soon skip the meetings with the Sultan so he can stay on top of this . . . Good . . . Yes? . . . Certainly, you can't be dragged into all these details. I'll keep him off your back."

"Pretty neat," Loggerman's aide said. "Do you want the Secretary now?"

"No, let him wait. Come on, I'll buy you lunch."

The National Security Advisor wandered out of his office and down the stairs to the basement, his aide following along behind. Before entering the White House Mess, he turned right into a room that contained vending machines. He bought two apples and gave one to his aide. Next, he stopped and made an appointment to get his hair cut by the White House barber. When he got back to his office, he found his secretary anxiously waiting to report that the Secretary of Defense had called three times. "He's in a panic," she said.

"Fine, fine, get him on the line." He tossed the second apple to his secretary. "Now listen to this," Loggerman said to his aide. "Mr. Secretary, have you got a job at one of your department stores for a former government employee? . . . Listen, I laid it on the line. I said you were absolutely right. Well, he finally backed off . . . yes, you can do it that way, but only on the ICBMs. For everything else, he said you better 'eyeball every one' . . . no, if you want to survive I'd stay away from calling him. He doesn't like losing an argument . . . One other thing, he'd like you to skip the Sultan's meeting so you can stay on top of this thing. Right. Stay in touch." Loggerman put the secure phone back in its cradle.

"That was brilliant," said Loggerman's aide. "He's in your debt."

"It's better than that," Loggerman said, unlocking the bottom drawer of his desk and taking out a box of Cuban cigars. "He's now reluctant to call the President. And the President doesn't want to talk to him, either. Instead, they'll go through me." He inhaled the moist aroma of the Churchill-sized Cohiba. "That's called control."

The ferry from Meersberg sliced through the furrows of light reflecting off the water from the Belvedere at Constance. At the rail, Terence Culver lit a cigarette with a flip-top Ronson embossed with the seal of the 92nd Ranger Battalion. He recognized the thick-set young man who climbed out of a tan Mercedes, the last car to come on board.

Horst Bauer approached Culver carrying a briefcase in his left hand and with his right buried in his raincoat pocket.

"Hello, Terry, are you all right?"

"Fine, Horst." They spoke in German and did not shake hands.

"I've brought ten thousand dollars in cash and the text of what you are to say in the next phone call." Culver took the briefcase.

"That's not what you promised."

"You know, Terry, some of my colleagues doubted whether you had it in you. They still wonder if this might be a hoax. I have assured them of your integrity, but they insist that the weapon be put in our custody. Once you do that, you and your girlfriend Graciela," he nodded toward the car, "can be out of it."

"Where is she?"

"Safe with us." Horst Bauer led Culver toward the car, keeping his hand in his pocket. "In exchange for the weapon, you will get what I told you, five hundred thousand dollars in US bearer bonds, several sets of identity papers for both of you, and the location of several safe houses to help your escape."

Through the dark gray tint of the Mercedes windows, Culver could see Graciela sitting in the right front seat. There was fear on her face and a man in the seat behind her.

"I want her now." Culver dropped the briefcase, grabbed Bauer's right arm, and twisted it behind him. His hand was empty. He had no weapon.

"You must learn to trust your friends," Bauer grunted. Culver could see the man in the car press a Walther PPK against Graciela's head. He let Bauer go.

"You'll be together when I get what I'm paying for. The exchange will take place at the chalet in Kitzbühel at noon tomorrow."

"I can't do it that fast."

"Monday, then." He slammed the car door.

The ferry banged into the dock at Allmansdorf. Culver watched helplessly as Bauer's car turned left into Switzerland. He sat on a cold stone bench with the briefcase in his lap, and waited for a bus to take him back to Munich.

12

Ezrum, Turkey

At a lonely nuclear storage site in the barren mountains of Eastern Turkey, an overaged Major leaned on his desk and stared at the report. "It might as well be my retirement orders," he said to himself as a Second Lieutenant and a Staff Sergeant stood at attention before him. "How in the hell could this happen?"

There was only the sound of the wind blowing through the plywood walls of the prefab headquarters building of the 720th Atomic Weapons Custodial Unit. "As the Lieutenant explained, sir," the Sergeant spoke up, "it's because we keep the weapons disassembled for security reasons, sir. So that these Islamic terrorists and the Turkish Army, neither one can get their hands on a working weapon."

"But you are not explaining why I have eighteen weapon cases and only enough components to make sixteen complete weapons," the Major said with forced patience. "And you are not explaining why my inventory says I'm supposed to have seventeen. I've got the goddamned little stainless steel plate with the serial number for one of the weapons, but nothing else!" The Major was now shouting.

"The core probably went back to the depot in Izmir." The Sergeant brightened. "They should be able to find it."

"I've just talked to Izmir, and they made it very clear that they are too damn busy with their own inventory to save our ass," the Major snapped.

"Couldn't we just say it's here until we find the rest of it?" the Lieutenant suggested.

"I came out here six months ago to clean up this crap hole." The Major leaned forward and started shaking his fist. "Most of you jerk-offs were stoned on hash half of the time. Now I'm the one who's facing a court-martial."

He sat down heavily. Time was running out. He knew he had no choice but to send in the report. Well, the choice is clear, he thought to himself, I can lie, or I can go back to Tupelo, get me a pickup, and haul stuff.

Diego Garcia, the Indian Ocean

A huge, dark shadow in the water slid past the reef and into the lagoon. Aboard the Trident ballistic missile submarine *Nevada,* the Chief Operations Officer, Jay Berkely, briskly handed a message to the Captain.

"We just got this order over the blue-green laser link. It's not enough that we've got a major medical emergency that's pulled us away from our deployment zone, now we've got to play chicken-shit housekeeping games."

Captain Paul Nuzzo read the message. "No problem. We can do a weapons count in twenty minutes."

"But how are we going to report? We're still on patrol. We're not authorized to break radio silence, and the nearest bottom plug is back in the deployment zone, eighteen hours away."

"I'm sure the British Commander here at Diego Garcia can help us out." The Captain snapped shut his logbook. "As soon as we surface and dock, invite him aboard."

The Captain's first hint of trouble came when the Royal Navy Commandant refused. He insisted that the American Captain call on him.

"I'm afraid that what you're asking is quite impossible." The Commandant poured a tumbler of gin over a single cube of ice and held it out. The American Captain accepted it, noticing that the skin on the Englishman's hand—like that on his face, for that matter—was blasted by too much sun and too many juniper berries.

"I grant you that we do have this informal arrangement which enables you Yanks to use this island for certain purposes, like the emergency appendectomy for that unfortunate ensign of yours. But Her Majesty's government has publicly assured Parliament that this island will not be used as a nuclear base. And that has been interpreted as precluding the relay of any encrypted operational messages from either your submarines or bombers."

The Captain strained to distinguish the quiet-spoken Commandant's heavily inflected English from the clamor of the gooney birds nesting on the metal roof above their heads. "I could send something unclassified, but a coded message to the US Navy Annex on Grosvenor Square in London? Quite out of the question."

The American stared out the window. Across the lagoon an airfield shimmered in the tropical sun. He did not know why the Navy wanted a report on the status of the D-5 warheads, but if he failed to respond, he knew he would trip every alarm bell from Pearl Harbor to the Pentagon.

"Perhaps there is something else I could do for you," the Commandant smiled vacantly.

"Yes, there is," the Captain replied. "You could get me a little tonic water for this drink."

Schloss Ludwigshof, West Germany

"If there's anythin' outa order at the storage site, I'll teach these custodial weenies what it's like to be real soldiers," Colonel Holsey Handyside pledged to his orderly, as they strode across the parade ground toward the nuclear weapons compound at the edge of the base. Handyside was the Commanding Officer of the 92nd Ranger

Battalion headquartered at Schloss Ludwigshof, and he had little use for the nuclear custodial team, which primarily supported other army units in southern Germany.

"I'm sure nothing's wrong," his orderly said. "We've got this no-notice exercise because they failed to meet the deadline on the computer inventory check."

"So I get to be the goddamn mattress," Handyside bitched. "The head weenie's in the hospital from eatin' raw clams in Greece. His Deputy Commander bombed outa the Service a month ago an' we've got no replacement. The whole damn show's run by that Mexican bitch who's only a Spec 5, and you," he slapped his orderly across the chest with his swagger stick, "you go and let her take leave and she's overdue gettin' back. This ain't just a peacetime army, it's a fuckin' Club Mediterrenay."

They arrived at a double steel fence that enclosed a converted barn set half into a hillside. An original part of the estate of Schloss Ludwigshof, the barn concealed a cave that offered a perfect environment for aging the pungent cheese which, for two hundred years, gave the Schloss its minor fame throughout Bavaria. In 1945, when the US Army seized the estate and turned it into a Ranger base, the cave provided an ideal place to put munitions. Eight years later, it became one of the first storage sites for the thousands of US tactical nuclear weapons that were pouring into West Germany.

"Open up and let me in, goddammit!" Handyside barked into a microphone and grimaced at the video camera guarding the outside gate. It opened to a second gate, where he had to take off his right glove and place his palm on a cold glass plate that was read by an optical scanner. The inner gate clicked open, and the Colonel and his orderly carefully made their way up a serpentine path set off by bright yellow flags that marked the safe passage through the mine field surrounding the barn.

"This place is just a pain in the ass in every way," Handyside said in greeting the two custodial guards waiting at the reception desk. "Open the vault."

One of the guards picked up a phone from his console and pushed a red button. "Comcenter? This is the storage site. We're closing off the alarms for Colonel Handyside's inspection." Behind him the other guard was repeatedly trying and failing to work the combination lock on a small steel door set in the wall.

"Come on, for Christ's sake," Handyside said.

The combination finally caught, and the door opened to reveal a bank of switches. The guard turned off four of them.

"Can we get goin' now?"

"Yes, sir, you just have to sign these forms." He held out a clipboard. "I'll fill them out for you later, sir." Handyside gave a grunt of appreciation, and slashed an illegible mark across the page.

The storage area was protected by a foot-thick steel door of the type popular at local banks in the United States in the 1950s. In the decades since having replaced an ancient oak door, the massive steel vault had settled into the soft Bavarian earth. The top now tilted forward almost three inches.

As one of the guards spun the large wheel in the center, he shouted, "Stand clear!" The second guard stepped up to help control the rapidly opening door. It caught Handyside as he was moving away and almost knocked him down.

"Why the hell don't you get that fixed?" he swore. "It's gonna kill somebody. Get in there and get started."

While Handyside waited just inside the vault with one of the guards, his orderly and the other guard began at the back of the cave and worked their way forward. They checked the weapons against a copy of the master inventory that had been sent from Washington. The site held a total of fifty-eight nuclear weapons. Four Ground Launched Cruise Missile warheads were stored in separate nests dug into the walls at the bottom of the cave. Next, thirty-three atomic artillery shells for the 155mm and eight-inch Howitzers were placed at wide intervals on racks that lined each side of the cave for 150 yards.

It was crucial to keep the weapons physically separated. If they came too close together, a subcritical mass could be created that would result in a "neutron flux" that could be lethal to the personnel in the vault. A wide yellow stripe was marked on the floor of the cave. Weapons transported in and out had to hew closely to this stripe to avoid the possibility of a partial. The custodial guards called it "the yellow brick road."

The Atomic Demolition Munitions were stored at the head of the road, just inside the mouth of the cave. The big, one hundred-kiloton ADMs, used by combat engineers to make craters, start landslides, or knock down forests, were housed in steel drums set precisely in white painted circles along one wall. The Special ADMs, which were man-portable and used by the Rangers, sat in suitcaselike containers or hung in pouches against the opposite wall. Colonel Handyside paced back and forth between them across the yellow brick road.

"Hurry up," he called out. "I always feel like my sperms are bein' cooked in this place."

His orderly and the other guard emerged from the depths of the cave and quickly counted the ADMs.

"Well?"

"All present and accounted for, sir."

Malmstrom Air Force Base, Great Falls, Montana

Almost a half inch of snow had collected on the four members of the custodial team as they stood outside the special-access compound that screened the Stealth Bomber squadron from the rest of the air base. The Major in command of the custodial team was shouting into a metal box on the gate.

"Request denied? What the hell do you mean request denied? You've got twelve weapons signed out and we've got a top priority order to inspect them."

"You do not have the necessary clearances," a disembodied voice came from the speaker, "and we have no authority to admit you."

"Clearances? Clearances?" He was screaming now. "I'm calling the Base Commander. He's going to cut you a new asshole!"

"As you wish, Major."

The Base Commander shrugged his shoulders helplessly. "I only have so much authority over those Stealth Bomber people. I'll send a message to SAC, but you better check with your own folks in Washington."

Admiral McCollough grew increasingly angry as he read the message from the Custodial Unit at Malmstrom AFB. It was bad enough that the Navy seemed to have lost contact with one of its Trident submarines; now the Air Force appeared to be deliberately sandbagging the inventory.

"This is the third message I've gotten like this from one of my custodial teams at an Air Force base," McCollough complained to the Secretary of Defense. "I'm sorry to drag you into this, but the Chief of Staff of the Air Force and the Chairman of the JCS both claim you're the only one who can explain this to me."

There was such a long silence on the other end of the line that McCollough shook the phone to see if it was working. "Can you hear me, Mr. Secretary?"

"Yes, yes. Either I or someone else will get right back to you," he said abruptly, and hung up.

The next call McCollough received came from Karl Loggerman.

"Having a little trouble with the Air Force, Admiral?" He could hear the forced heartiness in Loggerman's voice. "Well, don't worry about it, we can just assume those weapons are safe and sound."

"Excuse me, Dr. Loggerman, but I can't assume any such thing. If you want to give me a written exemption, that's fine, but otherwise I'm obliged to tell the President whether the weapons are there or not."

He could hear Loggerman sigh. "The problem, Admiral, is that they are not. What I'm about to tell you is specially compartmented information which you are not, and which you will not, be authorized to receive. I'm putting myself out on a limb, and I'm counting on your discretion. The weapons are aboard aircraft engaged in a special armed airborne alert." Loggerman became formal and precise. "In view of certain recent dramatic Soviet gains in antiballistic missile defense, we've been compelled to put these aircraft on patrol where, if need be, they can urgently attack these Soviet ABM systems."

"But that's nothing new," McCollough protested. "We've had armed patrols over the Arctic ocean in the past. I appreciate the sensitivity of such an alert, but never before has this been a reason to keep it a secret from my Agency. I still have jurisdiction over the security of those weapons."

"Admiral," he could now hear the irritation in Loggerman's voice, "those weapons are beyond your jurisdiction. They're at forty-five-thousand feet over the heart of the Soviet Union."

Los Alamos, New Mexico

Jason Winniker, the former Chief of the Los Alamos Nuclear Weapons Laboratory, sat in a wooden armchair directly in front of the new Director of the Laboratory.

"Sorry to call you out of retirement after only two weeks, but we're having a problem with the provenance of some of our devices. Despite our professional differences, I hope I can count on your help on this." The new Director, who was twenty-seven years old, was showing an uncharacteristic modesty in asking anyone for assistance, particularly his predecessor.

"What's wrong?" Winniker asked.

"We're having an inventory on a somewhat crash basis. There are, according to our records"—he poked a teetering stack of files, log books and computer printouts—"eleven devices we cannot account for. We thought maybe you could help us."

I should have known it was a setup, Winniker thought. Claire, they're going to blame me for something else. He was talking silently to his recently deceased wife. He had been doing more and more of that lately. They're going to hound me right into my retirement. A wave of depression swept over him. He stared at the floor.

"Jason, you've got to help us. These records go back to 1943. The early years are a shambles. There's not even a record of turning over Fat Man and Little Boy to the Army, though obviously they were dropped on Hiroshima and Nagasaki."

"Let me see what's missing," Winniker relented, and took a sheet of paper the Director held out to him.

"Right here, Audrey I." The paper trembled as he pointed to the first device on the list. "We made it in 1952, but it didn't go to test. It was renamed Ellen II for a 1958 test, but it wasn't exploded, only irradiated by Ellen I. Then, I think in the late seventies, we remanufactured it into a trigger for one of the Askok hot X-ray series. I can't remember if that was canceled by Carter or not."

While Winniker's memory was good on the early years, the more recent lineage of nuclear devices eluded him. He had dominated the Laboratory for almost fifty years, but after the death of his wife his intellectual and physical strength had declined, while his views became more outspoken. The previous Administration, in one of its last acts, had abruptly dismissed him.

Winniker considered himself disgraced, and expected to be rehabilitated by the new Administration. When the call had come from the new Lab Director that morning, he had accepted eagerly. But vindication was not on the agenda. As the deadline to report to Washington approached, he could explain what had become of five nuclear devices, but was unable to account for half a dozen others.

As he drove home in the gathering darkness, Winniker was overwhelmed by feelings of humiliation and helplessness. Stopping at an overlook, he gazed down at the mesa on which Los Alamos Labs had been built, and remembered when it was covered with spruce, Douglas fir, and aspen. Now, it was a twenty-first-century jumble of windowless buildings and ventilation ducts, eerily lit with the orange light of sodium vapor lamps.

Going to the trunk of his car, he took out an old .30-06 lever-action Winchester he used for hunting deer. "Six of my nuclear weapons missing." He shook his head. "I'm so tired of it, Claire." He cracked open the lever and closed it. "Don't be mad at me, too. I just want to be with you." He put his forehead against the cool open mouth of the barrel for a moment. "Claire," he whispered, then pressed the trigger.

13

The moon shone brightly on a modern horseshoe-shaped building situated in a wooden park on the outskirts of Moscow. In an austere conference room on the tenth floor, Alexander Antunov sat patiently waiting for his meeting with the Chairman of the Committee for State Security. Antunov was Head of the North American Department of the First Chief Directorate KGB. He supervised both the clandestine collection and the analysis of intelligence on the United States and Canada.

The conference room was long and narrow, its blank walls paneled in blond wood to match the table. Recessed fluorescent lights gave the impression of daylight, though Antunov's digital watch told him it was 1:27 A.M. On the table in front of him were two thin files.

The top folder contained three reports. The first was a message from the Soviet Communications Intelligence Collection site at Siete Millas, Cuba. It transmitted the text of a call to the White House from Hamburg, West Germany, which had been intercepted off of Comsat IV. The second document contained an analysis of the increase in signal traffic between Washington and US Special Ammunition Storage sites. The third was an eyes-only message from the Soviet Ambassador to Washington reporting on an unusual meeting with the American President.

A door opened at the far end, and the Chairman of the KGB entered with his uniformed bodyguard. Antunov stood up. "The important thing is to make sure that this is not a provocation," the KGB Chief said without preliminaries. "What are your recommendations on that?" He sat down and indicated that Antunov do the same.

"I take it that Comrade Chairman has read the reports," Antunov began. "There is no independent confirmation that an American weapon has been stolen. I have queried Department V of the Operations Division about the activities of the liberation, and other armed struggle, groups in Europe and the Middle East with which they have contact, but they have not responded.

"As for the Americans, the Ambassador's report makes the President sound quite tentative about the threat, but our Signals Intelligence indicates that they are making systematic inquiries at every nuclear stockpile site in the world. That suggests they are taking the matter seriously."

"It also could be a deception." The KGB Chief stared at him intently. "The Ambassador believes that the President is using this as a pretext to establish direct contact with General Secretary Chalomchev. It's our responsibility to ensure that he's not being entrapped in some way. We do not want to be tricked into a meeting. Our policy is to let the new President wait until his eagerness produces some important concessions. By the way, your dossier on him is not very revealing."

Antunov knew that the last remark was a rebuke. "His rapid rise to power has naturally limited what we know of his political views," he explained. "That's why I believe it's essential to gain access to his closest advisors. We have an unprecedented opportunity with this agent." Antunov slid the bottom folder across the table. The KGB Chief did not open it.

"The agent is a journalist," Antunov continued. "He has worked part-time for both the CIA and MI-6 and was editor of one of their jointly controlled propaganda operations in London, World Photo Features. After that was exposed a few years ago, he was unemployed. Our European Department recruited him to put disinformation back into NATO intelligence channels. It's good fortune that he turns out to have a high-level contact in the new American Administration. However, the European Department is concerned . . ."

"I've read their reservations. Is he reliable? Could he be a triple?" He pushed the folder back to Antunov.

"He works for money. We can only establish his bona fides by testing him in more demanding assignments. This one is ideal. It's entirely defensive; it reveals nothing of our own plans and priorities."

"It's your responsibility." The KGB Chairman stood and walked to the door. He turned. "Report to me every four hours whether or not there are any developments. And do not worry about Department V. I will handle that aspect."

As he gathered up his papers, Antunov could not keep from wondering when the Chairman for State Security had come to personally look after Department V.

14

At 10:30 P.M. that evening in Washington, the corridors of the Pentagon were quiet except for a section of the outer "E" Ring, where the Secretary of Defense has his offices with windows overlooking the Potomac river boat basin. He sat behind a huge ornately carved desk that had been stolen from a Mexican Governor during General "Black Jack" Pershing's punitive expedition against Pancho Villa in 1916. The

Secretary found it comforting to run his hands over its rough and worn surface, especially when he was the recipient of bad news.

"It's like an adolescent nightmare." The Secretary shook his head. "Every time we slay one dragon, two more appear. And Jason Winniker killing himself, my God. I guess I have to give Loggerman a preview." He buzzed his orderly.

He and Admiral McCollough sat in silence as the call was placed by the Corporal in the outer office. "I'll bet he's at the State Dinner for the Sultan of Muscat," the Secretary said with a touch of envy. They continued to wait. He stroked the desk impatiently. He looked at the clock and then at his watch. "The NSC meeting is in forty-five minutes. What's the chance of any new developments by that time?"

"I don't think it'll change much either way," McCollough replied, "except I hope we hear something from the Trident submarine."

15

The National Security Advisor downed a glass of St. Barthelme Chardonnay '79 to congratulate himself on the success of the Sultan's visit. US deployment rights in Muscat were secure for another five years. The State Dinner was going smoothly. The Sultan's wife seemed pleased.

He glanced around the State Dining Room at the sea of round tables, each festooned with spring bouquets of tulip, hyacinth, daffodil, and flowering cherry. The shimmering candelabras, set on the heavy French linen, cast a festive and golden glow. At every place setting, a gilt-edged engraved card announced the menu and the wine list—cold salmon mousse with the Chardonnay, venison Sauce Chasseur with a Chappellet Cabernet Sauvignon '75, and Schramsberg Special Reserve for the dessert and toasts. But the splendor of the occasion failed to quell the unfamiliar stab of anxiety Loggerman felt when he thought of the NSC meeting and the call he might receive that night. He took a second glass of Grgich Hills.

Like the Cabinet officers and other senior officials present, Logger-man was the host of his table. He had arrived late, as usual, to avoid standing around awkwardly and to make his entrance more notice-able. He was disappointed that one of the chairs was still empty. He asked the attractive Dallas clothing designer on his right if she could tell him the name on the place card.

"A Mister Gordon," she responded.

A cloud passed over Loggerman's face.

"Isn't it unpatriotic for someone not to show up for a State Dinner? And for a Sultan, too!" There was a hint of flirtation in her voice.

"Arabs have been out of fashion since the end of the oil crisis," Loggerman said absently, still pondering "Mr. Gordon." He then picked up her mood. "But you're right, most red-blooded Americans would kill to come to the White House, even for potluck with the Sultan of Obscurity."

"I wonder why I was invited?" she laughed.

"Undoubtedly, to add glamour to the evening," he smiled. She beamed. Loggerman knew that the hacks were paying off some obscure political debt.

"Do you know everyone at the head table?" he asked. She shook her head.

"To the President's right is the Sultan, of course, then the Secre-tary of State and his wife, and the Muscat Foreign Minister, and then Kay Graham, owner of *The Washington Post* and *Newsweek*. She's standing in for the First Lady, who's in Chile leading a delegation to the inauguration of their new President. Next to her is the Speaker of the House, and then the Chief Justice of the Supreme Court. The woman on the President's left is the Sultan's wife. She's an American."

"Isn't she Hope Sheffield of the Connecticut Sheffields?" asked the New York socialite on Loggerman's left.

"Yes," he replied, "and when she married the Sultan, the New York papers said *he* was the social climber." They all laughed. Loggerman was pleased to be able to use the one-liner his staff had solicited from a New York gag writer earlier in the week.

"Dr. Loggerman, did the Sultan say anything about oil prices?" It was the sleek investment banker accompanying the socialite. She tapped him on the wrist for breaking the taboo against trying to do business.

"The value of Muscat lies in its geography, not its geology," Loggerman gracefully dodged the question. "It has no oil, just a strategic location. But you should be telling us where the world economy is headed."

"All our economists give contradictory advice."

"I've never trusted economic forecasters," Loggerman said. "They're like someone standing at the back of a train and trying to figure out where it's going by looking at where it's been."

The banker raised his glass to salute Loggerman's remark, as the waiters began to clear away the first course. The National Security Advisor reflected to himself that the train analogy applied to the Defense Department. It operated on the fallacy of the last move. The weapons had always been secure. So it argued that they still must be secure.

The refusal of the Secretary of Defense to report on the inventory was ominous. As the hour grew late, Loggerman knew there was a growing certainty of trouble. If he had good news, the Defense Secretary would be trying to call off the NSC meeting.

Up to that point, it had seemed to Loggerman less like a crisis than a game. But he knew that phase was coming to an end. The implications of a real stolen nuclear weapon made the pang of anxiety return. He looked up to order a third glass of wine and was startled to find Sean Gordon drawing back the empty chair at the table.

"So, it *is* you! Back from the dead." The charm had gone from Loggerman's voice. "To what do we owe this honor? Don't tell me you're here to ruin Muscat like you did South Africa." He tried to make it sound light. He failed.

"I'll leave that up to you, Dr. Loggerman." Gordon smiled and sat down. "Actually, I came back to Washington because I'd heard that the standards of journalism had greatly improved since you took a job in government."

"So has the quality of our intelligence since you retired—" The National Security Advisor was interrupted by a slight tap on his shoulder. A military aide in white tails leaned over him. "Sorry, sir, but there's an urgent call for you."

He put down his wine glass and ostentatiously excused himself from the table, enjoying for a moment the evident importance of being called away from a State Dinner.

"I just hope it's not Armageddon or something, Dr. Loggerman." The Dallas designer pressed the back of his hand to her full and freckled breasts. He pulled away instinctively.

As he hurried along to his West Wing office to take the call on the secure line, Loggerman ruminated on Gordon's presence. Was this the hacks getting back at him? Did the President know he was here? Then he admonished himself. He had much more important things to worry about than a washed-up spy. Whatever the reason, it couldn't have anything to do with the stolen bomb threat, Loggerman was sure.

The call was from the Secretary of Defense. Loggerman listened speechless to the preview of his report to the President.

"I guess I would lay it out just like that," he finally said hesitantly. "Don't pull any punches. Isn't the Trident thing worrisome? Should we undertake a search?" The Secretary's negative reply did not surprise him.

"All right, we'll wait on that, but be sure to bring it up in the meeting. What about Winniker? Should the President send a message of condolence to his family? . . . Right, that would draw attention . . ." He knew it was a dumb idea as soon as it was out of his mouth. He groped toward the main issue, regretting the two glasses of Chardonnay.

"Has this changed your mind about the threat?" He listened to the response, rolling his eyes to the ceiling. "I agree that if we don't get another call, there's no need to go into a crisis mode. But if we do, I don't see how we can treat this as a crank situation—not given the outcome of your inventory . . . Yes, I understand that there are possible explanations, but if I can give you some advice, Mr. Secretary, I think . . . Fine then, you keep your own counsel." They both hung up.

"Stubborn bastard," he said out loud. He then told himself to calm down. He had to get his plan back on track. The crisis was not pulling the Administration together, and he was growing anxious at the thought of trying to cope with a major threat while the top of the government was in such disarray. If he could raise the stakes high enough, the President would have to centralize control, and he would be back in the driver's seat. He knew the boy bleeding-heart running the State Department would not recognize the profound strategic implications of the crisis, and the Secretary of Defense did not think there was even a problem. Loggerman would make his case, but he knew he needed to move fast to build support.

"Try to reach the Director of the CIA before he leaves his office," he called out.

"He's already on his way," one of the secretaries answered through the open door.

"Let me know when he gets here. Try the Chairman of the Joint Chiefs."

As he waited for the call to go through, Loggerman began to dictate a memo into his tape machine.

"This is to the President, Top Secret Eyes Only. Subject: Tonight's Meeting; Action Agenda. Paragraph one.

"Your premonitions about the seriousness of the stolen bomb threat appear to have substance. I will let the Secretary of Defense fill you in. Paragraph.

"In light of his report, you will need to get the following out of the meeting. Colon. Subparagraph:

"One. A consensus that the threat is real. The SecDef may still disagree on this basic point. We will not be able to deal successfully with this crisis if we are divided. Subpara.

"Two. A review of the implications. They are profound. I will speak to this. Subpara.

"Three. Basic decisions on how to respond. You should be guided by the principle that this country does not give in to blackmail. Subpara.

"Four. Allocation of responsibility. We must have centralized control. The stakes are too great for business as usual. Full para.

"All this assumes we hear again from the caller. If not, comma, we will still have a mess to clean up given the results of the DoD inventory."

Loggerman gave the tape to his secretary, who was still holding on the signal line. "Type this right away, put it in an envelope eyes-only for the President and get it into his speech folder at the table."

She nodded and said, "It's the Chairman of the JCS." She put him through.

"Hello, Karl." His voice was breaking up.

"Where are you?"

"In my car on the way over."

"We can talk more when you're here, but you got my note on the meeting?"

"Yes, and we've been trying to help McCollough. Pretty wild stuff."

"Wait till you hear the full report. What I'd like you to do is address the military consequences. And I'd like your support in making sure this thing's run right."

"Okay, but it'll just be me speaking personally, not for the Joint Chiefs."

Loggerman frowned. What bureaucrats the military were, he thought. "That's fine, see you then."

He looked up, surprised to see that the CIA Director had come into the room.

"Odd time for a meeting, Karl." He draped his six-foot-four-inch frame over the couch near the fireplace.

"You received my personal note?" Loggerman asked.

"Yes, but surely there must be more to it than just this anonymous phone call."

"No, except that when we ask the Pentagon where all their atomic bombs are, we don't get very good answers. If this were true, who could be behind it?"

"You mean the Russians? Qaddafi? The Red Army Faction? The Islamic Jihad?" The Director spoke through his teeth without moving his jaw.

"The Russians," Loggerman prompted.

"Odd that you should say that. I've done a little checking. They probably intercepted the call you received last night. They're clearly following this inventory you're conducting with great interest. And I'm sure they enjoyed listening in on your conversation with the Chairman of the JCS just now."

Loggerman flushed at the reproach. "How did you know about the inventory?" he countered.

"We watch them watching us. You'd be surprised what we learn that way."

"I'm sure." Loggerman felt another twinge of anxiety. "But what about the Russians?" he pressed. "Are they involved?"

"No direct evidence as yet."

"And circumstantial evidence?"

"The chief circumstance—they're our enemy."

16

Sean Gordon blinked several times to help his eyes get reac-customed to the candlelight of the State Dining Room. The President and the Sultan had finished their toasts, and the floodlights were receding behind doors in the tall, square columns that graced the walls. As the TV crews packed their gear, two dozen violinists from the Air Force Strings swirled into the room playing Moussorgsky's *Carpathian Dances*.

Gordon was relieved at Loggerman's exit halfway through dinner. After he left, the others asked Gordon if he and the National Security Advisor knew each other well.

"I know him," Gordon had replied.

"I understand he's actually European Royalty," the New York socialite pressed.

"He used to tell people he was from a Dutch noble family, the van Loggermans," Gordon confirmed. "But he doesn't make that claim anymore."

"Is that why," she asked maliciously, "he's often called 'the short count'?"

Gordon almost bit through his wine glass. He laughed and began to relax.

When the violins switched to *Malagueña*, Gordon saw the President and the Sultan rise and thread their way out of the room, accompanied by the Secretary of State and the Foreign Minister of Muscat. By White House protocol, he knew that the dinner guests would be entertained while the two leaders went up to the third floor private quarters for a personal talk. As he settled back to enjoy the music, the white-gloved hand of a woman military escort put a note in front of him.

"Come to the second floor ASAP. Use the stairs." It was unsigned, but Gordon recognized the President's handwriting.

He was standing by himself at the head of the circular staircase, apparently lost in thought.

"Mr. President, we have to stop meeting like this."

"Sean! God, it's good to see you." The President shook Gordon's hand vigorously and then impulsively he grabbed his shoulders in a bear hug. "Did you get the material I left for you?"

"Yes." Gordon extracted himself from the President's embrace. "What happened to the Sultan?"

"I invited him into the elevator, pushed the down button and said goodbye." Gordon saw the President smile genuinely for the first time that evening. "He'll be in Blair House in thirty seconds. What a statesman. Each time I shake hands with him I have to count my fingers."

Gordon could hear the door of the small elevator open, and they started toward it. "It's so good of you to drop everything and come all this way at the request of a paranoid President. You know I always respected your decision to walk away from all this Washington craziness, particularly after what the press did to you, but dammit, man, I really need you."

Gordon looked skeptical.

"If you read the stuff I left in your room, you probably think I've gone overboard like everyone else." As they entered the elevator, a Secret Service agent emerged from a doorway and crowded in behind them.

"But the more I get into it, the more concerned I get." Gordon remembered when the President used to complain about the constant presence of the Secret Service, but now he continued to talk as if the agent were not there. "I want to fill you in on the political situation before we get to a little meeting I've called in the Sit Room."

"Mr. President, I don't think it's a good idea to bring me any closer to Karl Loggerman."

"Well, I've got a little surprise planned for him tonight, and besides, nobody believes that stuff he wrote about you."

"Maybe not, but there's a reason I'm teaching in La Jolla and not at Harvard."

"He goes around saying that you had planned to kill him." The President searched Gordon's face for a reaction.

"Good, I hope he still believes it."

The elevator opened into the White House basement. The sound of violins drifted down the main staircase.

"Sean, I had to put him in that job. I needed someone to balance the Secretary of State. You know what I've been trying to do. My predecessor"—the word stuck in his mouth—"left this country totally polarized. I meant it when I promised a government of national reconciliation."

They went through double doors into a glass-enclosed porch that connected the Mansion to the West Wing. Gordon was struck by the heavy humidity and the sweet perfume of the potted flowers.

"So I brought them all into the government." The President picked up the pace. "Left, right, center, Republicans, Democrats, Independents, you name it. But the fighting didn't stop; it just moved indoors. I'm just a referee. The back stabbing, the bad-mouthing, the leaks, it's making me look like a wimp."

The President stopped at the end of the long colonnade that ran beside the Rose Garden. It had turned cold. Gordon could see the President's breath as he spoke.

"I had the shortest honeymoon on record. It didn't even last until I got back to the White House from being sworn in on Capitol Hill. They say I'm too cautious or too erratic, that I'm not leading, that I'm not in charge, that my inexperience shows. If this bomb thing is true and gets bungled like everything else we try to do, I'll be a lame duck for the next three and a half years."

The President pulled open the glass door, climbed a short ramp and then descended a set of stairs into the West Wing basement. They passed the White House Mess and stopped at a heavy oak door with a small brass plaque that said SITUATION ROOM. The Secret Service agent rang the buzzer.

"Don't you also have to worry about overreacting?" Gordon asked. "It sounds like plenty of your friends would be happy to see you play the fool."

The President nodded grimly as they stepped inside. "I knew you'd get the feel of things right away."

17

The room was barely a dozen feet wide and only half again as long, dominated by a large teak conference table. Three of the walls were paneled in dark walnut squares, many of which concealed the paraphernalia of crisis management—four video monitors, two projectors, an intercom, a four-color printer, a bank of telecommunications terminals, and the controls for manipulating images on a large screen hidden by a curtain that covered the fourth wall. Despite the heavy air-conditioning, Gordon found the atmosphere thick and slightly damp. It was a room designed for close-quarter political combat.

Gordon recognized each of the NSC members—the young Secretary of State and the Director of Central Intelligence, who sat on the President's left; and the Secretary of Defense and the Chairman of the JCS, who sat on the right. Karl Loggerman was at the opposite end of the table from the President and staring at Gordon in evident surprise. An Admiral that Gordon did not know, and the FBI Director, and the Secretary of Energy, none of whom were NSC members, sat away from the table along the walls. With that as a cue, Gordon took a seat against the curtain behind the President.

"I want to thank you for coming at this unusual hour, but we may have an unusual situation. Before we get started, I want to introduce you to Sean Gordon. Some of you"—he nodded at the CIA Director—"may know Mr. Gordon from his distinguished career in the Clandestine Service. Others"—he glanced at Loggerman—"may recall his excellent work for me during the Senate probe of intelligence failures after the Mexican Coup." All of them except Loggerman gave Gordon a perfunctory nod.

"You are all aware of last night's caller, who indicated that he would phone again about now." The President took Loggerman's memo out of the inside pocket of his tuxedo jacket and spread it on the table. "Since there are differences over whether this is serious, I want your views. Mr. Secretary, Admiral, why don't you and the Director," he waved at the FBI Chief, "join us at the table. While we wait, you can tell us the results of the inventory."

"Mr. President," McCollough began as he changed seats, "we had to query several thousand facilities throughout the world to ascertain the location of the nearly thirty thousand nuclear weapons in our stockpile. The scale and speed of the inventory has probably introduced certain errors into the results—errors that minute by minute are being ironed out—"

"What's the bottom line?" the President interrupted.

"Yes, sir." McCollough ran his tongue over his lips. "As of 24:30 hours, or ten minutes ago, we could not verify the location of seventeen weapons."

Gordon saw the President's shoulders sag. "You've got to be kidding!" the Secretary of State burst out. The Secretary of Defense stared at the table.

"The unaccounted-for weapons," McCollough continued, "come in almost every category except operational strategic missile warheads. The largest group of missing weapons—"

"You can't say they're missing," the Defense Secretary insisted.

"Go on," the President overruled him.

"The largest group comes from the weapons labs, and most of them are very old. So it seems likely that those are a problem of record keeping. The rest are a mixed bag, some strategic and tactical bombs, a nuclear depth charge, some missile and artillery warheads."

"It's my firm view," the Secretary of Defense intervened again, "that these, uh, unlocated weapons are an artifact of the hasty inventory. We keep excellent track of all of our weapons, it's just that we've lost track of some of our tracks," he concluded earnestly.

"What about the Trident submarine?" Loggerman asked with feigned innocence.

"That's a perfect example." The Defense Secretary jumped on the question. "Up to a few minutes ago, we thought that one of our Tridents in the Indian Ocean was missing. We'd lost contact. But it turns out that it had an emergency and had to put into Diego Garcia. The damned British who run the island wouldn't let our boys use their commo links to answer our inventory request, so we thought the whole sub had somehow vanished. Well, I was just handed a message from the sub relayed by the crew of an SR-71 that lands on Diego Garcia, and I can report that everything is fine. I'm sure we'll find that the rest of these so-called missing weapons are fine, too."

"Mr. President," McCollough added, "we've done a computer regression, and it does tell us that the number missing is within the range of statistical uncertainty, given how fast we had to do this."

"So you're saying that despite a computer check that showed dozens of weapons missing, and a physical inventory that reveals seventeen nuclear weapons missing, and a mystery caller that claims to have at least one of our weapons, you think everything is fine. And if he calls again, we can just relax because it's a joke?"

"No," the Defense Secretary replied, "we simply don't know if it is or not."

"I see. And when might we be fortunate enough to know?"

Gordon could tell from the President's increasingly polite tone that he was getting very angry.

"A few days to a week," McCollough responded.

As the President started to speak, a buzzer sounded. He opened a drawer in the conference table and took out a telephone receiver.

"Switch it in here to Loggerman's phone and also put it on the speakers."

The National Security Advisor took a phone out of the drawer at his end of the table. The curtains covering the wall behind the President parted to reveal a large screen and several speakers. They heard the crackle of a telephone connection and white noise like roaring wind. A young man's voice came on the line sounding unnaturally close. The ends of his words were clipped off.

"Dr. Loggerman?"

"Speaking."

"Since you're taking this call, you obviously know that my message yesterday was not a hoax. So listen carefully, I have instructions that must be followed precisely."

"Who are you?"

"Don't interrupt or I'll terminate this call. Here are our demands.

"First, you must begin to withdraw all nuclear weapons from Europe within twenty-four hours.

"Second, removal of the entire stockpile must be completed within seventy-two hours thereafter.

"Third, if you fail to carry out these instructions on time, the weapon will be detonated in a major city in Western Europe.

"I want to emphasize that I'm not operating alone. If any effort is made to find me or my associates, the weapon will be exploded. You should know it continues to be one-point-safe.

"As soon as these instructions are fulfilled, we'll arrange for the weapon's disposal."

The line went dead.

The group sat stunned.

Finally, the Secretary of State asked, "Admiral, what does 'one-point-safe' mean?" He was searching for solid ground.

"The weapons are designed so that if they suffer a shock, or a fire, some of the high explosive that starts the chain reaction can't go off. Part of it's safe, so there can't be a full nuclear explosion. He's apparently trying to reassure us it won't detonate accidentally."

"How considerate," said the President.

"How often do you get a threat of a stolen weapon?" the Secretary of State asked.

"It's not very common. Maybe two or three a year. Usually, it's easy to establish that it's a crank. I think the last one we had, a few months ago, the caller said he was from Saturn."

"This guy didn't sound like he was from outer space," the Secretary of Energy commented. "He sounded very competent."

The FBI Chief nodded in agreement.

"Mr. President," the Secretary of Defense said, in a tone of resignation, "I guess prudence requires that we proceed on the assumption that the threat is genuine." Gordon saw him look at Loggerman, who gave a tight, satisfied nod. In the deep silence that followed, Gordon watched the enormity of the Defense Secretary's judgment register on the faces of the others.

"If I may, Mr. President," Loggerman moved in quickly, "I'd like to outline the broader implications of this crisis in order to help structure our decisions. It seems likely now that the missing weapon was taken from the NATO stockpile in Europe . . ."

"There are seven unaccounted for in Europe, eight if you include Turkey," McCollough added.

"If he has the support of others in Europe," the National Security Advisor continued, "it's more than likely the terrorists have links to the Soviet Union. In any event, the demands for a US nuclear withdrawal are the same as those made by the Soviets for decades—it objectively serves their interests."

"Wait a minute," the Secretary of State said sharply. "Let's not jump to conclusions. I hadn't heard a thing about any of this until the dessert course this evening. It's a little soon to start weaving theories."

The youngest man since Thomas Jefferson to hold the office, the Secretary of State had been the junior Senator from California, and the President's principal rival for the nomination. Articulate and mercurial, he still retained a large political following among the younger and more populist members of his party.

"I think we've had these weapons in Europe far too long," he added. "Most of the Europeans don't want them there, either. They've been demonstrating against them for years. And hell, almost half the Senate would like to bring our troops home, too."

"That's exactly why this situation is so dangerous," Loggerman shot back. "The issue here is the NATO alliance. I grant you there are radicals," he nodded imperceptibly toward the Secretary of State, "both in Europe and in the United States, who think that NATO's out of date, that we can deal with the Russians with diplomacy and wishful thinking. But NATO's prevented another World War for half a century. And our troops and nuclear weapons in Europe are the glue that holds NATO together.

"If we give in to these demands, the Congress would never let us leave our troops behind defenseless. If we retreat in the face of a terrorist threat, even of this magnitude, our allies would never again believe we'd stand up to the Russian Army. They'd have to strike their own deal with Moscow, and we'd be out in the cold. Mr. President, you don't want to go down in history as the man who presided over the collapse of the greatest alliance of free men the world has ever known."

"But if this atomic bomb goes off," the Secretary of State countered, "we'll be responsible for destroying the very people we're supposed to protect. Then NATO really will be finished. Just the revelation that even one US weapon is missing, not to mention seventeen, would wreck American credibility in NATO and everywhere else in the world."

"I agree with Dr. Loggerman," the Chairman of the JSC said tersely. "If we cave in, we lose Europe. There would be a massive shift in the world balance of power. The Russians would feel free to challenge us anywhere. America would be placed in great jeopardy."

"I'm not suggesting we cave in—" the Secretary started to reply, but the President cut him off.

"NATO's vital, and no one wants to see Paris or London get blown away," the President declared. "But the United States doesn't give in to blackmail, period! Now, I want to know what we do."

The President looked over at the Defense Secretary, who had been silent during the debate between Loggerman and the Secretary of State. "This remains a defense matter," he said. "We're charged by law to maintain the security of our nuclear weapons. If one's missing, we have the responsibility and the capability to find it."

"Our Nuclear Emergency Search Teams are trained to find lost weapons," the Secretary of Energy spoke up.

"It's stolen, not lost," the Defense Secretary retorted.

Gordon recognized the iron law of bureaucracy at work; faced with a tough question, a committee invariably argued over turf.

The President turned to the Secretary of State, who leaned back in his chair displaying the crimson lining of his tuxedo. "I don't share all of Karl's views"—he prepared to shift ground—"but he makes a persuasive case that this is a NATO crisis and an extremely delicate political operation. We don't want," he glanced at the Secretary of Defense, "MPs in combat gear or NEST teams in antiradiation suits stumbling around all over Europe.

"Our response to this crisis must be carefully coordinated with our allies. We'll need their help. They are the target and should have something to say about all this. I recommend that I be authorized to conduct urgent consultations in the NATO Council, and in London, Bonn, and Paris. We would need the help of other agencies," he covered the concession with a bright smile toward the CIA Director, "but I think it's clear that the State Department is the most qualified to manage a NATO crisis with the necessary political sensitivity."

"And the CIA?" the President asked.

"We have the ability to try to recover the weapon on a clandestine basis." The CIA Director bobbed his head as he talked. "Equally important, we must find out who is behind this, and what their motives are. I'm not trying to reopen the debate, Mr. President, but if this person is working with others in Europe, the odds are that they have links to East Bloc intelligence services. Are these terrorists on their own, or is this a Soviet challenge? The answer will be central to how you ultimately respond. CIA has the best chance of finding the answer."

The President finally looked to the National Security Advisor.

"Each of you is correct," Loggerman said smoothly. "You all have crucial and unique roles to play. But these efforts will require centralized coordination."

The Chairman of the JCS said, "I agree."

"And Mr. President, I don't wish to be alarmist," Loggerman went on, "but this incident could . . . it's potentially the crisis of the century. It must be run from the White House. I guess I don't have to tell you who I have in mind for the job." He smiled. The joke did little to ease the tension.

"I'm glad no one here is trying to pass the buck," the President said with a hint of sarcasm. "I agree with Dr. Loggerman that this operation must have a central crisis manager in the White House." He paused for effect, "and that's going to be me. Mr. Gordon has agreed to assist me."

Gordon was as surprised as Loggerman. The Secretaries of State and Defense glanced at Loggerman, who sat rigid, trying to show no reaction. They then turned and looked closely at Gordon for the first time.

"You all will continue to carry out your statutory responsibilities," the President picked up again. "There'll be plenty to do. Karl, you'll remain the point of contact if this terrorist calls again. I also want you and the Secretary of State to assess the Soviet role. The CIA can referee. Mr. Chairman, I want the JCS to develop a plan to *look* like we're responding to these demands without doing so—and without scaring our Allies. And I want you," he turned to the Defense Secretary, "to keep searching for these goddamned missing weapons.

"Mr. Gordon will have the task of finding this caller and his friends and any weapon they have. You're all to coordinate through him. He's to have full access to any and all of the government's resources on an absolute priority.

"One thing more you should all understand about Mr. Gordon: He's a personal friend. I trust him. Sean, please give us your thoughts on how we should proceed."

Gordon felt a little like the fish that burst when pulled up too fast from the ocean bottom. But he knew he could show no hesitancy.

"I know that parachuting a new player into a crisis like this can only make your lives harder. Mr. President, we'll have to develop a plan of action tonight. We're not going to sleep much over the next several days, and that's going to cloud our judgment. It's essential that you get some rest, so that you can be fresh.

"But before you go, there's one crucial issue that has come up here and requires absolute clarity. This crisis will become totally unmanageable if it becomes public. So far, we've been plain lucky. If this story gets out, the public in Europe will panic. Our Allies would be forced to go after these terrorists, and the weapon, if there is one, may be set off. Their help could make some things easier"—he nodded to the Secretary of State—"but we can't risk widening the circle. For the present anyway, we've got to try to handle this ourselves. And we must all make the most solemn commitment to maintain the utmost security."

"I'm certainly for that," Loggerman said, the challenge in his voice unconcealed. "But isn't it a little naive to think this secret will keep? And when it leaks, what do we say? That we're so irresponsible that we can't locate over a dozen of our nuclear weapons and have to assume that at least one is in the hands of terrorists? No, we must expect a leak and have an explanation that doesn't destroy NATO. Even the Clandestine Service leaks. You, above all, Mr. Gordon, should know that."

Gordon refused to be baited. "What do you recommend?"

"I go back to my point concerning the Russians. Whoever these terrorists are, they're serving Soviet interests at least indirectly. Even if there's no provable connection, our most vital interest requires that this entire incident, whether real or a hoax, be laid off on the Soviets. It is the only way," Loggerman concluded, "that we are going to hold NATO together."

"So?" Gordon prodded him.

"So, instead of counting on a pledge of secrecy as if we were Boy Scouts, Mr. President, we must plan for a leak. We should even consider leaking it ourselves so that we can at least control the spin on the story."

Gordon glanced over at the President, who waited for his response.

"Mr. President, I do not believe that the best way to deal with these terrorists is to get into a slinging match with the Soviets. We risk a deeper crisis and we may even need their help before this is over."

"I second that." It was the Secretary of State.

"We'll have plenty of time for pointing fingers when we find out who's behind this," Gordon added. "Yes, we need a cover story. But I see no way that talking to the press, deliberately or otherwise, can do anything but make our job impossible."

The President looked slowly from Gordon to Loggerman and then at the rest of the table. "I was a newsman long enough to learn that the ship of State is unique," the President began quietly. "It leaks from the top. Our Administration has been bleeding to death because of leaks. Every one of you, except Sean and maybe the Admiral, has gotten used to telling the press our innermost secrets on a daily basis. Don't bother to deny it. Often it's necessary, or it seems so." His tone was conciliatory.

"Well, that crap stops right now!" He slammed his fist down. "I want the Bureau," he pointed at the FBI Director, "to monitor the phone calls of everybody involved. There'll be no civil rights for anybody in this operation. I'll use all my authority, including the emergency powers of the presidency, to punish anyone even suspected of leaks.

"Now, I'm going to get a good night's sleep." They all stood as the President rose to leave. "And I'm going to pray that in the morning I don't read about this meeting in the newspapers."

When they sat down, Gordon moved into the President's chair. It still felt warm. The faces of his new colleagues ranged from hard to cold. Admiral McCollough broke the ice.

"I suggest that we continue to use the cover story for the inventory, that we're conducting an exercise . . ."

As he spoke, a door behind Loggerman slid open and the Situation Room duty officer handed him a yellow telephone call slip.

"Mr. Gordon," the National Security Advisor interrupted, reading the note with evident pleasure, "you've had a call from *The Washington Post*. Walter Pincus saw you on the list for the State Dinner, and he wants to talk to you about the story behind the death of a mutual friend, Jason Winniker."

II. SUNDAY

18

"If he's dialing direct from Europe, it has to go through London Toll," Gordon explained to Admiral McCollough as the car passed the darkened Jefferson Memorial and mounted the ramp to the southwest freeway heading toward Andrews Air Force Base. "Don't let the State Department or the lawyers at Justice screw up the request to the British for a backtrack. Have the National Security Agency use their own channel to contact their counterparts at GCHQ Cheltenham. They should do it, no questions asked."

"Won't they record it?" the Admiral asked.

"They're not supposed to, but probably. If we don't make a fuss, they may treat it as routine and not look at it for weeks. It's our only hope of tracing the calls."

Gordon had quickly made McCollough his deputy. If Gordon was to direct the search from Europe, he needed an ally in Washington who understood the system. Despite the fact that the Admiral was an unknown quantity to him, Gordon judged that as a military officer, McCollough would know how to give and take orders. And unlike the civilians, he probably had no political axe to grind. Loggerman was so relieved that Gordon was leaving town that he did not object to the Admiral's operating out of the White House. Then Gordon had rapidly brought the NSC meeting to a close before too many questions could be raised to unravel the President's decisions.

The lighted dome of the Capitol seemed to float by the car windows in the early A.M. darkness. Gordon began to think aloud.

"What if we put ourselves in the place of the terrorists? Which of the missing weapons would we want to steal?"

"You can forget the depth charge at that Dutch naval base," Admiral McCollough said. "It's much too big for one or two, or even three or four people to handle. They'd need special equipment. That goes for the B-43 and B-28 bombs missing from Lakenheath and Norvenich." He struggled with the small gooseneck lamp behind the seat to make it shine on the papers in his lap. "Ditto the Ground Launched Cruise Missile warhead at Comiso. All those weapons, plus the warhead for the Nike air defense battery in Liège, are protected by Permissive Action Programs. The PAPS would inert them if they're not handled just right."

"So that just leaves the two artillery shells they can't find at Ramstein?"

"Yes, and incidentally, that raises the possibility that the terrorists have two weapons."

"You're full of good news."

"I really haven't answered your question, either." The Admiral paused. "You realize that the Secretary of Defense could well be right, that the missing weapons are just the result of the rushed inventory."

"Spare me—"

"I don't mean there's no stolen weapon. I'm trying to say that the odds are only fifty–fifty we've discovered it. I wouldn't steal any of the weapons on this list."

"Don't keep me in suspense."

"I've never pictured myself as a terrorist, but I'd steal an ADM."

"What's that?"

"An Atomic Demolition Munition. It is designed to be set off by one person, on the ground, just like dynamite. It has a timer and a remote detonator. One version, the SADM, is man-portable. Hell, these others"—he slapped the folder—"won't go off unless they're a hundred feet under water or a thousand feet in the air. The two artillery shells can't be armed except by being shot from a cannon."

"But no ADMs are missing."

"We're checking again."

The car turned off Interstate 409 and onto Suitland Parkway, an old-fashioned divided highway built during the term of Franklin Roosevelt before the second World War. Gordon fell silent for several minutes.

"Maybe it would be easier to focus on finding the people rather than the weapon," he finally said.

"It had to be an inside job," the Admiral concluded. "We'd know if force was used. The caller, he sounded American. I'll have the FBI linguist check the tape and also get a voiceprint . . ."

"Go over all your personnel records. Check everybody who resigned, was fired, transferred, disciplined, or anything. Go back six months, further if you have to."

A huge water tower signaled their arrival at Andrews AFB.

"What should I do about that reporter at the *Post*?"

Gordon felt a stab of guilt. Walter Pincus had been one of the few people in town who defended him when he had been under attack by Loggerman.

"How about something unusual for Washington?"

Admiral McCollough cocked an eyebrow.

"Not answering his phone call."

As the guard waved them through the gate and onto the base, Gordon had one more item on his agenda.

"You may not need this, but let me give you a few tips on handling Loggerman . . ."

19

The National Security Advisor sat behind his desk, framed by the tall, night-blackened windows. He hated to wait for anyone, but he decided to stay until Admiral McCollough returned from Andrews. He was determined to get their relationship straight from the outset.

Nothing had really changed because of the meeting, Loggerman assured himself. Gordon had not been brought into the White House, but sent on a mission abroad. He could not do anything from the field except manage his own activities. He, Loggerman, was still the National Security Advisor, still responsible for coordinating the State and Defense Departments and the Intelligence community.

But how did the others see it? Would they think he was being eclipsed by Gordon at the most crucial moment the Administration had faced? They all knew about the bad blood between them. If Gordon succeeded, would they think that Loggerman would be on his way out? Would they take longer to return his phone calls? Have subordinates respond to his requests? He had to be alert to the subtle signs that power was shifting away from him.

Damn the President! He had made him look like a fool. Nothing the President did was impulsive or accidental. It had to be deliberate, a shot across his bow. But he warned himself against paranoia. The President always tried to keep everyone off balance. He simply doesn't appreciate how difficult it makes my job of buttressing his leadership, Loggerman thought bitterly. And now it was mandatory to pull the government together and enforce discipline. Loggerman was determined to play that role, even if the President did not appreciate it. And the first priority was to reassert his own authority, starting with Admiral McCollough.

Loggerman's intercom buzzed.

"Admiral McCollough's here," Suzy Marcos said.

"Come on in, Chip," Loggerman said heartily, without getting up from his desk or asking the Admiral to sit down. "We've cleaned out an office for you down in the Sit Room."

"I appreciate that, sir."

"Don't thank me. I've had to send my military aide packing across the street. It's just another debt the Navy will owe the Army."

They exchanged ritual chuckles.

"I've also set up a special series of messages from the Sit Room just for your use. Of course, I would expect to clear them," Loggerman added almost casually.

"Excuse me," McCollough became wary, "you want to approve any messages I send out? Even messages to Mr. Gordon or instructions he may have me relay to others?"

"It's just a formality," Loggerman responded, still casual. "I am, after all, in charge of the Situation Room . . ."

"But Mr. Gordon is in charge of this operation, reporting directly to the President. And I am responsible to him. I can't have two commanding officers, especially not in an emergency like this."

"I'm sure the President did not have in mind your operating on your own out of the White House. In fact, he doesn't even know you're here." Loggerman's tone had turned waspish.

"Then let's ask him what he intends," said McCollough smoothly. "I've set up a briefing for him at 6:30 A.M. through his Appointments Secretary. I can raise it then."

Loggerman paused. He did not know what the President would say. He did not need another humiliation. "We don't have to trouble him with that," he said, backing off. "I just want to be sure I see all the message traffic, to ensure coordination."

"No problem, sir." McCollough eased into a posture of military subordination.

Loggerman did not see him to the door. He was raging inside. After McCollough had gone, he pushed the Sit Room button on his intercom.

"Duty Officer."

"I want all of Admiral McCollough's telephone calls monitored. Make only an original copy and give it to me."

"Uh, sir, I'm not sure I can do that . . ."

"Why not?" Loggerman shouted.

"That would be a surveillance, which requires approval by the White House Counsel . . ."

"What about this caller? You taped him!"

"We have standing orders on threats. But Admiral McCollough, he doesn't—"

"Then just give me a list of who he calls." Loggerman slammed the phone down before the Duty Officer could refuse.

Agitated and angry, he paced around his office. His authority was already slipping. Kids in the Situation Room were telling him to take a flying fuck. He had to calm down. Get control of himself. He needed some rest. He should go home. It was late.

He stopped at the door. What was Henry Kissinger's advice to him? "Remember, even paranoids have enemies." He had the Secretary of Defense in hand. The Secretary of State was next. Turning back to his desk, he wrote a note in his diary for the next day. "Call Walter Pincus at *The Washington Post*."

20

Graciela felt Horst Bauer push himself inside her. She gazed vacantly at the dust dancing in the first rays of light to penetrate the dark bedroom of the chalet. Concentrating on the beams and the knotty pine boards in the ceiling, she tried not to think.

When first she loved him, she used to shake with excitement when Bauer entered her. Later, when love turned to hate, she still could not help but respond. Now she felt nothing but his thickness and weight. Bauer manipulated her with love, then fear, and finally force. He had taken her body from her.

She retreated within herself. She reverted to the little girl she had been, who would stare at the shadows of rustling palm fronds that moved across the walls of the tiny stucco house in East Los Angeles as her stepfather worked in and out of her, spurring himself to a climax by shouting, "My little whore . . . *tu me chingas bien!*"

She always tried to dream of the gardens of the great house in San Marino where she and her mother lived caring for an elderly woman who had brought them from Mexico. When the woman died, a small inheritance helped Graciela's mother buy a four-room pink bungalow in the Boyle Heights district of Los Angeles.

Graciela's mother worked long hours at a convalescent home and expected her daughter to cook, clean, study hard, and stay away from what she called *los mojados*—the wetbacks—who were her neighbors. She never spoke of Graciela's father; when once asked, she said, "He doesn't exist for us now."

When Graciela was eleven, her mother suddenly married an Ecuadorian who called himself "El Condor" because he claimed that, no matter how drunk, he always found his way home. As soon as he got a green card, which made him a permanent resident alien, he began sliding down the employment ladder. His first job as an auto mechanic ended when he dropped an engine on the hood of a car. He failed as a gas-station attendant, and finally found a career in a car wash.

Graciela's mother never criticized him—even when he came home as he often did, late and drunk and mean. She knew nothing of the afternoons when he returned from work early to catch Graciela making dinner or doing her homework. He always made her keep on her dark blue jumper with its crest from Immaculate Heart Junior High School.

One Saturday, staying away from home because her mother had to work, she sought the cool sanctuary of the local Catholic church. In the confession box, she felt comfortable with the warm voice of the new priest on the other side of the screen. When she seemed unwilling to leave the booth, he asked her if she wanted to tell him something more.

Her mother first accused her of lying, then of provoking her husband. The Catholic Relief Services found her a foster home. But she was even more lonely. When she turned seventeen, and before graduating from high school, she joined the Army.

It gave her back her pride. Surviving boot camp, and excelling in computer school, she was initially assigned to the Army Logistics Command at Ft. McNair near Washington, D.C., and six months later she was transferred to the Quartermaster's Office at Pirmasens, West Germany. But in the American military ghetto of West Germany, she felt as isolated as in the barrio of East Los Angeles. Her experiences with the enlisted men she met were uniformly brief and disastrous. She felt drawn to those who abused her.

Horst Bauer seemed different. He walked up to her in a *Bierstube* near the base and introduced himself in near-perfect American English. "Hi, I'm Horst"—he smiled broadly—"how do you like me so far?"

Graciela liked him fine. He was strongly built, with dark, wavy hair and bright, impish blue eyes. Only the thin lips set in the square jaw hinted at the cruelty to which she was fatally attracted.

Bauer took her away from the Army and showed her Europe. They caught the last of the spring skiing in Kitzbühel, downing *Glühwein* on the terrace of the Alpenhaus, plowing through plates of pastries at Café Langer, and dancing through the night at the Take Five. On a cool, misty Sunday on the Rhine boat, they emptied three bottles of Moselle gliding under the Lorelei between Cologne and Mainz. He introduced her to *Der Rosenkavalier* at the opera house in Karlsruhe. They made love slowly throughout a rainy weekend in the tower suite of the Weisses Rossl overlooking St. Wolfgangsee. She had never been so happy. She did not want to ask him too closely where all his money and spare time came from.

After three months, Bauer asked only one favor. His reasons made no sense to her, but she did it anyway. He then disappeared for more than a year.

Bauer was moving faster now, the sweat from his forehead dampening her breasts. She wanted to think of Culver, but that made her feel ashamed. When they first met, she saw him only as a gawky Second Lieutenant, and her indifference turned to anger when he continually shirked his duties as Deputy Commander of the Custodial Unit at Schloss Ludwigshof. He took little interest in his responsibilities, and did not even bother to explain why he disappeared so often on long leaves. But Bauer saw him as an ideal target: few close friends, poor performance record, no evident female relationships.

He also was so painfully shy he seemed impervious to Graciela's flirtations. But on an excursion to Berlin for custodial personnel hosted by the West German Army, Graciela was the only one he knew, and they soon became inseparable.

On the last day of the visit, they ditched the tour group in the labyrinth of hallways at the Akademie der Kunst and walked hand in hand through the Tiergarten. Despite the cold, they sat on the outside benches at the zoo, where suddenly he kissed her, while she laughed at the seals, her mouth open, their teeth clashing. They spent a long twilight afternoon eating finger sandwiches, drinking Berliner Weisse, and trying to learn to waltz at a thé dansant in a café at the Europa Center. Over coffee and schnapps, he said he was afraid he would love her, and she told him not to be afraid.

They tried to get a room at the Hotel Kempinski, but they were turned away. Culver's resentment increased his ardor. At last they found a small hotel on Mommsenstrasse, occupied primarily by Turks and tarts from the Kurfürstendamm. In the faded elegance of the darkened room, Culver's excitement collapsed.

Amazed to find a man intimidated by her body and not somehow enraged by it, Graciela felt suffused with a new sense of power. She caressed him softly and patiently, until at last he was able to make love. Culver was hers. And she was his.

Bauer grunted to a climax and fell over on the empty side of the bed. She immediately went to the bathroom, stopping momentarily to look out the window at the bright morning landscape. The mountain peaks looked clear and clean in the sunlight. She hurried into the bathroom to wash.

Bauer lit a cigarette. He went to the window to open it a crack and let in the cool breeze blowing down from the alpine meadows. He tried the bathroom door and found it locked.

Up in one of the high meadows, Culver sat with binoculars trained on the chalet. The meeting with Bauer on the ferry on Lake Constance had taught him a lesson, so the guards stationed outside the house were no surprise. But he was unprepared for the two naked figures that he saw, one after the other, at the same second-story window. The shock was not a jolt. It was the death of feeling that comes when one's most secret fear is confirmed.

He went back to his car. He had a lot of work to do before meeting Bauer on Monday with the bomb.

21

The aircraft slid effortlessly past Mach 1. Strapped into the rear seat of the FB-111, Sean Gordon felt the pressure of the continuing acceleration as he watched the lights of Nantucket, Hyannis, and then Provincetown vanish under the left wing. In the clear and moonless night, the dome of stars cast shadows in the cockpit. The nonreflecting canopy made him feel he was riding in open space.

He focused on the raster display that all but blocked his view forward. The screen was empty except for a lone incoming track that the air controller in Gander, Newfoundland, identified as a Federal Express cargo flight. On a combat mission, his would be the hot seat of the two-man strategic bomber. Digitized radar tracks, terrain contour projections, electronic countermeasures suites would appear in different colors on separate segments of the screen. The glowing blue-green bezels on the right would give the status of the half dozen B-83 hydrogen bombs or AGM-69A Short Range Attack Missiles that would be carried by the aircraft in an atomic strike. Gordon appreciated the irony of starting his mission as the payload of a nuclear delivery system.

Europe lay three hours and one midair refueling ahead. He tried not to think about the odds of finding a nuclear weapon and neutralizing a terrorist group in some unknown place in Europe without the help of Allied police or intelligence. Under the NSC's strictures, Gordon was limited to support by Defense Investigative Service, US Military Police, and local CIA stations. The Alert Company of the Delta Force and a Department of Energy NEST team were being prepositioned at Upper Heyford, England, for contingencies, but were too overt to be used in the search.

He planned to begin by trying to find the two missing 155mm nuclear artillery shells at the depot at Ramstein and see where the trail would lead. He had always operated alone and on instinct. After almost two years on the beach in California, he wondered whether those instincts were still there.

Gordon's last mission, which had ended his career, had begun the same way as this one—an urgent night flight across the Atlantic in a military aircraft. Then as now, he was being asked to cope with a crisis so obvious and long in arriving that it came as a surprise. His destination had been South Africa in the midst of revolution; the task, to gain control of Pretoria's secret nuclear arsenal before it fell into the hands of terrorists.

Acting under presidential instructions, Gordon first tried to buy the weapons for the United States, but he found the political price too high—military intervention on the side of the whites in the civil war.

Panicked by satellite photos showing preparations to move the weapons out from the storage site near Randfontein in the Kalahari desert, the NSC approved Gordon's alternate plan.

A bleep on the heads-up display shook Gordon from his reverie. The aircraft on the screen was closing fast. The pilot's voice crackled over the intercom.

"We've got a Concorde II off the left side at about ten o'clock."

It flashed by in an instant, the little postage-stamp windows glowing like a string of Christmas lights. Dawn made a red crease in the horizon. Morning came early at forty-five thousand feet.

Gordon knew he should sleep, but instead he squirmed in the cramped cockpit. He was also discomforted by another parallel with his last mission—a lack of resources. His plan to seize the South African weapons had to cope with the fact that, despite one million men and women in the US Armed Forces, only a single company of the Delta Force was ready for immediate deployment on a day-to-day basis. He needed help, and the only ones willing to give it were the rebel forces of the African National Congress.

In early morning darkness, two platoons from the Delta Force parachuted onto the airstrip at Randfontein and seized the control tower before an alert could be sounded. Minutes later, two C-5Bs laden with six hundred ANC soldiers were on the ground, and the troops were moving toward the storage bunkers. Heavy firing erupted from the massive fortifications. Automatic Belgian cannons ripped apart the first ANC assault. The second wave, attacking from the rear, broke and ran when the troops stumbled into a mine field.

Fearing the operation was about to fail, Gordon cursed himself for holding back half of the Delta Force. Then a squad of ANC cut through the perimeter fence and a Delta Force team was able to launch a TOW wire-guided missile at the pillbox defending the east flank of the storage site. It exploded like a beer bottle on a stove.

ANC troops swept through the gap and overran the site. Slipping satchel charges into every orifice in the fortifications, the Delta Force had the bunker open in five minutes and six refrigerator-sized weapons rolling toward the airstrip.

In the growing light, Gordon's satisfaction was marred by the heavy

ANC casualties and the sight of the surviving South African troops being lined up for execution.

"Is that necessary?" Gordon asked Colonel Okwege, the ANC commander.

"We paid a heavy price." He gestured to the landscape littered with hundreds of ANC troops. "But don't worry. We'll save some of them to teach us how to use the weapons."

Without surprise, Gordon had looked toward the runway. ANC soldiers had encircled the aircraft and seized the nuclear weapons from the Delta Force.

A red warning sign snapped Gordon back to the present. Flashing letters cautioned INTERCEPT COURSE, while the raster monitor displayed a blip with an arrow indicating the direction and speed of the approaching aircraft. The pilot came on the intercom.

"Either the Greenland air force is about to shoot us down, or we're about to gas up. Hit your IFF."

Gordon pushed the Identification Friend or Foe button. A pulse of radio energy carrying a digitally encrypted message flashed toward the blip. In a microsecond, a return pulse showed up on his screen in green. "It's NATO Friendly," Gordon reported.

He felt the aircraft slow rapidly and descend. Buffeting, and the whine of hydraulic pumps, told him that the swept wings were moving forward for subsonic flight. In a second, a faint dot in the morning twilight mushroomed into a KC-135 tanker aircraft. The FB-111 passed over it, went into a wide left-hand turn, and settled in behind.

"Give me the fueling probe," the pilot ordered.

Gordon pulled back a lever and saw an indicator light confirm that the probe was extended. A three-foot-diameter funnel on the end of a heavy hose uncoiled from the rear of the tanker and came whipping and bouncing toward them. Nudging the aircraft forward, the pilot jammed the nose into the funnel, engaging the probe. Three tons of JP-4 immediately began coursing through the hose at one thousand gallons a minute.

Gordon's nightmare of South Africa was momentarily eclipsed by the realization that he was hurtling along at 350 knots, tied by a forty-foot hose to a flying bomb five miles above the Atlantic Ocean. He closed his eyes, only to see the grinning face of Colonel Okwege as he waved with his AK-47 ordering the C-5Bs to take off.

Once airborne, Gordon had had the Starlifters make one slow pass over the ANC convoy to identify the trucks carrying away the nuclear weapons. The soldiers had fired up at them without effect.

"If they get them sons'a bitches too close together, we won't have to worry about gettin' 'em back," said Colonel Peckwood, the Delta Force leader. "Should I radio the rest of the company?"

"Tell them the ANC is taking the road south and should be at the Bravo location in about an hour. Have them drop there ASAP and we'll link up in about twenty," Gordon ordered.

Gordon's planning had prepared for the possibility that the ANC would double-cross him and take the weapons for themselves. With even one nuclear bomb, the rebels could threaten Johannesburg and end the civil war on their terms. That was why he had been confident of ANC help, and why he had kept two platoons of the Delta Force in reserve aboard a third Starlifter parked on a nearby dry lake. A full company from the Delta Force, he hoped, would be enough to handle the ANC forces after they had been decimated by the assault on the storage bunkers. Still, the odds were ten-to-one.

He watched without pleasure as Colonel Okwege drove his convoy into the ambush waiting in the steep ravine. A HOT Missile slammed into the lead truck. The second and third vehicle plowed into the fireball. Firing from concealed positions, the Delta Force raked the convoy, sparing only the trucks carrying the weapons. With impressive discipline, the surviving ANC troops tried to charge up the steep slopes. But one of the C-5Bs appeared over the rim of the ravine and unloaded ten thousand rounds a minute from a pair of GAU 88s. The carnage made Gordon want to throw up.

In short order, the Delta teams had wrapped the weapons in harnesses and attached them to balloons that carried a cable three hundred feet into the air. Flying slightly above stalling speed, the Starlifters yanked the weapons off the ground and reeled them in. Using a special shock-absorbing polyester cable, Gordon was snatched up the same way. As two of the aircraft headed for McGuire Air Force Base in Delaware, the third C-5B returned to the Randfontyn to await the Delta Force.

A sudden jolt and the FB-111 disconnected itself from the umbilical of the tanker. Saluting with a waggle of the wings, the pilot opened up the throttle, kicking in the afterburner and again pushing Gordon into his seat. Climbing at twenty degrees, the fighter-bomber folded its wings back and rose rapidly through layer upon layer of brightening clouds. They leveled out at forty-three thousand feet in between two sheets of stratus that seemed to Gordon to create an enormous room stretching endlessly in every direction. Over the Faroes VAR, the pilot altered course to 105°, heading toward the northern tip of Scotland and the North Sea coast of Europe.

The moment Gordon had returned from South Africa, he had been rushed to a private meeting with a grateful President, who had said that he would receive America's highest secret award—the National Security Medal.

"Mr. President, I'm genuinely honored." Gordon felt overwhelmed by fatigue and stress. "I don't know what to say . . ."

"Some good's got to come out of this. Have you seen what's been happening? You've been out of touch." The President snapped on the video monitor set in the wall of the small study next to the Oval Office. Tapes assembled by the Situation Room staff showed looting, burning, and killing as white resistance collapsed, and mobs from the shantytowns went on a rampage of revenge. For Gordon, it brought back images of piles of dead black and white soldiers.

"They're trying to hang this around my neck. Look at the papers." He tossed Gordon a copy of *The Washington Times*. "They're saying I 'lost' South Africa. And we can't even brag about what you've just done."

"I'm sorry, sir . . ." Gordon did not know how to comfort him.

"Well, I've only got a year to go, and then somebody else gets to be the national fireplug. The presidential campaign's already under way. That's what this is all about, attacking me to undermine the Vice President's candidacy," he said, as if Gordon needed the reassurance.

The next day, Sean Gordon awoke to an early morning phone call from his ex-wife. He was pleased that she might have learned of his award and was calling to congratulate him. Instead he heard concern in her voice.

"Have you seen *The Washington Times?*"

"No, it comes in the afternoon at the office."

"Get the morning edition, and if you want to have dinner with some-one tonight, I'm free. Call me."

Enveloped in the haze from rush-hour traffic, Gordon stood in his running suit on the corner of Wisconsin and M Street in Georgetown staring at the paper he had just withdrawn from the vending machine. Two pictures dominated the front page: a telephoto shot of Gordon getting into an Agency car on West Executive Avenue, and, next to it, a wire service picture of a heap of white South African schoolchildren slain by black tribesmen. The headline read, SECRET WHITE HOUSE ENVOY HELPED REBELS. The story reported that Sean Gordon had met secretly with ANC military leaders to assure them of the US President's support.

The next day's headlines in *The Washington Times* were worse. Under the banner THOUSANDS SLAIN BY REBELS it charged, "ANC Saved by US Strike on SA Nukes." Quoting former South African officials and unnamed sources in Washington, the article asserted that Gordon convinced the President to save the ANC from certain defeat by destroying the whites' ultimate defense. The stories were written by Karl Loggerman.

The White House dismissed the reports as distortions and refused further comment. But Gordon's award ceremony was postponed indef-initely. The Agency immediately sent him abroad on a three-week inspection trip and, when he returned, assigned him to a management review committee.

Shunted from one high-sounding "housekeeping" job to another, he felt like a walking dead man. He knew that, while politicians thrived on controversy, for civil servants—let alone CIA officers—notoriety ended careers. Gordon looked forward to a threatened congressional investigation to clear his name, but the few remaining friends on the Hill advised him that it would be a circus that could only hurt him more. Together with the White House, they managed to quash the hearings on the grounds of national security.

Gordon pushed the painful memory aside. Looking down through the broken clouds, he could see the coast of Friesland. The pilot re-ported that they would land in twenty minutes.

When he had taken an inventory of his life, he had discovered little but memories, memories he could not share, and in any event no one to share them with. He had found himself questioning his accomplishments. He felt that all he really had ever done was to keep worse things from happening. Initially, he had wondered how he could have been so naive to sacrifice family and friends for that. As time passed, however, he realized that he had made deliberate choices. He had allowed himself the furtive self-importance of knowing powerful secrets. His legendary disdain for bureaucracy selfishly had ignored the fact that he would not have succeeded without the support of those he called "the gray grinds." He prided himself on taking risks, and they had finally caught up with him. He had been riding for a fall.

After moving to La Jolla, Gordon had started rebuilding his life by getting to know his son, Ted. One twilight evening, during a week of backpacking along the Big Sur coast, they had sat in a high meadow, the surf crashing a mile below. His son asked if he was bitter.

"I used to be. You know, outraged that lies could change my life. But as I've always told you, if you pick a career in government—"

"Don't expect justice," Ted finished the homily. They laughed.

"I'm sorry I never asked before, but was it hard for you?"

"Sometimes," Ted replied. "Mostly the kids just stayed away like somebody in your family died. I couldn't blame 'em. It's hard to relate to having your dad called 'Mr. Atrocity.'"

Gordon still flinched at the label. "Well, I haven't lost faith," he said, sliding into another mock solemn adage, "that we're put on earth for a reason . . ."

". . . even if you've got to make it up as you go along," Ted concluded. They both had laughed again.

The tires screeched as the FB-111 bounced onto the runway at Ramstein Air Force Base. Before the chocks had been jammed under the wheels, a blue Air Force Chevrolet rolled up and a frantic-looking Captain leaped out saluting and waving a red dispatch case.

"I have a flash White House message for a Mr. Gordon from Admiral McCollough."

22

It was good news, but Gordon reread the message with growing despair.

TOP SECRET/RYMLAND NOCOPY
TO: Gordon
FM: McCollough
SITTO-1

TWO ARTY SHELLS RAMSTEIN LOCATED. MISSING BOMBS LIKELY ACCOUNTING ERROR. DEPTH CHARGE FOUND AT UK ROYAL NAVY DEPOT PLYMOUTH. REINVENTORY OF ALL ADMS SHOWS NONE MISSING. ONLY CURRENT PERSONNEL LEAD IS SPEC 5 GRACIELA MORENA AWOL FROM SAS SITE SCHLOSS LUDWIGSHOF. SADMS STORED THERE BUT ALL ACCOUNTED FOR. GLCM WARHEAD AT COMISO STILL NOT FOUND. GOOD LUCK. CHIP.

"Sir, we have a T-33 standing by to take you to Comiso or a chopper to Schloss Ludwigshof," the Major explained.
"How far to Comiso?" Gordon asked.
"About two hours."
"Let's do Schloss Ludwigshof first."

23

For the third time, Gordon paced the full length of the storage bunker, checking the weapons against the computer printout.
"Just like I reported," Colonel Handyside said, "they're all here."
"Let me see a record of all inventory actions over the last six months."

Gordon sat at Sergeant Graciela Morena's battered metal desk and pored through a black logbook.

"She kept this book?" Gordon asked Colonel Handyside.

"That was her job."

"She herself was involved in a lot of these actions—moving, maintaining the weapons?"

"This ain't the Pentagon. We can get short-handed. She pitched in, but she doesn't do this stuff alone," he added. "There's always somebody and even a couple of somebodies with her. We never, ever, compromise the two-man rule."

Gordon started searching the desk. In the top drawer, he found paper clips, white-out, stubs of pencils, ballpoint pens with clotted nubs. The rest of the drawer contained unclassified memos and instructions, a PX guide, and a pair of lift tickets from Kitzbühel, which he put in a plastic bag. The upper-right-hand drawer held rubber stamps, Kleenex, and a tan telephone directory. The middle drawer was full of stationery. In the large bottom drawer, he found more personal articles: a pouch with soft-rubber galoshes, a box of tampons, and a neatly folded scarf. He opened the top drawer again and slid forward the tray with the pens, pencils, and paper clips and found a card from Auf das Rio Grande, a TexMex restaurant in Wiesbaden, and a box of matches from the Café Hafstnähe in Munich. Under them, he found a thin envelope with a photograph of a group of military personnel posing before the wall in Berlin. He put all three items in the plastic bag.

"Let's see her room," Gordon ordered.

It seemed more like a cell. The walls were painted concrete block, hung with government-issue travel posters of the French Quarter in New Orleans, Arizona's Sonora desert, and the Olympic peninsula. Her personal items were neatly arranged in a plywood dresser. Some surprisingly expensive-looking clothes hung in the closet. Gordon made a note of the labels and emptied the pockets. He put some fuzz from the pocket of a white wool blazer in his plastic bag. The dressing table contained a bank book and a few personal papers, which Gordon also placed in the plastic bag. There was no passport.

"Is this GI drill?" he asked Colonel Handyside. "Have you some regulation against personal things?"

Colonel Handyside looked perplexed.

"You know, books, magazines, letters, snapshots. Hell, stuffed animals. There's no personality here."

"You might check her footlocker. It'd be under the bed."

It was locked. The Colonel's orderly pried the top off with a crowbar. Inside it was stuffed with souvenirs: an empty bottle of Moselle wine, tickets for the Jägerball in Vienna, a porcelain windmill with Amsterdam painted on the base. Then a brass replica of the four horses on the façade of St. Mark's Basilica in Venice, a white leather bible from her First Communion, a base metal copy of the Eiffel Tower, an Immaculate Heart yearbook, and a photo album.

Sitting on her bed, Gordon slowly leafed through the pictures in the album. Attractive enough in uniform, Graciela was striking when made up and dressed in civilian clothes. She had large brown eyes, luxuriant hair, a wide, sensuous mouth with fine, even teeth. High and prominent cheekbones sculpted her face, giving her a haunted air. A snapshot on a beach revealed a frail but full-breasted figure.

"She looks very young."

"She's twenty, maybe twenty-one." Colonel Handyside sifted through a personnel file he was carrying. "Yep, twenty."

"She carries a lot of responsibility for a kid."

"We expect boys even younger to use these nukes."

"Who's this? He shows up here and here and here," Gordon said pointing to pictures of a tall red-haired young man. "From this one, it looks like they're pretty good friends."

"His name's Terence Culver. He was a Ranger doing TDY with the Custodial Unit."

"Can I talk to him?"

"He's gone."

"What do you mean? Transferred?"

"No, out. Busted. Well, not court-martialed, but we didn't let him re-up. Got into some trouble. Nothing to do with nukes." Colonel Handyside began to fiddle with his swagger stick.

"Colonel, I want the whole story," Gordon said evenly.

"Can't do that, Mr. Gordon. I've got no authority."

Gordon snatched the swagger stick and poked him in the chest. "Cut the crap—"

"Culver was 'black.' It's all I can say. You'll have to talk to EUCOM."

"Screw EUCOM. Get me an Autovon channel to the White House and get me that logbook again."

24

Admiral McCollough shook his head in disbelief at the two sleepy faces in front of him in the Situation Room. His voice had the edge of anger that comes from a night without sleep.

"You used one of *my* custodial slots to hide an Army intelligence agent without even telling me?"

"Your predecessor okayed it a long time ago. It's so tough to get good cover for our people," the Deputy G2 from the Army Staff explained nervously.

"And you're not exempt like the Peace Corps," said CIA's Deputy Director of Operations. "I guess nobody thought you'd object."

"Object? Why would I object to having some cowboy, some marginal psychopath with a hero complex, secretly bypass all the indoctrination, all the checks, all the psychological testing? Hell, we're only talking about protecting nuclear weapons."

"It isn't Culver's sanity that's at issue, Admiral," the CIA's DDO interjected. "It's his loyalty. Look." He handed over a green-colored file.

Admiral McCollough read through it for several minutes. "I remember something about this. The Czech government accused us of sabotage and then it all quieted down."

"It was a joint operation with the British," the Deputy G2 added, "re-equipping our stay behind networks with some new communications gear. They walked into a trap. The British agent was killed. Supposedly, this Culver commandeered a locomotive and then ran it off the rails into an apartment block, killing a lot of people. There was a hell of a stink. The NSC," he paused to look around as if to make sure Loggerman would not hear him, "clamped a lid on it."

"Everybody thought Culver was buried in the rubble," the CIA man continued, "but then a week later he showed up half-drowned on the Austrian side of the Neusiedler See. Our British friends thought his escape was a little too miraculous—so did some of us at the Agency. Our British cousins said they had evidence he'd been doubled."

"And so you let him just walk out the door."

"He got some wall-to-wall counseling, if you know what I mean," the army officer said, "but he denied everything. Claimed the British agent blew the operation. We had nothing to try him on."

Admiral McCollough snapped the speaker phone on and pushed the button for the Sit Room Duty Officer. "Get me Gordon on secure."

25

"Look at this: dozens of instances where the two of them handled weapons alone." Gordon shoved the logbook across the conference table to Colonel Handyside in the Base Operations Center. With growing impatience, he waited to resume contact on the Autovon phone. The connection had been broken three times in ten minutes.

"What is the problem?" he asked the communications officer sitting at a nearby console.

"Higher priority calls." He shook his head.

"I'm supposed to have the highest priority."

"All I can tell you is I once worked a trip for the Vice President, and while he was talking on Autovon to the President, *they* got bumped by a higher priority call. Okay, here we are again."

Gordon shook his head as he listened to Admiral McCollough describe CIA's views about the link between Culver and East European intelligence services.

"There's something strange in that story all right, and I'm not just talking about this guy Culver." Gordon turned to Colonel Handyside. "Did you keep him under surveillance?"

"Only as long as he was here. For our own protection. There wasn't any requirement from EUCOM."

"Chip, I hate to add to your burdens, but could you dig into this some more? If Culver's our man, the only way I'm going to find him is to know everything I can about him. Check with Army Intelligence. They should have a voiceprint you can use to check against our caller. And for God's sake, get me a link on the Agency's Bluebird satellite. The bomb could go off while I'm waiting for some general's wife to finish placing her commissary order—" The line had already gone dead again.

Gordon hung up and stared at Colonel Handyside. He gestured to the communications officer to leave the room. "Let me tell you how it adds up," Gordon said. "We have a man with a motive. We have an accomplice. It's clear from the record that they had plenty of opportunity. So much for the two-man rule, Colonel. Anybody ever consider that, in today's army, two 'men' might fall in love?"

"It's a hell of a theory, Mr. Gordon," Colonel Handyside responded. "Except that there's no weapons missin'. You counted 'em yourself."

"Maybe. Let's go back to the site. I want to see every weapon the two of them ever touched."

26

Bumping along in the Hummer toward the helipad, Gordon thought the crisis could well be over. Once again, he had found that every weapon at Schloss Ludwigshof was in place. The most recent message from McCollough reported that the weapon missing from Comiso had been found packed aboard a Navy supply ship in Naples. If Culver's voiceprint matched the caller, they could write it all off as a hoax or Soviet disinformation.

Still, Gordon felt uneasy. He had a premonition that he was onto something, and years of intelligence operations taught him to trust his feelings. What if Culver was not bluffing? What if he had been too clever? On the other hand, what if he, Gordon, was just reluctant to let go of the assignment? He should be overjoyed. Why was he steeling himself against disappointment?

As he walked toward the Blackhawk warming up on the exercise grounds, he glanced over at the jump tower and the platoon of men taking turns leaping off. They carried mortars, heavy machine guns, even shoulder-fired Stinger antiaircraft missiles.

"Colonel," he shouted over the beats of the helicopter, "how do you use a SADM?"

"Just strap it to your chest with a harness. Then you can jump with it. You set it off like any other explosive. Bigger, o'course. Use it against a bridge or a dam or to start a landslide."

"Do you practice jumping with the SADM?"

"No, we've got dummies to practice with . . ."

Gordon spun around and bolted back toward the Hummer. A half hour sifting through the records of the Quartermaster's Office and they found it: a dummy SADM signed out to Terence Culver on February 28. Handyside was defensive. "Well, we didn't inventory 'em 'cuz they're not weapons." Gordon flipped through the printout of the nuclear inventory to February 28. There was nothing. But on February 29 he found an entry indicating that a 6.5-inch mortar warhead, an ADM, and a SADM were removed from inventory for an orientation lecture for newly assigned personnel. The record indicated that the weapons had been checked out in the custody of Morena, Revson, and Witall—and returned by Morena and Culver.

"I want to look at that weapon."

A technician flanked by two custodial team guards placed the SADM on Graciela Morena's desk. He unzipped the flaps of the green canvas harness and revealed a dome-shaped device of gleaming titanium. It was scarred by the dents and scratches of heavy use. "Run the counter over it," Gordon ordered.

The technician waved a black probe over the SADM. He checked the connecting wire between the probe and the box on his belt. After adjusting the dials on the box, he tried again. Finally, he placed the probe directly on the metal casing.

"Still nothing," he reported.

"Open it up."

As he removed a circle of bolts from around the perimeter of the dome, the technician explained that dummy SADMs were almost ex-

act replicas of real weapons because the men had to practice maintenance in the field. He carefully inserted a special fork-shaped
hydraulic tool into a square hole at the apex of the dome. The dome
popped off to reveal a foil-covered sphere embedded in a maze of wires,
batteries, and fusing devices. After fifteen minutes of carefully discon-
necting the wires, he could finally open the core. Lead buckshot
poured out.

Gordon's message to the President was short:

THREAT REAL. McCOLLOUGH WILL BRIEF ON WHO AND HOW.
LOCATION OF TERRORISTS AND WEAPON UNKNOWN. GORDON.

27

All along he had been the one who thought the threat might
be genuine, and now he found it hard to believe. How will it all end?
the President asked himself. He shuddered in the crisp morning air.
He was standing on the terrace of Aspen Lodge, a copy of Gordon's
message in his hand, looking out at the Catoctin Mountains spread
beneath him. Spring had drawn pale green gauze over the dark winter
woods, and splashed the hillsides with pink and white dogwood.

On impulse, the President had flown up to Camp David after the
NSC meeting the night before, hoping to relax. But he had slept badly,
and not at all after being awakened for Gordon's cable. The same
question kept turning over in his mind, "How will it end?"

He went back into the lodge for a sweater, climbing a ramp put in a
half century earlier for Franklin Roosevelt's wheelchair. FDR had conducted much of World War II from here, the President thought. He
built it, and called it Shangri-la.

Camp David is a 1,400-acre hilltop sprinkled with log-sided lodges,
each named after a different tree, connected by paved paths named
after local birds. Except for Aspen, the lodges are spartan. The senior

White House staff slept in bunk beds. VIP accommodations, Dogwood and Birch consisted of only three rooms—two barely large enough for double beds, the other a sitting room with space for a couch and two chairs. Heads of State, flattered at being invited to Camp David, usually ended up complaining.

"Marine Two should be here in about fifteen minutes, sir," the Secret Service man on duty at the bedroom door reported.

"Fine, put them in the conference room in Holly." He pulled the heavy Icelandic sweater over his head. "Let's go for a walk," the President said.

How did Roosevelt think it would end when he ordered the bomb to be built, the President wondered. Did FDR worry about the implications? It was wartime. He had faith in the alliance with Russia and hope for the United Nations. He was flat wrong, but was he ever in doubt?

For twenty years, when he was a television journalist, the President had stated his opinions on the nightly news with clarity and certainty. Now that he had power, reality had lost its edges. Truth blurred with hope and fear. Decisions became a cascade of unknown consequences, each choice a trapdoor, all advice a ploy or a gambit, every friendship an exercise in access and influence. He had belittled Jimmy Carter for constantly saying, "I feel comfortable with that," when he was manifestly insecure. Now, he respected the fraud required to build and maintain a façade of presidential leadership.

The President recalled a story Clark Clifford had told him about finding Harry Truman alone in the Roosevelt Room one afternoon, sitting with his head in his hands, after a meeting on the Berlin blockade. Truman had looked up at Clifford and said, "You know, there must be a dozen men right here in Washington more qualified to do this job than I am."

At a small overlook, the President stopped. On the horizon, silhouetted against the rising sun, a single hill rose out of the flat Maryland plains. From there, Confederate troops had planned their strike on Washington. Instead, they were destroyed at Gettysburg.

"How will this end?" he asked himself again. The President wanted desperately to talk with his wife, but she was airborne between Lima and Santiago. He had never felt so alone. When he heard the sound of a helicopter, he turned back toward Holly.

28

The beating of the helicopter blades only made Loggerman's headache worse. He had had three hours of fitful sleep. Now his throat was raw from arguing with the Secretary of State above the noise of the engine. The waves of anxiety were contained only by the reassuring thought that the President had asked him to come to Camp David to discuss the terrible news from Gordon.

It was no longer a game. Strength, he told himself, would be the key. He himself had written that early in a crisis, when events were still in flux, bold action could be decisive. This would be his guide.

Perhaps, at last, the President would appreciate the importance of control. Dissent in the Administration would now be dangerous.

He looked over at the Secretary of State, eyes closed, apparently dozing. Undisciplined actions could send false signals. It was essential to send the *right* signal to the Soviet Union, and fast.

Terence Culver's involvement made it an open-and-shut case, Loggerman concluded. Friends close to British intelligence had sworn to him that Culver had been doubled before the Czech incident. That made Soviet complicity more than circumstantial. Now, perhaps, the President would see the importance of bringing the Soviets to account.

Suddenly, Loggerman's self-righteousness collapsed. This was real. A nuclear weapon was missing and in the hands of a madman—or, worse, a terrorist. For a moment, he felt overwhelmed.

The Secretary was not sleeping. He had retreated inside his own head. A voice kept saying, it's not happening. You'll have to pretend it's happening to do your job, but it's not actually happening.

He loved politics. The people, the crowds, the debate, and, he admitted, the celebrity. This was not the politics he knew. It was like being in some third-world country where people in public life murdered each other. Or killed others, countless others in this case. He opened his eyes and looked over at the Admiral in his fresh, starched uniform. He appeared as calm as Loggerman looked agitated. Calm and caution, that's what the President needed. Prudence and judgment. For the first time, the Secretary wondered if he was old enough for the job.

Admiral McCullough had remained silent during the shouting between Loggerman and the Secretary of State. It was a little early in his opinion for tempers to be so frayed. Things could get a lot worse, and probably would. The pressure of the last few hours was not like combat. There was no action to provide relief, no plans to give the comforting illusion of control. Just pressure to the point of implosion.

The door opened and a Marine Sergeant came out of the crew compartment.

"If I may have your coffee cups, gentlemen. We land at Camp David in two minutes."

29

"There's no denying who's behind it," Loggerman summarized his argument. "It's an unparalleled act of aggression. Every President is tested early in their term by the Soviets. This is your test."

The Secretary of State drew adjacent triangles on a pad of yellow paper. Admiral McCullough sat quietly at the end of the table. Chattering birds could be heard through the open window. The President got up and helped himself to another cup of coffee from a silver urn set against the pine-paneled wall.

"What does the State Department think?" he asked.

"Nobody knows anything about it but me, and I have no way of knowing whether this Culver is a Soviet agent or not. He made a hell of a ruckus in Czechoslovakia, but that wasn't exactly an attack on us."

"I've talked with the Secretary of Defense and the CIA Director. They all agree with my assessment," Loggerman interjected.

"That the Soviet government has deliberately organized a theft of an American nuclear weapon and intends to blow it up on NATO territory if we don't withdraw from Europe? I think it's totally far-fetched."

"Where do your conclusions lead you, Karl?" the President asked. "What are you suggesting that we do?"

"I think it's essential to make clear to the Soviets that we're onto their game and that we hold them fully responsible."

"What if the Russians have nothing to do with this?" the Secretary interrupted. "We'd be telling them something they don't know."

Too late, the President thought, reflecting on his secret conversation with the Soviet Ambassador.

"And they could use it against us, as you have pointed out so eloquently," the Secretary added sarcastically.

"That's why we need to put the fear of God into them."

"All we know," the Secretary countered, "is that an American has stolen an American weapon and wants the rest of America's weapons out of Europe or he'll destroy America's friends."

"And the Soviets are just innocent bystanders, I suppose," Loggerman shot back.

"I resent having to defend those bastards in the Kremlin, but where are the facts?" The Secretary had decided to lose his temper, but his anger at Loggerman was genuine. "All we have is a *suspicion* that they're involved, and a *theory* that they stand to benefit. They would be running enormous risks, and that's not usually in their game plan."

"They wouldn't see much risk if they knew what you were recommending," Loggerman flared.

"I'm not going to take this—"

"What *are* you recommending?" The President's question brought the exchange under control.

The Secretary hesitated. "Nothing," he knew, would not be an acceptable answer. Crises required action. "We could state the facts we know for sure and ask them about their role."

"I'm sure they'll tell us the truth," Loggerman scoffed. He had the Secretary on the defensive, and decided to press for a decision. "It's the classic terrorist ploy, Mr. President. Some dispicable thing happens, but nobody did it. The stakes are too high on this one for us to play charades."

The President sat thinking about his private conversation with the Soviet Ambassador the day before. He had, in effect, already tried the Secretary of State's approach, and had received no answer.

"You both want to send the Russians a message." The President suddenly looked very tired. "Draft something and I'll look at it. I'm taking a swim."

As soon as the President stepped outside, Loggerman produced several sheets of paper from his briefing folder. "I have a draft we can start from. Of course, it's open to changes." His tone suddenly became friendly and accommodating.

The Secretary read it quickly, then began dictating a new opening, with Admiral McCollough acting as stenographer. Loggerman accepted all of his changes until they got the last sentence. It read:

> Accordingly, the United States government holds the Union of Soviet Socialist Republics responsible for any and all consequences arising from this grave act of aggression.

"Replace 'act of aggression' with 'incident,'" the Secretary said. "There are international law implications to the word 'aggression.' And take out the word 'grave.' The whole thing's serious enough without getting theatrical." Again, Loggerman agreed.

"One last fix," the Secretary added. "Instead of 'holds' them responsible, let's insert the phrase, 'wants to know why it should not hold' the USSR responsible and so forth—"

"No," Loggerman stopped him. Having made all the concessions on minor points, he now drew the line. Twenty more minutes of wrangling slowly moved the Secretary off his position. The sentence had been entirely reworked and their differences were reduced to one word: "The United States considers the Union of Soviet Socialist Republics [a/the] party responsible for this incident, and, accordingly, for any ensuing consequences."

They took the issue to the President, who was dozing fitfully on the sun porch of Aspen Lodge. The President pulled his reading glasses out of the pocket of his red plaid Pendleton shirt. Wearily, he concluded, "Let's give this one to the diplomats, shall we, Karl? 'A party' leaves us a little more flexibility."

Loggerman nodded obediently. But as he turned away, he could not suppress a slight smile. There are no articles, no "a" or "the," in Russian. The message would be transmitted in Russian and convey exactly what he had intended.

"Put this on the Hot Line to get their attention," he said to Admiral McCollough.

30

The Hot Line has no terminal in the White House. At the height of the cold war, when President Kennedy and Nikita Khrushchev agreed to install it, influential members of the US defense establishment feared that the President would use it to strike secret bargains with the USSR behind their back. To undercut such opposition, JFK handed the system over to the military.

Admiral McCollough gave the message to the clerk in the communications trailer near the helipad, who passed it to the White House Situation Room via a scrambled, long-distance Xerox link. The Sunday Duty Officer punched it into his terminal at one of two triangular work stations, and in a flash the text was transmitted across the Potomac river to the Pentagon through an underwater cable pressurized to detect any physical intrusion by hostile intelligence.

The young Air Force Captain on duty at the National Military Command Center stood on a glass-enclosed balcony overlooking a room the size of three basketball courts. The floor was crowded with desks, which at that hour on a weekend were lightly manned. Video monitors on each desk displayed reports from military commanders, key geographic areas, and intelligence installations, including direct readouts from spy satellites. Any item of interest was relayed to the Watch Officer and projected on huge overhead screens. During a crisis, ranks of military brass planned to sit row-on-row in the balcony, following developments on the screens and issuing orders through the telephones at each seat.

That morning, the screens were largely empty. When a bell went off, the Captain pulled the message out of the printer labelled WHITE HOUSE and showed it to the Senior Watch Officer. Opening a small door set unobtrusively on one side of the balcony, they entered a small room jammed to the ceiling with stacks of electronic communications equipment. At the end of one aisle, a Lieutenant j.g. sat in front of two keyboards reading *Aviation Week*. The keys on the left were Cyrillic and formed part of an enormous black iron apparatus that looked like it belonged in an old Western Union telegraph office.

"We've got you a real message for a change," the Watch Officer said. "You can put aside the poetry." For more than twenty-five years, the military headquarters of the US and USSR had tested the Hot Line every day by sending ten lines of poetry—a convention conceived by the Soviets as providing the least opportunity for the transmission of American propaganda.

"How's the cultural exchange program going?" the Air Force Captain asked.

"I'm trying to subvert them with Frank Zappa lyrics, but all I ever get back is Pushkin. Let me see what you've got."

Thirty minutes later, two copies of a translated version went out over the old vacuum tube–powered communications console provided by the Soviet Union. One passed through land lines from Washington to the AT&T building in lower Manhattan. There it switched to a dedicated circuit on underground and undersea cables linking St. John's Island, Nova Scotia, Iceland, Liverpool, Glasgow, Copenhagen, Uppsala, Helsinki, Leningrad, and, finally, Moscow.

The other copy was transported on K-band microwave to Ft. Meade, Maryland, where it was beamed up to a passing WWMCCS satellite and then bounced higher to a Soviet Molnya transponder in geostationary orbit. The message traveled by downlink to an antenna farm south of Moscow. Hard copies of both messages poured out of identical NEC 741 printers in the Kremlin and at Soviet General Staff Headquarters at Stremski fortress in Moscow's 17th District.

Immediately, the General Staff Duty Officer made five copies. One went by wire to Zavedovo, the dacha of the General Secretary of the Soviet Communist Party, Ivan Chalomchev. Three motorcycle dispatch riders delivered the other copies to key members of the Defense Council: the Defense Minister, the Foreign Minister, and the Chairman of the Committee for State Security.

The Duty Officer personally carried the Hot Line message to the Chief of the Soviet General Staff who, though it was late Sunday, was as usual in his office. The D.O. stood at attention while Marshal Ogorodnik read it. When the Marshal came to the last line of the message, it was difficult for the Duty Officer to tell if he was grimacing or smiling.

31

Gordon held the phone tightly to his ear, trying to decipher McCollough's voice through the whoops and howls of the State Department's voice-scrambling system. He sat at a wooden table inside a small clear-plastic cubicle suspended within the communications vault of the US Consulate General in Munich.

"Aren't they getting a little ahead of themselves?" Gordon paused, then repeated, "Ahead of themselves. I'm not saying Culver's not working for the Russians, but he's been acting pretty strange if he is.

"First of all, he registered with the Consulate and the West German police. Yeh, just like he's supposed to. We've been to his apartment. He was there recently, maybe only hours ago. It's a dingy couple of rooms in Schwabing, the student district. CIA and DIS are going over his stuff, but nothing unusual stands out. He's apparently been trying to get a job using his language skills. There's a file of want ads and letters.

"The interviews with the other custodial people didn't tell us much," he said in response to a question from McCollough. "Except for each other, Culver and Morena kept pretty much to themselves. The Defense Investigative Service is checking anyone who worked with her at Pirmasens but our only lead right now is the photo album. The MP lab is doing the fibers and fingerprints. Nothing's very promising. How are you doing on Culver and the Czech story?

"I see. Okay, I'll handle that part. Let me know as soon as we get an answer to the Hot Line message.

"No, nothing but wait and pray for a lead. I'm going down the street to the Vier Jahreszeiten, eat a couple of pounds of white asparagus at the Waltherspiel, call my lady friend in California, and then sleep like a stone."

32

"Sunday evenings are sacred," Fyodor Kazmasin muttered to himself as he prepared the round, green-baize table for the meeting. It was fine for these high officials to miss the first telecast of Stravinsky's *Sacre du Printemps*, he thought; they probably had seen it in Paris, or from the party boxes at the Bolshoi, or had video recorders. But a steward, even a Chief Steward, had only this one chance.

At each seat, he put a new pad of unlined paper embossed with a gold hammer and sickle, together with a freshly sharpened pencil. Every place also received a saucer and a glass in a metal holder for tea. Kazmasin then placed bottles of soda water and fruit juice, along with two glasses between every other seat. A waitress came in and set up a samovar while Kazmasin unlocked a cabinet in one of the blond teak walls, took out six small glasses and a bottle of Moskovskaya Vodka. He dusted them off and set them on a silver tray in the center of the table. Since it was past seven o'clock, protocol required vodka, but anyone less than a member of the Politburo would jeopardize their career to drink it.

Fyodor Kazmasin stepped back to inspect his work. They had forgotten the cigarettes! He shouted to the waitress, who quickly produced a half dozen packs of cigarettes, and a box of matches and an ashtray for each place. Now all was in order. Kazmasin calculated that he might still catch the second act. Opening a recessed panel by the door, he adjusted the lighting, switched on the recording machine, and advised the orderly standing guard that the room was ready.

"The purpose of our meeting is to exchange information and advise the Defense Council on the appropriate response to the American President's message," the Chief of the International Directorate of the Communist Party announced from the chair. "What does the Committee on State Security know of this so-called operation?" He looked across the table at the KGB representative.

Alexander Antunov slowly opened the file in front of him while assessing his colleagues around the table. The late hour on a Sunday and the importance of the President's message had produced an unusual gathering of widely different ranks. Some had the authority to speak for their Ministers, others did not. In either case, the unprecedented situation freed them to speak their minds—always a dangerous situation in Antunov's view, especially if their Ministers later felt compelled to back them up.

To Antunov's right sat Dimitri Fyakov, a Special Security Advisor to the General Secretary, and an old friend of Antunov's from their days together at KGB training school No. 311 in Novosibirsk. Antunov had great affection for him, but years of service to the most powerful men in Russia had turned Fyakov into a wraith, oddly devoid of human substance.

The place on Antunov's left was occupied by Valerin Kuznetsov, Second Deputy Foreign Minister. An expert on the United States, he was a career diplomat with no political weight. To his left, sat three generals in ascending order of importance. Antunov knew Major General Serge Kirillin of the GRU quite well from intelligence committee dealings. Bright and ambitious, Kirillin had once become the youngest general in the Red Army because of his superior intellect. Now he was beginning to realize he would go no further for the same reason.

Lieutenant General Boris Zamyatin from the Policy Directorate of the Defense Ministry was an unknown quantity. Antunov judged that he was mostly just serving his time in Moscow until he could arrange a command of a Tank Army. The most senior person at the meeting, including the Chairman, was General Constantin Krushenko, Vice Chief of the General Staff. Antunov knew him only by reputation, which was that Krushenko's idea of strategy was ten thousand artillery pieces, wheel-to-wheel, all firing at once.

Finally, the Chairman. He would have his work cut out for him tonight. Relentlessly calm, fair, firm, and faintly avuncular, he had been Chairman for so long he had no other personal characteristics. Even his round, wide body conformed to the requirements of the chair.

And how did they, in turn, measure Antunov? He hoped to be seen as a complete professional, in addition to engendering the touch of suspicion and fear that every KGB officer learned to enjoy.

"We have no direct connection to this Culver," Antunov began. The Chairman wrote the word "direct" on his pad, followed with a question mark.

"He was, however, the principal American agent exposed by our counterintelligence during an operation with the British in Czechoslovakia. Unfortunately, Lieutenant Culver, who is a member of the US Special Forces, managed to avoid capture by the Czech authorities. It is our understanding, however, that he was punished for the failure of his mission and the diplomatic furor it created."

"You said 'direct' . . ."

"Yes, Comrade Chairman. According to established policy, Department V attempts to monitor the activities of all armed struggle groups in Europe, particularly in West Germany. One of these groups was the Kolmar Fraction, a descendant, an offshoot of Baader-Meinhof, organized by one Horst Bauer. Herr Bauer was responsible for the destruction of the US Army's General Abrams Hotel at Garmisch-Partenkirchen. After that attack, which was not authorized by us, we severed all connections with him except to facilitate his escape and domicile in South Yemen."

"What has he to do with this?" the Second Deputy Foreign Minister asked impatiently, as if he did not want to be tainted by knowledge of such activities.

"He returned to West Germany a few months ago under the recent political amnesty of the Bonn government," Antunov continued with his fastidious presentation. "Since we have no working relationship, we have only occasional reports on his activities. But they suggest that he has been recruiting new agents and reactivating old confederates. The woman, Graciela Morena, mentioned in the message as Lieutenant Culver's accomplice, may be one of those. She was involved in the Garmisch attack."

"Where does he get his money?" the Chairman asked.

"While he was exiled in Yemen, he developed contacts with several Arab governments and acted as a courier for some Palestinian groups. We surmise the money comes from them, but we cannot be certain."

"Is he behind this incident?" demanded General Zamyatin.

"We don't know," Antunov replied.

"I see no basis for the American allegations that we are responsible," General Krushenko said flatly.

"Let's let the GRU speak," the Chairman insisted. Representing the authority of the Party, he was never intimidated.

"We have not completed our inquiry," General Kirillin said without apology. "But we also see no reason to tolerate these charges."

"We should recommend rejecting the American President's message." Lieutenant General Zamyatin concurred with a third military voice.

"We would also respectfully point out," Major General Kirillin continued, with a touch of obsequiousness befitting his more junior rank, "that this incident offers an unprecedented opportunity. The news that an American nuclear bomb is missing will provoke a major crisis of confidence in NATO. If it goes off, the peoples of Europe will rise up and sweep away these NATO puppet governments and drive the Americans off the continent."

The generals from the Defense Ministry and the General Staff began to slowly nod their heads.

"A word of caution, Mr. Chairman." Antunov raised his hand to interrupt. "I would remind the committee that Lieutenant Culver is an enemy intelligence officer. We have no independent information that he stole a weapon, and we cannot rule out that this is an elaborate deception. You will note that the Americans are setting the stage to blame *us* for this incident. That will not cause a revolt in NATO. Quite the opposite."

"All the more reason to move quickly," the Vice Chief of the General Staff observed.

"I don't think," the Deputy Foreign Minister spoke up, "we can exclude the possibility that this is a genuine terrorist incident—perhaps like Garmisch." He smiled accusingly at Antunov. "Of course, we should reject any suggestion that we are linked to it, but we could have a problem if this Bauer is involved. I also have to report that yesterday the American President forewarned our Ambassador in Washington that something like this could be happening. I believe the KGB also has recordings of the telephone threats made to the White House, and unusual military communications—"

"Yes," Antunov answered, "but that doesn't prove anything . . ."

"A provocation is not in keeping with our observations of the President's policy or temperament," the Deputy Foreign Minister added. "He's been trying to establish negotiations."

"And so now he's trying to force us into talks?" It was a statement put as a question from Lieutenant General Zamyatin.

"Or it could be forces within his Administration," the GRU General interjected. "He's not fully in control. This Loggerman has the soul of a provocateur."

"My point precisely," Antunov said.

"So it's either an historic opportunity, or a provocation," the Vice Chief of the General Staff observed, "but in either case, prompt and decisive action to defend our security is required."

"It's equally likely that this is a typical American mess," Deputy Minister Kuznetsov countered tensely, "but no less dangerous for that if we make a precipitous move. Caution is indicated."

"We all agree," the Chair interposed himself, "that the allegations of Soviet responsibility should be firmly rebuffed. Beyond that, I will report your views to the Defense Council, and I assume you will brief your superiors."

To Antunov's surprise, he then slammed his hand on the green-baize table, abruptly closing the meeting. The tea, soft drinks, vodka, and cigarettes were all left untouched.

33

"And that lapdog Fyakov, he said nothing?" Marshal Ogorodnik, the Chief of the General Staff, drew in on a Belomorkanal, a cigarette that was two thirds cardboard tube, one third tobacco.

The Vice Chief shook his head.

"We thought Chalomchev would be so decisive when he became General Secretary." He exhaled; clouds of blue smoke drifted up to the vaulted stone ceiling. Freezing rain began to rattle on the narrow medieval windows. The rumble of the barges on the Moscow river could be felt through the brick floors of Stremski fortress.

"He's all television and public relations. He talks of action, reform, change. But nothing happens. Well, he can't avoid making a decision this time." He rubbed his hand over the liver spots on his bald head. "Get me that coward of a Defense Minister."

General Krushenko winced and looked at the clock. "It's after eleven," he noted.

"Then start with his girlfriend's apartment."

"I do not want the Foreign Ministry making excuses for the Americans." The irritation was clear in his voice. "That just plays into the hands of Marshal Ogorodnik and his Neanderthals." The Foreign Minister sat huddled by the fire in the study overlooking Gorky Street. A heavy afghan covered his lap.

"This could not have come at a worse time. The cranes are coming home to roost. Fyakov did not reveal his hand?"

"No," Deputy Minister Kuznetsov replied.

"That means the General Secretary is uncertain or possibly even afraid." The Foreign Minister reached out a bony hand, grasped the poker, and stirred the fire.

The Defense Minister put the phone down. "I don't feel well." He allowed himself to sink back into the chair's soft, tapestry-covered pillows.

"I told you not to eat the smoked eel." Galina Tryanova pressed her breasts against the back of his neck and ran her hands down his heavy chest. "You need a hot bath to relax."

"No, I must go." His voice betrayed more anxiety than resolution. He stood up. "There will be an important Defense Council meeting early tomorrow."

"I'm not keeping you." She pulled away abruptly. As she crossed in front of the cut-crystal lamp, he could see her full figure outlined through the thin silk of her caftan.

"But you could do something for me, couldn't you?" He reached out and caught her wrist. "To help me sleep later?" he pleaded.

She stepped close to him, staring impassively into his eyes. Her hand reached down to his groin. He sighed. She dropped to one knee. "Show it to me," she ordered.

Antunov hurried from his apartment building into the open door of the long black ZIL. Grains of freezing rain fell from his hat. "I've just come from Zavedovo," the Chairman of the KGB said, as usual without a greeting. Antunov could barely see his face in the darkened limousine. "The General Secretary plans to pre-empt any disagreement in the Defense Council tomorrow. He also feels we need more information." The Chairman's silence did not invite comment.

The car had pulled into the priority lane reserved for high level officials in the middle of the street. Soon, they were speeding at 100 kilometers per hour over ice-slicked roads toward the KGB Headquarters in the suburbs.

"He is using our channels to send a message rejecting the President's charges. But he's also offering to help the Americans." Antunov was startled and began to object, but the KGB Chief continued, "I have volunteered your services." He looked at Antunov for the first time and allowed himself a smile.

"Do not misunderstand the reasons," he added quickly. "This is not a goodwill gesture."

To Antunov, it smelled like a desperate act.

"The General Secretary"—the KGB Chief paused to select his words carefully—"feels somewhat isolated by our military colleagues. He wants direct contact with the Americans and an independent assessment of their motives. He also wants the KGB involved so we will stand by him in the Defense Council. I wish to preserve the flexibility of the KGB until we know more or until . . ." He let the sentence fade out.

"Forgive me, Comrade Chairman, but I do not like it," Antunov protested. "They will exploit my presence somehow—"

"Then you must turn the tables on them!" snapped the KGB Chief.

They rode in the night without speaking. Antunov had no choice in the matter. "What are the arrangements?" he finally said.

"We will not know until the Americans reply. They probably will tell us to go to hell. Has the agent in London been activated?"

"Starting tomorrow, I was going to begin the process. Working through the European Directorate is somewhat delicate—"

"Do it yourself. Immediately. Whatever is required!" His tone made clear there could be no excuses.

34

It had been a long time since he had opened his eyes and not known where he was. Gordon stumbled toward the knock on the door. Only when it opened inward and he found himself looking at yet another door did he fully realize that he was in a hotel, in Munich, on assignment. The communications Duty Officer from the Consulate General apologized for waking him. Gordon looked at his watch. It was 5 A.M.

"You have a call on secure."

Gordon couldn't find his shoes. As he stumbled around looking for them, he put on a wrinkled shirt. He had to remember to buy some clothes.

"Are these yours?" the Duty Officer held up a pair of Johnson and Murphys. Gordon had left them in the hall to be shined.

Except for one Marine guard in a steel-reinforced reception booth, the Consulate was deserted. The call was from the President.

"Sean, I'd like you to do me a favor."

What am I doing now, Gordon stopped himself from asking.

"I'm sorry I didn't tell you about the Hot Line message," the President said without a trace of apology. "Anyway, the Soviet Ambassador just delivered an answer—or at least a reply. We're meeting on it in ten minutes, and I expect some fireworks. They claim they've got nothing to do with it."

"Surprise," Gordon said.

"But they've offered to help us. They want to send someone to work with you."

"Wait a minute." Gordon was waking up. "That's crazy!"

"Why?" The President's voice went cold.

"We're talking KGB, not the Boy Scouts. It's an intelligence fishing expedition."

"How can it hurt? You've worked with them before. Taking out that Pakistani nuclear plant—"

"That was different. They could be behind this one! If they don't know anything about it, how can they help?"

"You sound just like Loggerman."

"Mr. President, I'm against it."

"Listen, Sean, I'm trying to keep this from turning into an East–West crisis, but everything and everybody's pushing me in that direction. I need a line of communication to the Russians, and to build some kind of backfire against the Hotspurs who allegedly work for me. Whatever they can learn from us is nothing compared to avoiding a nuclear war. Maybe it'll build a little trust. We're having a NSC meeting in a few minutes and I want you on the speaker phone sounding enthusiastic."

It was an order, not a favor. "All right, but on one condition. I'm not playing hide-and-seek over here. If he gets in my way, I take it I have your permission to kill him?"

The President paused. He knew that Gordon's light tone meant he was serious. "Give him at least one break. Their KGB people will contact the Agency folks in Munich so you can link up.

"One more thing, Sean. Why do you think Chalomchev didn't use the Hot Line and wants me to communicate only through his Ambassador? Loggerman says it's a tactic to denigrate our concern . . ."

"Mr. President, I wouldn't worry about that stuff at this point. Maybe he just wants to keep his military out of it. The key is Culver. Is he working for the Soviets or not? Why's he doing this? I have to know everything I can about him. Would you get all the files turned over to Admiral McCullough, including all the White House records on the Czech incident? Loggerman's, too."

"Yes, sir," the President said mockingly. "It's nice to be working for you again."

Gordon started to smile, and then the uneasy truth of their conversation sank in: If the President needed his help to handle the NSC, he was not in control.

III. MONDAY

35

The President had made the wrong decision. He was playing into the hands of the Soviets. It was a catastrophic decision.

The thoughts kept circling in Loggerman's head as he paced the length of his apartment, from the Oriental bedroom to the heavily paneled English study, through the living and dining areas covered in a white Berber carpet with white leather sofas. He was fighting shock.

He admitted to himself that the President's earlier decision to bring in Gordon had come as a surprise, but at least it made a certain sense. Accepting assistance from the Soviets was plain foolish. Had he heard nothing Loggerman was saying?

Perhaps he should resign. But in the middle of this crisis? Impossible. That would be a disservice to the country. After all, what might the President do next? He'd become unpredictable. Maybe even dangerous.

Loggerman stopped pacing and looked through the plate glass windows at the Potomac. The lights from the skyscrapers in Arlington scribbled multicolored streaks on the dark waters. To his left, the Lincoln Memorial went dark, signaling that it was past midnight. He could not sleep.

The meeting had been a disaster. The Soviet reply was contemptuous and sarcastic, yet the President had seized on the one straw the Kremlin offered—they would send someone to help Gordon. Loggerman believed that only further demonstrated their complicity. It was probably part of the plot! Sickeningly clever, he had to admit, but the President couldn't be made to see it. And Gordon just went right along with it. Clear evidence he's angling for my job, Loggerman thought bitterly.

To get some fresh air, he slid open the door to the narrow terrace. The lower pressure created by the building's air-conditioning sucked in the wind at gale force. He stepped outside, pulling his red velour robe around himself.

The National Security Advisor kept rerunning the arguments he had made in the NSC. How could the Russians be held responsible for this threat if they were helping us? If the terrorists were caught, the Russians would take credit for saving our Allies from us! Their ass-kissing brand of détente would get a boost in Europe. In the meantime, the US would still pay politically for having lost control of one of its nuclear weapons. And if we didn't find it, the Russians would get kudos for trying, and all the fault would be ours! The Atlantic Alliance would collapse like a house of cards.

Loggerman suppressed a shudder. He could not get the President to think in geopolitical terms. Vital American interests were at stake, and the President worried about casualties. Half the meeting had been spent on how many people the SADM would kill in various European cities. It was their luck that the stolen weapon was the new, improved SADM, with a yield of at least ten kilotons.

Still, the President was focusing on the wrong things. Loggerman knew that under pressure some men had a tendency to concentrate on the trivial, on the routine. It was a form of psychological reassurance. That's what the President was doing. It could be fatal to the country.

But what could he do? He returned to the living room and sat on the couch. It sighed under his weight.

A majority on the National Security Council agreed with Loggerman, but that meant nothing. The President had the only vote that counted.

That was not the way the National Security Council was supposed to work. James Forrestal, Dean Acheson, and others designed it in 1946 to compensate for the weaknesses they saw in Harry Truman.

He would be President, but they would run America's foreign and defense policies from the NSC. Truman saw through it. He attended only one meeting and then downgraded the operation by making the Secretary of State the Chairman. Now the NSC had become the routine way for Presidents to get advice and give orders.

Loggerman wondered, was there a way to turn the clock back to the original concept? He had the Defense Secretary under control. He needed to work on the Vice President. The Secretary of State he would take care of in his lunch with Pincus. With these tantalizing thoughts in his mind, he drifted off to sleep still sitting up on the sofa.

36

In Moscow, shafts of morning light stabbed through the thick blue cigarette smoke that hung like an inversion layer below the crystal chandeliers of the two-story conference room. The meeting had started out tense, then became restless, finally soporific, as the Chairman, General Secretary Ivan Chalomchev, ponderously led the Defense Council through a protracted discussion of the production problems of the SS-29 mobile ICBM. Chalomchev was determined to dull the anticipation of discussing the American President's Hot Line message by dealing first with every other item on the agenda.

During a desultory discussion of flight test failures, an orderly brought the Foreign Minister a note which in turn he passed to Chalomchev. He read it with satisfaction, and quickly ended the discussion of the SS-29.

"Our last issue is the matter of the message from the President of the United States." The men at the table tried to shake off their torpor with gulps of coffee and seltzer and freshly lit cigarettes.

"I already have taken the liberty of answering by rejecting it out of hand." There was a stir among the members of the Council. "Does someone object to that?" He glared at the group. "Does someone believe there is merit in the President's accusations?"

A wave of "nyets" swept the table.

"Good. I am deeply suspicious about this matter. We must be on our guard for the possibility of a provocation or entrapment. I therefore arranged to place one of our top officers from the KGB into the midst of the American operation."

"This is a penetration?" the Defense Minister asked.

"No," the Chairman of the State Security responded. "We have just received word that they have accepted our offer of assistance."

More murmurs eddied up and down the green-baize table.

"Has the KGB considered"—the Chief of the Soviet General Staff pointedly avoided the Chairman—"that this could be seen as an admission of complicity in these events?"

"Our sole purpose is to obtain information to safeguard the security of the state and to thwart any machinations the Americans may plan," the KGB Chief replied primly.

"You're giving credence to slander," Marshal Ogorodnik shot back. "We're helping them because we're involved! That's what they will say!"

"They're saying nothing. They're desperately afraid the story will get to the Western press and that their European Allies will go mad with fear and recriminations."

"And why shouldn't we let the world know all about this?" the Defense Minister asked, prompted by a nudge from Marshal Ogorodnik.

"Because we do not know what has actually happened," the General Secretary broke in. "That is why I approved the dispatch of one of our most capable intelligence officers." He stressed the word "approved" just enough to shift responsibility to the KGB Chief. "We will meet again when we have more facts to discuss. All of our options remain open."

He stood up and the meeting was over. As he walked toward the door, he could not avoid overhearing someone in the cluster of military officers muttering the phrase, "violation of collective responsibility."

37

It was 6 A.M. in Munich. Unable to go back to sleep, Gordon considered calling Laura in California, where it was the middle of the evening. But after failing to reach her earlier, he was afraid he would still not find her home. He remembered his ex-wife telling him, if you worry what she's doing at night when you're traveling, she's too young for you.

He walked the seven blocks to Westenriederstrasse, where the 7th Army MP Headquarters stood across from the old city wall. The cool and misty rain the Germans call a *Spritzregen* felt good on his face. His footsteps echoed off the eighteenth- and nineteenth-century façades. The glistening streets were quiet and dark. An occasional empty tram, its warm lights glowing inside, glided smoothly by.

The city seemed orderly, serene, safe. It was not the Germany described by the President's National Security Advisor in the heated discussion he had just heard. The Germans were unreliable, unstable, neurotic. The Russians, implacable. America, fragile. The world was governed by conspiracy and force. Under the growing pressure of the crisis, Gordon could see every suspicion, prejudice, fear, and ambition rising to the surface.

How, Gordon wondered, had Loggerman come to be regarded as an intellectual? How could any ideologue be an intellectual? They didn't try to make sense of things. Their minds were like assembly lines churning out new models of the same old idea. No matter what the question, Loggerman had the answer: the Russians did it; America was in jeopardy: bold action was required.

He had to stop indulging his anger. Loggerman was not his problem. Finding the bomb was his problem. And now he would have a KGB agent on his back as well. What a vote of confidence from the President.

Whoa, you're starting to think like Loggerman—paranoid, feeling sorry for yourself. Maybe you've been out of the business too long, Gordon thought. Got a case of beachbrain from staring at the Pacific ocean?

He went back over the steps already taken to see if he had left anything out. All the basic police work was under way by the Defense Investigative Service, but that could take a long time and did not guarantee success. When the Italian Red Brigades kidnapped General Dozier, it took six weeks to find him, and then the police had a tip. Gordon had less than seventy-two hours.

He needed a breakthrough. He had to think strategically, not like a policeman. Terrorists operated as if they were intelligence agents. In fact, Culver was one. He would use all the trade craft of intelligence. He would not just wander aimlessly around Europe with the SADM in a suitcase. There had to be safe houses, cutouts, dead-drops, multiple identities, deception, cover, false flags. There had to be a plan. Gordon had to mount a counterintelligence operation.

Turning left onto Weinstrasse, Gordon caught sight of the Isartor, a squat and sinister medieval keep guarding the eastern route into the old city. He remembered the first axiom of counterintelligence: penetrate communications. If he could do that, he could unravel Culver's network, uncover his group's infrastructure, run them to ground. Good in theory, but how to apply it in this situation? Apart from Graciela, Gordon did not even know if Culver had a group.

Gordon climbed the steps of Number 3 Westenriederstrasse, an imposing Romanesque building that had formerly served as the Munich headquarters of the Gestapo. Built in 1158 by Henry the Lion, duke of Saxony, it had always been a jail. Even Adolf Hitler spent a few hours in its dungeons, dressed in pajamas and bathrobe after he was found hiding in the attic of a suburban farmhouse following his abortive Putsch in 1923.

The US Army seized it in 1945 for the Military Police, and in the early 1960s converted the upper floors to offices for the Pentagon's Defense Investigative Service, reserving the mezzanine for a forensics laboratory and the first floor and the subbasements for the MPs. To Gordon, the heavy stone walls and low, round ceilings reeked with the cold, damp smell of human cruelty.

The forensics lab blazed with light. Gordon was greeted by an elderly German in a regulation white lab coat. "Dr. Waldbaum," he said, bowing slightly. As they shook hands, Gordon noticed the concentration camp number tattooed on his wrist.

A half dozen assistants, some Americans, some Germans, manned the equipment. A gas chromatograph, used for spectrographic analysis, glowed in one corner. A section of wall, covered with glass tubes, was devoted to the examination of blood samples. A bank of computers lined the opposite wall. Microscopes of various descriptions sat on islands in the middle of the room. Gordon recognized the large steel box at the end of the room. It served as a chamber for discharging firearms and detonating small samples of explosives.

"I do not know exactly what you are looking for, and I have been told not to be too curious." The old man's eyes glinted mischievously. "So I'm not sure I've found all there is to find."

"I appreciate you working all night," Gordon said.

"For me it's easy. I don't sleep anyway. For the young ones, it's hard. Come, we start with fingerprints." He spread a set of enlargements onto a light table. "From the articles you collected in Sergeant Morena's room, we could obtain thirty or so prints. Most of them naturally were of the girl. The next most numerous belonged to Lieutenant Culver. By the way, the prints taken from his apartment are all his, except some found in the bathroom. Chemical analysis suggests the presence of silica from scrubbing powder, so we believe they are from his *Putzfrau*—housekeeper, isn't it? But still we check.

"Now, these from the Morena samples turn out to be other members of the custodial team. The only odd print is this one. We have a right thumbprint from the photograph of Culver and Morena together, the same thumb and forefinger from the lift ticket, and a print of the forefinger and fragment of a palm on the match box from the Café Hafstnähe."

"Can you get an ID on it?"

"We have asked the Bundespolizei."

"Put it on the network to Interpol, and also send it flash to the FBI marked SOG/COB Rymland," Gordon said.

"Certainly." The slightly indulgent tone had gone out of Waldbaum's voice.

"Here we are doing fibers analysis." He pointed to two men peering through microscopes. "Frankly, we do not know what we are doing, and could use some guidance."

"I'm trying to find Culver, Morena, and possibly others. Anything that would identify the others or suggest who they might be, or where . . ." It sounded awfully vague even to Gordon.

"I don't think the fibers will help us, but we will keep looking for something unusual. We will also examine the soil vacuumed from Lieutenant Culver's carpet to see if peculiarities can suggest anything about travel or another location."

He walked over to the bank of computers and tore off a long sheet of fanfold paper. "The PTT provided us with a list of calls made from Lieutenant Culver's apartment, going back three months. He didn't use the phone much. Mostly to Schloss Ludwigshof. But there are these calls to big companies . . ."

Gordon looked at the sheet. It cited each call by date, number, duration, and charge. "He was looking for a job," he explained. "Not very helpful."

"It depends what you are looking for. Would you like some coffee?"

Gordon nodded gratefully, and they went to Dr. Waldbaum's office. Among piles of books and documents, he found plastic cups, sugar, and nondairy creamer. Waldbaum drew coffee from an electric pot on his crowded desk and cleared a place for Gordon to sit on the brown leather couch.

"Black," Gordon said.

They drank their coffee in silence.

"Professor," Gordon finally spoke.

"Doctor is good enough," he smiled.

"Doctor, then. Do the Germans also keep track of pay telephone calls?"

"I believe so. They keep meticulous records of almost everything, except of course who ordered the extermination of the Jews." The bitterness was in his words, not his tone. "The PTT will give us such records, I should think. What would we do with them?"

"If you wanted to communicate by phone and not be tapped, what would you do?"

"Use a pay phone, certainly."

"Right, and if you were really cautious, you wouldn't use the same one every time."

"That would be prudent," Dr. Waldbaum agreed.

"But that might help us."

The old man looked perplexed.

"If the same number is called from a large number of pay phones in Culver's neighborhood, it could be what we're looking for." He put down his empty cup. "Let me know what you find. I'll be upstairs in the DIS vault."

38

Gordon sat at the gray metal table with the personnel files of Graciela Morena and Terence Culver spread before him.

Why would they do this, he asked himself. Nothing in the girl's record suggested a radical. She had done well in school and in the Army. No trouble with the law. No discipline problems in the service. Never previously AWOL. Apparently, a frequent churchgoer. The only unusual item was that she had been in a foster home from age fifteen to seventeen even though her mother was alive. He made a note to check why.

Culver's file was more extensive. Born in Council Bluffs, Iowa. Two years of community college. ROTC. Parents divorced. Brother killed in action in Guatemala. Boot Camp and advanced infantry training at Ft. Ord, California. Ranger training, Ft. Benning, Georgia. Assigned White Star counterinsurgency team Medellín, Colombia, for one year, followed by OCS at Ft. Collins, Colorado, then six months Ft. Myers near Washington, D.C. Member US Military Assistance Advisory Group, Khartoum, Sudan. After fourteen months, medical transfer to Walter Reed Hospital. Three months medical leave and subsequent assignment to Schloss Ludwigshof, West Germany. Awards: a Purple Heart and two Distinguished Service Medals.

Gordon noted the asterisk on the awards citation and turned to the classified annex. As he had anticipated, the second Distinguished Service Medal came from a "black" operation in Ethiopia. Culver had saved the life of his Commanding Officer when they walked into an ambush set up by the people they were helping—the Eritrean Popular Front. Gordon wrote down the name of Culver's Commanding Officer, Major Dwayne Babitch.

Reading through the evaluations, Gordon saw something of himself in Culver. "Contemptuous of authority," "impulsive," and "impatient" appeared as often as "dedicated," "resourceful," and "outstanding." As Gordon knew, that combination could earn enemies. But that did not make Culver a terrorist.

In fact, it made no sense. Gordon had read the dossiers of scores of spies and defectors. They came in many varieties. But a young man and woman with successful service records, apparently in love, with everything going for them, fit none of the patterns. Still, there was the Czech operation and the suspicion that he had somehow been doubled. Gordon made another note: "How?" Maybe my new friend in the KGB could tell me, he thought.

"Excuse me," the clerk interrupted, "Dr. Waldbaum is here to see you."

"I have a list of matching numbers," he reported. "Unfortunately, there are over two thousand of them."

Gordon tried to remain positive. "Can't we eliminate certain obvious repeats? It's a student area, so you can leave out the university numbers, the restaurants, movie houses, discos, sports arenas, you know."

"Yes, of course we took that liberty and we are still working on the list. But it still has more than five hundred numbers."

Gordon could not hide his disappointment.

"I have some good news, too. Interpol wired us this." He handed Gordon a list of names and several blurry photographs. "He has many names," Dr. Waldbaum said.

The list read:

Heintz Bader
Heinrich Bator
Horst Bauer
Helmut Beser

Bernard Heitz
Berndt Hönzollern
Bertram Honig

and twenty-three others.

"All aliases of the same man, but, apart from the picture, no information on him," Dr. Waldbaum added. "Interpol says to contact the Bundespolizei."

"Terrific!" Gordon exclaimed. "What do the German police say about him?"

"They have declined to give us any information until we inform them of the purpose of our inquiry."

Gordon's enthusiasm vanished. "Dammit! That's a sure sign he's political." Gordon stared at the pictures. An intense dark-haired young man stared back.

"Also, you should know that none of the repeat telephone numbers are registered in any of these names."

"I'm not surprised. Tell me again where you found his prints?"

"On one of the photographs, on the lift ticket, and on the match box from the Café Hafstnähe. It's not far from here."

"See if anyone in the café recognizes him, and check the pay phone, too. See if there've been calls to Culver's number and to the pay phones in his neighborhood."

"There can only be a few," Dr. Waldbaum said. "They have only just started installing pay phones that accept incoming calls."

"That should make it easier," Gordon said. He put the pictures and the list in an envelope. "You can reach me in the Research Section of the Consulate General."

Dr. Waldbaum gave him a knowing smile.

Gordon got off on the fourth floor, and pushed the bell next to a Dutch door marked RESEARCH DEPARTMENT. A pretty young woman opened the top section of the door.

"I'd like to see the Base Chief. I'm Sean Gordon."

She registered no reaction. "Could you wait, please?" She closed the door.

A moment later, the whole door opened and a large, heavy-set man stood there. "Christ's sake, Sean!"

"Billy Kelly!" Gordon feigned surprise. "Are you still here? I thought your successors had just taken over your name."

"Never! We're all declared here. Us elite even get to use our real names. I got a message you were coming." Kelly grabbed his hand and dragged him inside. "I've an office set up and some fancy commo gear should be arriving anytime. I heard you were already in the building last night. What kind of horrible thing has you consorting with the State Department and MPs?"

"That's not the worst of it." Gordon suddenly felt happy; he was home. "It's a nightmare. And I need your help. Can you run these names through your index? *Don't* check with Langley."

"Typical Gordon operation, I see."

Billy Kelly had ruled the Munich CIA Base for almost ten years. During that time, it had become the most active CIA post in Europe, eclipsing both Berlin and Vienna. Many believed Munich owed its success to proximity to Eastern Europe, the influx of refugees, and the presence of Radio Free Europe. But Gordon knew the secret was continuity. Unlike Billy Kelly, most senior officers of the Clandestine Service rotated to new assignments every twenty-four months in search of promotions.

Some of Kelly's files went back to 1945, before the CIA was created. They took up almost the entire top floor of the old Consulate General, but in the new building on the corner of Königinstrasse and Von der Tannstrasse, reports were filed in an IBM mainframe that automatically transmitted duplicates to the master computer banks in Washington. But like his predecessors, Kelly had a few files he refused to put into the machines for fear of electronic penetration or because the reports were too tentative, speculative, or sensitive to share with Washington.

The IBM printer started chattering almost immediately.

"Our computer knows him," Kelly said. "Oh-oh. There's a whistle on him. See the icon next to the name Horst Bauer? It says to look at our consular records."

*   *   *

After an hour of argument and a call to the Consul General, the head of the Consular Affairs section finally agreed to show Bauer's file to Sean Gordon. He tilted his wire-rimmed glasses to peer around at the nondescript conference room. He had never been in the CIA section of the consulate before, and was evidently disappointed not to find whips and chains or at least thumbscrews.

"He was a US citizen, you see. Well, not actually. His father was American, but he failed to spend enough time in the United States. In fact, he failed to spend any time there, so he has forfeited his citizenship. But, he has the right to emigrate whenever he chooses without quota restriction."

"If he's German, then we can go after him again," Kelly noted. The Consul looked pained.

"Do you have an address for him?"

"It's in the file."

"Thank you," Gordon said, dismissing him. The folder, so precious to the Consul, contained only two pieces of paper. A birth certificate indicated that Bauer was his mother's maiden name, and that his father, a US Army noncom, was named Jackson. The other document was a citizenship registration form signed on Horst's behalf by Corporal Jackson. The address was eleven years old.

Gordon turned to Kelly, the friendliness gone from his voice. "Okay, Billy, let's see his file."

"You don't think," he said in mock innocence, "I'd ever target an American—"

"Cut the crap! You've wasted a precious hour."

"Sean, if you could tell me what this is all about—"

"You're going to hold out on me unless I do? Okay, it's about whether you get on the afternoon flight to Washington and never come back." Gordon reached for the phone. Kelly surrendered.

Kelly opened a small safe in his credenza. Then he closed the heavy drapes to block the view out over the twin domes of the Frauenkirche.

"Believe me, I haven't looked at this in a long time," Kelly said with a note of contrition as he leafed through Bauer's folder. "Let's see, we first started tracking the kid when he was only sixteen. We had no idea he was American. Here, look for yourself." He handed it to Gordon. "In fact, he was very anti-American, became a leader in the antimissile movement by the time he was eighteen. Then, I remember now, he fell in with a rough crowd. I wasn't about to destroy this stuff, because he might decide to become an outfielder with the Yankees. He disappeared after the Kolmar radicals blew up the General Abrams Hotel in Garmisch a few years ago."

Gordon stopped at the last document. It was only a few months old.

Secret
MF/WHISTLER -19   Source Grade A
NODIS OUTSIDE BASE   Info Grade B
Subject: Activities of BAUER, Horst (See Aliases)
Source -19 reports subject has established management consulting firm with offices in Vienna and Munich since return from Middle East. Origin of funding unknown. Subject has placed previous confederates on payroll. Sought to recruit source.
   Source reports subject's political orientation unchanged. (See MF/OVERLAY-22. KOLMAR FRACTION SEEKS OUSTER OF US TROOPS: GERMAN UNIFICATION.)
Request guidance re: recruitment.

"Did you?" Gordon looked up.

"With all that's going on here? No, we just alerted the German police."

"And now they won't tell us anything about him."

"I could do a little work." It was a peace offering.

"Do that." Gordon accepted it. "Also check out the mother's address. And ask the commercial officer to come up here with all his business directories, especially new businesses and management consulting firms."

Kelly's secretary interrupted. "Mr. Gordon, there's a courier here for you."

The envelope contained a list of eighteen phone numbers with the date, cost, and duration of the calls from the pay phones in Culver's neighborhood. An attached note requested Gordon to contact Waldbaum.

"You were correct," Dr. Waldbaum exclaimed as if praising a star pupil. "Telephone calls were made from the Café Hafstnähe to Culver's apartment and to the two nearby pay phones that take incoming calls. These two telephone cabins were also frequently called by other pay phones in the vicinity of the Café Hafstnähe. No one at the café would identify Bauer or Culver or the girl. The eighteen numbers are all in that same locale as the café. It's a fancy district near the consulate, the Englischer Garten. They were called repeatedly from pay phones in Culver's neighborhood, particularly the return-call cabins."

"Get the MPs out here right away. Check each address. Talk to the neighbors, but don't approach the target under any circumstances—"

"The German Police won't like us doing this—"

"Screw the German Police."

"You will have to explain to them, then," Dr. Waldbaum rang off, his sense of propriety offended.

An hour later, Gordon sat amidst a stack of thick reference books and ring binders trying to match up the names and officers of any new consulting firm with one of Bauer's aliases or with any of the eighteen phone numbers. He was getting nowhere. He stared at the list again.

ENGLISCHER GARTEN DISTRICT

Numbers Dialed from Pay Phones in Schwabing District
(In Order of Frequency)

Name	Number	Date	Duration	Charge
Gross, L.	22-45-73	3/18	00:06:24	3.10
		4/12	00:02:48	1.00
		4/12	00:00:33	1.00
		4/23	00:08:05	3.90
		4/28	00:04:19	2.40
		5/2	00:01:50	1.00
		5/9	00:02:53	1.00
		5/16	00:09:11	4.10
		5/21	00:02:05	1.00
		5/21	00:00:23	1.00
		5/23	00:04:05	1.30
Mannlicher, V.	78-99-01	3/13	00:05:15	2.55
		3/16	00:09:38	4.25

ENGLISCHER GARTEN DISTRICT (*cont.*)

Name	Number	Date	Dura-tion	Charge
		3/25	00:02:56	1.00
		3/29	00:01:37	1.00
		4/10	00:12:19	5.15
		5/9	00:00:08	1.00
BGE	42-14-53	3/30	00:00:10	1.00
		4/15	00:00:12	1.00
		4/26	00:00:11	1.00
		5/5	00:00:09	1.00
		5/7	00:00:13	1.00
		5/17	00:00:10	1.00
Feuer und Draggen, GmbH.	78-08-00	3/2	00:02:42	1.00
		3/9	00:01:31	1.00
		4/18	00:11:05	4.80
		4/20	00:03:15	2.10
		5/18	00:02:10	1.00
		5/21	00:01:55	1.00
Albrecht, K.	22-73-24	3/11	00:02:20	1.00
		3/19	00:02:45	1.00
		4/4	00:01:52	1.00
		4/27	00:02:05	1.00
		5/19	00:02:58	1.00
		5/20	00:01:12	1.00

And the list went on with thirteen more names, the numbers burning holes in Gordon's retinas.

How long would it take for the MPs to check out all these numbers, he wondered. More than a day? And they could still miss Bauer. Maybe he was wasting his time on Bauer. No, he had to be the man behind the threat, the man with the network and with the money. Culver had no resources. He was living in a dump and looking for a job. Maybe Kelly could get something on Bauer out of the Bundespolizei, but if he had use to a clandestine source, how long might that take?

He felt discouraged, frustrated. He thought of trying to call Laura again. But it was 3 A.M. in California. If there were no answer, would she be asleep, or— He turned back to *An American's Guide to Small Business in Munich.*

Gordon's stomach was telling him to eat lunch, and his jet-lagged eyes were forcing him to sleep when Kelly stuck his head into the conference room and announced, "I've got something for you."

He handed Gordon a slip of paper. "I can get the whole file by tomorrow, but I thought you'd want the name of his company—Beratungsgesellschaft Europa."

"Dammit!" Gordon swore, "It's not on the list."

"Let me see." Kelly took the list. "Look, it's right near the top, BGE."

"Oh." Gordon was embarrassed.

"See, all the calls to BGE are extremely short—less than fifteen seconds. They're just bell-ringers," Kelly explained. "You just call and ask for the wrong person and they know to call you back from another phone."

"Jesus," Gordon said, "I should've seen it right away." I've lost my touch, he thought. "I must be going blind!" he mumbled.

The phone on the conference room wall rang. Kelly answered it.

"I see." He put his hand over the mouthpiece. "It's Waldbaum. The MPs have found Bauer's place, too."

"Same address as yours?"

Kelly nodded.

"Tell him we'll meet them there." Gordon was already moving out the door.

39

"Looks like they left in a hurry," Kelly observed.

It was an expensive duplex apartment. The two-story living room, with floor-to-ceiling windows, overlooked a huge eighteenth-century park. The lights burned in every room. The bed was unmade. Drawers hung open in the bedroom, bathroom, and kitchen. The automatic coffee maker was on, and the glass pot filled with a hard, black crust. A team of MPs dusted for prints and collected assorted flotsam for their evidence bag.

"Have you seen this, sir?" an MP asked.

In a back bedroom Gordon found a high-back armchair, tape sticking to the arms and front legs.

"And we found this." The MP showed him a vial of sodium pentothal and a syringe.

"Looks like somebody's not cooperating," Gordon said to Kelly. "What do the neighbors say?"

"Nobody knows a thing," the MP said. "We're checking to see if he had a car."

Gordon went back into the living room and sat down in a soft, down-filled sofa. He felt very tired. After all the effort, it seemed like a dead end. He looked at his watch. Thirty hours had passed since the last phone call from Culver. He had spent an entire day fruitlessly tracking Bauer and was no closer to Culver. About sixty hours remained before the deadline. He had no more leads.

"Dr. Waldbaum is here."

Gordon started. He had drifted off for a moment.

"Yes, ask him in."

The midday sunlight pouring through the picture windows gave the old man skin of parchment. He sat on the edge of an overstuffed chair, clutching a folder.

"The DIS found Frau Bauer right away. It seems she was not very friendly. She claimed not to have heard from her son for several years. Our inquiry was the first sign she's had that he's even alive. DIS will continue surveillance there anyway."

Gordon nodded wearily.

"I also have something that might be useful. I don't know." He spread the file on the glass coffee table. "I took the liberty to match all the calls from the pay telephones in this neighborhood with those in Lieutenant Culver's district. Again, there are many repeats, but I thought you should see the results."

Gordon glanced down the list of several dozen names and numbers, some outside Germany—in Copenhagen, Denmark, Paris and Strasbourg, France, and several to Vienna and Kitzbühel in nearby Austria. They meant nothing to him. He shook his head.

"Perhaps, Mr. Kelly's associates could check in these cities while we check here," Dr. Waldbaum offered.

"No." Gordon walked over to the window and gazed at the snow-covered Alps floating over the haze of the city. "We can't afford another wild—" He then remembered something, something he had found in Graciela Morena's desk in the custodial compound, something Bauer had touched that tied him to Waldbaum's new list of phone numbers.

"Get me Colonel Handyside at Schloss Ludwigshof," he told an MP.

"Colonel, I'm advising you that you'll soon get a critic message from the JCS via EUCOM. Be ready to move a dozen men in civilian clothes. They should look like hikers and tourists. Have them take passports and the heaviest, uh, equipment they can get in their luggage." Gordon paused. "No, we don't have time for the NEST team. Are you a fighter or a bullshitter?

"Good. We'll rendezvous at the civilian airstrip at Bad Tölz at 13:30. Yes, you'll get the orders, just be ready . . . What? . . . You'll get the details later, but you'll need passports because we're going over the Austrian border—to Kitzbühel."

Gordon turned to Kelly and started giving instructions. "I need to charter an aircraft with at least twenty seats. Dr. Waldbaum, can you track down the address for the number in Kitzbühel? Let's get back to the consulate. I've got to make a secure call to the Chairman of the JCS."

"Sean, before we run off in all directions at once, I have a question," Kelly said. The young woman from his office had appeared with a dispatch case. "The local KGB Rezedenz says you're supposed to meet an Alexander Antunov arriving on the three o'clock plane from London. What am I supposed to do with him while you're hiking in the Alps?"

"It's a golden opportunity," Gordon replied.

Kelly looked baffled.

"Recruit him."

40

Reginald Weede left his office at *London Financial Week* and hurried up St. James's Street. He had to stop and wait in the rain in front of White's as a fleet of Daimlers unloaded a covey of junior Government Ministers, each rebuttoning their double-breasted suits as the doormen waved umbrellas over their heads. By the time Weede reached Piccadilly, his fawn suede shoes were stained dark by the blowing drizzle, and the faint crease in his trousers vanished altogether a foot above his cuffs.

Moving gracefully for a heavy man, Weede cut across the traffic to the fountain. He entered the maze of small streets behind Shaftsbury Avenue and worked his way northeast into Soho, stopping occasionally to see whether there was any chance of being followed. In an alley, under a red-and-white sign that read ASIA GARDEN—ORIENTAL MASSAGE, Weede pressed a buzzer and was admitted discreetly.

Except for a towel across his middle and the Rolex that he checked every few minutes, he now lay naked on his back on the massage table. Normally, Weede disliked having women touch him. But somehow, he did not mind the blunt fingers of the squat Korean girl. Except each time she tried to work upward from his ankles, he would raise his head and order her back, saying *"Shiatsu! Shiatsu!"* a word he knew had something to do with feet.

Weede hated face-to-face meetings. They were too risky, except in an emergency. But what could be the emergency? Had he been blown? He giggled at the double entendre to reassure himself.

Never would he have picked a massage parlor. Evgenyi might think it clever, he thought, but you never know who you might run into in such a place. Better to select a locale where one could be certain of the class of clientele, like the Pelham bus or the bookmakers in Shepherd's Bush. He checked his watch.

He sat up. "Tub, tub." The girl looked confused.

"Oh, bath! Yes, please. This way."

She led him down a dark corridor toward the sound of rock music and turbulent water. The mirrored walls were covered with mist from the large, round Jacuzzi. Weede entered gingerly, then settled on the first step. The masseuse unzipped the front of her white nurse's uniform.

"No, no! I only want to relax. You go." Obediently, she gave him a stack of towels and closed the door behind her.

With his eyes closed, Weede drifted into that first zone of sleep where hearing shuts down. Evgenyi had to call his name twice.

"What?" Weede started. "Evgenyi, what time is it?" He lifted his Rolex out of the water.

Evgenyi Kolkoff, an Assistant Director of the Soviet Purchasing Mission, AMTORG, squatted up to his neck in the bubbling water. "I have a new assignment for you, Rege."

"You know, you could exchange a few pleasantries before plunging into business." The rock music seemed to be louder. "I think you rather enjoy the tawdry aspects of your profession."

"As you realize, I am often followed by your people. Today, I believe I've been left alone, but I could be wrong. We should complete our work before my escort from the Special Branch shows up and arrests us for playing three men in a tub." Kolkoff prided himself on making small jokes with English references.

"Three?" Weede rose out of the water.

"Yes, I want to introduce you to someone." He gestured toward the door. As it opened, steam condensed from the contact of the outside air with the humid atmosphere of the Jacuzzi. Alexander Antunov emerged from the billowing clouds and sat on the edge of the tub.

"It's a pleasure to meet you, Mr. Weede." He did not introduce himself.

"Charmed, I'm sure," Weede said coolly. He hated surprises.

"We were very pleased with the way you handled the Czech matter," Antunov continued. "It blew back on the Americans just as you said it would."

Weede tried not to show his pleasure at the compliment. "And now what do you have in mind?" He decided that taking the initiative might put this person in his place.

"We want you to visit your friends in Washington. We want certain information," Antunov said simply.

"Just a moment. My specialty is *dis*information, a little rumor-mongering, that's all. And that's all I get paid for, too." Weede was becoming petulant.

"You will be well compensated for this assignment."

Yes, two free air tickets to the Bulgarian Riviera, Weede thought. "And if I refuse?"

Antunov just looked at him. It appeared to Weede that the man's bones were, like a Russian wolfhound's, too delicate for his hard-muscled body. Like a wolfhound, Weede concluded, he probably made no sound when he killed.

In ten minutes, Antunov told Weede all he needed to know about the operation.

"I must emphasize the importance of your task," the KGB man concluded. "There are things of which you do not know."

"Rest assured," Weede said grandly as the two left. But a twinge of fear stayed with him. He slid into deeper water and watched his stomach rise to the surface. He tried to think of food.

41

At noon, all the bells in Kitzbühel chime. The first is always a small pair of sopranos in the half-timbered towers of the Spitalkirche. The last is a basso in the belfry of St. Andreas in the town center. In between, glockenspiels of every timbre and intonation peal in a strict order established by a diplomatic codicil signed by Protestants and Catholics at the end of the Thirty Years' War. The only interloper in this medieval carillon is the bell on the roof of the railway station. A nondescript modern instrument, its only distinguishing characteristic is that it, alone, rings out the true time.

When Graciela heard the bells, she could barely contain her excitement. She would soon be free of Bauer no matter what. As the car in which she was riding wound down the mountain, she kept her eyes focused on the railway station, her mind on Terence Culver. She did not even feel Horst Bauer's grip on her left wrist as he sat beside her in the rear seat.

The tan Mercedes 440 ES pulled up next to a blue BMW 745 in the vacant end of the train station parking lot. Culver leaned against its left rear fender. Graciela's heart gave a leap. He wore a new raincoat, unbuttoned, his hands buried in the pockets. When Bauer's driver started to open his door, Culver kicked it shut.

"Horst can get out by himself. You stay in the car, hands on top of the steering wheel."

Bauer opened his door. "Relax, Terry. Everyone gets a little tense at the time of such an important transaction." He tried on a reassuring smile that failed because of a hint of arrogance. He closed the door behind him, keeping Graciela in the car.

"Horst, I'm armed and I will kill you if there's the slightest sugges-tion . . ." He let the threat stay undefined. "Let me see the money."

"Don't you want your girlfriend first?" His scorn was now uncon-cealed.

Culver tried not to look at Graciela's anxious face in the rear win-dow. "The money," he insisted.

"I have what you want, but shouldn't we do this in a more private place?"

"No. Stop wasting time."

"May I open the trunk?" Culver nodded. "Driver," Bauer gestured to him. The deck lid made a popping sound.

Inside was an Italian leather shoulder bag. Bauer took it out and set it on the back of the BMW.

"Open it," Culver said.

Bauer unzipped one of the compartments and started to reach in-side.

"Very slowly," Culver ordered.

Bauer's hand came out grasping twenty-, one hundred-, and thou-sand-dollar bundles of US currency and US Bearer bonds in five-thousand- and ten-thousand-dollar denominations.

"Would you like to count it?" Bauer smiled again.

Culver glanced toward the depot. More cars were arriving for the 12:14 train. He shook his head.

"And here are the passports I promised. Six of them. Out of friendship, I'm also including some addresses where you can be safe, at least temporarily. Now, what am I paying for?"

Culver opened the trunk with his left hand, keeping his right in his pocket. The lid swung up to reveal an olive drab metal box with rounded edges about the size of two five-gallon fuel cans. Steel handles were fastened to each end, and the number 364-C5/1 was stenciled in white on the side.

Bauer bent over to inspect a small plaque attached to the case on one end.

> US MIL SPEC 1956: 2764A/12-46
> TYPE: W-54S SADM
> US Dept. of Energy Control No. 864121973
> US Army Lot No. 364-C5/1

"I want to look inside it," Bauer said.

"Shall I dismantle it for you?" It was Culver's turn to smile as Bauer glanced uneasily at the growing crowd in the parking lot.

Bauer tried to lift the SADM. "Heavier than I thought," he grunted. "Maybe Fritz could—"

"Keep your goon in the car. Graciela can help you."

She got out and started to run toward Culver, but stopped short when he motioned for her to stay out of the way of the MAC-10 machine pistol he flashed under his raincoat. Obediently, she joined Bauer to carry it from the BMW to the Mercedes. She, too, seemed surprised at how heavy it was.

"How does it work?" asked Bauer.

"Like any other explosive." Culver opened a small door in the side. "This switch lets you arm the weapon. These two lights show that the primary and secondary circuits are working. The third light is the power-supply indicator. You have to wait thirty seconds for a diagnostic check, then this one comes on and you move the switch over to this position to enable it. That there's a timer. As you can see, it works

up to twelve hours. Here you have the input for the remote detonator."
Culver handed Bauer a heavy shoebox-sized canister. "The receiver is
this part with the wire antennas. It plugs in here on the weapon. The
other antenna's for the transmitter. It will work up to five miles, further if it's line-of-sight. These leads and lights are for testing the
batteries in the remote detonator, receiver, and transmitter."

"It looks very complicated," said Bauer. "Perhaps Graciela should
stay for a while to teach me to use it." He was smiling again.

"Oh, no . . ." Graciela started to back away.

"Actually, that might be a good idea," Culver said without emotion.

"What are you saying, Terry? You can't leave me here!"

"It's too dangerous for us to travel together. They're going to be on
the lookout for two of us."

"No, I won't!" She started to cry, but her protests were drowned out
by the sudden arrival of the train. Culver picked up the leather bag and
started moving toward the depot.

"Here." He tossed Graciela the keys. "Keep the car. I'll get in touch
when I've set up something safe," he said without conviction.

Bauer started to put his arm around her to draw her back to the
Mercedes, but she broke free. Clinging to Culver, she kissed him
fiercely and whispered, *"No me olvedastes. Dame tu promesa!"*

Culver hesitated. *"No mas,"* he finally pleaded, his voice cracking.
The bell at the station signaled the train's departure. He pushed her
away, backed up a few steps, then turned and ran for the platform.

As the train made its way down the valley, Culver stood on the
observation deck of the last car. For as long as he could, he watched
the tan Mercedes make its climb back up the mountain.

42

"It's our alpine club," Gordon explained to the German rental
agent standing next to the Dornier 120, as a dozen men loaded their
gear in the back of the aircraft. The agent looked doubtfully at the riot

of civilian clothes in which the Rangers tried to conceal their military identity—Levi's and sheepskin jackets, Italian leather jumpsuits, J. C. Penney's blazers and slacks.

He shrugged. "Have your pilot report to me with his license. You're cleared for takeoff in five minutes."

As soon as the twin prop jet was airborne, Colonel Handyside made his way forward to Gordon.

"Well, General," he said with frank scepticism, "what's your battle plan?"

Gordon had a Michelin map spread out on his knees.

"As far as I can tell," Gordon said, "Bauer's chalet should be here." He pointed to a one-lane road high above Kitzbühel that petered out where it encountered a mountain stream.

"Here, I got some pictures EUCOM says might be the place." Handyside unlocked a zippered folder and took out a black envelope. "They're Faxes from the satellite and so the quality's for shit, but it gives a general idea of the area."

"Pretty open country." Gordon shook his head.

"It'd be better to wait till dark. Gotta have some surprise," Handyside noted. "Why the hell don't we just bomb the crap out of 'em?"

"Because we don't know if Bauer or Culver or anybody else is there. It could be a family from Cleveland."

Handyside snorted.

"What have you told the troops?"

"Just that it's a counterterrorist action. My boys are up for it," he said, showing enthusiasm for the first time.

"We'll settle on tactics after we check it out," Gordon concluded. "I'll tell the pilot to make a few passes over the area. Have the men get a good look at the target, so we're all working from the same sheet of music."

43

"Admiral, have you ever been to a congressional prayer breakfast?" the President asked.

"No, sir." The two of them were standing with Karl Loggerman under the Harry Truman balcony at the south entrance of the White House.

"It's a gathering of the impious to importune God for the impossible. Like everything in Congress, it's a deal. You pray, you eat. It's only a drop-by for ten minutes. Why don't you ride along with me." It was an order. "Karl, make sure everything's ready."

A faint blush of embarrassment spread over Loggerman's face as the door slammed and the President's motorcade pulled away. Walking up the driveway toward the West Wing, Loggerman tried to console himself with the thought that staying behind would give him a chance to work on the Vice President.

Inside the car, the President quickly scanned Admiral McCollough's report on Gordon's plans.

"Sean asked me to emphasize, Mr. President, that the Kitzbühel operation could be a wild goose chase."

"That's exactly his problem. He's a total romantic, but tries to conceal it by denying the power of hope. So why is he doing it?"

"We know that Bauer has leased this chalet in Kitzbühel through a dummy corporation. But whether he's there, or Culver, or the bomb, we won't know without going in. We've brought along the Rangers just in case."

"Do they know how to defuse it?"

"A couple of custodial people from Schloss Ludwigshof are with them. They've also given Sean a crash course."

"We'll get real-time reports?"

"I hope. We have an AWAC in the air over southern Germany, linked up through one of our satellites. It's supposed to be able to pick up CIA's secure voice equipment from the plane or the ground."

The President leaned back in an effort to relax.

"God, I hope this is it."

"It's a long shot, sir."

"You've had breakfast?"

Admiral McCollough nodded.

"Me, too." The President paused as the motorcade drew up to the service entrance of the Congressional Hyatt Hotel. "Maybe we should pray anyway."

From behind the pilot's seat, Gordon could make out the north-ernmost ridge of the Alps. The mountains, gray and white, rise abruptly out of the dark green German forests. Formed 250 million years ago, when Africa jammed the Italian peninsula into the under-belly of Europe, the Alps spread north in a series of concentric granite wrinkles ending in the plains of Bavaria. A long finger of Austria snakes westward up the last major valley and divides Germany from Italy and much of Switzerland.

The rain and light snow of the night before had swiftly moved east. The afternoon was bright and clear except for the clouds and mist filling the deep valley of the Inn river. The limestone massif of the Kaiser Gebirge shone brightly in the sunshine and served as the gateway to the smoothly rounded Grasberge, the cow-pasture moun-tains of the Kitzbühler Alpen.

Gordon took his bearings from the towering Kitzbühler Horn. Rotat-ing the map in his lap, he pointed the pilot to turn more south from southeast.

"What's the evidence again that the Russians are in on this?" Bleary-eyed and not yet awake, the Vice President kept rubbing his face as if to arrange the parts in better working order. He sat to the right of the President's vacant chair while a technician fiddled with a speaker phone. Other members of the National Security Council drifted in and out of the Situation Room.

"First, there's the demands themselves," Loggerman explained pa-tiently, "and the disaster this whole thing could be for NATO. Admit-tedly, that's circumstantial, but it's a fact nonetheless, and more important than all the others. Then there's Culver and his questionable past. Now we find the link, Horst Bauer. Terrorist. May have killed over a hundred GIs and dependents in that terrible bombing in Germany a few years ago. Reportedly seen at terrorist training camps in Yemen. He has the typical profile for connections to East Bloc intelligence. Finally, we have the Russians' reaction to our message—'We didn't do it, but we can help you out.'"

The Vice President was having a hard time absorbing so much news. He was a species long thought extinct in American politics—a Vice President with no higher ambitions. His job was to balance the ticket. Beyond that, he viewed his job as OJR—On the Job Retirement.

Always overweight, he had gained another fifteen pounds in the few months since the inauguration from the endless round of ceremonial lunches and dinners. As he bit into a cheese danish, the significance of what he was hearing began to dawn on him.

"This could lead to war," he said, trying out the words, not yet believing them.

"That's why it's imperative that we show firmness and resolve. This is a purposeful challenge by the Soviet Union, not some accident or random terrorist act—"

"I think the patch is operational, sir," interrupted the technician.

"Gentlemen, we have contact with the plane," Loggerman called out to the others.

"Well, let's cross our fingers," the Vice President said lamely.

From the map and the Xeroxed satellite photos, Gordon concluded that Bauer's was the large chalet at the end of the one-lane paved road that ran toward the Trattalm. A typical two-story Bavarian design, it had a balcony that ran around the entire second story. The only unusual feature was the configuration of the driveway, which suggested a garage under the house. Looking down from fifteen thousand feet he could see no car or any other sign of activity, except a thin wisp of smoke emerging from a chimney on the west side of the house. Patches of snow covered the ground, but the road was clear.

"We've located the target," Gordon said into a small microphone, "and see nothing unusual at this moment. I'll give you an update in a minute." He shut off the mike.

"Can't be too subtle with this one," Colonel Handyside said. "I say, bring the main group right up the road like they was tourists. And send four men around that hill to flank the house from the rear. We all pull up, get out, look confused, ask directions, get close. On your signal, four of us go in the front door and windows, two go up onto the balcony and two blow open the garage. If they start shooting first, the four at the rear burst in the back. Ditto, vice versa."

"What about the custodial people?"

"Put 'em in the last car out of the line of fire."

Gordon could see no better alternative. "Let's do another orbit so everyone knows their assignment, then go down for one close look."

It was hoke, hype, and hypocrisy, and the President loved it. Back in the real world, he thought to himself, smiling and shaking the hands that reached out to him as he made his way among the tables in the Grand Ballroom.

"You're lookin' good."

"Feel like I'm out of solitary," he responded honestly, grasping the rough right hands of professional politicians.

On the dais, he gave the presiding reverend a two-hand shake and then waved to a starburst of strobe lights fired from the wall of photographers to his right.

"Mr. President," intoned the reverend, "let us pray."

He bowed his head.

"We're going to swing out around the Hahnenkamm. That's the mountain behind the chalet." Gordon's disembodied voice emerged from a speaker in the middle of the table. Loggerman pointed to a relief map propped on an easel at his end of the room. "Then we'll make one run down the river valley at three or four hundred feet to get a close-up. But we don't want to raise suspicions, so only one pass. We'll go right into this grassy field. It usually just handles gliders, so it may be rough. Then we pick up our vehicles and should be in place for the assault in fifteen minutes."

There was a click and a hum, and the connection seemed broken. "Mr. Gordon, can you hear me?" the Secretary of State said.

"Yes," Gordon's reply was noisy but clear.

"What about Austria's police and customs?"

"No customs here. We hope to get in and out before the police get back from lunch."

"Describe what you see," urged the Chairman of the Joint Chiefs.

"Nothing yet, we're still behind the mountain. This is all open pasture. Some streams and fences. Snow at the higher elevations. The chalet is quite remote, maybe four miles up the road from Kitzbühel.

"Okay, we can see it now. Uh-oh. That's what I was worried about." A pause was punctuated by indistinct whisperings. Concern swept the faces at the table. "They've got lookouts at each corner of the balcony. Makes things a lot tougher, but at least we know somebody's home."

"Maybe they should wait until the NEST team gets there?" the Defense Secretary cautioned.

Loggerman frowned. It was a typical Pentagon response: When in doubt, add more resources. "Anything else we should know?" he asked, ignoring the Secretary.

"Don't think so. Hey, wait! Tell the pilot to bank right." More indistinct sounds. "Something's going on. Somebody's running down the hill from the house. Now there's others. Tell the pilot to make another pass."

The NSC members could hear the sound of a protesting voice.

"Screw surprise," Gordon said impatiently. "Yes, it's a woman running like mad and three men chasing her. They're firing at her—"

The door to the Situation Room opened and the President stepped in. "What's happening?" Loggerman pointed to the speaker on the table. The faces around it were hard with tension.

"Shit, they caught her. Christ, I wish this thing were a helicopter. Oh, my God! Oh, my God . . ."

"What is it? Sean, this is the President."

"An explosion! A huge explosion! The chalet is—unh!" They heard a roar through the speaker. "That was the shock wave. The chalet's gone, vanished. That can't be—"

The men at the table looked fearfully at one another.

"There was an enormous flash, but still not— Tons of debris raining down, hitting the plane. Wait . . . We've got the counter out. No sign of radiation. We're okay . . . can't be nuclear. I don't know what the hell—"

"Was the bomb in there?" asked Loggerman.

"I don't know. But it had to be conventional. We don't have any readings. If the case were blown apart, we'd still get some clicks, wouldn't we?" Gordon asked.

"I think so," McCollough answered.

"You're all okay?" the President asked again.

"Yes, but the chalet is just a massive hole in the ground."

"What do we do now?" the Vice President wondered.

"The girl and the men chasing her are on the ground. I don't know if they're dead or not. I'm putting three men out on chutes to help them. Pray they're alive."

44

Loggerman could not wait to give the President the news. The monitor on his credenza indicated that he was meeting with a delegation of Western Governors in the Cabinet Room.

"Pass him this note," Loggerman instructed Peter Andretti, the President's Appointments Secretary.

"He doesn't want to be interrupted," Andretti replied. He remained sitting behind the tiny desk stuffed in the cubbyhole he occupied between the Oval Office and the Cabinet Room.

"Yes, he does. And if you won't do it, I will."

Reluctantly, Andretti took the note, squeezed around his desk, and disappeared into the Cabinet Room. He was doubly irritated that the note was in a sealed envelope, suggesting that he could not be trusted.

The President came through the door with an anxious look on his face.

"Has he found it?"

Loggerman looked uneasily at Andretti.

"Well, tell me!" the President insisted impatiently. Loggerman was shocked that he had let his Appointments Secretary in on the secret.

"No. Mr. Gordon hasn't found the bomb."

"Is the girl alive? Any other survivors?"

"The girl's alive but unconscious. So are the men who were chasing her."

"Does anybody know what happened?"

"No, not yet," Loggerman responded.

"Then what the hell's the urgent development?" the President exploded.

"Sean Gordon's in jail."

The President looked at him, unbelieving.

"He's accused by the Austrian police of dropping a bomb on Bauer's chalet. All the Rangers are under arrest, too. We have a major diplomatic incident on our hands and"—Loggerman paused—"*and* a real risk that the whole story could come out."

"Can't we get them released?" asked the President.

"The State Department's working on it, but they're arguing among themselves whether Consulate General Munich or the Embassy in Vienna should deal with the Austrians."

"The State Department?" The President said incredulously. "Gordon's not some kid with a backpack full of hash. Get the CIA on it."

"They have similar problems. Austria is the Eastern European Division and they have to send someone to Kitzbühel all the way from Vienna, even though Munich is closer. And State has been trying to block the CIA. Of course, they don't know what this is all about. I insisted with the Secretary that no one in the department be told about this. Still the Assistant Secretary for Consular Affairs claims that the arrested Americans are State's turf."

"Karl," the President said slowly, "are you enjoying this?"

"Mr. President," Loggerman started to protest.

"I want Gordon out. Immediately!" The President grabbed him by the lapels. "Your job is to get that done. Understand!"

The President slammed the door to the Cabinet Room before Loggerman could stammer, "Yes, sir."

*   *   *

Billy Kelly had already figured out a way around the bureaucracy. His emissary arrived in Kitzbühel at three-thirty in the afternoon and by four had met with the local authorities to persuade them to release Gordon on his own recognizance.

Gordon sat in a cell in the basement of the Rathaus, disgusted with himself. The President, he decided, had made a fatal mistake in giving him the job. He had lost his edge, and worse, he had run out of luck. Anyone should have seen that from what had happened to him over the last few years.

The Austrians, after discovering the Rangers' weapons, had put them all under arrest. They had singled him out for the full terrorist treatment, confiscating his clothes, and giving him a vicious rectal examination. He was freezing, sore, and had no idea what was going on. Kelly had not been in his office to take the one phone call he was allowed, so he'd left a message. Since then, nothing.

"Herr Gordon, you have a visitor," the guard said.

He did not recognize the sandy-blond man with the humorless eyes and faintly Asiatic cheekbones who was let past the bars.

"I am Alexander Antunov." He stuck out his hand. "I have instructions to be of assistance to you."

With freedom came hunger. Gordon realized he had not eaten in almost a day. They stopped at Satamperl, a small *Beisel* in the *Vorstadt*. The schnitzel was half grease, but he bolted it down. Though devoid of customers in the middle of the afternoon, the restaurant, warmed by a log fire, felt cozy.

"I told them the truth." Antunov sipped his Kleiner Brauner. "That our two governments are cooperating in search of a terrorist group."

"That story didn't impress them when I used it," Gordon responded, downing another boiled potato.

"I admit that our people in Vienna also contacted certain persons in the Interior Ministry and they talked to the City Fathers, but only to vouch for my bona fides."

"Which are?" Gordon stopped eating and looked up.

Antunov ducked the jab. "I told them that the Soviet Union placed a high premium on security cooperation and that their record on this matter would weigh heavily on my government's position on whether to vote against Kitzbühel as the site for the next Olympic winter games."

Gordon guessed that he meant they already had some local politician on their payroll. He filed it away for a later counterintelligence report, and buttered a crescent-shaped *Salzstangerl*. He loved the taste of the bread's crunchy salt crystals against the sweet flavor of the fresh alpine butter. He felt a long way away from tofu, bean sprouts, La Jolla—and Laura.

"I appreciate what you've done to get me out," Gordon said, honestly. "Now, what can you do to help find Culver and the bomb?"

"We know something of him from his operations against us and our friends in Czechoslovakia. Also we have," he paused to select his English words carefully, *"resources* here in Western Europe that may prove of use. But let me be frank. We do not know if all this is a trick designed to expose those resources. What concrete assurances can you give me on that point?"

"None. Look, a missing US nuclear weapon is not something to brag about. The President of the United States took a big risk in telling your government about it, particularly when it looks like the people who stole it are friends of yours."

"They are not linked to us in any way."

"And what 'concrete assurance' can you give me of that?"

Antunov paused. "None. But we are alerting all of our resources in an effort to locate Mr. Culver. Why have you not notified the police?" he asked, to regain the initiative.

"Mr. Antunov, both of us are trained to ask questions to which we already know the answers. Let's not waste time practicing."

The waitress intervened to clear the table. She wore a tight green dirndl that made the tops of her breasts roll like pails of milk. Gordon ordered a coffee *mit Schlagobers*.

"Did you learn anything from the survivors?" Antunov asked.

"Only that they survived. All of them were unconscious up to the time I was arrested. One got a splintered timber through his back. I don't think he'll make it. Did your deal with the police include getting Graciela Morena out of here?"

"Yes. But they wouldn't let Herr Bauer go, since he's not an American. He's in critical condition in any event. Your troops will stay here as well. They are a token of your 'good faith.'"

Gordon waved for the check. "Let's get to the hospital."

She looked beautiful. Her tawny skin made a rich contrast to the starched white pillows; her dark eyes, dilated by the concussion, were black as fear; and the high cheekbones accentuated her helplessness. Gordon felt something stirring inside him that he pushed to one side.

"I guess I'm lucky," she said weakly. The pain from her broken ribs and left forearm showed on her face.

"Can you answer some questions?" Gordon asked.

"I'll try. I'm a little confused. The doctor says it's the concussion. That's why he won't give me anything more for the pain."

"What happened?"

Tears filled her eyes. "I don't know."

"Take it slow. We know all about you and Lieutenant Culver and the Special ADM," Gordon said gently. "What we want to know is where the bomb is now?"

"I don't know," she said again. "Terry gave it to Bauer. I was trying to escape, and then I don't know what happened . . ."

"There was an explosion. It wasn't the SADM. There's no sign of it."

"Is Bauer—?"

"He's alive. Worse off than you. Broken collarbone, maybe skull, too. He's still unconscious. Was Culver in the chalet?"

"Terry's gone." Her voice had become a whisper.

"What do you mean?" Antunov said sharply, speaking for the first time.

"He gave us the bomb. At least, the case. But it seemed too heavy. Maybe that's what went off. He left me behind with it. I don't know why he would do that . . ." She started to cry.

Gordon took her right hand. "You must know how important this is." She nodded, tears still flowing. "Anything you could tell us about where he might be, or the bomb?" She just shook her head slightly. The tears stopped.

"What about the deadline and the demands?" Antunov asked. "Is Lieutenant Culver committed to them, or is it Bauer?"

"It's all Bauer's idea," she said bitterly. "Terry just did it to prove something. I don't know, though. He's so angry. Nothing was working out. I'm so worried about him." The tears came once more. "He's changed. I think he may be a little crazy, now."

45

That was the last straw, Loggerman thought angrily, his limo edging its way through lunchtime traffic in Georgetown and onto Canal Road. Never again would he be blamed for the Secretary of State's incompetence. First, he has the gall to criticize Gordon's hot pursuit of Bauer to Kitzbühel on the grounds that it violates Austrian sovereignty—but says so only after it failed. Then, the State Department drags its feet on Gordon's release. They could never do that without the Secretary's tacit approval. And on top of that, the President blames me, Loggerman thought bitterly, while the Russian gets the credit for getting him out!

The Secretary of State is becoming a menace, Loggerman said to himself. He's flaky and reinforces the President's indecisiveness. If the country is to get through the crisis safely, he has to be neutralized. That thought fortified Loggerman for the risk he was about to take by having lunch with Walter Pincus of *The Washington Post*.

The city gave way to parkway and finally countryside before the heavily armored Chrysler rolled into the dirt parking lot of the Old Angler's Inn. It stopped in front of a terrace filled with tables that surrounded a large fountain. Most of the patrons were couples enjoying the fine weather and taking a break from the Washington routine as well as from their spouses. The maître d' showed Loggerman to a secluded upstairs room. Walter Pincus was already waiting for him.

They joked and fenced through an arugula salad and linguine with white clam sauce for Loggerman, minestrone and veal paillard for Pincus. Over coffee, when the reporter raised the "subject" of the lunch, the suicide of former Los Alamos Director Jason Winniker, Loggerman brushed it aside.

"I don't know why he did it. Maybe he'd heard what the State Department's up to."

Pincus smelled fresh bait, and knew he would get more by not going after it. He asked another question about Winniker. Again Loggerman tried to move the subject back to the State Department. On the fourth go-around, Pincus signaled for the check and Loggerman's voice took on a slight edge of urgency.

"You don't know the abuse I've been getting from the State Department," he said.

"They haven't said anything to me," Pincus replied, giving only the faintest encouragement.

"Have you been talking to the Secretary about nuclear weapons in Europe?"

It was all going to be laid out. Pincus just waited.

"Do you realize he wants to withdraw all of our nuclear weapons from Europe? He says Americans are willing to help defend Europe, but don't want to start a nuclear war in the process. And he ties it all to terrorism. He claims the weapons are too vulnerable. He wants a big study and is accusing me of dragging my feet because I want the Pentagon to answer his questions first—especially about the terrorist threat."

"You've had worse fights than that, Karl." Pincus still appeared unimpressed.

"I've had to have the President himself clamp down to keep him from raising it in NATO and scaring our Allies to death."

"Might be worth checking out. Mind if I call you later on it?"

"No, no. Keep me out of it. We never had this conversation."

Loggerman could relax. Mission accomplished. He poured the complimentary snifter of Sambuca into his coffee and watched the three beans swirl toward one another in the middle of his cup.

46

Gasthaus Eikenberg sits on the northern edge of Cham, an undistinguished village in the otherwise picturesque Bavarian forest that runs the length of the Czech border. Frau Eikenberg, who operated the inn with ruthless efficiency, was one of the resources Antunov had mentioned to Gordon. She did not consider herself a spy, any more than she would accept the label of police informer for also keeping the West German border police, the Bundesgrenzenschutz, apprised of unusual visitors. To be sure, she was paid by the GRU and not by the border police, but the small sum of money did not go directly into her pocket. It helped maintain her standards of service at the Gasthaus. More important to her was the implicit insurance policy her dual role provided in case of an invasion from the east. Most of her family had perished during the second World War, and she intended to survive the next one.

The GRU, Soviet Military Intelligence, employed Frau Eikenberg to help keep watch over the activities at the US nuclear storage site across the Regen river in the nearby woods. She seldom had much to report, but today was different. Heavy American trucks and armored personnel carriers had been driving through town toward the storage site for the last twenty-four hours. According to her standing instructions, she had phoned a travel agency in Nuremberg with an ostensibly routine inquiry, and now expected a visit from her control officer. He was a fifty-year-old East German who had come west ten years earlier and specialized in tours of the Bayrischer Wald along the Czech frontier.

When Frau Eikenberg answered the bell at the front desk, she was disappointed to find that it was not her control officer, but a tall young man in motorcycle leathers seeking a room for the night. His Austrian passport identified him as Dietrich Aufenaker from Lintz. His German was impeccable but clearly not Austrian. Now she had something to report to the German border police as well.

"You must park your motorcycle in the back. Dinner will be served in an hour and a half," she said officiously. Noticing that a shoulder bag was his only luggage, she asked for payment in advance. He paid in dollars. His bag seemed to be full of cash. When he climbed the stairs out of sight, she reached for the phone. As it rang at the local border police station, she wondered whether her GRU contact might also be interested in the young man.

Terence Culver was faintly surprised by the absence of fear and doubt. By taking action, everything had become clear. After weeks of torment and anger, he felt calm for the first time. The churning thoughts had stopped. The storm raged around him, but he was in the eye. He had even managed a short nap, but he wanted to check on whether his threat was being taken seriously.

The powerful BMW K-100 felt good between his legs as he accelerated away from the Gasthaus and over the Regen river bridge south on the E12. Where the road divided, he took Route 20, then, after climbing three kilometers into the hills, turned onto an unmarked but well paved lane. He opened up the visor on his helmet to let in the cool forest air. The trees crowded close to the road. After a kilometer, he began seeing military vehicles parked in the woods on either side, only partly concealed by the spring foliage.

Rounding a corner, he suddenly ran into a roadblock. A jeep was parked across the road, with a 20mm machine gun on a tripod pointed right at him. A half dozen nuclear custodial personnel flanked the vehicle. In the distance, Culver could see the earthen dome of the nuclear storage bunker. The gates stood open and a line of trucks pulled inside. He could not quell his excitement. Were they moving the weapons out?

"Where are you going?" a black sergeant asked in passable German. Culver responded in perfect *Hochdeutsch*.

"I'm looking for the road back to Roding. Am I in an exercise zone? I'm sorry. I saw no signs."

"Let me see your papers."

"Excuse me, you are Americans, no? You have no right to ask me for papers," Culver said.

The sergeant hesitated. He looked at the lieutenant sitting in the jeep. The other custodial guards trained their weapons on Culver.

"You speak English?"

"*Nein*," Culver replied firmly.

"I'm not gonna argue with you," the sergeant said in English. "*Schnell!*" he barked and held out his hand.

Culver got off his motorcycle and opened one of the plastic saddlebags. He took his time rummaging in it, looking up from time to time and counting a total of twelve trucks and four APCs, and two "turtles," which transported warheads for the Pershing II Missile. It looked like a redeployment was under way, but he could not get close enough to be certain. Finally, he handed over his passport.

"Mr. Aufenaker, you wait right here."

He leaned against the back of his motorcycle, hoping to look relaxed.

They were taking a long time with his documents. The name Aufenaker was repeated several times on their radio, but he could not hear the rest of the conversation.

What are you trying to do by acting smart? Culver asked himself. Do you want to get caught? Maybe Bauer's passports were a setup. Or they could be no good, bad forgeries, or taken from known criminals or in the alert books of every major government as false or stolen papers.

His right hand rested on the saddlebag with the MAC-10 machine pistol. They were all Americans. They could have been his buddies in Boot Camp. But if he had to, he would use it.

"The widow Eikenberg is always good for a schnapps," the Oberleutnant explained to his relief at the Cham Bundesgrenzenschutz office. "I'll check on this Herr Aufenaker on the way home." Maybe get a quick feel, too, he thought to himself.

But he had to wait. When he arrived at the Gasthaus, the buxom widow was huddled in her office with another man. She emerged looking flushed and excited.

"Who's that?" the Oberleutnant asked peevishly.

"A travel agent from Nuremberg. My place is becoming very well known." She opened an ornately carved wooden cupboard. "Mr. Aufenaker, he has gone out"—she poured him a Dornkaat—"but I don't think he's important. I hope you don't mind," she smiled. "It was just an excuse to see you."

The Oberleutnant knocked back the schnapps and held out his glass for another. "When will he be back?"

"He said he'd be back for dinner. That's in an hour."

"Let me see his room." She seemed in a good mood. He hoped that if she escorted him upstairs, they might be alone, and then, one never knew with her . . .

The pilot put the US Air Force DC-9 carrying Gordon and Antunov on the runway at Munich-Riem airport. Graciela Morena was taken from the litter on the wall of the aft cabin and carried on a stretcher to a waiting ambulance.

"Put her in the consulate infirmary," Gordon ordered the corpsman.

Kelly stood waiting at the foot of the stairs. "I have a message from Antunov's people. They think they've spotted Culver in a little town up on the Czech border. We've got a helicopter ready . . ."

As the UH-60A Blackhawk started to lift into the air, it paused for a moment. Gordon slid open the door.

"Billy!" he shouted, "they wouldn't let Bauer go! Get some surveillance on him!"

"Okay."

"I'll tell you everything when I get back!"

"Good hunting!"

The helicopter rose swiftly into the afternoon sky and headed northeast.

After Culver had waited thirty-five minutes, a major with a clipboard arrived in another jeep with two more guards and another lieutenant. They conferred with the sergeant for several more minutes.

"Herr Aufenaker, sign this." The sergeant spoke in German again. "It says you voluntarily identified yourself and that we didn't invade your privacy. Then you can go."

Culver signed it with relief.

On his way back to the Gasthaus, he told himself that the activity at the storage site might be a normal exercise or even a charade for his benefit. Still, the promise of revenge felt good. He stopped on the bridge over the Regen river and killed his engine.

The water was dark and swift. He looked upstream where the river disappeared into the dense pine-forested mountains. It seemed right to him that the circle of betrayal should wind back to this place where it had begun only a few months ago, the jumping-off point for the debacle in Czechoslovakia.

For more than a year Culver had been running a forward network in Czechoslovakia. Like Frau Eikenberg, his agents were to report on Soviet military activities, but because of the higher risks, they were confined to alerting the West only of an impending surprise attack. Despite spy satellites, radar, and electronic eavesdropping, night and bad weather could still conceal a military buildup. And the best source was still someone on the spot.

Unfortunately, Culver's agents could not simply pick up the telephone and have him pay a visit. They used radios. But their radios were old, bulky, hard to conceal, and easy to locate while broadcasting. The radios had undone more than one agent in recent years.

For several months, Culver had been arranging with the British to smuggle in new microminiaturized radios with a "burst" communications capability. His jumping-off point for Czechoslovakia had been Cham.

Culver remembered the feel of the ultralight aircraft in his hands as he had followed the Regen river valley at dusk under a lid of clouds. He had cut the engine shortly before the guard towers, and sailed quietly into Czechoslovakia below the Osser's three-thousand-foot peaks. His Czech contact, Nadya Zakostelsky, waited for him in an isolated pasture in a remote corner of a collective farm near Domažlice, a railroad town where they were to rendezvous with a British team.

The plan had had all the elegance of MI-6. The British had hidden the new communications gear inside a van full of computer equipment that the Russians were illegally exporting from Great Britain. Piggybacking on a GRU operation ensured only perfunctory inspection of the cargo at the Czech border. There, the van would be hoisted onto a flatbed railcar for transport by train to the Soviet Union.

Culver had carried the vital parts, a handful of extremely high frequency oscillators embedded in gallium arsenide wafers. He, Nadya, and the British team were to enter the van in the marshaling yard at Domažlice. While the train traveled deeper into Czechoslovakia, they would separate and assemble the gear. At a preselected point, the train would be halted briefly by a truck stopped on a grade crossing. That would give the group an opportunity to escape with the equipment.

Everything worked smoothly. Culver was happy to see Nadya, a blond woman in her early thirties whose father had been killed during the Soviet invasion of 1968. She had served as his principal contact inside Czechoslovakia for over a year. Their relationship was strictly professional, but her fatalistic jokes, her flirting and teasing, even the way she often treated him like a boy, made Culver very fond of her.

Culver had not met his British counterpart. He proved to be an unsmiling thick-set man in his late twenties, who introduced himself only as Arnold. He was accompanied by an older Czech who said his name was Franz. Quickly, they located the flatcar and van at the head of a line of propane tank cars.

They completed their task swiftly. Only slightly behind schedule, the train slammed on its emergency brakes. The four of them jumped out and began unloading the equipment as Franz dashed into the darkness to contact the truck. Suddenly, Culver, Arnold, and Nadya were blinded by floodlights. A voice over a loudspeaker announced in English that they were under arrest. They were ordered to place any weapons on the ground.

Culver watched Arnold lean over and drop a Czech Mauser. Nadya shouted out that she was unarmed. Culver removed a MAC-10 machine pistol from his jacket, and with the muzzle pointing at himself he squatted down to place it on the ground. With a slight twist of his hand, he pointed the muzzle past his head, toward a tank car, and pulled the trigger with his thumb.

The Teflon-covered bullets punched through the aluminum-clad tank as if it were wax. The exploding gas blew out the floodlights. Culver had spread himself on his stomach. Arnold and Nadya were knocked flat. Culver smothered Nadya's burning hair and got her moving away from the exploding tank car. He tried to help Arnold onto his feet, but the British agent grabbed him, swearing, and knocked him down. Confused, Culver rolled away and started running after Nadya. He looked back to see Arnold pointing his pistol at them. He fired and Nadya tumbled to the ground. Other shots began to ring out. Culver dove between two boxcars as another exploding propane tank silenced the firing.

Culver ran to the front of the train. He decoupled the engine, then ordered the trainmen out of the cab. The diesel-electric engines were still running. Culver pulled away in a shower of fragments from the tank cars that were exploding like a string of firecrackers.

A mile down the track, Culver slowed the engine, then put it on full throttle as he leapt to the ground, hoping the Czechs would chase it half the night. Later he would learn that a few miles away it had jumped the rails, killing dozens of innocent people who slept in a trackside apartment house. He shuddered at the memory of the pictures.

In less than a week, Culver had managed to slip back into the West over the Hungarian border. He'd expected to be treated as a hero. Instead, he had been slammed into the stockade, and his nightmare had begun in earnest.

He kick-started the BMW. No more betrayals, he vowed. Nadya was dead. Graciela and Horst must be dead by now. Soon, I probably will be, too, he thought, popping his bike into gear. But not before I finish what I've started.

As she bustled about the dining room setting the table, Frau Eikenberg's thoughts dwelled on the Oberleutnant and the way his mustache tickled her neck. She looked up to see Herr Aufenaker's motorcycle parked next to the front door. "I told him to put it in the back," she said crossly. The GRU man had warned her to be careful of him. Well, that didn't mean letting him make his own rules in her house. And where was the Oberleutnant? "Probably sneaked home to his skinny wife after he got what he wanted," she muttered as she climbed the stairs to Herr Aufenaker's room.

But when she knocked and then opened the door, there was the Oberleutnant. His left hand was full of passports and packets of US currency. His right held a gun trained on her guest.

*   *   *

"This is impossible!" Gordon had lost all patience. He was shouting at Admiral McCollough over the radio as the helicopter approached Cham from the south following Route 20. "Everytime I want to get EUCOM to assign me forces, I have to go through Washington. We've got fifty men at the SAS site near here and I can't get any help from any of them!"

Antunov listened to the exchange with a slight smile on his face.

"Then the two of us will go in after him by ourselves," Gordon continued, looking over at Antunov. "We'll find out, but according to our friends he doesn't have it with him. Cross your fingers. This guy could just be a magazine salesman."

When Frau Eikenberg opened the door, Culver saw the Oberleutnant's eyes shift toward her. He dove forward. The policeman slammed against the armoire. His gun flew backward, crashing through the window and onto the street. Floating twenty-dollar bills filled the small room. One blow from the back of Culver's hand and the Oberleutnant was out.

Kicking the door shut, Culver whirled on Frau Eikenberg. She made no sound. She was already on her hands and knees, collecting the twenty-dollar bills.

The helicopter descended into the parking lot behind the Gasthaus. Gordon and Antunov walked briskly through the back door. No one was at the reception desk. Gorman opened the registration book; Aufenaker, Room 2E. Antunov quickly scanned the dining room. Both of them raced up the stairs.

Gordon knocked once. There was a muffled reply. Together, they kicked in the heavy pine door. On the bed they found Frau Eikenberg tied with bed sheets face down upon the still unconscious Oberleutnant. Twenty-dollar notes were scattered on the floor. Gordon heard the sound of a motorcycle fire up outside. He rushed to the open window in time to see the motorcyclist disappear down the road toward town.

"That's him!" Frau Eikenberg managed to sputter.

In less than a minute, they were airborne again.

"Make a big sweep," Antunov suggested. "Try to pick him up on the outskirts leaving town."

"That looks like him!" Gordon pointed to a motorcyclist turning onto the Ostmarkestrasse.

"He's going too slow," Antunov noted. "He does not look like someone escaping—"

"He's moving now. He must have heard us."

They chased him through the villages of Miltach, Kötzting, and Lam while Gordon, on the radio, argued through layer after bureaucratic layer at US Army European Headquarters trying to get help. They would get back to him.

"Mr. Gordon," Antunov spoke up, "he is not carrying any nuclear weapon on that motorcycle, if I am correct? So why do we not shoot him?"

"Maybe it's not him."

Antunov looked at Gordon coldly.

"And if he's killed, we still don't have the weapon. It could be set to go off by itself!"

"I can assure you that when he slows down on one of these turns, I can shoot the motorcycle out from under him."

Gordon searched Antunov's flat eyes. Did he want an excuse to kill Culver and eliminate the man that could prove the Soviet connection? Maybe that was why they were so anxious to be helpful. On the other hand, if he let Culver get away after the Soviets had found him, they would be convinced the US was playing games. Before he could answer Antunov, the radio crackled to life. Gordon listened intently, started to protest, then said simply, "Thanks"—without a trace of gratitude.

Antunov looked at him expectantly.

"They'll do their best to set up a roadblock between Schönberg and Tittling, about twenty-five kilometers south. They've no idea how long it will take."

"Mr. Gordon, it's getting dark."

He knew Antunov was right. They had to risk trying to stop him. He looked down at the road.

The motorcycle had disappeared. So had the road.

"Where the hell did he go?" Gordon exclaimed.

"Tunnel," answered the pilot. "This is the Grosser Arber." The helicopter shot upward. "It's over six thousand feet. We have to turn west to make sure we don't cross into Czechoslovakia. They like to shoot us down over there."

Once over the twin stone spires, they had a clear view of the road as it emerged from the mountain and wrapped around a dark lake. A few cars and a tour bus were visible, but no motorcycle. They hovered over the mouth of the tunnel.

Several minutes passed. Finally, a car with a trailer appeared. They had passed it earlier.

"He turned around," Antunov shouted.

"Or he's hiding inside. Put me down. I'll start through this side. You check to see if he doubled back. If you find him, stop him any way you can, but keep him alive. If you kill him . . ." Gordon did not have to complete the threat. "Am I supposed to take orders from this Russian?" the pilot asked.

"Absolutely," Gordon shouted; he jumped to the ground.

The tunnel was unlit. Water streamed out of the rocky walls and dripped from the ceiling. As an occasional car passed, its headlights revealed a curving road ahead. After ten minutes, Gordon thought he could make out a figure moving carefully toward him along the opposite wall. He stood still.

A large truck came up behind him, and he pressed against the rocks until it went by. Gordon then ran forward a few yards, hoping that the truck's headlights would blind his quarry. Then he waited for another vehicle from his end of the tunnel and, when it had passed, he ran again, repeating the process several times.

There was a long gap in the traffic, and Gordon, peering out from behind a boulder, strained to see ahead. Several cars came toward him, but they revealed nothing. A tour bus roared down Gordon's side of the tunnel. As it went by, he started to run once more, but he tripped on something and fell. In an instant, someone was on his back.

His arms were pinned behind him. A flashlight shined into his face. He heard a sigh of disappointment.

"It seems we've lost Lieutenant Culver," Antunov said.

47

"It's all there in my report." Alexander Antunov spoke loud and slowly, so that Dimitri Fyakov could hear him over the encrypted telephoned circuit.

"But what is your assessment?" Fyakov persisted. "Is this a deception or a provocation?"

"I don't know yet. There was no sign of a bomb. On the other hand, if the Americans are trying to appear disorganized, they are very convincing."

Antunov was speaking from the headquarters of the Soviet Liaison Mission, located in a small palace surrounded by gardens on the outskirts of Munich. A relic of the Four-Power Occupation after the defeat of Hitler, the Mission consisted of eight four-man teams of Soviet Army officers ostensibly exercising the rights of conquest by patrolling the West German autobahns. In reality, the Mission provided a legitimate base for illegal military intelligence operations. All of the officers were GRU.

"Alex, are you alone?" Fyakov asked. "Do you think this line is secure in *every way*?" He accented the last phrase to indicate to Antunov that he was primarily concerned about the GRU.

"Yes. We can never be sure about the Americans, but everyone else, yes."

"I want to give you a feel for the situation here," Fyakov explained. "It's extremely delicate. Thankfully, the military has confidence in you personally, but they remain opposed to your assignment with the Americans. So far they are cooperating, yes?"

"They told us Culver was in Cham."

"Good."

"Are they still saying that we should expose the whole thing?"

"Yes, and now they argue that 'holding the USSR responsible' could mean that if a NATO city is destroyed, the Americans might attack us in retaliation."

Antunov saw the logic. The United States could hardly blame the USSR and then do nothing if Hamburg or Munich were obliterated.

"I appreciate you telling me this," Antunov said carefully, wondering nonetheless why he was being told.

"I do so because we are friends, and I believe we can count on you."

The "we" had to mean the General Secretary. Antunov braced himself.

"There are other aspects I cannot go into," Fyakov continued, "but suffice it to say that provoking premature action by the Defense Council could have unpredictable consequences. Because of this, we would appreciate you trying to buy time for the situation here to . . . stabilize."

Antunov hated vague orders. They were a formula for disaster. "I'm not sure I understand. Am I to continue to support the Americans?"

"Of course. Fully. But I want you to think first of the General Secretary."

Pressing for further clarification, Antunov knew, would be fruitless at this stage. As an intelligence officer, he knew how to read between the lines. Even as personal friends, Fyakov's calling him directly was unprecedented. Obviously, serious conflicts existed in Moscow. The General Secretary's instructions were too sensitive to go through normal KGB channels. Unfortunately, they also seemed too sensitive to be explained. "I will do my best, Dimitri Andreyevitch."

"Mr. President, I have no direct authority to command the local US forces," Gordon explained. "An entire battalion sat on their duffs a few miles away. It's been hours, and I've still no confirmation that the roadblock's set up. A lot of good it'll do now."

Tired and mad, Gordon had already briefed Admiral McCollough and Loggerman, and was trying to maintain his patience with the President. "You've got to give the European Command standing orders to do whatever I say, no questions asked. And they've got to report every incident directly to me. I just learned that a Custodial Unit actually had him—"

The President interrupted him.

"Sure, I can wait." Gordon tried to calm down. He was so close.

Now, back to square one, he sat staring at the clock in the Consulate General in Munich. It was almost midnight. Culver could be anywhere. The President's Appointments Secretary came on the phone.

"Sean, this is Peter. We've got this whacko on an incoming line. Hold on, I'll try to cut you into it."

"Are you Lieutenant Terence Culver?" Gordon recognized Loggerman's voice.

"Not anymore. You all fixed that." The fury in Culver's voice penetrated the noise of the three-way connection.

"I'm gonna make this short. If you make one more try at catching me, the weapon goes off! Period!"

"We're doing as you asked," the President broke in, but Culver had already hung up.

"Was the call long enough to get a trace?" Gordon demanded.

"We'll soon find out." Admiral McCollough spoke up.

Fifteen minutes later, Gordon learned the call had come from Venice.

48

"Has Loggerman seen this?" the President asked Admiral McCollough.

"No, he's been out on the tennis court. I have to warn you, the JCS will be unhappy, because it messes up their neat organization charts. But Gordon gets the clout he needs with our commanders in Europe."

The President hesitated, then scrawled his signature across the bottom of the document.

The light on the President's telephone console flashed.

"The Secretary of Defense is on secure," Peter Andretti said. "Seems agitated."

He was. "Mr. President, we're in deep trouble."

"That's true." He sighed, wondering where the Secretary had been the last forty-eight hours.

"I mean, new trouble. It's the old trouble, but it's new."

The President decided to wait until he got himself straightened out.

"What I mean is, *The Washington Post* has the story!"

The President's heart sank. "Wait, let me put you on the speaker phone. Admiral McCollough is with me."

"Mr. Secretary," McCollough identified himself.

"What's going on?" the President demanded.

"We just got a call from that reporter at the *Post*, Walter Pincus. Naturally, I didn't take it. My press spokesman did. He knows nothing about all this, of course. Anyway, he says, and I'm quoting his notes, Pincus claims he knows all about the terrorist threat and the nuclear stockpile in Europe, and he wants a comment. He says he knows State's top leadership thinks the weapons should be withdrawn, but that Defense and NSC are against it. He wants a comment or he will have to go with the story as is. See what I mean?" the Secretary concluded anxiously.

"Run that by me again more slowly and let me get my secretary to take it down." The President pushed the mute button on the speaker and ordered McCollough to find Loggerman.

"I predicted that something like this would happen." Loggerman, in tennis whites, stood in the middle of the Oval Office wiping his face with a towel. "Mr. President, you're going to have to take strong action against whoever leaked it."

"That's very helpful, Karl."

"I wonder," Admiral McCollough intervened, "whether Pincus really knows what we know." The President's silence encouraged him to continue. "What the Secretary's notes don't say is that a US nuclear weapon is missing. And that's crucial. He has the scent of it, but he's got it wrong. He could think it's a policy fight. Right now it sounds like all he's got is, ADMINISTRATION WRANGLES OVER NUKES IN EUROPE."

"McCollough may have a point," said the Defense Secretary through the speaker phone. "My man didn't say anything about a stolen weapon, and I couldn't ask him—"

"The main thing is to avoid giving him any more information that could lead him to the real story," McCollough added.

"That puts a premium on shutting off the source," Loggerman as-serted himself. "Once we do that, maybe we can exploit the story."

"How?" the President asked.

"We've needed a cover story all along, and this might be the oppor-tunity for one."

"For example?"

"You can say you're deeply concerned about the possibility of a terrorist incident involving our weapons in Europe. So you've ordered a study and a program to test the security of our storage sites. But you don't want to go public, because that'll cause panic in Europe and boost the prestige of every terrorist from Londonderry to Beirut."

"I'm supposed to tell the *Post* that?"

"If you talk to the *Post*," McCollough warned, "even off the record, you'll also be asked if there've been any real threats."

"Why bring me into it at all?" The President started digging in.

"You're the only one who can get them off the scent," Loggerman insisted. "And you'd have to say there's no real threat."

"I'm not going to lie to the press," the President said flatly. "Dammit! Who would be so stupid as to leak a story like this?"

"Analyze the message," Loggerman suggested. "Who's the hero?"

The President looked at the notes again. The words, "State's top leadership thinks that the weapons should be withdrawn," jumped right out at him.

"I guess I have to talk to the Secretary of State." The President sounded dejected. "Give me some privacy."

The Secretary of State's formal office, used primarily to receive vis-itors, was long and low-ceilinged. Reflecting the Secretary's western political roots, it was decorated with Indian artifacts and pottery, paint-ings by Georgia O'Keeffe, and statues by Remington. The famous Indian portrait *End of the Trail* hung behind the large oak desk that had been made for the President of the short-lived California Republic and donated to the State Department by the heirs of Leland Stanford.

When the President rang, the Secretary was shaving in his private bathroom concealed behind rosewood panels to the rear of his desk. He started at the distinct rasp of the direct White House line.

"Mr. Secretary," the President began. His formality was unusual, and a bad sign. "We have a problem with *The Washington Post*."

"I was just about to call you about the same thing," the Secretary said quickly.

"Oh?"

"Walter Pincus. He said he had a story that the State Department was urging that our nuclear weapons be pulled out of Europe."

"Did you personally talk to him?"

The Secretary hesitated. "Yes," he admitted.

"And what did you say?"

"I denied it. I had to. He was going with the story if I didn't."

"And what did you deny? That there was a problem? That a bomb had been stolen? Or just that you were advocating a pullout?" The anger was clear in his voice.

"Mr. President, I was extremely careful. I didn't say anything about a stolen bomb. But he planned to write about a terrorist threat to our nuclear inventory!"

"And you said what? I want the whole story, goddammit!"

"I said that I was concerned about terrorism, too. He wanted to know if I had differences with Karl and the Secretary of Defense on this issue and I told him no. He said nothing about a stolen weapon. He doesn't have a story."

"The hell he doesn't! Before he just had rumors, now he's got *you* on the record. I can see the headline now, SEC STATE FEARS A-BOMB TERROR, DENIES US PULLOUT. In case you hadn't noticed, we've been trying to keep the public calm but make Culver think we're getting out. Now you've done the reverse!"

"Mr. President, I don't know what to say."

"You've already said too much." He paused, and when he came back on the line, his voice was etched with regret. "You're the only one that's been on my side in the NSC. Now, you've put me in an impossible position. I laid down the law. No talking to the press on this, period."

"Surely, Mr. President—"

"Surely shit! The Secretary of Defense didn't talk to Pincus! I didn't. Loggerman didn't. Neither did the Admiral or anyone else . . ."

"Somebody else did!"

"And you did! Everyone's waiting to see if I'm as good as my word and fire you."

The Secretary of State paused before replying. He looked out his window past the Lincoln Memorial, the Potomac river, and to Arlington Cemetery in the distance. "Mr. President, you have my resignation whenever you want it."

Donny Graham, publisher of *The Washington Post,* knew that he was being "taken up on the mountain," and he had to admit the President was good at it. Graham had long since emerged from the shadow of his powerful mother, Katharine Graham. He'd spent years in the lower ranks of the paper—police reporter, sports, deskman, production, and had earned a reputation for being smart, fair, and never having killed a story.

"I won't ask you not to print it," the President had begun. "As a former journalist, that's the last thing I'd do. I just want to give you my perspective from the Oval Office."

The President had launched into a long monologue about the burden of preventing nuclear war. They sat in the wingback chairs on each side of the fireplace, the burning logs popping and bursting, as if to punctuate the President's speech.

"The easiest thing to do would be to turn a blind eye to the risk of nuclear terrorism. Assume everything's fine, and sweep the questions under the rug. But I can't in good conscience do that. Yet, every time we even try to study any nuclear problem, much less make some small change, it touches off a furious debate. The Russians jump in with a propaganda barrage, and we have another crisis in NATO. People don't like to think about nuclear weapons, and they don't like people who *do* think about them. But I must, or the world could perish.

"So these studies have to go forward, and I'll make whatever changes I believe are needed for America's survival. I'm prepared for a public debate. But God almighty, I wish the press would at least let us do our homework first. It's downright misleading to tell only part of the story and give the impression we're suddenly concerned about nuclear terrorism. Hell, we're always concerned about terrorism.

"Donny, I give you my word that we'll grant the *Post* a full exclusive before anybody else. I'm not trying to avoid informing the public, I'm trying to keep from misinforming them, frightening them to no purpose on a life-and-death issue."

"Has there been an increase in the terrorist threat to our nuclear weapons?" Graham bluntly asked.

"That's what we're trying to find out," the President hedged. "And I'll be damned if I'm going to say anything until we know for sure what we're talking about and it's safe to do so."

"Mr. President, I appreciate your giving me your personal thoughts on this," Graham responded politely. "I understand your concerns. You should know that someone very high up in your Administration gave us this story."

"Are you going to run it?"

Graham took a long time to answer.

Walter Pincus was waiting outside in the car when Donny Graham left the West Wing. "So?"

"We don't run the story."

"What? You're kidding!"

"No President goes to all that trouble to stop a story about some studies—even about nuclear terrorists. Keep digging. There's something more important going on, and I want you to find out what."

Now it's just a matter of time, the President thought as he gazed out over the darkened White House lawn. The *Post* will figure it out. But maybe I've bought a few days. And after that . . . he let the thought drop.

He bit the end off his cigar and lit it. The first one of the day. Somebody besides the Secretary of State had talked. As Loggerman said, "Who's the hero?" Who benefits? "It sure isn't me," he said aloud. He stood alone in the Oval Office, and knew he was now isolated in the National Security Council.

49

Loggerman divided up embassy dinner parties into three acts. For the first act, cocktails, he often had his staff consult with joke writers in New York and Los Angeles for topical one-liners that might end up in the press along with his name. Tonight he would content himself with expressing the Secretary of State's regrets that he suddenly had to leave that evening for the Law of the Sea conference in Caracas.

The second act, the actual meal, was entirely predictable—a pinkish roast with small potatoes, carrots, and peas served from a large silver tray always held up by an aged waiter who looked like he was collapsing from the effort. And the conversation usually proved excruciating. He would be bounded on each side by the wife of a Washington "somebody." Invariably, he found them to be empty-headed women that the "somebody" had married before coming to Washington.

He liked act three best. After dinner, the embassies all adhered to old-fashioned protocol. The women excused themselves and went off to chat about the difficulty of getting good help, while the men adjourned to the library for the serious talk of the evening. Loggerman always prepared carefully for the after-dinner discussion. Tonight, however, he had not planned one of his famous impromptu lectures. He had set himself a far more delicate task.

The Belgian Embassy library was his favorite. The heavily carved wood paneling gave a sense of grandeur and security that particularly appealed to him. The room also opened onto a terrace that could be used for more private conversation. Loggerman's suggestion to the Chairman of the Joint Chiefs of Staff that they catch a breath of air was a time-honored signal for a confidential talk.

"I'm glad to have a minute with you, Karl," said the Chairman, taking the initiative. "This order of the President's to put Gordon in the chain of command has the chiefs in an uproar. We have statutory responsibilities. We realize there's an emergency here, but that's no time to get your lines of authority all fouled up!" He was hot.

Loggerman did not want to admit he knew nothing about it. "Tell the Chiefs I'll check into it." Guessing, he added, "This was hatched by Admiral McCollough, and we just assumed he'd touch base with you."

"Well, he didn't," the Chairman said, only slightly mollified.

"But that raises another point." Loggerman moved the conversation onto his track. "As we get closer to the deadline and the risk of an explosion, more and more responsibility will fall on you and the military."

"I'm glad somebody understands that," the Chairman said gratefully. "We've already done some contingency planning on what to do if the damn thing goes off. But since we don't know where it might happen, it's hard to judge our requirements for rescue, medical teams, decontamination, and all."

"I'm glad you're on top of that." Loggerman did not want to get bogged down in a discussion of the military's favorite topic—logistics. "But I think some *strategic* contingency planning is also required."

The Chairman looked at him quizzically.

"If the weapon goes off, what do we mean by holding the Soviets responsible?" Loggerman asked. "More to the point, what do the Soviets *think* we mean? Will they assume we'll attack them in retaliation? Will they try to pre-empt us—strike first? We need to look at the options."

Even on the darkened terrace, Loggerman could see that the Chairman had paled. The sound of cars passing through the woods on the Rock Creek parkway rose from below.

"God forbid it comes to that," Loggerman added. "But we've got to think this through. I don't want to send out a study directive from the NSC. That'd be leaked all over town. I know the President would be grateful if you could do some options work on your own."

The Chairman straightened. "Can do."

IV. TUESDAY

50

At night, Venice rises like a mirage out of the oily black waters of the lagoon. Gordon stood next to the Captain as the *motoscafo* from the airport skimmed across the treacherous shallows and buried pilings toward the spires, domes, and bell towers emerging on the horizon. Under the overcast sky, the city was outlined against the dark by the soft glow from street lights in a hundred small *campos*.

When Gordon learned that Culver was in Venice, he felt a stab of hope. It was the best place in Europe to try to capture him. Only one long causeway with a highway and railroad tracks connects Venice to the mainland. Departing boats could be easily spotted on the broad, flat surrounding lagoon. But he immediately realized that Venice could be the worst city in Europe if the weapon went off.

With nearly four hundred thousand people inhabiting its 117 islets, it had the greatest population density in the Western world, except for midtown Manhattan. And its ancient buildings would not withstand a blast like steel-reinforced concrete.

Venice is also a treasure house of Western culture. Titians and the Tintorettos hang in the Doges' Palace. Golden Byzantine mosaics line St. Mark's vaulted ceilings. Bellinis and Carpaccios adorn the walls of the Galleria dell' Accademia. Byron, Ruskin, Henry James, Thomas Mann, and Ernest Hemingway walked many of its four hundred stone bridges. Venice itself is a work of art, a city out of time, the last place on earth at the end of the twentieth century where mankind could still live and breathe the High Renaissance.

Detonated in Venice, the SADM would instantaneously destroy a thousand years of civilization. It would cover the ruins in mud so radioactive that they could not be approached for another ten thousand years. And that, Gordon knew, would not be the worst of it. The fireball would suck up millions of tons of water and deposit it back on the mainland. The deaths from radioactive contamination along the heavily populated Veneto region and into the Po valley could rise into the millions.

The speeding *motoscafo* started planing and bumping on the hard, glossy surface of the water. Out of concern for Graciela Morena's broken ribs, Gordon asked the Captain to slow down. She lay strapped to a stretcher attended by a corpsman in the tiny cabin below. She wanted to cooperate, and Gordon hoped she might provide insights on Culver's motives and patterns of behavior. If he could be found, her presence might prove crucial in dealing with him.

Gordon decided to check on Antunov at the back of the launch. He appeared to be lost in thought, staring back toward the lights of the oil refineries of Mestre.

"Do you think he's still here?" Antunov asked as Gordon sat down.

"The real question's whether the weapon's here."

"But Lieutenant Culver is our best lead, no?"

Gordon nodded. "There's a good chance he's here. It's hard to get off Venice after midnight. No trains, no buses. No departing flights. We had to raise hell to get our military aircraft in before daylight."

"What about a car?"

"The car rental places are closed. If he took a boat to the mainland," Gordon gestured toward the wilderness of docks, industrial plants, and tank farms, "where would he go at that hour? Besides, he's had a big day. He has to sleep sometime."

"You have not done so."

"I get to sleep now, while you go to work," Gordon smiled. "What's your first step?"

"I go directly to the Union hall. Every crew member of the *vaporetti*, the *motoscafi,* and the gondolas will get a copy of Culver's picture."

"There had to be some reason God let the Communists run the biggest union in Venice," Gordon joked. Antunov did not smile.

"The biggest problem is gondolas. All other boats have radios and can contact me aboard the *Rostov.*" Antunov planned to use a Soviet "fishing trawler" anchored in the lagoon as his command post.

"At sixty dollars an hour, it's very unusual to see a gondola cross something as wide as the lagoon," Gordon noted. "I'll have the US Navy catboats keep watch."

They had entered the Grand Canal. Black gondolas, nestling together at the docks like sleeping birds, bobbed in the wake of their launch. Rising water flooded into the main floors of the opulent sixteenth-and seventeenth-century palazzi. The canal was empty except for a garbage scow working its way slowly toward them. As it passed by under the Rialto bridge, Gordon asked, "Are those boats covered? What about commercial delivery boats in general?"

"All taken care of," Antunov assured him. "And you are set also?"

"We have the Navy Shore Patrol watching the train station, the bus terminal, and parking garage at the end of the causeway. We've even got people *on* the causeway in case he decides to walk."

The *motoscafo* had passed under the wooden foot bridge of the Accademia and was beginning a maneuver to bring the vessel up to the dock next to the Gritti Palace Hotel, which Gordon planned to make his headquarters. There was no US Consulate in Venice. It had been closed for more than a decade. Under pressure to cut its budget, the State Department had proposed the shutdown itself, not dreaming that the Congress, which loved being taken care of in Venice, would ever agree. Unfortunately for the Foreign Service, they had.

Gordon had wanted to use the Navy frigate *USS William Kidd* as his base of operations, but it had to anchor far out in the lagoon. He needed a centrally located hotel with a good telephone system and a staff accustomed to unusual demands. The Cipriani had too many movie stars and too much press. The Danieli generated a depressing Gothic gloom. The five-hundred-year-old Gritti, with its comfortable rooms and reputation for total discretion, was Gordon's choice. It was an illusion, but he welcomed its feeling of permanence.

As the doormen carried Graciela and the baggage and equipment up to a third-floor suite, Gordon completed his arrangements with Antunov.

"You can speak to me at any time through these." Gordon handed him a radio with a short, rubbery antenna. "Here, take two in case one breaks."

"All of our plans assume Lieutenant Culver will try to leave Venice," Antunov observed. "What if he stays? What if he simply hides in some small hotel until the deadline? What do we do then?"

"Frankly, Comrade, I don't know."

Graciela was in her bedroom asleep. The corpsman snored on the couch. The concierge had arranged for a very cold and dry Tanqueray martini to be delivered to the suite. It would work faster and cleaner than a sleeping pill. Gordon sipped it as the sky and water over the lagoon to the east began to brighten with morning. The phone rang.

"Your call to California, sir, we have the party on the line."

"Laura!" He felt enormous relief.

"Sean! God, I've missed you. I'm sorry you couldn't reach me. I've had a terrible time."

"Are you all right?"

"Yes, but the house is a wreck. It's been raining ever since you left. The hillside came right in the back door. Everything's ruined. I've saved some pillows, some of your clothes and files. I took them to your office. Until today, I've been sleeping at the faculty club while I shoveled everything out. God, it's a mess!"

"Don't worry about it. I love you," he said. "I'm sorry I'm not there." Even discussing a domestic disaster was a comfort.

"Oh, Sean, it's so good to hear your voice!" She sounded warm and sexy despite her travails.

"It's wonderful to hear you, too."

There was a pause while they both luxuriated in re-establishing contact.

"I'm sorry for rattling on like that," she said, her voice growing huskier. "I want to know what you're doing."

"I really can't say . . ."

"Well, where are you? Washington? The man on the phone sounded foreign."

"Laura, I can't tell you."

"You can at least tell me when you'll get back," she pleaded.

"I just don't know."

"I see. Fine." Her voice was dead cold. "Well, I won't keep you from whatever it is."

"Please, don't . . ." Gordon had had the same conversation with his ex-wife a hundred times. He never knew what to say.

"Sean, I don't know where you are, but it's getting late here. I've worked hard all day."

"Sure, I understand. I'll try to call tomorrow." He paused, wanting to say more. "Goodnight."

"Goodbye," she replied.

51

    Culver could not sleep. The calm of the day before had become a panic that attacked in the night. He lay on his bed in the Pensione Zambianco breathing in slowly, counting to ten, holding his breath for another ten, exhaling slowly for ten more counts, then starting over until the black dread receded. Occasionally, he would drift off to sleep, only to bolt awake in terror from a dream that was all chaos.

It had been a mistake to stay in a place he had shared with Graciela. In the dark, his mind served up images so real he could almost feel them. Graciela's breasts swayed above his face as she pressed down to envelop him, her eyes open in unseeing passion, her hair suddenly thrashing across his chest as primeval sounds escaped her throat.

He started to get hard. Then the anger came in a flood. He tossed and turned, remembering the fear and humiliation of trying to sleep on the couch with a pillow pressed over his ears to keep from hearing the sounds of his mother and sister "entertaining" their boyfriends in the bedrooms.

As the anger drained away, his fear and dread began to seep back. They'd almost caught him last night. They had no intention of doing what he had demanded. They were planning to betray him again. But this time they would regret it. This time they would pay.

Then why the panic? Culver told himself to be logical. He had nothing more to lose. He had faced death dozens of times before without panic. But then he had had a mission. His murderous feelings had been sanctioned.

He had a mission now, too, he insisted to himself. The most important ever. And they could not stop him. As he drifted, exhausted, to the edge of sleep again, he knew it was time to finish the job. Otherwise, he would lose his mind.

The hard knocking brought Gordon instantly awake. Laura had been there and his son, too . . . but the dream vanished. The corpsman stuck his head in the door.

"Sir, a messenger is here from the *Kidd*."

Gordon felt like he was alert, only his mind was not working. He shook his head. Wrapping himself in one of the Gritti's warm velour robes, he shuffled into the sitting room. He took an envelope from the ensign and asked him to have a seat. It contained the manifest of Alitalia AZ 206, the 10 P.M. flight to Venice from Salzburg, and a message from Kelly.

```
       TOP SECRET/RYMLAND NOCOPY
       FLASH/NIACT
       VENICE VIA CINCUSNAVEUR
       FOR GORDON EYES ONLY
       MUNICH 879
    SUBJECT:   REPORT ON BAUER GROUP
       BAUER NOW CONSCIOUS BUT REFUSES TO TALK. ONE ASSOCIATE
    DIED THIS A.M. OTHER CONFEDERATE ABLE TO PROVIDE SOME
    IDENTITIES GIVEN CULVER BY BAUER. DOCUMENTATION IN-
    CLUDED CREDIT CARDS AS WELL AS PASSPORTS. IDENTITIES FOL-
    LOW SEPTEL. KELLY.
    (NOTE: MSG RELAYED WHITE HOUSE FOR MCCOLLOUGH AS
    TOSIT-4.)
```

Gordon sat down at the writing desk near the French doors. The sunlight falling on the gleaming inlaid ivory, silver, and mother-of-pearl hurt his eyes. He opened a thick leather folder and took out sheets of onionskin paper embossed with the crest of the Gritti Palace. As usual, the expensive stationery was accompanied by a cheap ball-point pen.

He quickly wrote a note to Admiral McCollough.

Top Secret/Rymland NoCopy
Flash/Niact
White House For Adm. McCollough Eyes Only
ToSit-5 Ref. (ToSit-4) Munich 879

Subject: CULVER Identities.
Reftel reports IDs given Culver by Bauer include credit cards. Contact all credit card companies ASAP to arrange real-time readout from their computer verification systems of purchases made by anyone using identities SEPTEL. Also, run Agency namechecks on all passengers Alitalia AZ 206. Manifest sent SEPTEL. Gordon.

He folded the message into the envelope with a copy of the manifest and gave it back to the ensign. Picking up the phone, he ordered coffee, grapefruit, and croissants, and asked the concierge for an airline guide.

The six hot jets of water in the green marble shower began to clear out his sinuses and the vagueness in his head. He adjusted the spray so that only one pulsating stream beat down the back of his neck.

He could not wash away the feeling that he was making a mistake. Cham made sense. Culver was checking on the withdrawal at the SAS site. But why would he come to Venice? Had he hidden the bomb here? He felt at a disadvantage; he did not know his quarry. Venice could be a diversion while the SADM sat in a locker in the Munich railway station, its timer inexorably moving toward detonation. If they couldn't locate Culver in the next few hours, more drastic efforts to find the weapon would be required.

Gordon stepped out of the shower and took a heavy towel off of the chrome warming-pipes. He heard the bell to the suite. Someone answered the door and he could hear his breakfast being set up.

When Gordon emerged from his bedroom, he found Graciela serving a piece of his croissant to a cat on the narrow, flower-packed balcony.

"You're feeling better?" he asked.

"Very much, thank you. Look at this poor cat, it had to jump from the other roof to get here. It must be starving." She wore a thin robe supplied by a secretary at the consulate in Munich. The tape around her ribs was visible, as was much of the rest of her. She was such a young girl, Gordon thought as he averted his eyes. "Have you had anything to eat?"

She shook her head. He ordered her a full breakfast and, when it arrived, suggested that the corpsman take a walk.

"You've got to help me understand Culver. I need to anticipate his actions. Why, for example, would he come to Venice?" Gordon reached out to hold the grapefruit as she tried to eat with only one hand. "Look at the airline schedules." He opened the guide on the table with his other hand. "He had a lot of other choices—Copenhagen, Frankfurt, Strasbourg. Why here?"

"I don't know, Mr. Gordon."

"Had he been here before, do you know?"

"Yes, we came together once. It was wonderful." Her eyes started to cloud over.

"Where did you stay?"

"A little place. I don't remember the name. Near where the Jews live. They said it was the first ghetto ever."

Gordon went to the bookcase. The shelves held volumes on Venice in a dozen languages. He took down the Michelin Red Guide to Italy. She did not recognize any of the names listed for Venice.

"It wasn't much of a place, I guess," she apologized.

He called the concierge and had Graciela describe it to him.

"It's probably the Hotel Azzurra or the Pensione Zambianco," he said.

"Zambianco, that's it!" she said, excited.

The concierge said he could make a discreet inquiry about Mr. Culver.

He rang back in less than five minutes.

"They have someone, a Canadian by the name of David Breckenridge, who fits that description."

Gordon checked the Alitalia manifest. David Breckenridge had been on flight AZ 206.

*   *   *

As the morning grew brighter, Culver hoped his nameless fears would ease. But the smallest things started the panic again. The streaks of light quivering on the ceiling, reflections off the canal outside his window, could be conjured as snakes. Culver knew they were not snakes, but his mind dwelled on the idea. It wanted to see serpents writhing in the light. Ordinary objects, the doorknob, the billowing curtain, the pattern in the wallpaper took on a sense of menace. It was not in his control. He could hear his heart pounding. Adrenaline surged through his bloodstream and made his body start to tremble. He had to get away from that room. He had to get out!

Pulling on his shirt and jacket and grabbing his shoulder bag, he rushed into the hall, down the winding stairs past the reception desk, and out into the narrow alleyway. He still felt trapped. If he reached out, he could touch both walls. The sound of arguments and crying children and the smell of cooking smothered him. He started to run, twisting and turning through the crowded *calles*, desperate for a breeze, searching for more than a sliver of sky above his head. People shouted after him. He tried the breathe on a ten count and still run, his heart racing. He sloshed through the passageways inundated by the high tide, the odor of fetid water up his nose, the buildings growing more decrepit.

Then he began to notice the cats. Dozens of them, scores of them huddling together, seeking higher ground. Emaciated, hungry cats— some could hardly walk they shook so hard with disease. They growled and hissed and crowded the doorways, stairs, and window ledges. Their matted fur was covered with bare spots and mange. Some had five and six toes. They filled the dry spots in the alleys crying and howling, clawing back at him as he pushed through.

He broke into a small square, a *campo* full of cats, their eyes bright with malice, screaming and dashing from one side to the other in waves of hysteria. Culver backed up a flight of steps, some of the cats clinging to his legs, biting. He turned and found the door to a small church. He fled inside, kicking away the cats, slamming the door behind him.

Safe at last in the cool, dark sanctuary, he forced himself to breathe evenly. His heart beat more slowly. Sliding to the floor, he tried not to think of anything, just absorb the quiet and the dark.

He drew in the damp aroma of the church. There was another scent, too. And the quiet seemed strangely restless. As his eyes became accustomed to the gloom, he could see that the floor of the church was covered with something, a something that was moving.

Cats. Hundreds and hundreds of cats. A silent circle of glowing eyes surrounding him. He could hear their claws on the stone, the guttural noises growing in their throats. He saw the tails whipping back and forth. Culver started to struggle to his feet. A huge cat sprang forward. The others surged toward him, scratching and tearing. He yanked open the door. A horde of cats waited outside. Kicking and stomping on the soft, screaming bodies, Culver tried not to lose his footing as he scrambled back down the steps. Faster and faster, he ran down a narrow passage toward the light, desperately trying to shake loose the cats clinging to his back and hair. The tiny alleyway ended suddenly at the lagoon. He stopped. In the distance above the hazy water, he could see the mainland. He sensed the cats closing in behind him, and jumped.

Antunov winced as the American radio crackled to life. "This is Cowboy calling Indian. Cowboy calling Indian. Come in, please." Gordon's voice was urgent.

"This is Indian." He stood on the bridge of the *Rostov*. "And I do not like these code names."

"Later. Right now I've a positive identification of the target. I'm at the Pensione Zambianco on the Calle del Traghetto Vecchio near the ghetto."

"He is there now?" Antunov asked with faint surprise.

"No, but he's not checked out yet."

"The weapon?"

"No sign of it. I searched his room. The people here say he ran out with only a shoulder bag."

"Is there something you want me to do?"

"No," Gordon replied. "I'm establishing surveillance at the *pensione* and directing the shore patrol to converge on this sector. But I thought you should know we have confirmation the target is here."

Antunov did not need confirmation. For five minutes, he had been observing Culver at four thousand yards through the ship's powerful binoculars and wondering what he should do. The target sat on the fantail of a garbage scow wrapped in a large blanket as the barge slowly made its way across the eastern lagoon toward Aquileia.

"Shall we launch a boat?" the Captain of the *Rostov* asked.

"Not yet." Antunov was in a quandary. He did not understand how to apply Fyakov's instructions. Cooperate with the Americans, but buy time. What did that mean in this situation? "I must communicate with my headquarters."

He made his way down into the interior of the ship. In contrast to the rest of the trawler, which was covered by rust-chipped paint and a thin black film of bunker oil, the communications room was spotless and furnished with the most modern equipment available to the Soviet military.

"I want a voice link to my headquarters."

The scrambled single-sideband signal was picked up simultaneously by the KGB listening post at the Soviet Embassy in Belgrade, Yugoslavia, and the GRU communications central in Tripoli, Libya. The GRU could not demodulate it, and the clerk aboard the *Rostov* selected the Embassy/KGB channel. The communications shack on the roof of the Belgrade Embassy opened a relay to the KGB radio site in Bratislava, Czechoslovakia, where the signal was patched onto a land line to Moscow.

"This is of the utmost urgency," Antunov addressed his assistant. "I must speak to Dimitri Fyakov. Arrange for him to call me immediately." As he clicked off, Antunov allowed himself to reflect that it was typical for the Kremlin to organize a vital operation so that they could call you, but you could not call them.

52

Sitting on the terrace of the Gritti, Gordon took another sip of the strong Italian coffee and opened the Canadian passport in the name of David Breckenridge. The face said Terence Culver. He was out in the city somewhere, but there was nothing more Gordon could do. Every available sailor from the USS Kidd had fanned out through the maze of streets with a picture of Culver and a packet of telephone tokens. Even the outlying islands San Giorgio Maggiore, Torcello, and Burano were all covered. If he did not have the weapon, this was the time to grab him. Could he have hidden it someplace in Venice? Gordon needed to talk to Graciela again. He gave a note to the waiter asking the corpsman to bring her down from the room.

While he waited, Gordon tried to relax by appreciating the passing parade on the Grand Canal. The *vaporetti*—steamboats that served as public buses—honked their way from stop to stop filled with handsome, delicate-featured Venetians. The long and powerful *motoscafi* shined with burnished wood, chrome, and sleek foreign passengers. The black gondolas came by, still mostly empty of tourists at that late morning hour. Perched on their platforms at the rear of the graceful shells, and making their odd, jerky movements, the gondoliers seemed to Gordon a triumph of art over science.

One of Gordon's university lectures used Venice as an example of the economic power of security. Modern economists consider defense spending wasteful, he taught, but in the Middle Ages, it was essential to prosperity. Created as a refuge from the barbarian invasions, Venice exploited its security to create wealth the way other states utilized their natural resources. Without fertile land or minerals apart from salt, and tucked away in the northern corner of the Adriatic sea, Venice had no geographic advantage over a hundred other Mediterranean towns and villages, except to be surrounded by water. To strengthen its security, it produced the strongest navy in the Renaissance world. At its height, the arsenal of Venice could produce a new fighting ship every day, and the Serene Republic held sway over much of the eastern Mediterranean.

Gordon's ruminations were interrupted by Graciela's arrival at the table in a wheelchair, accompanied by her guard-corpsman. She wore a sleeveless yellow sundress to accommodate the cast on her left arm and a sweater around her shoulders to keep warm on the shady terrace. Gordon ordered her a lemonade and asked the corpsman to give them some privacy.

"Would Culver really be willing to destroy this city?" he asked her. She just shook her head, not saying no, merely I don't know.

"Could he have come here without you knowing about it? I mean since he took the SADM."

"You don't understand," she said quietly. "He changed after he took the weapon, really after he came back from Czechoslovakia and they treated him so horribly. He was always private, I guess he had to be, but he got unpredictable, more secretive, strange. I still love him, you know," she added with a touch of defiance.

"So the Czech thing was the turning point?"

She nodded.

"Tell me," Gordon said gently, "everything you know about it."

The barge carrying Culver away was only a dot on the horizon by the time Antunov finally got through to his office again.

"What is going on?" he shouted into the mouthpiece. "I've heard nothing!"

"I spoke to Mr. Fyakov's assistant, who assured me that he would be told that you needed to speak with him."

"Call him again right now on the other line." Antunov's voice was low and angry. "Tell him that the person we want is within my grasp but slipping away. I need to know what to do!" he shouted in exasperation. "I'm staying on the line."

After a long five minutes, Antunov's assistant came back. "I have a message—"

"Did you speak to him yourself?" Antunov demanded.

"No, sir. His aide said he could not come to the phone. But he sent you a message."

"Go on!" Antunov made a mental note to fire his assistant.

"He said that the situation is even more delicate, and please think of the General Secretary."

"After the British agent attacked him, Terry was afraid to use any of the preplanned escape routes." Graciela had graduated to sipping a bright pink Bellini. "What's this made of? It's wonderful."

Gordon could not keep from smiling at her childlike enthusiasm in the midst of disaster. "Champagne and peaches," he explained. "It's the national drink of the Serenissima." He gestured vaguely to encompass all of Venice. The sun was growing hotter, and Gordon felt anything but serene with the absence of news on Culver.

"Anyway, Terry bought a bicycle," Graciela continued, "some old clothes, a cage full of chickens, and, instead of going back toward West Germany, he headed east figuring they wouldn't be looking for him in that direction. He just rode along on his bike like a farmer and got into Hungary pretty easily. But when he contacted the CIA in Budapest, they wouldn't go near him. The Agency put him in touch with smugglers to get him across the Austrian border, but they set him up. Terry had to swim across the Neusiedler See with the Hungarian police shooting at him from helicopters and boats and the guard towers in the lake. It was a miracle that he made it."

"That's what people say," Gordon said, noncommittally. If the story was even half true, Culver should not be underestimated.

Graciela worked slowly on a seafood risotto while Gordon picked at his fried calamari. As the afternoon lengthened lazily, Gordon grew increasingly anxious.

"I saw Terry when he first got back. When they drove him in the gate, he waved and looked so happy. Then I heard he was in the stockade and these big honchos from EUCOM came to the base. For three weeks he stayed in there. When he came out, he showed me his bruises. His promotion to Captain was canceled. They even told him he couldn't re-enlist. That really destroyed him. The Army meant everything. He was going to be a lifer. He didn't even get the honor of a court-martial so he could defend himself."

They finished eating. Gordon ordered coffee. Graciela ordered another Bellini.

"Why did he steal the SADM? Revenge?" Gordon asked.

"No, at least not at first. It was more like pride, like he was proving himself after all the humiliation. You know, they kept him working with the Custodial Unit until his enlistment ran out. It was like everything was normal, but it wasn't. He was confined to base. He couldn't even look for a job.

"We'd been lovers," she said without embarrassment. "But after being in the stockade, he stopped making love to me. One day, we were alone in the weapons storage vault. I was checking some numbers and . . ." she hesitated, ". . . and then he raped me. That's what it was like. He tore my clothes. Forced me to do things . . ." She shuddered at the memory. "Terry was so angry at everything, including me."

"Why you?"

"Because of Horst, I think. Maybe he figured out Horst was using me to get to him. I don't know. Anyway," she drew in a deep breath, "it was over in a minute. Then he started to cry. He said he needed help. He asked me what Bauer wanted."

"And what was that?"

"I didn't want to tell him. I said it was something crazy. Impossible. But he insisted. So I told him. Bauer wanted a nuclear weapon. And then Terry said it wasn't impossible. It would be easy. You know"—she shook her head—"it was."

The sun started dipping behind the round dome of Santa Maria della Salute, a seventeenth-century church erected to celebrate the end of the plague. Gordon asked her about her relationship to Bauer and she candidly described how they had met and how he had vanished after exploiting her.

"I didn't see him for more than a year. I was riding on a bus on the way to work at Pirmasens, when out of nowhere he got on and sat down next to me. I don't remember what happened exactly, but the next thing I knew I was kicking at him and screaming. The driver put us off the bus. And then I just collapsed. I loved him then, you know.

"For a while, everything between us was like before. Then he started after me to get a transfer to a Custodial Unit. When I refused, he turned nasty. He told me about Garmisch."

"What did you have to do with that?"

"I know only what he told me." She stopped talking and Gordon waited. "I gave him the key to the Quartermaster's Office," she finally said.

Gordon watched her carefully.

"It was stupid and wrong. Bauer did business with the Army, at least that's what he claimed. He said his competition was trying to ruin him.

There were letters in the office that injured his reputation, and he wanted to see them to find out what they were saying. I know it sounds phony now, but at the time . . ." Her eyes started to fill with tears. "Well, I did it anyway.

"That was more than two years ago. Last fall, when he was pressuring me to join a custodial team, he told me that I had made it possible for him to steal the explosives for Garmisch. If I didn't do whatever he wanted, he threatened to tell the Army. He said I would be shot or go to jail for life." She said the last part quietly, tears running down her face, and then looked up at Gordon as if to ask whether it were true.

He shrugged his shoulders. "None of us have much of a future if we don't find the bomb."

The waiter brought a phone to the table. Admiral McCollough was calling long-distance and in the clear.

"We can't get your secure phone to work, and I had to get you right away. The American Express computer popped up with one of the names. It looks like our friend rented a Hertz car in Klagenfurt, Austria."

"When?"

"Your time? About three-thirty in the afternoon."

"Today?" Gordon was stunned.

"I'm afraid so," McCollough said.

53

Admiral McCollough climbed up the ladder at the stern of the presidential yacht in time to hear Loggerman say, "I know I sound like a broken record about the Russians, but the only explanation is that this Antunov let him go."

The *Sequoia* sat anchored downstream of Roosevelt Island in the middle of the Potomac river. Bought for President Hoover in the depth of the Great Depression, it had faithfully served three generations of Presidents as the best deal-making salon in Washington. When Jimmy

Carter had retired it as an unnecessary luxury, Capitol sages had seen an omen of political naiveté.

For several years it remained in private hands, until a group of the former President's cronies bought it back as a donation to the government. No modern President could ask for a yacht, and Congress would never vote money to buy one. But the government would let the Navy provide for its upkeep, even if the annual cost of maintaining such an antique vessel was half the cost of a new one.

Admiral McCollough had never been aboard the *Sequoia* before. His practiced eye appreciated the mahogany hull gleaming through several layers of clear varnish. The brass fittings and hardware, mostly handmade copies of the originals, shone brilliantly in the morning sunshine. The President, in a straw hat and shirtsleeves, sat with Loggerman in a cluster of upholstered captain's chairs around a low table on the aft deck. The scene could have been 1935—except for the mast over the cabin bristling with radar, dipole antennas, and satellite dishes.

"Admiral," the President greeted McCollough with a note of despondency in his voice, "what does Sean think of Culver's escape?"

"He's very suspicious of Antunov, too."

"And what does the Russian say?" the President asked.

"He blames it on the Italians. Claims they're disorganized."

"Bigot," the President snorted. "All Russians are bigots."

"Mr. President, I think it's worse than that," Loggerman persisted. "You keep saying that all my arguments about Russian involvement are circumstantial. That may be, but the weight of circumstances has become overwhelming."

The President simply waited for him to continue.

"Antunov supposedly comes to help, but first he wants to shoot Culver, then lets him get away. There are only two explanations. First, they don't want us to find the weapon. Or, second, they're covering up. They don't want us to get our hands on Culver, because he can confirm that they are behind this whole thing. Unfortunately, the two explanations are not mutually exclusive. We need to draw the appropriate conclusions."

"And what would that be?"

"They want the weapon to go off."

The President looked incredulous.

"In any event, we have to plan on the possibility that the weapon could go off," Loggerman added quickly. "We've less than forty-eight hours until the deadline. We must think through our response if that happens."

The President stood up and walked to the rail. He watched two eight-man sculls from Georgetown glide silently past. The slight breeze from the south hinted of summer. Aircraft angling down the river toward National Airport swooped low overhead. A few black men on the opposite bank watched from the shade as their corks bobbed in the sluggish stream. The hum of traffic from the bridges filled the air.

"Sometimes I think I'm going crazy," the President said, mostly to himself. "It's a beautiful day. Everything's normal. I get up, exercise. I meet with people. Smile for the press. Sit in the sun. Wear a hat so I don't get any more little cancers. In a few minutes, I'm getting together with Senate and House leaders to work out a budget for next year. Only, in less than forty-eight hours there may be no next year. Staying in shape may be a waste of time. Solar radiation may be the least of my worries!"

"One nuclear explosion or even two will be a tragedy, but it doesn't mean the end of the world," Loggerman said. "It won't come to that."

"Karl," the President sat down again, "you didn't think it would come to *this*."

They were quiet for a while. The sound of water lapping against the hull made McCollough wish he were aboard his sailboat on a broad reach across the open Chesapeake.

"If even a single one goes off, it'll be the end of my presidency."

"With all due respect, I just don't think that's true," Loggerman insisted. "Not if it's a Soviet-inspired terrorist attack. Your presidency hinges on how you handle it. If you let it ruin NATO, destroy America's position in the world, encourage the Soviets to assault us elsewhere, yes, you could bring about World War III. But that's the issue, not whether one or two weapons go off."

"What are you trying to get me to do, Karl?" he said warily.

"Nothing right now. But we have to think through our response if the weapon explodes. The JCS has been developing some options . . ."

The President looked at him sharply.

"It's their job," Loggerman added defensively. "They have to prepare for contingencies. I think we should review their options as soon as possible."

"Admiral, what does Sean think of these options?"

"I'm not sure he knows anything about them, Mr. President." McCollough looked at his watch. "You could talk to him on the phone aboard the *Kidd*. He's getting a debrief on the Navy's view of how Culver got away. He wanted to talk to you, too."

The call went through quickly, but the transmission quality was poor. Gordon faded in and out.

"As far as I'm concerned, Antunov has used up his one dispensation." His voice emanated from the speaker phone on the low table between them.

"So you agree with Karl," the President said glumly. The National Security Advisor allowed a prim smile to surface. "And do you also think we need to look at our 'options'"—the President spat the word out—"in case the weapon goes off?"

"I don't know what you . . ." Gordon's voice disappeared and then came back, ". . . but I can think of one you need to look at right now."

"Go ahead."

"We don't know where Culver is. He could be in Italy, Austria, southern Germany, or even Yugoslavia. We don't know where the weapon is. It could be anywhere in Western Europe ticking away while Culver just leads us on a merry chase. We've got about forty hours now.

"I was against it before, but now we don't have any choice," Gordon continued. "We need help from the local governments. We can't do it ourselves. We should be checking every luggage locker west of the Elbe. The border posts, air, rail, and bus terminals should be covered . . ." he faded again, ". . . road blocks in thirty-, fifty-, and a hundred-mile circles around Klagenfurt. We should be flooding the area with pictures. His face should be on every television set—"

"That's all wrong!" Loggerman burst out. "You might win the battle against Culver, but lose the war with the Russians. I say again the bomb and the people who may be killed by it are *not* the issue. If you do what Gordon wants, it'll all be over for us in Europe."

"Mr. President, Mr. President," Gordon was trying to get through, "in accepting our weapons on their soil . . . Allies are trusting us to do the right . . . theories of international politics are secondary. Our first obligation . . . protect their people."

"We're not in Europe to protect Europeans," Loggerman emphasized. "We're there to protect ourselves. To keep the Russians from taking control of Europe's military and industrial power. We can't do that if we're kicked out. Do you think any Allied leader will stand up against the public furor?" Loggerman asked heatedly. "Politicians don't have any guts."

McCollough saw the President look at Loggerman with a flash of hate.

"Let's try to stay civil," said the President. "We'll have a full NSC review of our options, including Sean's, as soon as the JCS is ready. I hope someone comes up with better alternatives than I've heard so far."

54

"Please keep your coat on. Marshal Ogorodnik is hunting." The orderly showed Major General Kirillin through a warmly lit dacha and out into the darkened garden. He turned on a flashlight to lead the GRU Chief down a path that entered the woods. After a ten-minute walk they came upon a clearing. To one side, a tethered goat stood helpless, transfixed by three spotlights. To the right a twenty-foot-square shooting platform nestled among the trees.

General Kirillin climbed up the two flights of wooden stairs with trepidation. This was his first visit to the country home of the Chief of the General Staff, and he was not exactly bringing a present.

Marshal Ogorodnik was sitting in an overstuffed leather club chair. His principal deputy, General Krushenko, took up most of a heavily brocaded couch. Between them, a hammered silver tray was smothered with caviar, smoked fish, and sausages. In the middle stood a half-empty bottle of vodka frozen into a block of ice.

Oriental carpets from Bokara, Dagistan, and Shirvan covered the floor. Open to the forest, the platform had no walls, only a railing with several large-caliber rifles leaning against it. A second orderly in white livery hovered discreetly in the far corner.

"Come have a drink with us." The Marshal waved General Kirillin to a seat. "The hunting is lousy. We drink to celebrate."

"And if you shoot a boar?"

"We drink to celebrate," said General Krushenko. He emptied his glass for emphasis.

"There are developments?" the Marshal asked as he poured.

"Yes. The Captain of the *Rostov* reports to us that Comrade Antunov permitted the American to escape from Venice."

In the following silence among them, the sound of crashing could be heard in the woods. No one moved for the guns.

"Why would he do that?" the Deputy Chief of Staff wondered. "Is he a traitor?"

"Perhaps, but he made two calls to KGB Headquarters. Apparently he was under instructions."

"I know how those KGB bastards think," Marshal Ogorodnik muttered. "Suddenly it has dawned on them that we're right. Handing Culver over will be distorted by the Americans into a confirmation of our involvement. The world will be told that US pressure worked. The Soviet Union would pay for an American mistake. The KGB doesn't know what to do now, and they are temporizing.

"But thank you for this information," the Marshal smiled. "I will use it to tear off their balls. Now we shall see if the KGB will continue blindly following the Comrade General Secretary."

"There is something else you should know," the GRU Chief said uneasily.

Raising his glass, the Marshal indicated that he should drink first. General Kirillin put it down with one gulp. In the morning, he knew there would be blood in his stool from his ulcer.

"You will recall," he continued with a slight gasp, "that we have a standing order to avoid terrorist groups. They are the KGB's domain."

The Marshal nodded.

"Except in the case of West Germany," General Krushenko added in.

"Precisely. 'Armed struggle groups active against our enemies in a theater of possible military operations,'" the GRU Chief quoted from a Defense Council directive, "'are a legitimate source of potential support in the event of conflict.'"

"That is my doctrine. Why do you repeat it back to me?" the Marshal asked suspiciously.

"In accord with that policy, we have used our discretionary funds to support Horst Bauer."

"In the past, and besides the KGB also admits it once was involved . . ." General Krushenko was already formulating an explanation.

"And at present also." General Kirillin insisted, taking a deep breath. "In fact, we are his principal source of financial support."

"Why have you delayed telling me this?" the Marshal demanded. "Never mind!" He knew the excuses. Tightly compartmented activity. Failure of communication. Heads would roll later. "Did we know he was planning . . ." The Marshal did not have to complete the question.

"He was uncovering information on American nuclear weapons security procedures," General Kirillin said hurriedly. "This constituted vital intelligence. We never dreamed he could be successful . . ." His explanation petered out.

The Marshal said nothing for a long time, staring hard at the GRU Chief.

"Who else knows this?"

"No one outside a small group in my operations staff." He paused, then added, "except, of course, Bauer himself."

More noises came from the forest. The sound of rooting and snorting could be heard in front of the platform. The goat began to bleat and thrash in agony. Suddenly, it stopped.

Marshal Ogorodnik got up and went to the rail. He watched the four-hundred-pound wild boar in the spotlight feeding on the goat's entrails. Without turning, he gave his orders. "Make every effort to apprehend the American and his weapon. That will decisively strengthen our hand against the General Secretary."

He hoisted up the Ferlacher .868 caliber hunting rifle, rested it on the rail, and put a 200-grain bullet in the boar's brain.

"And eliminate Bauer."

55

Could his mind do that to him? Create such a powerful hallucination? For the thousandth time, Culver tried to push aside the fact that he had so few scratches. There were small marks on his ankles and the bottom of his pants were torn, but all the rest? It seemed so real. He was swept by a greater horror at the thought that it was not.

Again, Culver fought to focus his attention on the road. The concentrated effort of driving helped calm him. He was almost there. The hidden drive could easily be missed at night.

The sound of tires crunching on gravel always gave him a good feeling, a reminder of his grandparents' white-stone driveway in Council Bluffs. But the headlights of his rented Volkswagen outlined a dark three-story Tyrolean hunting lodge set back into the tall pines. Culver climbed out, stretched, and looked upward at the gray and white slab of mountains towering over him in the moonlight.

He broke a window to get inside. The huge top-floor room had the musty smell of damp ashes. He lit a lamp and was surprised to see that much of the furniture was missing. The cabinets were bare of food except for a few canned goods. The refrigerator held only a bottle of Williams pear brandy.

Culver was cold. He took several heavy swallows of brandy and shuddered convulsively. Not being much of a drinker, he could feel the alcohol by the time he got down to the second-floor bedrooms searching for a blanket.

The beds had been stripped. "Bauer should be punished for his lack of hospitality"—Culver laughed to himself—"only, he's already dead."

He found a down comforter in a closet, took another swig of the sweet brandy, and climbed back upstairs. Sitting by the silent fireplace, he tried to organize his thoughts.

He would eat something from the cans. Then he would get drunk so he could sleep. In the morning he would go down into the basement and open the trunk where he had hidden the SADM. He laughed again. Right under Bauer's nose. In his own hunting lodge! "Take that, asshole!" Culver said aloud. "Trick me, fool you!" he shouted up the chimney.

The anger intensified his hunger. He went to the open kitchen area at one end of the large room. He could not make the can opener work, but managed to get the lid off a jar of Vienna sausages. The matches on the stove would not light the burners. The gas was shut off. He ate the sausages cold, washing them down with pear brandy.

He remembered the meal Bauer had prepared the evening after an exhilarating day hunting on the Hochschwab. Culver had taken week-end leave from Schloss Ludwigshof. They had bagged two mountain goats and on the way back had to traverse the face of an ice fall with crampons and rope. Mysteriously, Culver's line had come undone, and he had fallen forty yards before halting, suspended in midair at the end of his lifeline. After a half-hour struggle, Bauer had managed to pull him to safety.

Back at the lodge, shaken and grateful, Culver had taken a long shower and emerged to find a splendid dinner: terrine of hare and crispy pork roasted on a spit, all washed down with light Austrian white wine in glass mugs. Even now, as he sat eating wieners clotted with gelatin, he could recapture the glow of well-being he had felt then, the triumph of the hunt, the thrill of cheating death, the warmth of companionship with someone who had risked his life to save his. And it had all been a setup for recruitment, a classic ballet of betrayal.

Bauer had explained over dinner that his mother never cooked. "She told me before I could hardly reach the top of the stove, 'I make the money, you can learn to make the meals,'" Bauer had said lightly. "You know, my father wasn't around very much. I never saw him after I was nine."

"He was an American?"

"Yes, and so were a lot of my 'uncles.' I had so many uncles. My mother worked at the US base near Stuttgart. Every weekend she brought home a new uncle. By the time I left for university, most of my uncles were black."

Culver remembered trying to fill the ensuing silence by talking about how his father had to leave the family behind in Council Bluffs when the auto assembly plant closed. He had gone to California to work in a defense company and, as soon as enough money could be saved, the family was to join him.

"But it never happened," Culver said. "One day I got back from school and found my mother all dressed up sitting on the floor of the living room. She had only one nice dress, dark blue with lace across the front. She was crying and holding an envelope against her cheek. When she tried to get up, I could see she was drunk. She fell against the coffee table and scattered these little porcelain dogs all over the rug. I was just frozen. She started yelling at me and waving the envelope shouting, 'This is your father! A thousand dollars, that's what he thinks we're worth, the bastard!'"

Culver's memory of telling Bauer the story was overwhelmed by the image of his mother on the floor, her shoes all twisted under her. He could feel the dread of realizing his father would never come back. He took another gulp of Williams pear brandy and remembered how Bauer had simply waited for him to keep on talking, and he did.

"We had to move out of our home into a little apartment. My sister slept with my mother, and my brother and I slept in the living room. Then my mother started bringing guys home from the restaurant where she worked. And so my sister would come to the living room and one of us would have to go and sleep in the kitchen. Pretty soon, my sister was bringing guys home, too. My brother got so sick of it, he joined the Army. He wouldn't even wait to graduate from high school. He died a year later, stepped on a mine in Guatemala. My dad didn't even come to the funeral. I couldn't believe it."

"You know," Bauer had said, "I used to think my mother was a whore. I hated her more than my father. But she was mostly just lonely."

"That's why I've made the Army my family," Culver had explained. "There's lots of people around, so you can't get lonely. But you don't get to know people too well, either, so you don't miss them when they get reassigned or killed."

When Bauer asked him what he thought of the Germans, Culver remembered saying that he didn't like them much, admitting that except for Bauer, he didn't know any. "But, they look at our cheap PX clothes and lousy haircuts and the pity's written all over their faces. I often wonder what the fuck we're doing here, when the people we're defending despise us."

"There's a reason for that," Bauer replied without taking offense. "Germany's not a free country. Oh, we look free. But in the most important thing, we're impotent. We're powerless to reunite our country, to become one people again.

"Just imagine America divided along the Mississippi, with two million German soldiers in the east defending you from the Russians in the west. On the German side you'd have all the freedoms you have now, except you couldn't put your country back together again. That really wouldn't be America anymore, would it? Just think how you'd look at those German soldiers. Even though they were saving you from the Russians, maybe *because* they were protecting you, the resentment would grow.

"I want to confess something," Bauer had continued. "I'm one of those Germans who wants all the foreign troops to go home. This is not just a hope, it's my passion. I'm not saying anything against Americans. You've done a lot for us, and I know you love your country very much."

"Sometimes," Culver had said in return, "it's the only thing that keeps me going." He remembered staring into his snifter and watching a drop of cognac race around the bottom as he twisted the glass in the firelight.

"We're very much alike." Bauer's tone had become fatherly. "America's my second country. But I had to decide who I am, and I am German. As a German, I'll have no say over whether there'll be another war in my own country. No German will have any say. I want to be a free German. I want to free my country of the Russians, but that means we must be free of the Americans, too."

He could picture Bauer watching him carefully, weighing his reaction. When Culver had opened his hands as if to say what can I do, Bauer made up his mind.

"Terry, I need your help. You know most American soldiers don't want to be here. More and more of your politicians ask why they keep a quarter of a million men in Germany. They want them to come home. I'm working with friends to help strengthen that political pressure. It makes sense for both our countries. A free and united Germany will be strong enough to keep the Russians out of Western Europe."

Culver took another gulp of Williams with the last cold, sticky sausage, and tried not to recall exactly what happened next. But the memory forced its way through. Bauer wanted the phone directory of all the US military officers stationed in West Germany. His words came back clearly. "I know it's only for official use, but I don't think it's really classified information. I would never ask for anything like that. We want to send some pamphlets. Political support from American officers is very effective."

Then came the clincher. "The second thing," Bauer had said casually, "is that I'd like to be able to communicate with you in a private way. I think that the time may come when that would be . . ." Bauer had searched for the right word, ". . . sensible."

"I understand," Culver had said quietly, but all the bells were ringing in his head.

"Terry," Bauer had said, "I need you."

Culver cringed at the memory. Tears came down his face as they had then. Gratitude. Betrayal. Loss. He had actually hugged Bauer at that moment. The oldest rule of tradecraft: You make them friends before you make them traitors. And the pitch was near perfect. A directory, nothing classified, but it was a hook. And if Culver then agreed to communicate secretly, the hook would be set.

He remembered feeling very drunk and going off to bed saying something like, "Horst, I'm a friend." But in the middle of the night, he had taken Bauer's car and left a note. It told Bauer that if he ever tried to contact him again, he would be killed.

That was before Czechoslovakia.

As he finished off the pear brandy, Culver thought that the worst of it was being set up by Graciela. Graciela, who said she loved him. Graciela, who introduced him to Bauer. Graciela, who he knew now had always belonged to Bauer, never to him. He heaved the empty bottle of pear brandy against the fireplace. He wanted to see the SADM.

Holding on to the railing to steady himself, Culver climbed down to the basement. He kicked in the storeroom door. Weeks earlier, he had locked the weapon in an army footlocker and stacked it under several of Bauer's trunks. The light failed to go on when he turned the switch. He groped about in the dark, but could feel nothing. Staggering back up to the top floor, he found the matches where he had left them in the kitchen. Despite the pear brandy, the panic was coming back. He crashed down the stairs again and struck a match. In the shadowy light, the storeroom looked vacant. Quickly, he lit a fistful of matches all at once. The room shone brightly. It was empty. Bauer's trunks were gone, and so was the weapon.

56

The moonlight tunneled through the darkness and spread across the foot of Horst Bauer's bed. The nurse was gently shaking him.

"You have to wake up for a few minutes, Herr Bauer."

He began to stir, then his eyes popped open wide.

"Just a few minutes every few hours." She turned on the bedside lamp and shined a small high-intensity light in his eyes to watch his pupils contract.

Bauer had noticed her before. In her early twenties, she was younger than the others, plain but more friendly.

He tried to speak, but the bandages and the thermometer made it difficult. The nurse gave him a pen and a notepad. He scribbled.

"I want to let my mother know I'm here. Would you mail a letter?"

"I'm afraid I can't do that," she replied. "The police wouldn't approve."

"Call her," he wrote.

"I'm not sure that's permitted, either."

"She'll be so worried. Nothing secret. Just let her know where I am."

The nurse finished marking on her clipboard and then paused to look at Bauer.

He wrote out a phone number.

"We'll see." She turned out the light.

57

The Joint Strategic Targeting Planning Staff, known by its unpronounceable acronym JSTPS, worked out of a large underground bunker forty feet under the front lawn of Strategic Air Command Headquarters, at Offutt AFB, Nebraska. In the maximum security conference room, Colonel Royce Van Lindt, USAF, and colleagues from the US Navy and Army prepared for a "murder session" with the SAC Commander. They had worked with their staffs straight through from the previous evening to prepare options for Rymland Express.

Van Lindt stuffed a camel filter into an ashtray in the lecturn and coughed. He had just showered, shaved, and put on a fresh uniform, but he still looked like he had been up around the clock.

"You know, this is the first time in years that I've told my wife that I had to work all night," he said to his Army and Navy teammates, "and I actually did. I'll tell ya, at my age, drinkin' and fuckin's easier." He was thinking of his broken date with the little Belgian number with the NATO liaison group.

He checked the microphone and slide projector.

"What have we left out?" The others shook their heads. "Okay, let the old bastard know we're ready."

General Phillip Tinguely, Commander of SAC, was a small, wiry martinet who fell short of becoming an ACE in Vietnam by one enemy aircraft, and was forever determined to make up for it. He viewed most of his Air Force colleagues as desk-bound pencil pushers, and himself as one of the few surviving warriors.

"I want this over by 18:30 hours." He had come to the briefing alone. "We have an appointment to brief CJCS at 22:00 hours in Washington. You may begin."

Colonel Van Lindt began his formal presentation by noting that their task was to develop target options and associated war plans to carry out a nuclear strike on Eastern Europe or the Soviet Union in response to a single Soviet nuclear attack on NATO.

"Why Eastern Europe? Russia's the enemy," General Tinguely immediately challenged him.

"To reduce the likelihood of a Soviet counterstrike on the United States. The National Command Authority may want an option that would confine the exchanges to Europe." The General nodded.

"Here is the target list." The room darkened and a slide appeared on the screen. "You can see they're divided by geography. The three columns to the right of each target indicates the prompt fatalities that could be expected with weapons of different sizes. As you can see, the population damage ranges from twenty-five thousand to more than three million. The last two columns indicate, on scales of one to ten, the relative economic and military value of each target.

"Why are there no purely military targets?" General Tinguely was playing at being a civilian.

"Because there are none. Virtually all the interesting Soviet Bloc military installations are colocated with urban areas. There really is no such thing as a surgical nuclear strike."

"That's hard to believe. Why not attack a nuclear storage depot or a missile site?"

"A depot attack might set off the other weapons stored there. Most of them are out in the countryside, but that much ground burst could produce substantial fallout casualties, in some cases well into the tens of millions. Even if we hit a depot in central Asia or the Far East, we could end up with sizable fallout over a wide area in China and Japan.

"As for missile silos, we have no single warhead missile accurate enough to have a high probability of killing a hardened Soviet ICBM. The M-X Peacekeeper could do it, but it has ten warheads. We would have to down-load the extra weapons and reconfigure the missile. That could take time, which I'm told we don't have."

"Why not the B-1?"

"One might not get through. If several were shot down, we'd lose more than we're trying to destroy. Let me show you the next slide, which indicates our optimum weapons choices."

Weapons Options

Weapon	Location	Yield	Remarks
Pershing II	West Germany	Multiple	EE/USSR coverage, quick response, high damage expectancy.
Lance	West Germany	Multiple	EE coverage only. Quick response. High DE.
8-inch Howitzer	West Germany	5-20 KT	E. German, Czech coverage only. Quick response. High DE.
F-15	UK/West Germany	Multiple	EE coverage only. Moderate response, moderate DE. Post-attack assessment.
FB-111	UK	Multiple	EE/USSR coverage. Moderate response. Moderate DE. Post-attack assessment.
Minuteman II	USA	250 KT	EE/USSR coverage. Quick response. High DE.
Peacekeeper (M-X)	USA	350 KT x10 WH	[Same as above.] Only against Moscow, Kiev, Leningrad, Volgograd.

"Are you trying to tell me we should use a Howitzer for this?" General Tinguely asked sharply. "How the hell did that get on the chart?"

"We believed," the Army Colonel spoke up, "that this could be a viable low-end option . . ."

"*We?*" the General said scornfully. "You mean the Army wants a piece of the action."

"Sir, the Pershings are Army."

"What are you going to do," he continued without acknowledging any error, "roll a Howitzer right up to the border and lob one over? Pray the wind is blowing the right way so we don't cover ourselves in our own fallout? Stupidest idea I ever heard. Take it off the list.

"Now where's the Navy? Why no carrier aviation or Tridents or cruise missiles?" The General was on a tear.

The Navy Captain stood up. "Sir, the carriers are too vulnerable to retaliation. They could even attack us with conventional cruise missiles and we might go down. That's four billion dollars and a lot of men. As for the Tridents, they're part of the Strategic Reserve. Not to be touched except for general nuclear war."

"But what about Tomahawk Cruise Missiles? They're extremely accurate and the submarines are at sea and invulnerable. The Russians would have no logical place to retaliate against, not Europe, not the US."

"But sir, the sub might give away its position by firing a Tomahawk."

"Put it on the list."

General Tinguely stared at the chart for several minutes. "Why no Ground Launched Cruise Missiles?"

"They'd have to go through the thickest part of the Warsaw Pact air defenses," Colonel Van Lindt explained. "We'd have to launch a flock of 'em to have high confidence of getting one on target. If they're going after the same target they might destroy each other. If they go after different targets, you could do a lot more damage than you want. Tomahawk's got some of the same problems. They're pretty stupid machines."

"Isn't that also true of the M-X? Too many warheads?"

"That's why it would be targeted only against cities defended by ABMs. We'd need to send at least ten warheads to be sure we get one through."

"What if they all get through?"

"Could happen. But they'd just make the rubble bounce."

"Okay, what *haven't* you told me about these systems?"

"The Pershing and the Lance are vulnerable to retaliation by terrorist groups. The aircraft are like the Ground Launched Cruise Missiles. We'd have to send several with fighter cover, AWACs, and back-up tankers. With all that stuff in the sky, we could end up in a pretty big air battle. The F-111s are our best bombers, but the British have to approve it, of course."

"Fat chance," the General said. "What else?"

Colonel Van Lindt put up another slide. "The biggest issue is how to keep the Soviets from counterretaliation, and, more generally, to prevent escalation to an all-out nuclear exchange."

"Good thinking," General Tinguely had turned sarcastic. "How?"

"Our doctrine says we have to convince them that if they retaliate, we are prepared to fight a nuclear war and prevail," Van Lindt replied, reaching for a cigarette but not lighting it.

"Like I said, how?"

"As this chart suggests"—he moved a shadow pointer over the screen—"we need to have our strategic offensive forces at the highest state of alert and bring the strategic defense shield to maximum readiness."

"That piece of junk." General Tinguely never missed a chance to disparage the space shield. "What kind of military leader delegates his command decisions to computers?" he said of his rival at the Aerospace Defense Command in Colorado Springs. But his real complaint was that the space shield had absorbed more than half of the Air Force budget.

"Do you have the Op Plans?" he asked, changing the subject. "Pictures of the Designated Ground Zeros, the Release Codes, and all the rest for each of these options?"

"Yes sir." Colonel Van Lindt pointed to a stack of black ring binders and bright red envelopes with large numerals printed on the outside.

"Good. Anything more?" The General looked at his watch.

"I just want to emphasize that if we execute any of these options, we must be on maximum alert first."

"Colonel," General Tinguely shook his head, offended, "don't insult my intelligence. Now, do *you* have any questions?"

"Yes sir. Rymland Express is just an exercise, right? I mean, why would the Russians use just one weapon against us?" Colonel Van Lindt asked. The others nodded. The SAC Commander shrugged.

"Beats me."

58

"Your guest has arrived, sir."

"Thank you. Send him up," Loggerman switched off the intercom.

When the bell rang, the butler hired for the evening answered the door. The National Security Advisor deliberately waited in the library, planning to make an entrance as soon as his guest had been given a drink and a seat in the living room. He always believed in entrances, particularly with old friends he had not seen in a long time. They were in the best position to spot signs of infirmity, depression, and other ravages of advancing age. Why else, he thought checking his tie in the mirror, do they always remark on how good one looks?

The butler came to the door of the library and nodded. Loggerman walked briskly into the living room, a generous smile on his face. He found that his guest had his back turned, looking out at the river.

"Rege!" Loggerman announced his presence. "What a wonderful surprise. It's been too long."

Weede turned around with a slight smirk, clasping a martini to his middle with both hands. "Power looks good on you, Karl. May I kiss your ring?"

"Genuflection will do. You have a drink? Of course you do." He turned to the butler. "I'll have the same, but on the rocks with lots of onions." He steered Weede to one of the sofas and took the one opposite. "Now don't tell me you've come all the way from London just to see me." Loggerman's speech always took on English inflection and cadence in British company. "What brings you to Washington?"

"A bit of spying, old man. Want to know what the Yanks are up to. You've been awfully quiet of late. My editor insists you must be up to something." Weede downed the rest of his martini and held his glass out to the butler for a refill.

"Well, I might have a story for you. But later. You'll have to work for it. Now, tell all the gossip at Whitehall . . ."

Weede finished three martinis and Loggerman two and a half before they sat down for the first course of Crème Sénégalèse with a bottle of cold white Dezaley from Switzerland. Over the main course of soft shell crabs amandine, they reminisced about their exploits together. Weede's favorite operation was against Salvador Allende, stirring up the foreign press, getting sympathy for the striking truckers.

"Damn smooth operation, that. Pity it was my last engagement with the firm." Weede demolished two soft shelled crabs and signaled for more. "Bloody Congress getting into the act with its dos and don'ts. Put me out of business, it did."

"I can always get you back on the payroll, Rege." Loggerman was becoming expansive.

"Needn't bother. I've more work than I can handle. Would you like to be back on the list at MI-6?"

"Could be a slight conflict of interest," the National Security Advisor replied.

"That's never stopped you before!" Weede laughed.

As the wine worked its will, Loggerman's pretenses eased. Soon he was admitting that his finest hour was in uncovering Billy Carter's links to the Libyans, courtesy of some Italian swindlers who wanted revenge against President Carter for being prosecuted in US Federal Court. They both agreed that their best collaboration was in bringing down Willy Brandt as West German Chancellor by exposing the fact that his private secretary was a spy and a homosexual.

"Rege, you took some personal risk in that one."

"Yes, some of my chums did feel that came a little close to home."

Over espresso and calvados in the library, the conversation turned philosophical.

"You don't see anything happening in Washington, Rege, because with one exception nothing *is* happening. It's all a charade. We've reached a critical point in American history, much as England did under Queen Victoria. The skill it takes to become President and to stay popular are totally at odds with what it takes to run a government and exert world leadership. Under our system, the President is supposed to be both the Head of State—the King, if you will—and also the Prime Minister. Well, if that didn't work for nineteenth-century England, it won't work for twenty-first-century America."

"Hm, quite." Weede refilled their calvados. "What's the one exception?"

Loggerman continued as if he had not heard the question. "Think of it, who were the most accomplished Presidents? Truman, Johnson,

Nixon. They did things, good or bad. And who were the most popular: Eisenhower and Reagan. Royal types, father figures. The same man can't do both jobs. Particularly with the demands of television and the collapse of the political parties."

"You said there was an exception," Weede tried again.

"We have to go back to the original intent of Washington and the framers of the Constitution. The President was supposed to delegate most of his power to the Cabinet. The Secretary of State was supposed to run things, domestic and foreign."

"Would that really be enough of a challenge for you, Karl?" Weede jested. But when he looked up from his drink, he could see that the National Security Advisor was pondering it seriously.

"You want to know what's going on?" Loggerman asked. "We're having a crisis. A quiet little crisis that just might fundamentally change everything—not the least how this country is governed."

"Tell me more, old friend."

"I can't get specific, Rege." Loggerman shook his head and waved his arm, his drink sloshing onto the coffee table. "But I'd like your reaction to something."

Weede nodded.

"If the Soviets challenged us in Europe, we would have to respond, correct?"

"Yes, that's good old NATO doctrine . . ."

"But assume the situation is ambiguous. If the Russians are blaming us, and we the Russians. We would still have to take action, right? Let's say something terrible happened to one of our Allies. If we failed to live up to the NATO Treaty just because we felt partly responsible, the alliance would collapse, wouldn't it?"

"I thought America was over its Vietnam syndrome," Weede goaded him.

"Everyone but the President is." Loggerman's face turned hard. "But I can assure you, we won't fail to act."

Weede had what he had come for. He rose unsteadily.

"It's late, you're welcome to stay the night, Rege."

"Thanks, old man, I thought you'd never ask. But just for a few days. And only on one condition. You've got to get me up early. I'm on deadline, you know."

V. WEDNESDAY

59

Culver somehow found himself up on the roof of his grand-parents' house, where he often went when he felt lonely. It must have been spring or summer, because the Missouri was only a narrow band of water above the tops of the trees. In the distance beyond, he could see the flat green plains of Nebraska that seemed to stretch westward forever. He could hear the moan of a barge on the river and the rush of a freight train along its banks. Then another familiar sound came to him; a car was coming up the drive—his grandparents, or his mother, or his father coming back, coming up the gravel drive . . .

Culver sat bolt upright. Dawn filtered into the room. A car engine shut off. He shook his head, and it felt like it had a loose weight sliding around inside. His mouth was thick and sweet. Suddenly he remembered where he was and stumbled to the window.

Peeking through the slats in the shutters, he saw a large man in a dark green loden jacket inspecting his car. Culver backed away, look-ing around for his shoulder bag. It was not there. He tried to remember if he'd left it upstairs. No, it was in the car! He returned to the window. The man was opening the bag. He looked at the bundles of cash and passports, then took out the machine pistol. Culver sat back on the bed and tried to think. He removed his shoes and belt. He could hear footsteps on the outside stairs and the clank of a key ring. A door opened on the second floor. Quickly, Culver climbed the stairs to the third floor. One of the steps creaked beneath his stocking feet. The other man stopped.

"Hallo! Wer ist da?" he called out in a heavy Austrian accent.

Culver quietly positioned himself inside a closet next to the landing where the stairs rose from below. Standing perfectly still, he could hear the man climbing upward with effort. He reached the top breathing hard.

Springing from the closet, Culver wrapped his belt around the man's thick neck and tried to twist him to the floor, but the man whirled and struck Culver across the chest with a massive forearm blow that sent him tumbling backward down the stairs. The MAC-10 slipped out of the man's grasp, clattering down several steps. As Culver leaped upward to grab it, they collided, and the two of them fell backward onto the second-floor landing, Culver pinned underneath. The man wrapped his huge hands around Culver's throat and began to squeeze. Squirming and gouging and kicking, Culver could not break free. He could feel his chest start to implode. The ruddy, sweating face hanging over him began to blur.

Suddenly he heard a strangled cry and was released. The man stood up wheezing heavily, then sat back on the stairs clutching his chest with one hand and rummaging in his coat pockets with the other. Frantically, he pulled out a vial of pills. Culver slapped them away.

"Bitte, Bitte! Mein Herz." He sounded like he was drowning. His hands waved desperately for the pills. Culver kicked them down the hall.

The man stumbled, fell, then crawled after them. Culver snatched up the machine pistol, snapped off the safety, and turned to fire. But the man had collapsed three feet from his pills.

Culver let out a sigh. He leaned against the wall. Then it dawned on him that the man might know what happened to the trunk and the bomb.

The narrow hallway made it difficult to turn him over. Culver could see that the man's face was pale and covered with sweat. Vomit dribbled off his lips. There was no breath, no heartbeat. After a struggle, Culver wrestled him onto his back, and using his fingers, cleared out the man's mouth. He put both hands over his heart and quickly heaved his full weight on top of him, then released. Nothing happened. He repeated the process several times with no result.

A convulsion suddenly contracted the man's body and he began to cough. Culver could feel the heart begin to beat irregularly beneath his fingertips. Soon it began to steady. Color came back to the man's face.

Culver realized that the man had to be in his seventies. He tried to rise onto his elbows, but Culver told him in German to stay down and not move. He would get him water to take the pills.

A half hour later, the man could talk. His name was Steinhof. But he did not want to talk about Bauer.

"You have an easy choice, Herr Steinhof," Culver said. "You can tell me what I need to know, and then I will take you to the hospital at Judenburg. Or, you can stay silent and I will leave you here to die."

Steinhof claimed not to know anything about Bauer. He was only a caretaker. Retired. He worked only part-time. Bauer had rented the hunting lodge for the season and the lease was up at the end of the month. Steinhof explained that several men had arrived a week ago and moved everything out. He did not know where they went.

"You won't even get a priest here," Culver said reflectively. "Do you want to die with a lie in your mouth?"

Steinhof began to cough again. He pleaded for another nitroglycerin pill. Culver shook his head.

"I swear to God I don't know where they took all the things. Maybe back to where the men came from." His eyes started rolling in his head.

"Where's that?"

"Vienna," he gasped.

Culver tossed him the vial. Yes, he knew that Bauer had a safe house in Grinzing. He and Graciela had stayed there when they went as Bauer's guests to the Jägerball.

"You rest now," Culver said. "As soon as you feel strong enough, I'll help you to the car."

He folded the seats down and made Steinhof lie on blankets in the back of the Volkswagen. It was a twenty-minute trip to the hospital in

Judenburg. The orderlies quickly transferred him to the intensive care ward. When they tried to locate the young man who brought him in, Culver had disappeared.

Two hours later, Steinhof had another heart attack and could not be revived. Disobeying the doctors, he had his final seizure while making one last phone call, to West Germany, to Ludwigsburg, to Birgid Bauer.

60

The Kremlin guard with his bright red epaulets on his wool greatcoat waved the long black ZIL past the Borovitski gate and into the Kremlin.

Inside the limousine, the Defense Minister was trying to encourage Marshal Ogorodnik into a more supple frame of mind.

"I agree the intelligence reports are most grave. But it's better to meet with the General Secretary privately than have an immediate confrontation in the Defense Council. You and I have come a long way together." The Defense Minister put his hand on the Marshal's arm. "Do this my way, and I can assure you of the correct political outcome."

Rumbling through the cobblestone courtyard, the car rounded the apse of a small chapel, passed more guards, and plunged into a garage underneath the wall of buildings that overlooked the river. From the basement, they rode in a high-speed, computer-controlled Otis elevator. When it had been released through American export controls as a special gesture to Gorbachev by Ronald Reagan, Marshal Ogorodnik had argued against accepting it.

The doors opened into the mirrored foyer of General Secretary Chalomchev's office. The only vestige of Kremlin tradition were the mirrors, which concealed armed guards. Otherwise, the General Secretary had departed from almost three generations of Bolshevik practice by moving out of a medieval stone tower secluded in the middle of the Kremlin to a spacious and light-filled suite atop the wall, which commanded a dramatic view of Moscow's southern reaches. That Wednesday morning, it was overcast and threatened snow.

The Defense Minister and the Chief of the General Staff were surprised to see the General Secretary accompanied by the Chairman of the KGB and Dimitri Fyakov. Chalomchev came out from behind his desk to greet them.

"What brings you both out so early on such a fine spring day?" Chalomchev said heartily.

"We are deeply disturbed, Comrade Ivan Illyich," the Defense Minister responded, "by the intelligence information we have received this morning."

Chalomchev glanced at the KGB Chief with a look that said, I told you so.

"There are many important items brought to my attention each day." The General Secretary flipped the edges of a stack of documents piled on his desk. "Which one concerns you?"

The Defense Minister could see the skin above Marshal Ogorodnik's collar begin to turn red. "The information from the agent that Comrade Chairman," he gestured toward the head of the KGB, "wisely sent to Washington."

"And what disturbs you about that?"

"It makes it clear we are headed for war!" Marshal Ogorodnik almost shouted.

"In our opinion," the Defense Minister added quickly, "the report makes clear that Loggerman is in control and pressing for retaliation against the Soviet Union."

Chalomchev sighed. "Why don't we all sit down, and perhaps the KGB will give us its interpretation."

"We consider the report ambiguous," the KGB Chief began. "Loggerman spoke in riddles."

"He said they would retaliate!" Marshal Ogorodnik exclaimed.

"We have rechecked the translation. Our agent speaks no Russian. The word he actually used is 'respond.'"

"Comrade General Secretary," the Defense Minister intervened again, "with your heavy responsibilities, we don't wish to quibble with words. His meaning, and intentions, seem plain. If the weapon goes off, Loggerman intends to attack the Soviet Union."

"We consider that important," Marshal Ogorodnik added with a trace of contempt.

"On the contrary," the KGB Chief stood his ground, "the most important information in the report is the existence of a split between Loggerman and the President, who evidently does not want to respond aggressively to this situation."

"But according to the report, Loggerman seems confident he will dominate the decision . . ." the Defense Minister persisted.

"Our analysis indicates that the American President is still firmly in control of his government," replied the head of the KGB.

"Then why is the Secretary of State sent off to Caracas in the midst of this crisis? He is an ally of the President, no?"

"That merely confirms our analysis that the President is confident of his command authority," the head of the KGB concluded lugubriously.

"Your analysis explains everything so well," Marshal Ogorodnik broke in, "perhaps you can also explain why your Colonel Antunov let the man with the bomb escape?"

The stone-hard face of the Chairman for State Security momentarily lost definition as a cloud of uncertainty passed over it. "I do not know what you are talking about."

"We have a report from the captain of the *Rostov* that Colonel Antunov deliberately let the American get away when he could have captured him," Marshal Ogorodnik declared. "And during that time, he was in touch with KGB headquarters—twice."

"Are you accusing me—" the KGB Chief started to rise from his chair.

"Comrades," the General Secretary interrupted, "this is no time for recriminations. I am sure the KGB will investigate the captain's story."

"A special board of inquiry should be established under the Defense Council," Marshal Ogorodnik insisted. The Defense Minister winced.

"Is it not my prerogative as General Secretary and Chairman of the Defense Council to make such a decision, Comrade Marshal?" His anger showed through his even delivery.

"If we could return to the question of the Americans," the Defense

Minister moved into the position of peacemaker. "If the KGB is correct and they are divided, that is all the more reason to pressure them by releasing the story. You remember what they did to us at Chernobyl by putting the news out first."

The incident stung in Chalomchev's memory. "I see nothing in this report which requires precipitous action," he finally said.

"Then you should look at *this* report." The Chief of the General Staff handed around flimsy sheets of paper from a teleprinter. "Our source is in the NATO liaison group at the American Strategic Air Command Headquarters in Omaha. Their Planning Staff is preparing 'special' options. What more do you need?" The Minister of Defense withdrew into a mortified silence.

Dimitri Fyakov spoke up for the first time. "This report only mentions 'unusual activity' at the Planning Staff. The 'special options' are categorized here as 'rumors.'"

"For rumors you would provoke a profound confrontation," the KGB Chief jumped in, still angry and seeking revenge for Ogorodnik's accusations. "Once the bomb theft is public, the Americans will have no choice but blame us and act on that charge!"

"They are blaming us already, and planning retaliation!"

"You've no solid evidence of that." The KGB Chief dismissed the Marshal's argument with the back of his hand.

"We know what the end point of confrontation will be," Chalomchev said flatly. "Let's try cooperation a little longer."

"Will you only be convinced when American warheads are flaming down through our atmosphere?" Marshal Ogorodnik was not giving up. "I'm telling you, as Chief of the General Staff, if we do not take precautionary measures, we could be caught as we were in 1941."

The reference to Hitler's surprise attack on Russia raised the stakes. The General Secretary got up and walked to the window. A snow squall was working its way up the Moskva river from the southwest.

He turned to the group, his voice grave. "The policy of the Party and the government is to avoid a nuclear confrontation if at all possible. And it will remain so as long as I am the General Secretary. If there are measures, self-defense measures that are not provocative, they should, of course, be undertaken."

He sat down at his desk, opened a folder, and began to mark on it. After a moment he looked up, as if surprised that everyone was still there. He gestured to Fyakov to stay, a signal for the rest to leave.

In their limousine, the Minister of Defense and the Chief of the General Staff sat without speaking. As they passed out onto Kutuzovski Prospekt, Marshal Ogorodnik lit a Belomorkanal. The Defense Minister steeled himself against the stench that immediately filled the car.

"So you see what a tactful approach gets us? We're still keeping the Americans' dirty secret for them. Stalin was made of steel. Brezhnev was a man of iron. Comrade Chalomchev is like lead."

"At least we can increase our military readiness," the Defense Minister said, trying to sound positive.

"If we don't disturb anybody. If the Americans don't complain. I tell you plainly, I'll be the one who decides what steps are required, not the Comrade General Secretary." He savored his cigarette for a moment, then spoke again. "Did it seem to you that Comrade Chalomchev was not surprised to learn about Antunov letting Culver go?"

"Our KGB colleague seemed shocked." The Defense Minister avoided a direct answer.

"Dzerzinski Square," the Chairman of the KGB ordered his driver. "And I want immediate telephone contact with Colonel Antunov."

He sank into the black cut velvet upholstery. No, the General Secretary definitely was not surprised at Ogorodnik's charges. And the GRU is spying on me, he thought. Two can play that game. He reached for the phone again.

"Also, I want to see the head of Department V as soon as I arrive."

"He wanted you to deny him the precautionary measures," Dimitri Fyakov was trying to reassure the General Secretary. "You had to agree or he would have had an issue to strengthen his position in the Defense Council."

"I am relying on you, Dimitri Andreyevitch, to make sure these protective measures do not get out of control."

Fyakov nodded and continued, "You have accomplished the most important thing. You have consolidated your control over the KGB. You are now protecting them, and so they must protect you."

A mile away, in separate cars headed in different directions, the Chairman for State Security and the Chief of the Soviet General Staff shared that exact same thought.

61

"Nothing. Not a peep, not a sign, nothing for the last eighteen hours," Gordon said. "Culver's vanished and we've only got until 6 A.M. tomorrow to find him." He was commiserating by phone with Billy Kelly from aboard the DC-9 that was parked on the ramp at the Klagenfurt airport. "Antunov is trying to ingratiate himself by dropping tidbits about Culver."

"Like what?"

"Like he was set up in Czechoslovakia."

"He has an interest in saying that," Kelly observed. "Can I talk to him?"

"He's trying to make a phone call to Moscow. Some strange little man showed up here with a message for him. He's probably a Soviet sleeper activated for the first time since 1945."

"How's Graciela doing?" Kelly asked.

"Fine." She was pacing up and down the aircraft from the galley in the rear to the crew compartment, then back again.

"It's not that big a town," Gordon continued, "but there's no way to search it without getting the Austrians involved. I brought along a half dozen crew members from the *Kidd* who speak a few words of German and had them check out all the hotels. Zero."

"Well, maybe Bauer will help us out," Kelly replied.

"How's that?"

"Our friends in the Bundes police have told us that Culver's name, description, and all his aliases are circulating on their network. On Interpol, too."

"Who the hell did that?" demanded Gordon. "Billy, if you . . ." He knew Loggerman would go berserk and blame him if he heard about it.

"Hold on! Some company went to the police claiming Culver defrauded them. Turns out the company is one of Bauer's fronts."

"I thought you had Bauer under wraps."

"I did, until this morning when an army of lawyers descended on us. They may get him out tomorrow, and they're talking about a press conference."

"But he's got a cracked skull!"

"It's a hairline fracture. He's already walking around."

"Well, tomorrow it may all be over. How did the lawyers get there?"

"Damned if I know. Someone in the hospital must have carried a message."

"Can you turn off the German police, Interpol, and all that?"

"That'd raise a lot of eyebrows. The best thing is to let it go. I'll have our friends inside the Bundespolizei alert us if they pick up the scent. Don't get your hopes up. They're not conducting a manhunt or anything."

"All right, but put this one in your special file. Anything else?"

"Remember the guy who gave us Culver's aliases? Before the so-called lawyers got in the act, we managed to sweat out of him the locations of some of Bauer's safe houses. They may not be the same ones he gave Culver, but I've put them all under surveillance."

"Where are they?"

"A couple around Munich. One in Frankfurt. One in Vienna. One in Zurich, and another in Brussels. The guy said there may be more that he didn't know about."

"Maybe Graciela can tell us something about them. Christ, Billy, we're clutching at straws!"

"Are you coming back to Munich?"

"Might as well. I figure he's got to be headed back to Germany, and besides, you're so good for my morale. We'll be wheels up by noon. I have to be in the consulate by 10:30 A.M. Washington time to set up an open line to an NSC meeting."

"What's the agenda?" Kelly asked.
"We're reviewing our options."
"How do they look?"
"Wonderful."

62

Alois Schlechta crossed the Dorotheergasse and opened the door to the Hawelka Café. He was greeted by the stale smell of the night before. A fashionable nighttime gathering place for Viennese writers, musicians, and intellectuals, in the light of day the Hawelka reverted to a threadbare coffee house. Even its renowned paintings by Hundertwasser, Fuchs, Hausner, and Hutte failed to lend much color to the scene. A handful of other customers sat quietly reading and sipping coffee, a few still nibbling on breakfast pastries.

As he always did each morning at eleven o'clock, Schlechta took an overstuffed chair by the window, being careful first to hang his coat on the graceful Biedermeier rack by the door. He had the soft hands and thick-soled shoes of a policeman, but his familiarity with actual police work was limited. He had spent much of his life standing surveillance. One of his few pleasures, apart from pastry, was "physical" interrogation. However, he was more familiar with the myriad ways to violate the law than to enforce it.

He sat down heavily and picked up a freshly ironed newspaper. Presently, he would order *Buchteln* with vanilla sauce and a *Melange,* a large black coffee that was a specialty of the Hawelka. After twenty minutes, he would pay the check, pick up his coat, and leave. If there were any instructions from his GRU controller, he would find them in the right-hand pocket.

He was not fond of his current assignment. Horst Bauer appreciated his importance. No Schlechta, no money. But the other ones, the young fanatics, they thought they could order him around. Someday, he sighed, he would have his revenge.

The waitress came over with the usual glass of water, but instead of taking his order, she surprised him by saying he had a phone call. It was from Munich. He was instructed to meet two of Bauer's associates arriving on Austrian Airlines flight 087 at twelve thirty-five. He should bring a van and a "full set of special equipment."

Schlechta looked at his watch. They gave him so little time to arrange everything! He left the Hawelka in a hurry, forgetting to check the right-hand pocket of his coat.

Culver felt a sense of release leaving the confines of the Alps. Making good time on National Route 17, he passed into ever-broadening valleys with quaint cuckoo-clock towns braced by mean factories with saw-toothed roofs—through Semmering and Wiener Neustadt, past Baden and the vineyards of Gumpoldskirchen. Entering Vienna on Triesterstrasse, he crossed the *Gürtel* under the elevated train that marks where the old city walls once stood. He then turned right onto Wiedner Hauptstrasse, heading directly to the Kärntner Ring. In an underground garage across from the State Opera House, he parked the car and made his way on foot down the Kärntnerstrasse.

The street was a wide shopping mall closed to all but pedestrian traffic and lined with every variety of store. Culver cashed ten thousand dollars into Austrian schillings at the Kreditanstalt on the corner of Krugerstrasse. Visiting several camera and electronics outlets, he found what he wanted at Heilango on the Graben—a Compaq portable personal computer. It took twenty minutes to fill out all the forms promising that he would not export it to the east. He also bought a pair of binoculars, a joystick, and a simple toggle switch.

He took the twenty-eight-pound, suitcase-shaped machine out of its box and lugged it back to the car, pausing only to deposit the instruction manuals and reference guides in a waste bin on the street. Once back on the Ringstrasse, he drove west to Währingerstrasse, where he turned left toward Grinzing. At a small hardware store near the *Gürtel*, he stopped and bought a set of tools, including screwdrivers, a pair of pliers, wire cutters, a soldering gun, assorted batteries, a spool of copper wire, and a chisel. Culver then proceeded up the Cobenzlgasse onto the Kahlenberg, where he had a commanding view of the city and the wine village of Grinzing immediately below.

He focused his binoculars on one particular garden. It was set among a row of large houses at the foot of the hill along the edge of the vineyards that descended from the Kahlenberg. Like the others, it was heavily landscaped with trees and shrubs and surrounded by high walls with heavy iron gates. But unlike the stately neighboring houses, it had only a small cottage with a large terrace next to an empty swimming pool. An outdoor privy stood partly hidden in the trees.

Culver knew the place well. He'd stayed there for several days with Bauer and Graciela when they had all attended the Jägerball the previous February. It had been a wild night of drinking Sekt and waltzing and drinking more Sekt and waltzing again. Culver, in white tie and tails for the first time in his life, alternated with Bauer in sweeping Graciela around and around the ballroom of the Hotel-Palais Schwarzenberg.

She'd worn a long red dirndl with a tight vest that pushed her breasts up against him. Culver remembered the smell of her hair and shoulders as more intoxicating than the sweet Austrian champagne. As the hour grew late, the whirling dancers got drunker and the frequent collisions more violent. At 5 A.M., Graciela refused to dance another step. She told Culver and Bauer to dance with each other if they wanted to treat the waltz as a contact sport.

And so they did. Immediately, they were joined by a half dozen other male couples in a Viennese version of slam dancing, crashing, spinning, finally winding up in a heap in the middle of the floor where one of the gentlemen, sickened by the champagne and the exertion, threw up all over everyone.

Before getting back into the car, Graciela made Bauer take off his smelly coat and Culver his stained pants. Much to the disgust of their driver, the garments flew from the Mercedes' antenna as the trio drove back up to Grinzing, Graciela in the middle, while Bauer taught them a chorus from Csárdasfürstin.

The image in the binoculars had become blurred. Culver cleaned the lenses and wiped his eyes, forcing himself to push away the memories. He concentrated on the garden. No one appeared to be using the cottage. It was shuttered, and the sliding doors to the swimming pool terrace were chained and padlocked. He knew how the security system operated. A simple shunt coupled to one of his batteries would enable him to circumvent the alarm.

He scanned the neighboring homes. An old woman on the porch of the house to the left was filling a stone planter with geraniums and petunias. The house on the right seemed empty. Time was running short, he had to take the chance. Culver returned to the VW station wagon and started down the mountain.

When Gary Bates joined the CIA, he had imagined physical hardship, abuse, and torture at the hands of the enemy, and even the threat of death. He did not reckon on endless hours of sitting in a darkened room, peering through slatted shutters into an empty garden. He did not expect that the greatest challenge of Clandestine Service would be to stay awake.

Bates had been bucking the system. Recruited from Hofstra to be an intelligence analyst on the "white" side of the CIA, he'd fallen in love with the covert, "black" side during his training course at the Agency "farm" at Camp Perry in Tidewater, Virginia. Unfortunately, clandestine skills did not come easily to Bates. As part of the training program, the Agency routinely sent their cadets to Stanleyville, a nearby town where the new recruits would exercise relatively harmless assignments. One of Bates' first tasks was to maintain twenty-four-hour surreptitious surveillance on a woman picked at random from a shopping center. It ended an hour and a half later when her boyfriend broke his nose and the woman called the Sheriff. Instead of simply accepting his fate and maintaining his cover as a tourist, Bates panicked and used his one phone call to dial a special number in Washington given to agency employees for use only in the most serious emergencies.

Consequently, Bates had spent the next five years analyzing Warsaw Pact force structures while pining for an overseas assignment. He finally got an opportunity to join the US Delegation to the Vienna Troop Reduction Talks, where his job was to expedite the flow of intelligence reports from Washington. At an embassy reception for the Delegation, he managed to corner the CIA Station Chief and volunteer for part-time clandestine duty.

His thirst for service went unrequited for several months. Suddenly, at 2 A.M. the previous night, the Deputy Station Chief had woken him up to ask if he could help on a "problem" starting at 6 A.M. He had accepted eagerly. Since that hour, nothing but a rabbit had moved in the garden next door. The whole place seemed closed, and the lawn in need of tending.

While he watched a station wagon thread its way down the hillside vineyards on a narrow farm road, Bates began to wonder about lunch and whether the old woman below might make him something to eat. He got up, stretched, and made his way downstairs to the kitchen. The old woman happily made a sandwich of rye bread, roast beef, and *Schmalz,* a tasty spread of thick pork fat that Bates could not resist. He climbed back up to the top floor with his sandwich and a bottle of *Apfelsaft,* and took his chair by the window. It all looked the same as before. The garden was empty. The cottage was closed and dark.

Bates finished his sandwich and was licking the *Schmalz* off his fingers when he noticed the edge of a station wagon barely visible over the outside garden wall. He remembered a vehicle coming down through the vineyard. Did it pass? He could not recall hearing it go by. Was it the same color? Could a car parked *outside* the garden be construed as unusual activity? He did not want to look naive on his first real assignment. No, he could not ruin the chance to redeem himself by acting overanxious. He decided to wait.

Alois Schlechta also waited. Austrian Airlines flight 087 was scheduled to arrive in ten minutes; he stood against a pillar outside the ramp leading from the customs area. In his right hand he held a sign saying BGE to identify himself to the two members of Bauer's group. He took a pack of Ernte 23s from his coat pocket and, putting it to his mouth, used his lips to draw out a cigarette. With his left hand he fished around in the pockets of his suit and overcoat for a lighter. Sticking the sign under his left arm, he began searching the right-side pockets. In his overcoat he felt a folded piece of paper.

He glanced around quickly and then opened it. As he expected, it was from GRU control, but the message surprised him—one letter, "A." It meant "emergency."

In all his years, Schlechta had never received such an instruction. He was supposed to act on it immediately, but he had let almost an hour and a half go by. Every minute would be a black mark against him. He had to call a telephone number that he was required to memorize each month. But after hundreds of them he'd started cheating by writing the number on a piece of tape, which he then fastened to the inside of his left shoe.

The ARRIVALS monitor indicated that OS 087 would land in five minutes. Rejecting the urge to take off his shoe there in the airport waiting room, he ran for the men's toilet. He emerged with the tape in his hand and headed for the bank of telephones near the car rental desks. The ARRIVALS indicator showed OS 087 as LANDING. He found a phone that would accept incoming calls and punched in the number. A voice answered and requested his number. He gave it and hung up. OS 087 changed status to ARRIVED. The phone rang.

The unfamiliar voice began by announcing the code word. Schlechta gave the required counter–code word.

"Do you know a member of your group named Terence Culver, an American?" the voice asked. "He used to be a United States military officer."

"I met him," Schlechta replied, thinking of the night of the Jäger-ball, "but he is not a member of the group."

"No matter. If you learn of his whereabouts you must immediately notify the number you just called. Understood?"

"Yes."

"Time is critical. If you locate him yourself, you must maintain constant surveillance. You cannot let him escape."

"I doubt I'll see him. He doesn't live in Vienna."

"Listen! Do not talk. Should you have an opportunity to gain custody of him, you must not fail to do so. Bring him to transit point 46," the code name for Bratislava on the Czech frontier, "or, alternatively, 22 or 17," the border crossing points for Prague and Brno. "You will identify yourself there with your counter–code word. If you need assistance, call the emergency number."

"Are there any reports that he's in Vienna?" Schlechta asked. He saw that passengers were clearing customs. Groups of people rushed to greet them.

"His location is unknown. Most important of all, he may have a device. It's absolutely essential to get control of it. You should also be aware that the device is extremely dangerous."

"What is it?"

"That's all I can say, except that this operation has the highest priority. You know what that means."

That I can finally retire, Schlechta dared to hope.

"Do you understand the instructions?"

"Yes."

The voice broke off without speaking further.

Schlechta rushed over to the arrivals area waving his sign. Perhaps his visitors would know something of Herr Culver's whereabouts. Two young men in jeans and leather jackets hailed him.

"Schlechta, where the shit have you been?" the tall one demanded. Alois recognized him as one of Bauer's associates. He did not know the short one.

"Excuse me, I was given so little time."

"Everything's ready?"

"Yes, the van's outside."

"Good. We must get to the house in Grinzing immediately," the young man said.

Panic exploded inside of him. Culver had searched the cottage carefully, all the closets and even cupboards, under the bed, behind the sofa bed, in the woodpile next to the fireplace. The trunk was simply not there!

He sat on the bed and tried to think. None of Bauer's trunks were there, either. Maybe everything had been taken to Munich or Kitzbühel. Maybe I've already blown the damn thing up, he giggled to himself. No, the man from Vienna had collected everything. That was probably Bauer's driver, what was his name? Schlecher, or something.

He needed to go to the toilet and remembered the outhouse. Lifting the curtains, he looked carefully around, and saw no sign of anyone in the vineyard or the neighboring houses. He slipped out the back door and quickly made his way to the privy.

After a few minutes, he re-emerged swatting at the bees circling his head. Halfway to the house, he noticed fresh ruts in the grass. They

led to a small toolshed locked with a chain. Culver picked up a cut log
from a stack of firewood and used it as a lever to rip the chain's
mountings from the wooden door. Inside, he found his trunk.

Culver dragged it back to the cottage. Nervously, he fumbled with a
set of keys, trying one after another. Finally he ripped it with a screw-
driver. Hidden and protected among wads of clothes, the Special
Atomic Demolition Munition lay wrapped in its canvas carrying harness.

Carefully, he removed the SADM from the trunk and set it on a card
table near the fireplace. Making sure the curtains and shades were
drawn, he switched on a lamp. His tools laid out, he loosened several
straps and slid the harness out from under the weapon. Culver put the
palms of his hands on the gleaming titanium case. He imagined that
he could feel the energy and power radiating from inside.

The W-54, as the SADM had been officially designated by the
Atomic Energy Commission in 1959, was a product of Los Alamos
Laboratories, one of the last designs personally conceived and carried
out by Dr. Jason Winniker. When he was only twenty-seven years old,
Winniker had determined that the critical mass required for a chain
reaction was not fixed. With a suitable design and materials (such as
boron to generate neutrons and beryllium to contain them), it would
be possible to induce the ignition of very small amounts of certain
nuclear materials—especially plutonium 239.

Winniker's basic design was proof-tested in 1960 at the Nevada
proving grounds following the collapse of the US/Soviet moratorium.
In the years that followed, the basic device was incorporated into other
so-called tactical nuclear weapons—including a nuclear air defense
missile launched from airplanes called the Falcon, and a nuclear ba-
zooka called the Davy Crockett. Fired from a recoilless rifle mounted
on the back of a jeep, the Davy Crockett proved tricky to handle, since
it had a maximum range of only two miles and a lethal radius of at least
a mile and a half.

The weapon that Terence Culver cautiously proceeded to dismantle
was a testament to nuclear bureaucratic politics. In 1953, when "Engine" Charley Wilson left General Motors to run the Pentagon for
President Eisenhower, he declared that the American taxpayer was

going to get more "bang for the buck." He meant more nuclear weapons, which were supposed to be cheaper than conventional arms. In fact, amortizing the enormous costs of nuclear weapons plants and paying for the added security and safety of atomic weapons made that claim dubious. But since the Atomic Energy Commission paid for them out of a secret budget that always sailed through Congress, they were free as far as the Pentagon was concerned.

So all three uniformed services jumped on the bandwagon, and every part of each service clamored for its own nuclear weapons. The pilots both in the Air Force and Navy naturally were equipped with a variety of bombs. But that was just the beginning. The submariners got nuclear torpedos, and the destroyer drivers got nuclear depth charges, and the antiaircraft teams got nuclear-tipped missiles to shoot down airplanes, as if what happened on the ground below was not their department. In addition to nuclear cannons, the Army artillery deployed short-range rockets like the Honest John. Commanders were afraid to fire the Honest John—legendary in its inaccuracy—even with its conventional warhead.

The infantry got nuclear mortars and Davy Crocketts, but the Corps of Engineers? They were the most politically potent group in the Army and could not be denied. But what kind of nuclear weapon made sense for a branch of the service that spent most of its time building roads and dams for favored Congressmen? An Atomic Demolition Munition, nuclear land mines, proved to be the answer. And for the Rangers and other Special Forces units, a man-portable junior version, the Special ADM. The addition of a lithium booster in the mid-eighties increased the yield by an order of magnitude.

At 58.5 pounds, the SADM was only barely portable. However, Culver was rapidly making modifications to make it weigh even less. He first detached the remote radio-controlled detonator, the M-4 coder/transmitter and the M-5 decoder/receiver, which together accounted for almost ten pounds. The batteries and the power supply for the radio shed another five pounds. Next, he disassembled the dome-shaped shield and exposed the "pit," the core of nuclear material surrounded by high-explosive lenses that were connected by a maze of wires to the fusing and firing mechanism. He extracted the arming system, but left the time detonator in place. Culver could not resafe the weapon; it would be permanently enabled. But as a safety measure, he would not connect the firing switch until later. In all, he saved another six pounds.

After putting the pieces back together, he found the weapon much more manageable. Culver then hoisted the computer onto the table and began pulling out its insides.

At the crack of ripping wood, Gary Bates realized that he had drifted off to sleep. He looked into the garden in time to see a tall, red-haired young man disappear into the shed. A moment later he reappeared carrying a footlocker.

Bates immediately snapped on his radio. "Timber One, this is Timber Two. Do you read me? Over."

"Loud and clear, Timber Two. Over."

"There is activity here. A woodsman has entered the forest. Over six feet tall, red hair. He's moving a large trunk. Over."

Static and a buzz filled Bates' radio, but no response. "This is Timber Two. Do you read me? Over."

"We read you fine!" the voice was impatient. "Hold on! Over."

Bates waited.

"Timber Two, repeat description of woodsman. Over."

He detailed Culver's features with a sense of growing excitement.

"Timber Two, you're to maintain surveillance at all costs. We're sending help. They will be on this network as Timber Three. Report any further activity as it develops. Confirm. Over."

"Confirmed. Over and out."

In Culver's experience, portable computers furnished an ideal means for transporting weapons and explosives by commercial airlines. The X-ray machines could not penetrate their interior, and luggage inspectors were always reluctant to open them up to look inside.

Culver snapped the case back together and lifted it off the table. Heavier than a Compaq, but acceptable. He shook it. Wired and bolted to supports inside, the weapon did not rattle. He set the case down and stuffed the canvas harness for the weapon into his shoulder bag. As he moved toward the back door, it burst open.

*   *   *

"Timber One, Timber Three, this is Timber One, I mean, Timber Two. Over."

"We read you," Timber One said.

"This is Timber Three. We read you fine. Over."

"More activity here. Three new woodsmen have appeared in a van. They've gone inside the cottage. They're carrying . . ." Bates groped for a euphemism and failed, ". . . guns! Over."

"Are you equipped, Timber Two?" asked Timber One.

"No," Bates said nervously.

"We'll be there in ten minutes." It was Timber Three. "We're at Neusdörferstrasse. Sit tight. Over."

"Okay, wait. They are coming out. Three of them have their weapons on the red-haired woodsman. They're moving toward the van. Holy shit, one of the woodsmen just shot the other two!"

"The redhead? Over." It was Timber One.

"No, of the three woodsmen, oh fuck this, the three *guys* who just showed up, one of them killed the other two and he's making the redhead dump their bodies down in the pool. Now they're headed toward the van."

"Is he carrying anything? Over," asked Timber One.

"Sure!" Bates exclaimed, "he's got a fucking machine gun!"

"No, I mean the redhead."

"He's got a big plastic suitcase and a shoulder bag."

"Where's your car? Over."

"In the driveway here. Over."

"Follow them. Don't let them out of your sight. Keep us updated on your location. Timber Three will try to intercept. Over."

"Okay, over!" Bates started running down the stairs.

63

"Mr. President, I'm all out of answers."

Pumping his stationary bicycle, the President shook his head at the defeat he could hear in Gordon's voice. Had he been wrong to depend on him? Maybe Loggerman was right and Gordon had been out of the service too long. Christ, what was he doing? Attacking those closest to him out of frustration and helplessness?

"Sean, I don't need answers. I just need an idea, a strategy. I don't know where else to turn. You know what the Pentagon's bringing into the NSC meeting?"

"Not exactly."

"The details don't matter, it adds up to World War III."

The President talked to Gordon through a headset which he wore while working out in a small gym on the third floor of the White House. He hated exercise, and the bicycle most of all. The Press Office had set up three video monitors in front of the bike so that he could be distracted by watching all the morning network news shows at once. Promptly, he discovered that when you struggle to pedal 40 mph, television is mostly commercials. He then got a telephone headset so he could exercise and make calls at the same time.

"In a few minutes, Loggerman'll be in here to give me a prebrief. He's going to tell me that when the weapon goes off, our 'options' are to attack Minsk or Pinsk. And all the other sheep in my Administration are going to sit there baaing and nodding their heads."

"You know my recommendations," Gordon responded.

"Isn't it too late? What have we got, sixteen hours?"

"If it's too late, it's too late."

The odometer reached 25 miles, and the President released the tension on the pedals. His heart rate was in the target range, 80 percent of maximum for his age. He slipped off the bicycle with a sigh. As usual, his legs felt like rubber. He knew he was supposed to keep walking, but instead sat down and rested on the Nautilus abdominal machine.

"Christ, I don't know what the hell to do. Chalomchev sent me another private message. The Russian Ambassador delivered it before breakfast."

"What did it say?"

"Nothing. He regrets Culver's escape from Venice. And he went on about the importance of working together 'to overcome all obstacles.' Is that their way of admitting responsibility?"

"Probably. And telling you he's got some 'obstacles' to working with us."

"Well, I was encouraged by it until I got CIA's morning brief. They think the Russians may be getting ready for a first-stage alert."

"How so?" Gordon sounded skeptical.

"Communications. Something about heightened communications security and readiness. I don't know, shit, I'm just a President. How do I know what that stuff means? I'm at their mercy, Sean. Where the hell are you, anyway?"

"I'm in the plane. We're just about to land at Munich and the pilot's going to have to shut down this commo link. Listen, have you talked to the First Lady?"

"No. She's still in South America. I don't want to worry her. I told her to take an extra day, stay with a friend of ours on Contadora—maybe she'll survive . . ." the President's voice grew hoarse.

"Talk to her. She's always been your best advisor. Talk to her. Mr. President, I'm sorry, but we're in the glide path . . ."

As the President started to get up and go to the telephone control panel, he saw Admiral McCollough at the door.

"We've got a report on Culver." McCollough waved a flimsy sheet of paper.

"Wait! Sean, don't cut off! There's news on Culver!" The President could hear Gordon order the pilot to tell the tower they would have to circle the field.

"It's from CIA Vienna," the President said. "They think they've spotted him at a safe house of Bauer's. He's got a big trunk with him. Sean, that could be the weapon!"

"I'm changing course for Vienna. And don't worry about your meeting. You won't need any options if the thing explodes there."

"What?"

"Austria's neutral. It's not NATO territory. If it's gonna go off, hope it's there."

The President felt sick. Vienna was an old friend. He and his wife had spent part of their honeymoon there, drinking in the fragrance of the Rosegarten at the Burghof, listening to the music of Johann Strauss under the stars in the Stadtpark, consuming sinful quantities of the pastries at Demel's, marveling at the white Lipizzaner stallions

STATE SCARLET / 236

dancing in the Spanish Riding School. These images and a hundred other sensations rushed over him. It made him feel ashamed, but he hoped it would end there, one way or another.

"Faster! You can go faster!" Schlechta jabbed his gun into Culver's ribs.

The van bounced over the streetcar tracks in front of the Franz Josef Bahnhof on Alserbachstrasse. Culver cringed at the sound of the weapon banging around in the back. His MAC-10 was buried at the bottom of his shoulder bag and out of reach.

They crossed the Danube canal on the Friedensbrücke. When they turned left on Klosterneuburgerstrasse, Culver noticed a red BMW following them.

Was it the same car that had been behind him through Grinzing? He glanced at Schlechta, who had not seemed to notice.

"Where are we headed?" Culver asked.

"Shut up," Schlechta replied.

"They've gone into the Prater on the Hauptallee," Bates reported on his radio. "Where are you, Timber Three? Over."

"Crossing the Rotunden bridge. We'll try to intercept you by the racetrack."

Culver was startled when a gray American Chevrolet swung in behind him.

"What are you looking at?" Schlechta demanded. He rolled down the window to adjust the mirror for a better view. "Are we being followed?"

Culver shrugged.

"I think he's onto us, Timber One."

The van, the gray Chevrolet with three CIA agents, and Gary Bates' BMW made a 70 mph parade through the park and out onto the new divided highway along the Danube. A huge petrochemical refinery loomed off to the right. The trio of vehicles reached 90 mph.

"Where are they headed?" Timber One asked.

"It looks like the airport."

*　　*　　*

"Do we have a secure voice link to the Embassy yet?" Gordon half-sat, half-crouched in the flight engineer's seat, his stance putting pressure on the communications officer. The aircraft was still ten minutes from the Vienna airport.

"No sir, only teletype."

It began to chatter again.

> Top Secret/Rymland
> Via Munich Flash
> Vienna sends
> Sit Rep 4. Also To Sit 18
> Target van (description Sit Rep. 2) intercepted by second operations
> vehicle. Proceeding east on NR 9. Likely destination, airport, ENDIT.

"Come to me, you son of a bitch," Gordon whispered. "You just come to me."

Along National Route 9, the Vienna airport spreads over fifteen thousand acres of a flat plain that starts east of the suburban brewery town of Schwechat and stretches without geological interruption into Hungary, across southern Russia, all the way to the Chinese border. Hurtling down the four-lane highway at the rear of the three-car caravan, Gary Bates was the last to see the curved-roofed hangar buildings rising on the horizon. Timber Three came on the air.

"Timber Two, we'll take him right at the entrance when he has to slow down for the speed bumps. I'll cut in front of him and you ram him from behind. Over."

"Hey! This is my own car!" Bates protested.

"Is that a Roger, Timber Two?" It was Timber One from headquarters.

"Roger. Roger. Over."

The three-hundred-meter warning sign for the entrance flashed by. Bates kept his eyes focused on the van through the windows of the Chevrolet. He would try to slide into the van broadside to save his engine. The Chevy pulled into the left lane. Bates braced himself. The entrance raced toward him, then swept by, and so did the exit.

"Where the hell is he going?" Bates shouted over the radio.

"We'll know in about a mile," Timber Three responded. "There's a fork in the road."

Culver had been at that intersection before. He had come up the road from the right after escaping from Hungary across the Neusiedler See. Now, he was being forced to take the left fork. Even without a road sign, he knew only one town lay ahead—Bratislava, Czechoslovakia.

I don't care what it takes, Culver vowed to himself, I'm not going back into Czechoslovakia.

"I don't care what it takes," Bates heard Timber One order, "he's not to go into Czechoslovakia. Over."

"Roger," Timber Two responded. "We'll try to force him off the road. Over."

Bates could see the Chevrolet start to close with the van. "Be careful. He's got a submachine gun," Bates warned.

Suddenly the Chevrolet veered sharply to the left. Its rear window blew open, and large chunks of glass scattered on the road. With a sharp whine a crease ran up the hood of Bates' BMW, and a bullet hole exploded on the passenger side of his windshield. He hit his brakes to avoid colliding with the Chevy. By the time they recovered, the van was a quarter mile ahead, and the border only two and a half miles away.

"He's packing some heavy artillery," Timber Three shouted into the radio.

"Casualties? Over."

"No, except maybe our radiator. We're going to try for his tires. Over."

"Don't blow him up. Over."

The road, which was built up several feet above the surrounding landscape of shallow quarries and gravel pits, had narrowed to two lanes. Culver had decided on a bootlegger turn, jamming the brakes and yanking the wheel to the left. If he was lucky, the van would do a one-eighty, ending up in the opposite lane headed back toward Vienna, and Herr Schlechta would be splattered all over the dash.

The gray Chevrolet was gaining on them again, and Schlechta had reloaded his Uzi. A truck passed. The road was clear and flat. As soon as I clear the small rise ahead, Culver said to himself . . . *Now!*

He started to turn the wheel, but before he could hit the brakes, he felt his rear tires collapse. The van fishtailed wildly, lurching to the left and then flipping onto its top and sliding backward down the road in a shower of sparks. Schlechta hit the roof, squeezing off a burst that sent bullets ricocheting around the inside. As if in slow motion, Culver felt the van rotate onto its side and watched the asphalt scrape past his shattered side window inches from his face. Finally, the van hit the shoulder, bounced into the air and came to rest down the embankment, its grill pointed into the air.

Schlechta stepped on Culver's head as he struggled to fire out his door at the cars that were screeching to a halt on the other side of the road. Culver grappled with his safety belt. It finally came loose, and he crawled between the seats to the back of the van. The portable computer case containing the weapon lay upside down but still intact. He found his shoulder bag jammed behind the spare tire. Bullets slamming into the side of the van thundered in his ears as if he was inside a bell. He could smell gasoline.

Pushing open the rear door, he slid down the embankment, pulling the weapon and his shoulder bag behind him. Schlechta, pinned down by the firing from across the road, shot back blindly. Culver dragged himself along the drainage ditch that ran next to the embankment, heading back toward the rise in the road. As he had guessed, the rise concealed a three-foot-high culvert. He ducked inside, resting briefly, the weapon cradled in his lap.

The firing intensified for a moment, and then he heard voices, American voices, shouting for them to give up. Hunched over, Culver started moving slowly through the puddles of water in the culvert, trying to keep the case dry and to avoid scraping it against the concrete walls. He came out on the other side of the road and saw several men who had taken cover farther along the embankment ahead of the BMW and the Chevy. He took the MAC-10 out of his bag. Inching toward them, he tried to conceal himself in the new spring weeds that covered the drainage ditch.

A second effort by the Americans to talk to Schlechta was answered with a heavy burst, giving Culver a chance to scramble up the bank to the BMW. The moment the Americans returned fire, he reached up and unlatched the door. As it opened, he found himself looking directly into another pair of eyes.

Gary Bates lay on the front seat of his car, trying, despite the gear shift, to wedge himself under the dash. He was so startled that, before he could speak, Culver had the muzzle of his gun in his face.

"Do what I say and I won't kill you. Don't even think of shouting. Your friends can't save your life. Here, grab this."

Bates helped lift the SADM into the car. One of the Americans waved at them in a questioning gesture. Culver climbed into the car and pushed Bates upright.

"Let's go! Now!" he ordered.

As the BMW pulled out, Culver emptied a clip from his MAC-10 into the rear of the Chevy and the underside of the van. Both exploded in flames.

64

"Don't they teach patience in your service?" It was the closest Antunov had permitted himself to making a joke. He sat at the table set up in the forward section of the aircraft while Gordon paced up and down the aisle. They had been parked at Gate 47 of the Vienna airport since landing twenty minutes earlier.

"I'm perfectly relaxed, Alexander. It's the US government that's getting nervous. How can a surveillance team just go off the air?" Gordon knew it was a bad sign, and Antunov's calm, gimlet stare irritated him. "Besides, how can you teach patience?"

"At our Academy we have an exercise for the first-year class. When it's below zero, they must go outside with two pails tied to the ends of a stick. The pails are full of water and the stick is held across the shoulders. The object of the exercise is to stand at attention until the buckets freeze."

"That builds endurance. How does it teach patience?"

"The fools pick the coldest days, hoping to get it over quickly. Sometimes it is so cold the buckets can freeze in fifteen minutes. But when they do, the cadet usually loses fingers or toes. The wise ones pick a warmer day, even if they must stand for hours."

"That reminds me of the story of the Siberian toilet," Gordon responded. Antunov arched his eyebrows, not knowing if he was about to hear a humorous story.

"This American couple was in Moscow trying to buy Russian antiques. But everything in the hard-currency stores had been made in Romania, and the glue was still wet. So they fell in with this hustler they met in the bar of the National Hotel. After selling them several hand-painted boxes and gilded icons, he said, 'I have something very rare and not so expensive, but only for connoisseurs of the real Russia—a two-hundred-year-old Siberian toilet.'

"They were intrigued, and so agreed to go to his apartment in the older section of the city. Instead of taking them inside, he went to a shed in the back, where he showed them the 'toilet.' It consisted of one stick eight feet long and another four feet long.

"'That's a toilet?' the Americans asked, and the antique dealer nodded. 'Well, how does it work?'

"'You take the long pole and stick it into the snow, so you have something to lean on.'

"The Americans were startled but began to grasp the geometry. 'What do you do with the short stick?'

"'Oh, that,' the dealer replied. 'You use it to beat off the wolves.'"

Antunov gave a short snort, but repressed a real laugh. "That is anti-Soviet slander."

"No, no. That's why I said it was antique. It's anti-Czarist slander."

"True. All right, I will now tell you a toilet story of modern Russia." Antunov was warming to the exchange. "A woman sends her son out with five kopecks to buy three newspapers—*Pravda* for the mother, *Izvestia* for the father, and *Komsomol Pravda* for the boy. But halfway down the stairwell from their eleventh-floor apartment, the boy meets his father climbing up, coming home from work. The father takes away the five kopecks and tells the boy that the radio is sufficient—"

"Mr. Gordon," the pilot interrupted, "there's someone from the Embassy to see you."

Gordon rushed forward. "Any news . . ."

The man in the black raincoat glanced first at Antunov. "The target escaped. We had him trapped, but he got away from us about the time you landed. He's got one of our people hostage."

Gordon sat down heavily on the arm of a seat. "I better call the President. Is there pursuit? Do we know anything—"

"Yes," he said in a tone that suggested they should talk privately.

"We don't have any secrets for Comrade Antunov," Gordon said wearily.

"Are you sure?"

Gordon nodded.

"Okay. We thought the man who had Culver was headed to the airport. But he kept on going right by. So we tried to cut him off. There was a firefight. One of our cars was knocked out. Somehow Culver escaped in the other one. The guy who had been with him was killed when the van blew up."

"The weapon . . ." Antunov started.

"No sign of it in the van. As far as we know, Culver's got it."

"Thanks," Gordon sighed, "I'd better call the President. Anything else?"

The Agency man nodded.

"Well?" Gordon demanded.

"They were headed for the Czech border."

Gordon looked sharply at Antunov.

"That's why we used force to stop them."

"You should have let them go," said Antunov. "We would have caught them at the border."

"But why," Gordon asked, "would they head for Czechoslovakia?"

"That's just it. When we dragged the guy out of the weeds, he'd been burned, but we recognized him. His name's Alois Schlechta. For years he's worked in Vienna as a bagman and all-around heavy for the Soviets."

"Sean." It was the first time Antunov had used Gordon's Christian name. "This must be a mistake. I am sure there is an explanation . . ."

"If there is, I suggest your General Secretary convey it personally to the President of the United States." Gordon paused. "Until then, get the fuck off my airplane."

65

Loggerman entered his office briskly and slammed the door behind him. He took the wallet-sized tape recorder out of his suit pocket, placing it on his desk. He dropped into his chair, swiveled around to his credenza, and snapped on the dictating machine.

"Notes for the book. Re: NSC meeting this date on weapon crisis. Paragraph."

He paused to collect his thoughts. The reels on the voice-activated dictaphone stopped turning.

"The meeting was a shambles," he began. "Everyone was tense, waiting for word from Vienna on whether we had finally cornered Culver. In the meantime, we were trying to brief the President on our nuclear retaliatory options in the event the weapon is detonated. At first, the President didn't seem very interested, and then he started taking out his frustrations on the Chairman of the JCS. For example:"

Loggerman rewound his pocket recorder. It squealed back and forth several times until he found the passage he wanted.

CJCS: As I indicated, we have a wide menu of nuclear strike options to choose from. Any option can be tailored to the scale of the damage we suffer if the weapon goes off, and we can execute in a manner that will minimize the risks of further escalation."
P: How are we going to do that?
CJCS: By demonstrating that we can do more damage to him than he can do to us, within any given escalation boundaries.
P: And what keeps them from crossing these "escalation boundaries" and doing more damage to us?
CJCS: The ultimate sanction is that we can prevail in a general nuclear war.
P: And what does "prevail" mean, when thousands of nuclear weapons are going off on each side?

CJCS: To prevail means to terminate the war on terms not un-
favorable to the United States.
P: Cut the crap. What the hell are you talking about?
CJCS: We'd end the war with more nuclear weapons than they
would.
P: Oh, great. That's very reassuring. It doesn't mean America would
survive. No. Nuclear weapons survive. What are you trying to do,
make sure that you'll still have a job?

"Since the President was getting personal," Loggerman resumed his
dictation, "I decided I'd better step in. I assured him that we had high
confidence in our ability to control a limited nuclear exchange. I emphasized our multiple and redundant systems to detect, assess, and
evaluate the scale of any Soviet attack. We had spent fifty billion dollars over the last five years on the most sophisticated communications
to ensure command and control over our nuclear forces. The Soviets
had done the same. Para.

"I said we have to assume neither side wants an all-out nuclear war.
There would be powerful incentives to respect escalation boundaries,
and we both have the technology to do so. Colon:"
Loggerman turned on the tape machine again.

P: Give me an example.
KL: Like what we're discussing here. This terrorist weapon goes
off. We're hurt, we retaliate, and that's it.
P: But the Russians say that's not it.
KL: Well, of course we have to expect they'll threaten back. It's a
bargaining process. Escalation boundaries have to be negotiated.
P: Look, Karl, we're having a helluva time trying to cooperate now.
You think it'll be easier to negotiate when we're throwing nuclear
weapons at each other?

Loggerman stopped the tape and thought for a moment about the
last exchange with the President. "Note to secretary, scratch that
excerpt."
"Paragraph," he continued. "The President asked whether the Soviets believed in what he termed 'this tit-for-tat stuff'? The CIA Chief
then really put the cat among the pigeons. I could see his jaw muscles
bulge as he gave his answer.

"'Soviet doctrine emphasizes pre-emptive nuclear operations,' he said without unclenching his teeth, 'particularly against command and control.'

"The President asked for a translation, and as usual, the Secretary of Defense picked the wrong time to be helpful.

"'He means decapitation.' And then, the Secretary drew his finger across his neck. The President nearly exploded."

Loggerman ran the tape again to make sure he got the President's words right.

> P: How the hell are we supposed to negotiate 'escalation bound-
> aries' when we're both going at each other like two headless
> chickens?

"Full para. I waited for the Chairman of the Joint Chiefs to speak up, but when he failed to do so, I had to intervene once again to explain that while both sides might have such capability in theory, decapitation would be an irrational strategy if both were trying to limit the conflict. Moreover, neither side could be sure that the other did not automatically go to all-out nuclear war if its leadership were killed. The President asked if we had such an automatic system. Para.

"It was at that point, before anyone could answer him, that we got Gordon's call from Vienna. As I feared, he reported that once again Culver had slipped through his fingers. More important was that the Soviets were clearly implicated. Para.

"Everyone was stunned. (Parenthesis. I must admit that I'm some-what baffled by the game the Soviets are playing. Close parenthesis.) The Vice President summed up our reaction. 'What the hell's wrong with those people?' he said. Para.

"Thinking that he had to answer the question, the CIA Director ducked behind an old intelligence cliché, 'They're always pursuing at least two lines of policy at the same time.' And then, of course, all the others had to chime in. 'They must take us for fools,' the Secretary of Defense said. 'Strength is the only thing they respect, Mr. President,' added the JCS, and so forth. Paragraph.

"The President seemed dazed."

A blinking light appeared on Loggerman's intercom, accompanied by a soft buzz. He ignored it and continued dictating.

"I explained to the President that the issue had now become American credibility. I said the Soviets don't think we mean business. We have to re-establish respect or they could make a fatal miscalculation. I tried to make the President understand that, if we kept dancing around, the crisis could get out of our control. We had to send back a strong signal in the only language they understand—military power.

"The President just sat there immobile, saying nothing. So I indicated to the Chairman of the Joint Chiefs to speak up."

The intercom buzzed again and Loggerman snatched it up. "Well, he'll just have to wait," he said, and he slammed down the receiver. He pushed the PLAY button on his pocket recorder.

CJCS: Uh, we need to take several steps, but we'd stop short of Condition Yellow. We can put together a prudent package to send the right message to the Russians, but stay out of the press here at home.
P: And why won't this give some jackass in the Kremlin ammunition to argue for a Russian alert to show us that *they* mean business?

"At this point," said Loggerman, briefly stopping the recorder, "the Secretary of Defense finally said something useful. Colon:"

SECDEF: Mr. President, I think we all feel as frustrated as you do. There are no *good* choices, but protecting our nuclear assets is paramount.
P: You're saying I have no other choice?
SECDEF: No, no. I'm just saying what's prudent from the Pentagon's perspective in the light of Soviet moves.
P: And that's it? Just declare an alert, wait till this asshole blows up his bomb and then we start World War III?

"[Brackets. Note how emotional the President had become. I could sense that several of us were beginning to be concerned about his"— Loggerman groped for the right word—"'solidity.' Close brackets.]

"I took that opportunity to explain that we also would have to send another message to Chalomchev. I distributed a text that I had already prepared before hearing the news from Gordon. In light of his report of

Soviet treachery, I urged that the message make clear that a nuclear detonation on NATO territory would be tantamount to an attack on the United States and would not go unanswered. Para.

"I could see the President didn't want to hear what I was saying, so I concluded, 'With all due respect,' I said, 'we've tried cooperation and been rewarded by duplicity.' Para.

"'Duplicity for sure,' Gordon then interrupted, 'but not complicity. What do you want the Soviets to do? They obviously don't have control of Culver. They were trying to snatch him, not help him escape.' And so forth. Para.

"'For all we know,' I countered, 'that was their plan all along—make themselves heroes and us fools.' I told the President that it was getting too late to psychoanalyze the Russians. Strong action was even more urgent in the light of Soviet behavior. Paragraph.

"Once again Gordon butted in. (Parens. Note: It's very hard to control someone who's on a speaker phone.)" Loggerman held the recorder up to the dictaphone to capture Gordon's faint words.

GORDON: Mr. President, I just want to remind everyone that, as far as we can tell, Culver and the bomb are still in Austria. I'm moving MPs to all the West German and Italian border crossing points. For the moment, there's not much chance of the bomb going off in NATO territory. You don't need to do anything rash.
KL: Isn't it true, Mr. Gordon, you don't know where Culver is?
GORDON: Yes, but—
KL: And we still have to deal with Soviet alert . . .
GORDON: It's not an alert yet.
KL: Let's ask the experts about that.

"I turned to the CIA Director, who at first tried to slide around the word 'alert' by saying the Soviets were 'taking steps to enhance their readiness.' He enumerated some EMCON—that's emissions control—measures, like shutting down all their mobile radars, and encrypting critical circuits. But he really got the President's attention when he reported that they'd quietly started to cancel military leaves, calling personnel back to their ships and air bases.

"'It's a signal to us,' I explained.

"'Well, they've got my attention. Dammit!'

"His curse hung in the air. From the Rose Garden I could hear the clatter of metal folding chairs being set up for some awards ceremony. A faint exchange of angry voices drifted in from the Press Room. The President put the draft message down and peered intently at each of us.

"I tried to conceal my impatience, and looked at the others. The face of the Chairman of the JCS was empty, awaiting orders. The CIA Director looked clinical and detached, as if he were observing a subject undergoing psychological testing. The Secretary of Defense seemed to be wallowing in the self-importance of participating in an historic moment. Paragraph.

"I thought, briefly, that we might get a firm decision from the President. Then he looked directly across the table at the Vice President. The latter's rheumy eyes and shake of the head in effect told the President, 'You're on your own.' Para.

"The President got up, and, without saying anything, headed toward the Oval Office. I asked if he could give us some guidance, and all he said was a curt, 'Thank you, gentlemen, for your advice and counsel.'"

Loggerman switched off the dictaphone, then turned it back on, adding, "Okay, that ends it." He picked up the phone and pushed the intercom.

"Now you can send in Admiral McCollough," he said to his secretary.

"He's gone to see the President," she responded. "But he left some cables for you."

Loggerman started walking faster the more he read of the messages. The first was from the National Security Agency.

```
NSA/CRITIC/TS
39756205734/RYMLAND
    TO WHITE HOUSE SITUATION ROOM FOR MCCOLLOUGH
FOLLOWING MESSAGE SENT FRG POLICE VIA INTERPOL 16:17
ZULU FROM AUSTRIAN NATIONAL POLICE:
REFERENCE YOUR ALERT 08371, BE ADVISED HUGO BROWN-
MILLER CLEARED VIENNA PASSPORT CONTROL AT 15:50 THIS
DATE. DESTINATION UNKNOWN.
```

NSA NOTE: SUBJECT NAME IS ALIAS FOR TERENCE CULVER.
SIT ROOM NOTE: MESSAGE PASSED VIENNA FOR GORDON 16:31
ZULU.

When Loggerman read the second message, he broke into a run.

    FLASH/TS/RYMLAND
    TOSIT 46
    FROM GORDON
SEARCH OF VIENNA APT NEGATIVE. CULVER MUST BE ABOARD
AIR FRANCE FLIGHT 421 TO PARIS WHICH DEPARTED HERE 16:35
ZULU. IN PURSUIT. ARRANGE SURVEILLANCE ON CULVER AT
CHARLES DE GAULLE APT. GORDON.

When the National Security Advisor entered the small study, he noticed that the President abruptly stopped his conversation with Admiral McCollough.

"Thanks for making the meeting, Karl. I always enjoy working for you whenever you have the time."

"I'm sorry, Mr. President. This is terrible," Loggerman said.

"Oh, don't take it too hard," the President replied. "Just don't let it happen again, if we live through this."

"No, I mean Paris, Culver going to Paris."

"It was never one of my favorites. Snotty waiters." He looked more closely at his NSC Assistant. "What's wrong, are you finally taking this thing seriously?"

"My cousin used to head the French General Staff. He once told me that if Paris were destroyed in a nuclear attack, their command system is automated to launch everything the French have against the USSR."

"Is that true?" The President looked at McCollough.

"There's been rumors for several years. We never got any hard evidence. But it fits their strategy and the fact that all their command and control is centralized in Paris."

"How many nuclear weapons do they have?"

"In the hundreds," McCollough said, "mostly from submarines."

"The Russians won't know whose subs are shooting at them. They'll think it's us!" Loggerman exclaimed.

"So much for escalation boundaries," the President said easily and was quiet for a moment. "You're right about one thing, Karl, it's getting away from us. If we just wait, we'll be overwhelmed. We need something dramatic."

Loggerman was surprised at how calm the President seemed. The news about Paris appeared to confirm something in his mind. The sarcasm remained, but the self-pity was gone.

"What'll we do?" Loggerman asked uncertainly.

"I suggest you and your Pentagon friends now have a few more options to consider. Go ahead with the operational planning, but I'll want to see them again. As for the alert, protect our forces, but I don't want anything provocative."

"And the message?" Loggerman asked.

"Send it."

"On the Hot Line?"

The President thought about Chalomchev's request not to use it. "Yes," he said.

Jeez-us, Loggerman thought as the meeting broke up, where did the President suddenly get such big balls?

The President walked next door to the Oval Office and stood at his desk staring at Harry Truman's sign THE BUCK STOPS HERE. He shuddered involuntarily, then pushed the intercom button for his Appointments Secretary.

"Peter, set up an immediate meeting with the Soviet Ambassador. Have him come to the east gate. I don't want anyone in the West Wing to see him. Take him to the family floor."

He paused.

"And put through a call to my wife. Secure, in the clear, I don't care which. But get her for me."

66

The pilot of Gordon's DC-9 spotted the Caravelle near Mulhouse.

"The ground controllers are telling us to back off and give the target at least a kilometer."

Leaning over between the pilot and copilot, Gordon nervously shifted his gaze between the Caravelle, the incomprehensible instrument panel, and the void of the clouds ahead.

"How's the clearance for Charles de Gaulle?" Gordon asked.

"Weather's marginal." He pointed down to a solid blanket pierced only by the tallest Alps. "This stuff stretches all the way to the Atlantic. We've only got five hundred feet at de Gaulle right now, and the ceiling's dropping. The airport's been open and closed all day. I don't know if either one of us will get in."

"Just make sure you're ahead of them."

The pilot nodded. "They're scheduled and have priority. So I have to work through USAFE."

With nothing he could do, Gordon sat back into the vacant flight engineer's seat and strapped himself in. Pulling on a headset, he had the Communications Officer give him a line to McCollough at the White House.

"Chip, what's the story on surveillance at de Gaulle?"

"I've got some Agency types racing out from the Embassy. We really don't have much in the way of military assets in France."

"How about radios?"

"You don't have the same frequencies. But they have your description."

"Their orders?"

"Find him and don't lose sight of him."

"We've got clearance from de Gaulle," the pilot announced.

"Okay, Chip, we're about to go in, over and out."

Gordon motioned to Graciela, who was standing in the doorway, to sit down and buckle up. He tried to see something out of the cockpit window. Suddenly, the tops of high-tension electric towers emerged from the clouds, followed by the flat, newly planted wheat fields around Roissy-en-France.

The ground was close.

Culver felt safe. He was strapped in his seat, the bomb nestled between his legs. The inspection of the computer case at Vienna security had only been perfunctory. The MAC-10 and the money had been checked as luggage. The flight had given him a chance to sort out his next moves.

He had been stupid to think that the US would simply roll over and accept his demands. Bauer had probably known that, and planned to detonate the weapon all along. The demands were just a charade for my benefit, Culver thought bitterly. Now, with both Soviet and US agents after him, he would have to change his strategy. Or just set it off. In any case, he had to ready the weapon for instantaneous use. And he needed to do that before landing in Paris.

But before he could persuade the stewardess to clear away the luncheon debris so he could get up, the NO SMOKING signs came on and the aircraft began its bumpy descent through the clouds. As the stewardess finally started to clean up his row, the pilot came on the air, first in French, then German, and lastly English.

"Due to poor visibility at Charles de Gaulle, our flight has been switched to Lille."

Lille, Culver wondered, as he felt the plane again fight for altitude. "Where is Lille?" he asked the flight attendant in his imperfect French.

"Don't ask me," she snapped, "I'm a Parisian."

"The hell with clearance, take off!" Gordon insisted. "Stay with him!"

They had been halfway down the runway when over his headset Gordon heard the tower instruct the Air France flight from Vienna to divert to Lille.

"Nobody's landing in this stuff!" Gordon shouted. "Go!"

"But the tower's still letting people down—"

"Then say a prayer."

The pilot pushed the throttle, and the big jet surged forward. Everyone in the cockpit strained to look into the foggy sky.

The aircraft rotated and leapt upward, driving at a forty-degree angle. Suddenly, a huge airbus materialized in front of them. "What the bloody hell?" rang out in Gordon's earpiece, and he was thrown to the left as the pilot banked hard right. The airbus banked left and slipped by them.

A stream of invective came from the tower in French and English. "*Il est fou!* Asshole! *Bête!*"

The pilot cut them off as he switched over to pick up Lille. "We almost got ourselves the London shuttle." He shook his head.

"Now call 'Mayday,'" Gordon ordered, "and get this baby on the ground ahead of that Caravelle."

Gordon could not see the blue runway lights until the wheels hit the ground. At the end of the airstrip, the plane turned left, taxied a few minutes, then stopped. Gordon was at the door when it opened, and rode the automatic stairs as they dropped down.

On the tarmac, he looked around. The fog was so thick he could not see the terminal building. An ambulance with a flashing blue light came out of the mist, the driver holding his door open in order to follow the yellow stripe on the road. Graciela, pretending to be sick, was loaded in the back. Slowly, the ambulance made its way to the terminal passing rows of grounded airliners from around the world looming over them in the fog.

The tiny provincial terminal was a madhouse. Gordon picked his way through the crush. Turbaned Africans in white robes formed protective circles to feed their children; women from the Persian Gulf slept together in a pile against the wall. Wearing chadors and beaklike nose coverings, they looked like birds in an overcrowded cage. American college students took up the most room, sprawled over the floor with their backpacks, duffel bags, box radios, and guitar cases spread out as if they were at home.

Pushing through the mob surrounding the information desk, Gordon got the attention of a harassed airport official who was grateful to be able to respond to Gordon's questions without lying. "Air France Flight 421 from Vienna to Paris?" He checked his console. "Oui, Monsieur, that flight just landed at Orly."

67

The FASTEN SEAT BELTS sign on the wall of the lavatory lit up as Culver was still trying to connect the wires to the toggle switch near the handle of the computer case. He had the weapon resting on top of the sink. A wire ran from the detonator to the inside of the computer cover, which he held in his lap as he sat on the toilet. The loudspeaker jabbered directly into his ear in three languages, ". . . to relieve congestion at Lille, we've been cleared for Orly, which has a one hundred–meter ceiling . . ." It made it hard for him to concentrate.

The weapon was already enabled. The question was whether the switch would be on or off when he attached the leads. He heard the sound of the landing gear coming down. With no time to disconnect the battery, he traced the wire back to the power supply to determine which lead was hot. The ground strip was fastened to the chassis of the weapon. He then tightened the screws on the "B" wire. Double-checking again, he slipped the "A" lead under the screw. As he started to tighten it, he felt an enormous crash.

The plane bounced twice on the runway before settling down. Culver caught his breath and finished tightening the screw. He hurried to get the cover back over the weapon. The plane had stopped and passengers were filing out by the time he got the weapon back into the suitcase.

"*Allo!*" There was a knock at the door. "*Y-a-t'il quelqu'un là?*" Someone in there?

Culver struggled to get the computer case out the door.

"Oh, it's you," said the petite, sharp-faced stewardess who had snapped at him earlier. "How did you get all this on the plane?" she demanded. "I'll take it." She reached for the computer.

"No, it's mine!"

"I'm not stealing it."

Culver yanked it back and she let go. The case fell to the floor and he tumbled over it, landing between two rows of seats.

The stewardess shook her head at him.

"It's a computer, very delicate," Culver said as he pulled himself up from the floor.

"Marie-Elise, send him down," a voice said from the bottom of the rear stairs, "he has to get on the bus."

"Well, *merci*," he mumbled, collecting the case and hurrying down the stairs.

"Don't tell me you go for big-baby Americans," the other girl at the bottom of the stairs said to Marie-Elise.

"Never," she retorted. "They have formidable equipment, but they don't know how to use it."

The bus to the terminal was packed. Most of the passengers stood. Protecting the weapon between his feet, Culver held on to a pole squeezed in next to a woman with several small children. He shut his eyes and tried to think.

With the deadline approaching, would they alert the French authorities? He had to assume so. The test would be getting through the airport. It was not the best ground zero, but if challenged, he told himself, he would let it rip right there.

Culver opened his eyes and looked down at the weapon. A little boy's hand covered the toggle switch. About three years old, he examined the switch with intense curiosity. Culver froze. Seeing his expression, the mother looked down.

"Pas toucher, Olivier."

The little boy ignored her. She insisted, and tried to pick him up. The child protested, *"Non, non,"* and held on to the handle of the case while clutching at the toggle. The mother began yelling and the child started crying.

"Never mind, leave him alone," Culver said in English, his French deserting him.

The mother slapped the boy across the head. He let out a howl and collapsed to the floor, still clinging to the toggle switch.

The bus stopped with a jerk. The little boy sprawled backward. The mother bent down and scooped him into her arms. The toggle was the last thing he let go.

"Pardon, Monsieur," the woman said, and she pushed past him out the door.

Culver stood there feeling his heart racing until the bus was almost empty. He then hurried forward to make sure he would not be at the end of the line.

To his surprise, he was waved through passport control with only a perfunctory examination of his documents. He quickly found his duffel bag in the baggage claim, and at customs he took the green NOTHING TO DECLARE door. He started to relax. Then someone tapped him on the shoulder.

"Alors! Your passport please," the customs officer said in French. His face had the deep lines of a heavy smoker. His yellow teeth confirmed it.

Culver drew out an American passport and handed it over. He rested his left index finger on the toggle. For a fleeting moment, thinking of the little boy, he wondered if the switch worked. Perhaps he'd connected it wrong, or maybe something had come loose when the stewardess dropped it.

"You are importing that computer?" the customs officer asked in French, then German.

"No," Culver answered in English. "I'm doing some work on vacation."

"Open it up," he ordered.

Culver lifted the weapon onto the metal-covered bench. He kept his finger pressed against the switch. If this is it, he thought, so be it. He turned the Compaq on its side and took off the bottom, revealing a keyboard, a screen, and two disk drives. The customs officer examined it.

"Come with me," he said.

Culver started to close it up. He would wait to the last possible second . . .

"Leave it there. Come along."

Culver did not want to let it go.

"Something wrong?"

Culver hesitated. "No," he said, and reluctantly followed him. They ended up at a cashier's window.

"You leave a thousand franc deposit." He scribbled on the receipt and stapled it into Culver's passport.

"If you leave France without that machine, it will be very severe. You forfeit the deposit and pay the duty plus a fine."

The old woman working the *garderobe* at the Louvre held up her hand. *"Non,"* she said flatly to Culver. "Only coats and hats. It's all these crazy terrorists. We can't accept packages of any kind."

He needed to get away from it for a while. But he had to stay away from obvious storage places like bus or train stations. And he was not going to tempt airport security again.

Forty-five minutes later, he finally found a place to leave the weapon. The manager of the Gaudéamus Bains et Douches near the Sorbonne pushed one-half of a claim ticket across the stained marble counter.

"Hey!" he called out, "don't you want to take a bath?"

"Maybe when I get back," Culver answered as he disappeared out the door into the afternoon mist.

Culver wandered the streets without a destination, finding Paris, on a foggy afternoon, mysterious, beautiful, and somehow comforting. He avoided the major tourist spots, drawn instead to the narrow streets where he and Graciela had walked together. The Rue Champollion on glowed with the marquees of a dozen tiny movie houses showing old American pictures seldom seen in the United States—Olsen and Johnson's *Hellzapoppin'*, Orson Welles' *Lady from Shanghai,* and a Jerry Lewis double feature.

He walked down the Rue de l'Ecole-de-Médecine, across the Boulevard St.-Germain, and into the market on the Rue de Buci, where he watched Parisian housewives stuff fruit, fresh chickens, and whole fish into their string bags. He gaped at the sight of a side of meat hanging in the window of a shop adorned with the head of a horse.

Wandering down the Rue Bonaparte and then up the Rue des Beaux Arts, he gazed into tiny galleries with façades of peeling dark green paint, baffled at some of the things they presented as art.

Across Pont Neuf on the Ile de la Cité, he found himself staring up at the fortress of the Préfecture de Police and imagining that inside a desperate search for him was being organized. It gave him a sense of satisfaction.

Gordon could see nothing out the train window. Damp cold seeped out of the wooden walls of the coach. The heat failed to work. Graciela grimaced in pain as each shock from the rails traveled directly up through the wooden seats. But she did not complain.

Again, Gordon checked his watch. It was 7:30 P.M. The French Army had cleared the terminal at Lille by herding the stranded passengers into trucks and buses and carting them to the railway station. Gordon and Graciela Morena rode in the ambulance.

A WWI troop train awaited them. The sign on the side of their coach proclaimed, 40 OR 8—forty men or eight horses. No cars were available for rent at the airport. Gordon thought of stealing one, but in the dense fog, the train promised to make faster time than the Autoroute.

"Can we ever find him now?" Graciela asked.

"We're getting the Agency to cover all the rail, air, and bus terminals. We've got the phone trace set up in case he calls again. Maybe you can help like you did in Venice."

"I already told you everything. We stayed at the Hotel St.-Simon on the left bank. We did the normal things, the Louvre, the Eiffel tower, the boat on the Seine, Notre Dame, and the Latin Quarter. I gave you the whole list." She looked like she was about to burst into tears.

"Are you hurting bad? This train . . ."

"No. I'm just afraid." She looked embarrassed. "I keep thinking we'll search and search and still not find him. But we'll be too close when the bomb goes off."

"If we're close enough," Gordon conceded, "we'll never know. It'll be instantaneous."

"You know, he didn't set it off in Vienna, despite his threats," she said, clutching at any hope, trying to defend him.

"He wasn't in NATO territory either," Gordon pointed out.

They sat in silence for a while. The train rattled over a bridge in the gray twilight.

"Could be we've been going about this all wrong," he said at last.

"You've an idea?"

"If we get the chance, maybe we should try to make him come to us."

It was growing dark, and the old man in the skullcap was eager to close the gates. Culver did not want to leave. For an hour, he had been sitting on the floor, his back against the rough stone walls of the Monument to the Deportation, France's Holocaust. Culver had stumbled upon the memorial, hidden below ground behind the Cathedral of Notre Dame like a shameful secret of Christianity.

He had been trying to imagine the effort required to exterminate so many people without atomic weapons. Horst Bauer once remarked to him that nothing was ever accomplished in German history without violence and death. Culver wanted America out of Europe's murderous entanglements. That millions might die was in keeping with European tradition.

"We must close now." The old man had come back for the third time. Peering at Culver in the darkening shadows he asked, "Are you Jewish?"

"No—not anything, really."

"Then why do you look so persecuted?"

When Culver failed to laugh, the old man's tone changed. "Do you need help?" he asked.

"No," Culver said, backing up the stairs. "There's nothing you can do."

"I can listen."

"No!" he shouted down the stairwell, turning to flee across the footbridge to the Ile St.-Louis.

He shunned the crowd spilling out of the Brasserie Alsace. He ran as if to escape the memory of standing at the bar with Graciela, drinking stein after stein of Mutzig, oblivious to time, waiting hours to share their first cassoulet and salad *frisée*.

Halfway down the Quai Voltaire, he stopped running and finally came to a halt under a flowering chestnut that hung over the river. He descended the embankment and stopped at the water's edge. The Seine was dark and gleaming. He wanted Graciela to be alive again, to be with him. He wanted to die himself. Not in vain, he vowed. But soon.

68

Antunov climbed down from the AN 124 as soon as it rolled to a stop on the tarmac at Ramskoye aerodrome. He was led through a huge hangar and then into a warren of small offices which served as the base Flight Operations Center. He knew he was home by the odor of modern Russia—the thick, strong, sweet scent of disinfectant.

"The orders are changed," the officer of the day abruptly informed him. "You will be traveling by helicopter."

Antunov did not know what the original plans were, much less what the change might mean. After reporting through the KGB Residenz in Vienna about the rupture with Gordon, he had immediately been ordered to Bratislava, where an aircraft had been waiting for him. An old KGB saying held that, ordered home from assignment, you always kissed lead. You just never knew whether it would be a bullet or a medal.

Back through the maze of cubicles and across the hangar, he arrived at a waiting ME 24 Hind helicopter gunship. In ten minutes, it covered the twenty-six kilometers to the southern outskirts of Moscow, where it hovered over a major intersection that had been cleared of traffic by uniformed KGB officers with machine guns. The helicopter settled into the middle of the street, and Antunov was ordered to get out and wait. The road to the east was empty. The other three were clogged with late afternoon traffic. But not one horn could be heard. The haze and stench of diesel oil hung over the silent, sullen jam.

After a quarter of an hour, a black ZIL appeared from the east. It was, as Antunov suspected, the Chairman of the KGB.

"They're counting daggers in the Defense Council," Antunov's Chief began as the car sped north at 90 mph.

"Unfortunately, we, too, are being forced to choose sides. I know you are a friend of Dimitri Fyakov. Comrade Chalomchev and I have been friends since our days in Komsomol camp together. So I want you to understand, I do not intend to let the Committee for State Security go down with him."

Antunov waited alone on a bench in the hallway outside the heavily carved brass doors that led to the Defense Council chamber. Occasionally he could hear raised voices from the meeting and once or twice a shout. On the opposite wall hung an enormous three-by-five-meter painting of the retreat of the American Expeditionary force at Bol'shiye Ozerki in 1919. The Americans were escaping across the snow-covered fields, and the foreground was piled with the bodies of Red Army soldiers. What lesson is this supposed to teach? Antunov wondered.

The 'door opened, and Dimitri Fyakov came out. He sat beside Antunov on the bench. He looked exhausted.

"They've lost all proportion." His voice had an edge of hysteria. "They're scheming to bring down the General Secretary, and they don't care if we end up in a nuclear war! The old Marshal thinks the answer to the latest American threats is more threats. He wants to call a strategic alert!" He put his head in his hands for a moment, then sat back erect. "You are crucial to us, Alex. You must protect us on Venice. And the General Secretary wants you to tell the Defense Council what happened in Vienna. We know it was not KGB. This Schlechta had to be GRU."

"Dimitri, I'll do what I can." He was a small fish in a tank with sharks. And he was supposed to think of the sharks?

Alexander Antunov sat down next to Fyakov along the wall.

"Comrade Colonel Antunov will now brief us on his contacts with the Americans," the General Secretary introduced him.

He kept the report factual, specific, and short. The Chairman of the KGB and the General Secretary both looked satisfied. "Do you believe the American allegations about Alois Schlechta?" the Chairman of the KGB asked as planned.

"All I know is that the man who captured Culver was headed toward Bratislava. The CIA claims he worked in Vienna for our government," he responded carefully.

"Comrade Antunov," Chalomchev tried a flanking attack, "are you suggesting KGB elements were involved?"

"No, Comrade Secretary."

"Then it would have to be the GRU," the Foreign Minister added in a frontal assault.

"Are you going to believe the CIA?" General Ogorodnik demanded.

"I do not know whether the CIA is correct," Antunov replied evenly. "I'm convinced that they believe it. The files should show—"

Major General Kirillin, Chief of the GRU, rose to his feet. "The question is not whether we sought to capture this madman and his bomb, it is why the KGB and you, Mr. Antunov, let him go!"

"Don't deny it!" Marshal Ogorodnik warned Antunov. "I have the captain of the *Rostov* downstairs."

"I did not let Mr. Culver escape," Antunov said flatly. "I was operating under strict instructions from the Americans unknown to the captain. They made it impossible to verify the identity of the one possible target we spotted." Despite the admiration on some of their faces, he knew that not one of them believed him.

Before General Kirillin could follow up, the Foreign Minister took the offensive. "Are you admitting that the GRU tried to seize the American?"

"We are checking. Our people are zealous. We circulated orders to apprehend him, so it's possible . . ." General Kirillin replied.

"But in cooperation with the US authorities!" the Foreign Minister jumped on him. "You had no orders from the Council to bring him east! Now the Americans are convinced we're behind it all!"

"Perhaps this would be a good time to dispose of one of the items on the agenda," the General Secretary moved in smoothly. "We can hardly consider the proposal," he nodded at the Marshal, "to expose this to the public when we do not exactly have clean hands ourselves."

A murmur of agreement swept the table. Chalomchev had stemmed the tide against him.

Antunov, who had been left standing, was now allowed to sit down. He was surprised at how easily Marshal Ogorodnik had been outmaneuvered, but as the Defense Minister began to speak, Antunov realized it was a tactical ploy. Schlechta could have opened up a dangerous line of inquiry into the GRU's relations with Culver and Bauer. Now the subject was closed, and the Council would be reluctant to overrule General Ogorodnik again.

"One tries to grab him, one lets him go. All this is really beside the point," the Defense Minister said. "The issue is the latest Hot Line message from Washington. The Americans wrongly blame this crisis on the Soviet Union. We don't know if they're malevolent or misguided, but we must respond firmly. It's the only language Americans understand. We have prepared an appropriate message and a list of military actions to support it." An orderly sitting behind him began to pass out copies.

Antunov read the draft message over the shoulder of the KGB Chief. The most important part came in the second paragraph.

> The Soviet government warns that any aggression against the Soviet State or that of its Allies will meet a stern rebuff from the full might of the people of the USSR. Our military forces have been directed to take all necessary measures to assure that our ability to respond is unquestioned . . .

While they debated the text, Antunov saw the door open, and someone waved for Fyakov to come out. He returned a few minutes later and whispered into the General Secretary's ear. As the Defense Minister's argument reached a crescendo, Chalomchev interrupted him.

"You want to send this Hot Line message? Fine. You want an alert? You say Vigilance Three will not be provocative? Fine."

The military officers at the table seemed stunned. The Foreign Minister, who had been supporting Chalomchev, seemed uncertain whether to protest.

"Now, for the moment, there is nothing else you want, correct?"

The Defense Minister nodded. Marshal Ogorodnik said nothing.

"Now I want your agreement on something . . ."

Fyakov leaned over to Antunov and whispered, "We've just received another message, a personal letter from the President of the United States."

69

"I make it a rule to know everything that's going on in my country," the American Ambassador said. "No US government operations are conducted in France behind my back."

Sean Gordon and Graciela had been driven to the US Embassy from the Gare du Nord and brought directly to the Ambassador's office. He was dressed in white tie and tails. At six feet three, with longish hair graying at the temples, he looked to be the model of a professional Ambassador. Gordon had often wondered if it were possible to become an Ambassador if you were short. This one, he knew, had a reputation for being tough, turf-conscious, and having served so many Washington masters that he had forsaken any interest in policy.

"For example," the Ambassador continued, ignoring the light flashing on his telephone console, "the CIA Station Chief here works for me, not you. He's not carrying out one more of your instructions without my say-so. I know all about your penchant for flying solo, Mr. Gordon. I give you fair warning. I represent the President of the United States in France, and I'll not permit amateur-hour follies around here." Then he smiled and offered the two of them a plate of finger sandwiches, which he had thoughtfully prepared for their arrival.

Gordon checked the time on the gilded Louis XVI clock on the mantel. Paris might cease to exist in about four hours. He was not going to spend the time in bureaucratic squabbles.

"You've been candid," Gordon sighed, "I'll be frank with you. I'm not going to tell you anything unless I need to or the President orders me."

The Ambassador's face began to turn red under his fading ski tan. The light on his console kept blinking.

"Let's not waste time arguing," Gordon continued. "Have your secretary put through a secure call to the White House."

"We don't have to . . ." the Ambassador started to back off.

"I'm not playing games. I've got to talk to Admiral McCollough. If you also want to talk to the President, it's okay by me."

The door opened, and a secretary put her head in. "Mr. Ambassador, do answer your phone. It's the White House on the line for Mr. Gordon."

Gordon's heart leaped. An open line could mean Culver. He snatched the phone off the coffee table. It was Peter Andretti.

"It's our friend again. We've been stalling to get you all patched together."

Gordon put his hand over the mouthpiece. "Mr. Ambassador, I need your phone!" He motioned Graciela toward the Ambassador's desk. "And give us some privacy."

"Just a minute," he protested, "this is my office . . ."

Cradling the phone on his shoulder, Gordon snapped open his briefcase, exposing a .45 Magnum. The sputtering Ambassador backed out the door.

Culver was already talking.

". . . a modification of earlier instructions. I want a *public* statement by the President announcing that all US nuclear weapons in Europe are being withdrawn. You must make that announcement by midnight tonight, European time, or I'll detonate the weapon."

"Mr. Culver, this is the President."

Culver let out a gasp.

"Mr. Culver," the President repeated, "we're making every effort to comply with your demands. But you don't know what you've set in motion. If you explode that weapon, it could start an all-out nuclear war . . ."

"That's stupid . . ."

"I agree! That's why I'm trying to get *both* sides to pull back their nuclear weapons. I'm leaving immediately to meet with the Soviet leader . . ."

"What?" The surprised voice was Loggerman's.

"But that will take time," the President continued. "Mr. Culver, are you still there?"

"Yes," he paused. "How much time?"

"At least a few days."

"Negotiations are always an excuse to do nothing."

"I can't even meet the General Secretary by midnight!" The President strained to keep from pleading.

"All right, I'll give you until 15:00 hours tomorrow afternoon. Make the announcement with the Russians, if you can. Or by yourself, if you can't. I really don't care which."

"Mr. Culver, don't hang up," Gordon broke in. "Someone wants to talk to you."

"Hello, Terry?"

"Graciela—" The shock was clear in his voice. "You're alive . . ."

"I'm here, in Paris . . ."

"Here?"

"Terry, I love you," Graciela said urgently. "Why did you leave me? Why did you try to kill me?"

Gordon looked at her sharply. It was not what she was supposed to be saying.

"You . . . you know why. You and Bauer!" Culver shouted.

"Terry, he forced me!"

"I'm glad I killed him!"

"But he's alive, too!"

Gordon closed his eyes. It was going all wrong.

"Alive? Here?" Culver sounded disoriented.

"No, Berlin. He's giving a press conference tomorrow about you!"

"Graciela, I loved you . . . how could you?" Culver was drifting away.

"Terry! I love you too! I want to see you!"

"No. You're with them. You just want the SADM . . ." His voice sounded as if he were no longer speaking into the phone.

"I don't give a damn about them, or the bomb!" she screamed into the phone. "It's you!"

There was no response from Culver. A long minute passed.

"Is he still on the line?" Loggerman asked.

"How the hell would I know," said the President.

"I don't think so," Gordon added.

"I'm sorry, I ruined it, didn't I?" Graciela started to weep.

"Nice try," the President said.

"Hello?" The voice was American.

"Who's this?" Gordon asked.

"Harry Bosworth, American Embassy, Political Section."

"Where are you?"

"Telephone cabin, in front of the Galeries Lafayette. I guess we just missed him, huh?"

Dressed in a raincoat, with his hair darkened, carrying a large duffel bag, Culver stayed away from the train stations, bus terminals, airlines, and rent-a-car offices where dozens of embassy personnel had been deployed. Instead, he took the métro to the Etoile, where he switched to the RATP Regional Express for St.-Germain-en-Laye. Once there, he had a twenty-minute wait for the regular SNCF train to Rouen and the Channel coast.

At 11:45 P.M., he caught the overnight coastal hydrofoil at Dieppe, stopping at Calais, Dunkirk, Ostend, Antwerp, Rotterdam, Gravenhage, and Amsterdam.

70

Loggerman seethed inside.

"You can't be serious, Mr. President, you'll be walking into a trap! This has probably been their objective all along. Get us panicked, then squeeze us for concessions!"

"You may be right, Karl, but you heard that screwed-up kid. You think he's part of a conspiracy?"

"They manipulate people like that."

The President was being conciliatory by walking the National Security Advisor back to his office.

"Look at Chalomchev's message." Loggerman unfolded the heavy paper with a gold hammer-and-sickle letterhead. The words were printed with the uneven stroke of a manual typewriter. "He accepts a meeting, proposes Spitsbergen, then rejects any responsibility for what's been happening. Not a word about Vienna. And then see, he plainly says, 'Any use of US nuclear weapons against the USSR or its Allies would be a catastrophic mistake that would not go unanswered.'"

"You said we had to expect counterthreats," the President reminded him.

"And not to have told me anything." The National Security Advisor shook his head. "It makes me feel you've no confidence in me."

"I have the greatest respect for your capabilities. That's why I want you to stay here and run the show."

Loggerman stopped in his tracks.

"You mean I'm not going with you?"

"Someone has to manage the crisis from this end, Karl."

"But who's going to advise you? About verification, negotiating tactics, weapon systems?"

The President took his elbow and got him moving forward again. "You'll need military advice . . ."

"I'd like a few of your senior staff people, and I'm taking Admiral McCollough."

Loggerman stopped again. "McCollough? That'll drive the JCS berserk! They consider him an apostate! Cut a deal with him involved and the chiefs will be in revolt!"

"I'm counting on you to keep that from happening."

Loggerman realized he was getting nowhere. He tried to speak more calmly. "You're leaving the country, going to an island in the Arctic Ocean, right next to the Soviet Union—"

"It's Norwegian territory."

"In name only! The Russians run it. And you might have to launch nuclear weapons at any time!" Loggerman argued.

"That's why I'm taking the KNEECAP."

"The 'Doomsday' plane?"

"That's what it's for, isn't it?" The President had lost his patient tone. "Enough. I want situation reports every hour including a detailed report on each alert measure we and the Soviets are taking. Tell the press I've come down with a cold and have gone to Camp David. Have the press office say there's a news lid. I'm letting all the domestic staff go home early. Call an NSC working group meeting as soon as I'm airborne to fill them all in."

"You'll need briefing papers . . ."

"Put together whatever you want, but keep the agencies out of it." The President motioned for Loggerman to go into his office. He shut the door behind them.

"One more thing, I gave an order that everything in the White House files on Culver's escapade in Czechoslovakia be given to Admiral McCollough." Loggerman nodded. "That includes your notes for your book." He pointed to a small green single-drawer safe with a combination lock that was tucked next to the door.

Loggerman flushed. "Uh, of course. I'll have my secretary make a copy of the relevant parts."

"Fine."

The President opened the door. "You really think it's a mistake to try to negotiate something?" he asked.

"It's always dangerous when the top leaders try to make their own deals," Loggerman insisted.

"Then I guess you'll just have to pray for your country." The President closed the door behind him.

Donny Graham came down from the publisher's suite to Ben Bradlee's fifth-floor office to make clear to everyone that it was the managing editor's decision. Bradlee had assembled *The Washington Post*'s foreign editor, the State and Defense Department correspondents, the Chief White House correspondent, and the National Security correspondent. Walter Pincus, as usual, was the last to arrive. As he shut out the chaos of the newsroom approaching its 7:30 P.M. deadline, he heard Bradlee say, ". . . that's the President's version. It's off the record. We can't use it. What do we know on our own?" He expected Pincus to speak first.

"The Administration's been in a stew for several days over some kind of terrorist threat involving nuclear weapons, probably in Europe. My sources at the weapons labs say that there was a snap inventory at Sandia, Los Alamos, and Livermore on Saturday, and the shit hit the fan. All I can get them to say is that some paperwork got fouled up.

"But it has to have a foreign angle. A top White House official told me that State and Defense were deeply split over withdrawing nuclear weapons from Europe."

"What do you have?" Bradlee turned to the Pentagon correspondent.

"There's an exercise involving our storage depots. It's pretty widespread. It was a no-notice exercise, but the unusual thing is that it was almost forty-eight hours before they informed NATO."

"I see the headline now," Bradlee said, "ALLIES IN THE DARK AGAIN. There's got to be more than that."

"Well, all day there've been reports that suggest our strategic forces could be going on alert. The Trident crews at Charleston were called back to their subs. Several Midgetman missile squadrons have deployed from their shelters and are out on the road. But I don't know how many. More B1s and B-52s are standing strip-alert at a few places I checked, but there's been no dispersal or airborne alert."

"What do they say—"

"The same thing in every case, an exercise. And even at pretty high levels in the Pentagon there's no sense of crisis."

"Have you talked to the Secretary?"

"I've tried for three days, but they keep saying he's busy."

"He's usually pretty accessible . . ."

"Talks your ear off," the Pentagon reporter agreed.

"What about the Hill?" Bradlee asked. "Has he been up there?"

"No," the National Security correspondent replied. "But what I've got from the Intelligence people fits in. Yesterday, they started getting some peculiar data out of the Soviets. Spy satellites changing their orbits, radars shutting down, that sort of thing. Then about noon today, everything stopped."

"The Russians went back to normal?" Pincus asked.

"No. The intelligence stopped being disseminated. My sources are pretty high-level to be suddenly cut off."

The group fell silent. They all knew that no news was bad news.

"What about State?" Bradlee finally asked.

"Quiet as a tomb."

"That's a sure sign something's cooking," the White House correspondent said. "They're always the last to know." The others laughed.

"I do have something on the Secretary's trip to Caracas and the First Lady's sudden stop in Panama. Neither one was planned. The Secretary left on two hours' notice, bitching that the President made him go.

Everybody in the First Lady's entourage was surprised at the trip to Contadora. She was saying how much she wanted to get home."

"That doesn't exactly add up to World War III," Bradlee grumped. "What about the Commander-in-Chief?"

"Loggerman's fine," the White House reporter said, "and the President's not doing too bad, either."

That got a rueful laugh out of Bradlee.

"Seriously. Nothing too odd, some new Admiral's wandering around. We're trying to get a fix on him. A couple of NSC meetings. Only thing strange about that is no leaks. And it's unusual for the President to go off to Camp David in the middle of the week. He even canceled a speech. But his cold's supposed to be pretty bad."

"He looked perfectly healthy to me last night." Donny Graham spoke for the first time.

They absorbed that for a moment, then Bradlee looked to his foreign editor. "Overseas?"

"I've been through all the dispatches." He riffled through the file on his lap. "There's nothing. The only thing faintly interesting is that one of these peace types is holding a news conference in Berlin tomorrow and is trying to build a crowd by putting out the word that he'll reveal that a US nuclear weapon's been stolen."

"I'll believe that one when he shows it to us," Bradlee said. "So what does it all add up to?"

A copyboy opened the door and handed Pincus a note.

"I tell you," Bradlee continued, "smoke. Even if we throw in what the President said. There's nothing tangible here. Gossip, rumors, studies, infighting, head colds, it's crap."

"What about the military movements?" the Pentagon reporter protested. "And the intelligence cutoff."

"Find out why it's happening and we've got a story. We need something solid that ties it all together."

Pincus held up the piece of paper he had just been given. "How about the fact that, at six-twenty-five this evening, the President's big white 'Doomsday' plane took off from Andrews Air Force Base?"

VI. THURSDAY

71

For more than a decade, the forty-mile-long antenna buried under the farms and forests of northern Wisconsin and the upper peninsula of Michigan had been broadcasting the same simple message—Condition Blue—the world was at peace. The Extremely Low Frequency transmitter was not the only means to communicate with US strategic missile submarines. Cables strung across the Norwegian fjords broadcast in Very Low Frequency to submarines in the Atlantic, but the signal could be jammed, and disrupted by nuclear detonations. ORICS, the Optical Ranging and Communications System that used blue-green lasers, could send messages via satellite, but only so long as the submarines and the satellites were in the right locations. TACAMO aircraft (Take Charge and Move Out) could transmit and receive signals from submarines cruising just below the surface of the sea. However, that made the subs more detectable and vulnerable. And most of the eighteen Boeing 707 TACAMO aircraft remained on the ground, as vulnerable to attack as the VLF stations and ORICS satellites.

Only the ELF was fully reliable and secure. The powerful and slowly pulsed radio waves caused resonating vibrations in the Laurentian Shield, a massive subterranean granite formation that covered much of Wisconsin, Michigan, and Minnesota. The resulting signal could be heard in every corner of the world's oceans.

The only drawback to such an extremely low frequency was the messages could not be complicated. The ELF served as a "bell ringer" to signal the alert stage and tell the nuclear missile submarines that they should tune into other communications channels. If the other links were jammed or inoperable, and the ELF alert was above Condition Blue, the submarine commander, together with three other senior officers, could execute their standing nuclear attack orders.

For two weeks, Condition Blue had been broadcast by the ELF as the number seven. At 00:01 ZULU the message changed to number three. According to the code books, that meant Condition Yellow— "Nuclear Attack Considered Possible."

Sunnyvale, California   00:02 ZULU

Hector Munos was worried. For the third time in two weeks, his course on real estate law at San Jose State had made him late for work. His supervisor had already given him a warning.

Two miles past the airport, he turned off the freeway toward a cluster of large white dishes sticking out of an industrial park dominated by the multistory manufacturing buildings of the Lockheed Corporation's Missiles and Space Division. He stopped at a gate with a sign that said Satellite Test Center, an officially misleading title for the Satellite Control Facility, which manages the on-orbit operations of most US government satellites.

"Must be having some kind of flap in there tonight," the guard said to Munos.

"Shift hasn't changed?" Munos asked hopefully.

The guard shook his head as he handed back Munos' pass. "But you're still late."

Inside the windowless stucco building, Munos found the quiet chaos of a major drill. The air was filled with the urgent clacking of keyboards at the control consoles that lined three walls and formed a center aisle. Though the night controllers had taken over, most of the day shift had stayed on to give advice and see what would happen. He could see his seat was vacant.

"Where the hell have you been?" Munos' supervisor cornered him at the coffee urn near the door. "You know Candy's got to go home and take care of her kids." Except for a sprinkling of military supervisors, the controllers were, like Munos, civilians under contract to the Department of Defense.

"What's the story?" Munos asked.

"Some asshole exercise. We've got to change the orbital parameters and frequencies of damn near the entire World Wide Military Command and Control System."

"I don't work on WIMEX."

"All SIGINT and ELINT satellites are being moved and the sleepers activated, too. You've got a lot of work to do on the DSPs."

Munos was the night controller for the Code 686 Defense Support Program. His satellites would provide early warning of a Russian missile attack by detecting the heat from a rocket plume at launch. He liked the job, not because it was important, but because the satellites needed little tending and he could study most of the night.

The chair still held the warmth of the woman on the day shift. The screen in the center of a bank of CRTs contained her log. She had been able to carry out the routine alert tests on DSP East and Pacific DSP East before rushing home. Munos now had the treacherous task of reactivating an older code 647 DSP which for many years had been sleeping in a geostationary orbit.

"I've never done this before," Munos said to his supervisor, who hovered over him as he pulled up the relevant commands from the computer.

"It's really unusual in a Condition Yellow exercise," his supervisor agreed. "Get a readout on the last activation to see what its quirks are. It had to be a couple of years ago."

A small box appeared on his computer screen and grew into a window containing a report on the six previous reactivations.

"They always had a lot of problems getting her going," Munos noted. "Why bother? We've got the new ones."

"They'll be the first to go. The Russians know where they are. If we're lucky, they've lost track of old 647."

After fifteen minutes of reformating the commands to ensure that the satellite would report its status after each maneuver, Munos called his supervisor back to the control console.

"I think I've got everything in the right sequence," he reported. "Cross your fingers."

"Don't sweat it." His supervisor said reassuringly. "If you break it, we'll just never know what hit us." And you'll be out of a job, he added to himself.

Munos pressed the transmit command.

<u>Geostationary Sector XVIII-E1,</u>
<u>22,000 miles above the Indian Ocean   00.26 ZULU</u>

Munos' message spurted into high earth orbit from the sixty-foot disk at the Sunnyvale Satellite Control facility. It bounced off the transponder on Defense Satellite Communications System's DSCS Eastpac and down to the Pacific Command's switching station in Wahiawa, Hawaii, where it was flung back up to DSCS Westpac. From there, it beamed across deep space directly to the dormant DSP 647.

Twenty feet long, nine feet in diameter, the old early-warning satellite stretched out two long arms with disk antennas attached to the ends. It then rolled over a quarter turn, little jets of gas yawning into the void. An electro-optical eye popped open and fixed on the sun. Slowly, the long, dark cylinder swung around until its twelve-foot Schmidt infrared telescope was properly aligned. A metal shield over one end of the satellite opened like an iris. The sun's rays flooded inside, exciting thousands of lead sulfide detectors.

The forty-foot dishes at the ground station in Nurrungar, a remote clearing in the jungle of Australia's Northwest Territory, first received the word that DSP East Code 647 was alive and well. Processed in twin IBM 360-75J computers, the signal was relayed by radio three hundred miles northwest to Adelaide, where it switched to an undersea cable which traveled the Pacific emerging from San Francisco Bay near the AT&T building by the embarcadero. From there, Pacific Telesis passed the message on its main telephone trunk line down the peninsula to Sunnyvale.

Hector Munos cheered.

His supervisor decided to give him one more chance.

Missile Warning Center
North American Air Defense Command,
Cheyenne Mountain, Colorado   00:32 ZULU

The message from the Code 647 satellite was retransmitted in near real time on a microwave link to Peterson AFB in Colorado Springs, and then passed by telephone wires up the mountain to NORAD's Missile Warning Center. It did not improve Captain Rasenbruck's mood.

"Great! It can see the sun," the Captain said. "But can that old turkey see a missile launch? Can it tell the difference between one or a hundred coming at us? We've got three other DSPs on orbit already." His voice rose in frustration. "What we need are *radars*."

The Condition Yellow exercise had caught the two officers and four enlisted men at the Warning Center with more than half their radars either inoperable or down for scheduled maintenance. The Center consisted of two steel-sided trailers suspended by giant springs and shock absorbers inside a huge man-made cave deep within Cheyenne Mountain. It was linked to the rest of NORAD by a network of tunnels that could be sealed off by massive steel blast doors twelve feet tall and three feet thick. Though responsible for warning of a Soviet rocket attack, the Center had no operational control over the systems that provided the crucial data.

"What does Fylingdales say?" Captain Rasenbruck demanded from his communications specialist. He stood in front of a polar projection of the Northern Hemisphere pointing at a red light in the north of England.

"The Brits are pretty huffy. They say it's not their exercise, and they can't drop work, and I quote, 'Every time some Yank General wants to sound the colours.'"

Captain Rasenbruck sighed. There was nothing he could do. "Why a yellow light on Cobra Dane?" He put his finger on   Shemya island in the Aleutians.

"They're expecting a Soviet missile test impacting in Kamchatka. That takes priority over an exercise."

Captain Rasenbruck continued around the perimeter of the United States. The radar at Clear, Alaska, was down for scheduled maintenance and could not be turned on for forty-eight hours. The PARCs at Grand Forks, Wyoming, had a computer malfunction and could not be on line for twelve hours. The prognosis was only slightly better for the PAVE PAWS radars at Otis AFB on Cape Cod and at Beal AFB in California.

"We've still got most of the DEW line and BEMEWs. And Thule's operational," Rasenbruck's deputy said optimistically.

"Terrific! Let's just hope the Russians don't send a flock of homing pigeons over to attack them, or we won't know what the hell's going on!" He looked at the map again and finally shrugged. "Well, let's just thank God it's only an exercise."

Room 306, Old Executive Office Building, Washington, D.C.   00:42 ZULU

Loggerman was impressed. The display on the wall of the Electronic Situation Room glowed in four colors providing a schematic of the US command, control, communications, and intelligence system. Unlike the cramped and spartan Sit Room located in the basement of the White House, Room 306 of the Old Executive Office Building had high, molded ceilings, heavy silk brocaded drapes, a broad mahogany conference table with brass antique inkwells inset at each place, and every available media display device. Built during the first Reagan Administration, the room was widely known as "Allen's Folly," after the President's first National Security Advisor. In building the room, Allen had made only two mistakes. The first was to let State, Defense, and CIA know he planned to have all their communications come through the new Electronic Sit Room. They immediately refused to cooperate. Even more important, the room was not actually in the White House, but in the large antebellum building across Executive Avenue. No Cabinet officers wanted to go to meetings in a place that former Vice President Mondale dubbed "Baltimore." Thus, only junior people showed up, undermining Allen's effectiveness and downgrading his status.

Now, for the first time, the full potential of the room was being realized. The rear projection screen enabled Loggerman to check on all US strategic weapons and command and control systems just as if he were the Commander of SAC.

MEECN, the Minimum Essential Emergency Communications Network—a two-way hardened teletype link between SAC Headquarters and the Minuteman silos—showed in green, indicating it was operationally ready. GWEN, the Ground Wave Emergency Network of seventy-five relay stations, each equipped with three hundred–foot transmission towers, showed 80 percent availability. The Fleet Satellite Communications System of the Navy and AFSATCOM, the corresponding Air Force System, were fully operational and linked up with MILSTAR, the Military Strategic, Tactical, and Relay Network. MILSTAR's three polar and four geostationary orbit satellites each reported that their systems for automatic evasive action in case of attack had been enabled.

With a hand-held controller, Loggerman flipped through several more displays stopping at one labeled ERCS. His aide, Colonel Brandt, explained that ERCS stood for Emergency Rocket Communications. The system consisted of old Minuteman III ICBMs with radios fitted in their nose cones. As a last resort, they would be fired straight up and would be able to broadcast launch orders for half an hour.

The upper-left-hand corner of the screen indicated that SAC's "Looking Glass" airborne command post had taken off from Ellsworth AFB, South Dakota, and two aircraft from the Airborne Launch Control System squadron had also converted to airborne alert.

"That blinking red indicator in the lower right says AMCC, what does that mean?" Loggerman asked.

"That the JCS is in the process of staffing up the Alternate Military Command Center at Ft. Ritchie, Maryland. That's their hardened site."

"And what happens to us?" Loggerman said, unable to hide the concern and surprise in his voice.

"We can relocate, too, if you think it's time."

"No, no. Everything's under control." Loggerman fell into an uneasy silence. "Well, except for some of the radars, it all seems in good shape," he finally said.

"They do a fine job," Colonel Brandt agreed. "Of course, none of this stuff will work if the Soviets strike first."

Alternate Military Command Center, Fort Ritchie, Maryland   00:47 ZULU

Sergeant Darnella Wilson was known as the "Queen of the Rock." For almost twenty years, as officers rotated in and out, she had managed to remain, largely because nobody else wanted to spend their days three hundred feet underground. She had become essential to maintenance and upkeep of the AMCC, and she felt very inconvenienced by the alert.

"Code Yellow, Condition Yellow, Mellow Yellow! I don't care what you call it," she said. "Plain decency would've given us some advance notice."

Colonel Kranich, who had helicoptered the seventy-five miles from Washington with urgent orders to get the "Rock" ready, was not interested in her complaints. A fastidious bachelor and graduate of the Citadel, he had made his career "kicking ass" as a general's aide. He hated the Navy, the Air Force, black people, and women in the military in ascending order of intensity. He was unfailingly polite to all of these until he lost his patience. Sergeant Darnella Wilson was a severe test.

"Sergeant, it's your responsibility, and that of your superiors, to have this place available for immediate occupancy," he insisted. They were standing in a huge room with row after row of desks. The low ceiling reinforced the sense of being hundreds of feet under ground.

"Hey, don't talk about my superiors. They don't know nothin'. And call me 'Queenie,' you expect t'get somethin' done around here."

"All right." He paused, trying one last time to be civil. "Queenie, I need some answers. What about water?"

"Well, we a little short there. Full complement, there's enough for two weeks, maybe. With this drought I had to use some water to keep these plants alive." She gestured to the forest of ferns and begonias on the desks.

"And the food?"

"Ain't nothin' I can do right away about the meat. It's frozen in five hundred–pound packages. As soon as it thaws some, I can microwave it. Canned and frozen vegetables okay. Salad fixins we'll get fresh as long as we can."

"Why does this list say you have ten thousand pounds of chicken?"

"This is Maryland! We *invented* chicken! Besides, now that all the big brass finally come hide out here, the cook says he's gonna have a chance to do his special recipe for Chicken Maryland."

"Oh? I cook that," Colonel Kranich said, trying to be friendly. "What's his recipe?"

"Well, first you got to preheat Maryland to two thousand degrees."

Headquarters of the Supreme High Command,
Gadanya Forest   50 km Northeast of Moscow
00:53 ZULU

Marshal Ogorodnik was satisfied with his inspection of the bunker for the Stavka VKG. However, he maintained his troubled frown.

"Now, a report on readiness measures," he commanded from his seat at the apex of the broad, crescent-shaped table. Below him, in the pit, a briefing officer moved to a large map of the Soviet Union.

"Three Railcar Command Posts have departed their staging areas," he began. "From Kazan toward the southeast, from Neperopetrovsk to the north, and from Hkaberovsk toward the east. The Stavka train from Irkutsk is delayed indefinitely."

"What's the matter?" demanded the Marshal.

"No locomotive. The local party chief is using it."

Marshal Ogorodnik flicked his wrist toward one of his aides, who quickly began scribbling a note.

The map changed to show a polar projection of the earth with Canada and the US at the top.

"We have fully coordinated all planning for the United States theater of military operations." He pointed to the initials TVD, which stood for *Teatr Veonnykh Deistvii*. "We have placed the three air armies at

Smolensk, Venitza, and Moscow on ground alert. We are in direct contact with PVO STRANY at their underground headquarters on the other side of Moscow."

"What are their plans?"

"They are coordinating coverage between the early warning radars"—his pointer tapped at Minsk, Novgorod, Tallinn, Pechora, Krasnoyarsk, Irkutsk, and Sary Shagan—"with the Cosmos 2117 and 2128 satellites. We are having some trouble with the ground station at Kalinin, so we must work through the one down here at Yepatoriya," he explained, pointing to a spot near the Crimea.

"If they use aircraft, we will bring the full weight of the PVO STRANY to defeat them."

"Including the Stealth bombers?"

"Yes sir, if we can find them."

The Marshal sighed. "Continue."

"If they use rockets, we can of course defend Moscow with our anti-ballistic missiles. The Space Defense system is only a prototype, but we will use the two lasers at Sary Shagan and the particle generator at Samipalastinsk if the targets present themselves in the appropriate aspect."

"And if the Americans are that stupid. What are the chances of intercepting them?"

"With the Moscow system, eighty percent."

"So, if they launch ten, two weapons will get through?"

"Actually, with decoys, many more could get through."

"All of them?"

"Once the radar is hit, yes," he admitted. "With the lasers and particle beam we can hit sixty percent of the objects, including decoys."

"So, there's no defense," Marshal Ogorodnik concluded.

"PVO STRANY also has developed a plan to use its aircraft to intercept single incoming warheads with nuclear air defense missiles."

"They'll do more damage than the Americans!" the Marshal exclaimed. "Tell them no! What of our offensive forces?"

"The Strategic Rocket Forces have instituted a limited alert. Crews are being called back to their submarines in Arkhangelsk and Petropavlovsk. The rail mobile missile squadrons are dispersing. The heavy ICBMs at Dombarovskiy, Imeni Gastello, and Zhangiz Tobe are proceeding toward full alert." His hand swung in an arch around the southern rim of the USSR "The rest of the SRF is being brought to a six-hour launch status."

"Good." The Marshal relaxed his frown and allowed himself a cigarette. "Anything else?"

"Yes, the counter-measures plan."

"Proceed."

"It has three stages. The purpose is to disrupt and confuse the American early-warning systems. First, we would ignite flare gases from the two refineries near our missile fields here in the south. That will overload their older infrared satellites. Their KH-12 photo reconnaissance satellites will confirm the existence of the fires, and they will not know if they are being subject to camouflage.

"Second, we request authority to begin deploying space mines from Cosmos 2261. We do not have enough mother satellites on station, so we would propose to launch another 2261 from Kapustan Yar. We will target the polar and geostationary orbits of Milstar."

"They are recallable?" asked the Marshal.

"It would take several missions for our space plane to collect them. But the mines would accompany the target from some distance away. The nuclear ones would get no closer than five hundred kilometers. Nothing would happen without further commands.

"We are also prepared to begin jamming on all the known frequencies of the other American satellites. Our agents inside the National Security Agency have given us an excellent list.

"Finally, we request authority to alert some sabotage assets that would be directed at American ground-based communications. We have in mind the satellite control facility in Sunnyvale, California, and the AT&T switching centers in San Francisco; Lyons, Nebraska; Fairview, Kansas; Hillsboro, Missouri; and Lamar, Colorado. This program would not be activated, only agents placed on notice that an operation was possible."

Marshal Ogorodnik was pleased with the plans. A substantial increase in capability had been achieved with just enough outward evidence for the Americans to take notice.

"Everything is approved." He paused. "Except for the sabotage teams. Let's wait a few hours for that."

72

US Embassy, Paris, France   01:16 ZULU

Sean Gordon began to write on plain white stationery with no letterhead.

Ted Gordon
Amherst College
Amherst, MA 01002
USA

Dear Son:

I was going to write you a short note, as I usually do, saying, "Sorry we haven't talked. I love you and hope to see you soon." But I may not see you soon, and I thought I owed you an explanation. I guess I need one myself.

At this moment, I'm searching for a disturbed young man, not much older than you, who has in his hands the power to set off a chain reaction of events that may engulf the earth in a nuclear war. But it is not his madness alone that has brought the world to this point.

Remember your history paper on the arms race in Europe before the First World War? What if scientists of that day had explained to the Czar, Kaiser, or King that they had invented a fantastic new weapon that could smash Moscow, or Paris, or Berlin, or London? How many would they have wanted? Four or five? A dozen to be safe? Two dozen to ward off any conceivable combination of enemies? Fifty to conquer the world?

Now that the world has a thousand times more than that, the quantity of nuclear weapons are another statistic that makes our minds numb. The number of cities and military bases in the US and USSR has long been eclipsed by the number of weapons. Instead of weapons, we're really deploying targets for the enemy. A weapon on one side merely justifies a weapon on the other; people are irrelevant. And, inevitably, out of the tens of thousands of atomic bombs in the world, one has finally found its way into the hands of a deluded terrorist.

You once asked me what would happen if a nuclear weapon went off by accident, and I said with complete confidence that beyond the immediate tragedy, nothing would happen. I had been taught that governments were rational. The threat of total destruction would force both sides to be cautious. That was deterrence, and we believed in it. As Churchill said, peace would be the sturdy child of terror. And if a few thoughtful people worried that deterrence might fail, and if we spent billions in the hope of finding a defense shield that would make nuclear weapons obsolete, most of us behaved as though deterrence would last forever.

Mankind continued to maneuver and fight, almost as if nuclear weapons had never been invented. I threw myself wholeheartedly into the struggle. There never was, and never will be any doubt in my mind that democracy is worth dying for. You know how much I love our country. Sometimes you must have thought I loved it more than I loved you.

I thought I could make a difference, could make a world that was a little freer, a little safer for you and, someday, your children. And to be honest, I liked my work. But now I can see that whatever any of us have accomplished pales to insignificance in the shadow of the growing mountain of nuclear destruction. Now a single explosion may trigger the final avalanche. In the ruins, there will be no freedom and democracy for us, no triumph of Communism for our enemies.

We've talked lately about going to church together, but somehow never found the time. If we're both lucky enough to survive the next eighteen hours, let's go and pray that the world will have learned something this time.

One letter can't make up for all the years we didn't have together. But if I don't survive and you do, try to share this with your mother. I want you to know that I always loved you both.

Sean

"Is there some way this can arrive before three o'clock tomorrow?" Gordon asked the embassy communications clerk.

"I'll make a cable, and it'll be there in an hour. Unclassified?"

"It's too late to be anything else."

73

Aboard VTA flight 7786 from Moscow   02:33 ZULU

Alexander Antunov could not force himself to sleep. Alternating blasts of hot and cold air from the overhead vent had him sweating one minute, shivering the next. The din from the four turbo prop engines made his teeth hurt. The seat would not recline. And, worst of all, he could not stop trying to remember the name of the large blond man in the first row of seats. From his bland features, Antunov judged him to be a Balt, probably from Latvia, but he could not place him.

There were no windows in the An-22 military transport. The Voyennotransportanya Aviatsia provided no food or drink service. The pallet of twenty seats was bolted to rails on the floor of the cargo bay, with only a hanging padded blanket separating the passengers from the wooden crates that filled the aft section of the plane. All the seats were occupied. Everyone, except the blond man and Antunov, was in military uniform.

He closed his eyes again and tried to focus on his assignment. It was simple in concept, but tricky to execute. He landed at Schönfeld Airport, East Berlin, where he would be met by a team from the Soviet Residency in Pankow. They would enter the Western sector and proceed to Templehof Airport to intercept Horst Bauer. Antunov had been assured that the East German air traffic controllers would delay Bauer's transit through the air corridor until Antunov could put himself in place. To avoid the scores of West German police at the airport, Antunov planned to seize Bauer someplace between Templehof and the Free University where the press conference was to take place.

Both the General Secretary and Fyakov had stressed that it was not enough to prevent the press conference. He must also capture Bauer alive. If Bauer could be forced to reveal the full extent of his connections with the GRU, the General Secretary might have a decisive political weapon against Marshal Ogorodnik and, as Fyakov put it, "his clique of military adventurists."

Antunov realized that the Chairman of the KGB had manipulated him into taking the side of the General Secretary in the power struggle, while he himself played a more cautious game. If Chalomchev prevailed, Antunov would be the symbol of the KGB's loyalty. If he lost, the KGB Chairman would excise Antunov like a nasty splinter.

With these unhappy thoughts, he began to doze off. But, after a moment, he awoke with a start. The Latvian was staring at him.

Defense Nuclear Agency, Ft. Belvoir, Virginia
03:27 ZULU

Sandy Warren sat alone in the makeshift operations center. He had been depressed since the focus of the search effort had shifted to the White House. Why had the Admiral left him out of it? Over and over, he told himself that McCollough had other fish to fry besides worrying about his assistant's ego. Still, Warren could not help feeling rejected and resentful. He stayed later and later at the office, as though his mere presence would create something to do. Besides, he knew his wife did not want him around the house when he was in one of his moods.

Make yourself useful, he said to himself. "Doing what?" he grumped. Warren got up from the long table and began prowling around the room, looking at the various intelligence reports tacked to the walls.

One item caught his eye. The NATO Headquarters at Casteau, Belgium, had reported that the NEDS 911 system at Antwerp had registered two dings earlier that evening. The NEDS 900 series of detectors had been developed in the 1960s as a way to monitor the presence of nuclear weapons aboard Soviet warships transiting the Dardanelles from the Black Sea. After the Three Mile Island disaster, a more sophisticated version, the NEDS 910 series, was developed by the Department of Energy. Unclassified versions were used for power reactor monitoring. NEST teams used a classified design, the 911, which was also deployed at US ports as a way to detect nuclear weapons aboard the increasing number of Soviet merchant ships entering American harbors. By the eighties, with the deepening European concern about anything nuclear, the NEDS 911 began to be deployed along the Baltic and Channel ports. However, the system generally proved useless and was often ignored. Though extremely sensitive, it averaged a false alarm every twenty-four–forty-eight hours.

Warren searched through the master stack of intelligence cables looking for more NEDS 911 reports. Since France refused to deploy it, he concentrated on Belgium, Holland, and England. Halfway through the pile, he found another NEDS 911. It was from Ostend at 02:13 ZULU.

Sandy Warren told himself to calm down. It could just be a coincidence. Besides, what boat could travel that fast along the coast? Maybe a car, but even so, the detectors were out in the harbors.

He sat back, disappointed. They simply had to be false alarms.

74

Spitsbergen, the Arctic Ocean   05:45 ZULU

The President's aircraft parked at the south end of the runway near cliffs that dropped to the sea. After landing, he tried to nap before the first meeting with Chalomchev. The pounding of the waves against the rocks did not help his fitful and nightmarish slumber.

Admiral McCollough's knock awakened him. He got up and started dressing. As he straightened his tie in the mirror of his cramped compartment, his eye fell on a stack of black ring binders Loggerman had given him before departure.

"Did you read the Briefing Books?" the President asked McCollough as he entered the small mess room where breakfast was being served. The Admiral looked startled. "Don't worry"—the President sat down—"I didn't, either. It amazes me. He only had an hour and he comes up with a four-foot stack of paper. Do you think he just cleaned out his files?"

The President's personal valet poured coffee and served a crenshaw melon.

"We also have messages from Loggerman," said Admiral Mc-Collough opening a manila folder.

"You mean instructions, don't you?" The President grimaced. A piece of melon slipped off his spoon. He let it lay on the tablecloth. "What does he say the chances are that the Russians will accept the proposal in my letter?"

"About as much as we have of accepting the Russians' excuses."

"Is that all he says?" the President asked.

"He sent a list of the Condition Yellow measures. They look reasonable, but Karl warns that we may have to do more, depending on the Soviet reaction. And then there's this." McCollough held up a twelve-page message; the fan folds fell to the floor.

"These are the points the NSC says the Soviets have to accept to make a mutual nuclear withdrawal acceptable to us."

"You know," the President paused, "there is no hope. Here we are on the brink of nuclear war, and my august advisors in the National Security Council act as though we're negotiating a lease."

"I wonder what kind of advice Chalomchev's getting."

"He doesn't need any," said the President, pushing away his half-eaten melon. "That old bastard could just tell his people what to do or ship 'em to Siberia. I, however, am merely the leader of the Free World. That means I barely control my own Administration, and forget the Congress. 'E Pluribus Unum' has been replaced by 'Every Man for Himself.'" The President stood up from the table.

"Any news from Gordon?"

"No, sir, he's just sitting and waiting in Paris. We've no more leads on Culver's whereabouts."

"I hope to God Chalomchev is not as pig-headed and blind as he seems," the President said as he stopped at the door. "I worry that he's got no idea what the world will be like if these weapons start going off."

"Do you want to get the staff together to review all this material before the meeting?" McCollough gestured to the Loggerman messages and the Briefing Books.

The President shook his head. "Let's not leave our game in the locker room."

Will the world come to look like this? General Secretary Chalomchev asked himself as he looked out of his aircraft at the north end of the windswept runway. The rocky slopes of Spitsbergen appeared devoid of vegetation. In the morning half-light, Chalomchev could not see the occasional tuft of grass hidden in a crevice or the lichens clinging to the frigid stones.

But he noticed the birds. There will be no birds either, he thought. They are so fragile. Birds would be among the first to die from the radiation, he had once been told.

Chalomchev had seen much of death. As he sank into the soft leather chair in the communications room, his mind wandered back to when he was a mere boy in the Great Patriotic War against the Germans. He had served in the Party Headquarters in Leningrad. Of the half million people living there before the Nazi siege, three hundred thousand had died, mostly of hunger and disease. And afterward, there was more death from politics. Chalomchev was always surprised at even the slight sense of lingering guilt.

Stalin had always mistrusted the economic and political power of Leningrad, and left the city to fend for itself. But it withstood the Nazis, and when the war was over, Stalin would not forgive the Leningrad Party leaders. Their heroism made them an even more serious threat. Stalin turned on Leningrad with a vengeance. Every Party member senior to Chalomchev was purged, executed, murdered. And as they said of Chalomchev's survival and subsequent rise to power, "It was no accident, Comrade."

So I have blood on them, said Chalomchev silently, looking at the back of his hands and how the hardening veins stood out. That is the burden of leadership, he assured himself. Americans talk so much about the value of human life, and yet they invented the atomic bomb; they entrust it to madmen, and now spin bizarre theories of retaliation. We have known revolution and war on our own soil. It is Russia that understands suffering, he concluded, and the true value of human life.

The Soviet General Secretary glanced again at the President's letter, rereading the last line. "In view of your historical support of nuclear-free zones in Europe, I hope you will agree that a mutual withdrawal of nuclear weapons offers a prompt and peaceful way out of this crisis."

How, Chalomchev wondered, could the President be so naive?

Despite the secrecy supposedly surrounding the meeting, the President was greeted by a sea of staff members as he disembarked his aircraft. There were a dozen Secret Service, eight White House Communications Agency technicians, three NSC staff members, two Sit Room communicators, an aide from the Military Office carrying the "football" with the nuclear release codes, four Philippine stewards, six secretaries, Admiral McCollough, an interpreter, and an official photographer.

The American group, with the President and Secret Service forming a nucleus, merged with an even larger Russian mass which had collected in front of Hangar B. The two leaders met and shook hands in a blaze of strobe lights from the official photographers. The President found Chalomchev's hands strong and surprisingly callused. The General Secretary wore a heavy coat and a gray fedora pulled down hard over his head against the wind. The President had decided not to wear a coat or hat, and thought he might freeze if they did not move inside quickly. But the General Secretary held on to his hand, smiling for his own cameras and making remarks that no one could hear over the noise of the crowd and the roar of the wind.

At last, the tall hangar doors opened a crack and they could slip inside. As the doors again crashed together, the men were enveloped in silence. The President tried a small joke to ease the tension.

"Now I know why my predecessors preferred meeting you in Geneva."

Chalomchev's smile for the photographers had vanished. He treated the remark seriously.

"We could not have met secretly in Geneva," he said heavily. "If you would permit the Norwegians to give us our rightful sovereignty over this island, we could provide more hospitality."

He's not going to make it easy, the President warned himself.

The others withdrew, and six of them sat down at a long wide table, which, in Soviet imperial style, had been placed directly in the middle of the cavernous hangar bay. The General Secretary sat Dimitri Fyakov to his left, and to his right Pyotr Nemchev, the renowned Soviet interpreter who had served every Soviet leader and known every American President for over forty years. The President placed Admiral McCollough to his right. The interpreter sat on the left. He would only take notes, since by custom Nemchev would do all the interpreting.

The President opened his hands and nodded in the universal gesture for the other side to begin. The Soviet leader looked left and right at his own aides, and asked, "Didn't the United States propose this meeting? Mr. President, you should speak first."

The President did not like the sense that Chalomchev was already taking control.

"My letter states our proposal. The demands this terrorist is making—"

"You've not found him?" Chalomchev interrupted.

"He's disappeared again." The President brushed the question aside.

A faint expression conveying disgust at American incompetence crossed the General Secretary's face. The President could feel his temper stir.

"The demand for a unilateral US withdrawal of nuclear weapons is impossible," the President continued. "However, if we take this opportunity to announce that we both will withdraw our weapons from Europe—"

"The American proposal is unacceptable," Chalomchev said flatly.

The President acted as though he had not heard the rejection. "The Soviet government," he continued, "has itself proposed nuclear-free zones—"

"You fail to understand the nature of our meeting here," the General Secretary interrupted again. "The Soviet government views these discussions as taking place under duress—in fact, under the threat of nuclear attack. Naturally, any agreement in such circumstances is out of the question."

The President stared hard at the General Secretary. "Then why did you bother to meet?"

"I could not forgo the opportunity to urge you personally to abandon this mad plan to attack the Soviet Union," Chalomchev responded, his voice rising. "You claim the right to attack us, perhaps kill millions of my countrymen, because one of your own bombs, stolen by one of your own people, goes off on your own side! If you do this, I guarantee that the Strategic Rocket Forces of the Soviet Union will inflict the most terrible retribution." He slammed his fat fist on the table. "Cancel this plan! Decency demands it!"

The President could feel himself shaking inside. He kept his hands spread on the table so they would not tremble. And what if I just overruled Loggerman and the rest of them in Washington, he suddenly thought to himself. If the damned thing goes off, we just try to hold NATO together the best we can. He searched the unyielding face of the Soviet leader. No, the President concluded, I can compromise, but I can't lose. Or this bastard will never stop pushing me.

"Decency?" the President began quietly. "You want to talk about decency? We wouldn't be here if your government wasn't supporting every terrorist who crawls out from under a rock and claims the right to murder innocent people in the name of revolution. You've supported Bauer for years! And still do, for all I know!"

"I will not listen to slander. The Soviet Union abhors terrorism in all forms—"

"You invited me to talk," the President shot back, "and you'd better listen up. I wanted to avoid a useless exercise in laying blame. Yes, the weapon's ours and we bear responsibility. But the trail of conspiracy leads directly to the Kremlin, and you know it."

"If you kill millions of innocent people, you will be the biggest terrorist in history. There's no logic to it!"

The President fought the urge to shout, innocent people? What about Afghanistan, and Hungary, and Czechoslovakia, and Poland, and Ethiopia and . . .

Admiral McCollough pushed a note in front of him. "He's had his outburst. Try again."

The President took an even breath. The walls and the high-arched ceiling of the hangar receded into the gloom. The huge space had become a small pool of light. Silence gathered around them. The President forced himself to be calm.

"The logic of our plan to retaliate against you is the same logic as your threat to retaliate against us. It's the logic of nuclear deterrence, and it has underpinned the balance of power that has kept the peace for a half-century." Christ, the President cursed himself, I sound like Loggerman.

"If this weapon goes off," he continued, "the balance of power will be destroyed. I can't permit that. I'm trying to preserve the balance, save the system that has protected both of us for so long."

"Forgive me if I sound like an old Bolshevik." Chalomchev sat back in his chair. "But maybe the system is the problem."

"Any alternate proposals you'd like to make," the President tapped his watch, "we've got a whole ten hours."

Chalomchev looked at him carefully for a moment, then theatrically opened his eyes in mock astonishment.

"Now I understand! You believe your own propaganda! You don't think that we have politics in Russia. You think we're a nation of children and I—Ivan Illyich Chalomchev—I am the big bully who tells the rest what to do. In Russia, politics isn't a game like in your country. Your President Nixon tries to usurp all powers of government and the worst that happens is that he must go and live in New Jersey. When Stalin did that, we had to kill him.

"I don't have the power to do half what you ask. And if I tried, I would be replaced without ceremony. Those who would take over wouldn't even sit down with you. They would answer your threats with a mailed fist!" The Chairman paused, breathing heavily. Then he broke into English for the first time.

"So in your court I am afraid sits the ball, isn't it?"

75

The White House   06:13 ZULU

The National Security Advisor was lying awake in the White House bomb shelter. Built in the second World War, it consisted of a cot, two benches, a sink, and a toilet in an eight-foot-square room lined with sandbags under the basement kitchens. They must keep this antique here to show to the tourists, Loggerman thought. It wouldn't protect the President from a Hessian cannonball, let alone a nuclear strike.

He hated the iron bedstead and other GSA fixtures. The thought of dying in an iron bed wrapped in army blankets was worse than the thought of dying at all. Loggerman wished he was in his own bed under his own down comforter with his cat. It was good of Rege to stay another night to care for the cat.

The heavy metal door opened. The Sit Room Duty Officer poked his head through.

"Your call to the President is coming in."

The National Security Advisor felt ridiculous running through the corridors to the West Wing dressed in silk pajamas, his slippers slapping on the carpet. He took the call in the Oval Office.

"Mr. President, did you get my messages? Oh, you've already met . . ." He listened to the President's report. He sounded terrible.

"I warned you they'd be unyielding," Loggerman finally said. "They take your proposal to meet and arrange a mutual pull-back as a sign of weakness . . . that you don't want to retaliate—" The President's response was so loud Loggerman jerked the phone from his ear.

"Of course," Loggerman tried to mollify the President, "no one *wants* to retaliate, but they think they can just pressure you into doing nothing. That's what the Soviet alert is all about."

"Yes, I've read the intelligence. I sent it to you . . . I know half our radars are out . . . It's a fire in southern Russia . . . No, we don't know if it's deliberate, but I doubt they'd burn up two refineries . . . NORAD doesn't know what the little objects are. Space mines are only one possible explanation . . . Yes, but two of five air armies are *not* on alert . . . Sure, the JCS is worried . . . They're paid to worry . . ."

Loggerman listened, shaking his head impatiently. He sat down in the President's chair.

"Certainly, I take it seriously. But the Russians are just foot-shuffling. The point is political, to get you rattled."

"No sir, I'm not saying you're rattled. If you want, we can take some steps, too. The JCS would feel a lot more comfortable if we got all the Stealth bombers airborne and put the tankers on five-minute alert. And the Space Shield too, for what it's worth . . ."

Loggerman rolled his eyes in dismay as he listened to the President resist.

"Well, you can't have it both ways . . . Yes, State Orange is supposed to mean that nuclear war is *likely*, but those are only words. It can mean whatever we want . . . they're not threatening moves . . . yes, sir . . . fine . . . one last thing, did you include the troop cut?"

"It was in my message," Loggerman said, annoyance creeping into his voice. "The Joint Chiefs are going through the roof. They say they can't defend Europe without nuclear weapons unless the Soviets also pull out some troops . . . about fifteen divisions . . ."

Loggerman had to yank the phone away from his ear again.

"No, I'm not trying to make it impossible. That's why we've always opposed nuclear-free zones in Europe . . . Yes, it's complicated. If it was easy, Ronald Reagan would've done it . . . Well, if they show interest in pulling back the nukes, then hit 'em with the troop cut . . . I'll be here all night."

Loggerman hung up. He swiveled around and put his palms on the President's desk. It felt right to be sitting there. He told himself he had made the right choice, to stay in Washington and make decisions. The feelings of anxiety had passed. Whatever the outcome, he was confident he could play his part with dignity.

The Sit Room line chimed. "It's a Sandy Warren from the Defense Nuclear Agency. Do you want to take it?"

"No, not now," Loggerman said. "I ought to get dressed."

The Kremlin   06:51 ZULU

The Defense Minister arrived early and eased his bulk into the Chairman's seat. For the first time, he would lead the Defense Council. Without the crisis, the General Secretary would never have permitted it. The texture of the leather chair and the sweep of the long table gave him a feeling of power he found almost sensual. He let his mind linger on the fantasy of Madame Tryanova on her knees beneath the table ministering to him while he conducted the meeting.

"You look very happy." It was Marshal Ogorodnik. "I hoped you would come early. We must coordinate to ensure the proper outcome of this session."

"Yes, of course." The Defense Minister banished his erotic thoughts, hoping his embarrassment did not show.

"You've read the report of the Spitsbergen meeting?"

The Defense Minister nodded.

"Now there can be no illusions about what the Americans intend," Marshal Ogorodnik said, slowly walking around the table, the steel in the heels of his boots clicking smartly on the marble floor. "They plan to inflict a massive humiliation on us. This has been a provocation all along."

"The Foreign Minister believes that we should accept a mutual nuclear withdrawal—"

"Because the fool has often proposed it himself? Do you think we would have let him do that if we thought the Americans might agree? Mark my words, nuclear weapons are only the bait. If we show any interest, the President will insist we also pull out our troops. That's their real goal. To get us out of Eastern Europe and break up the Warsaw Pact!"

"I think he has the Chairman of the Council of Ministers convinced, and the Chairman of Gosplan is leaning—"

"And how many divisions do they have?" Ogorodnik challenged. "Anyone who accepts an agreement under American threats is a traitor! Even the KGB agrees with me. Look at their reports." He threw a black envelope on the table.

"You see, the Stealth bombers are airborne. And look, they are putting their strategic defense shield on alert."

"What does that prove?" the Minister asked doubtfully.

"We don't know where the Stealth bombers are!" Marshal Ogorodnik exclaimed. "Any minute, one could be right over the Kremlin ready to drop a nuclear bomb on us. And the defense shield is a deception. Our missiles can get right through it."

"Isn't that good?"

"No! Its true purpose is to destroy our satellites. Leave us blind and mute, unable to control our forces."

"Does our special source in Washington say they are planning a full-scale attack?"

"He doesn't know," the Marshal said contemptuously. "He believes they're trying to frighten us into thinking that they're prepared to do so. It amounts to the same thing."

"What can we do?" The Defense Minister suddenly did not want the responsibility of being the Chairman of the Defense Council.

"We must go to Vigilance Level Two. That will make clear that we cannot be intimidated. And that idiot General Secretary must stop encouraging them to think we are going to capitulate." Marshal Ogorodnik paused to light a cigarette. "He must be ordered to break off the talks."

76

US Embassy Residence, Paris   07:02 ZULU

Slumped on the couch in the library, Sean Gordon dozed fitfully, dreaming again and again of having an intense argument with Laura. Graciela was also asleep, her head in his lap. Though deeply disappointed by her breakdown on the phone with Culver, Gordon had tried to reassure her. Maybe they would get another lead. Maybe the President could work out something with the Russians. He had no faith in what he said, but in time she calmed down and fell asleep on his shoulder. Her warmth and softness stirred memories of Laura and pangs of guilt. He had felt emotionally exhausted and yet aroused at the same time, as if the prospect of death urged the body to keep the species alive.

The knock was soft but insistent. When Gordon opened his eyes, bright morning sunlight flooded through the tall French windows.

"Who is it?"

A young Marine guard peeked in the door. He saw Graciela curled up with Gordon and blushed.

"Excuse me, sir, there's a secure call. You can take it in the Ambassador's study."

It was Admiral McCollough. Gordon grew increasingly depressed listening to the report of the meeting with Chalomchev and of the growing mobilization on both sides.

"There's one ray of hope," McCollough added. "It's a long shot, but one of my staff guys just sent me a backchannel saying that several NEDS 911 detectors along the Channel coast have gone off in a sequence. At first, he thought they were random false alarms. But now he's got a set of readings that started in Ostend about 2 A.M. last night and go right on up to Amsterdam."

"When was that one?"

"An hour ago. But what could it be?" the Admiral asked. "No boat could move that fast."

"You're the expert." Gordon did not think much of McCollough's ray of hope.

"Except maybe a hydrofoil," the Admiral added.

Graciela came into the room rubbing her eyes. "Any news?" she asked.

"Nothing good, unless you know of a hydrofoil that runs from Paris to Amsterdam."

"Not from Paris, but from Le Havre. A sleeper that stops along the coast. Terry and I were going to take it once."

"Chip! That's it!" Gordon shouted into the phone. "We'll leave immediately for Amsterdam. Alert everybody. Move the NEST team—"

"Amsterdam?" Graciela put her hand on the mouthpiece of the telephone. "Amsterdam," she said again. "No. He won't stay there."

"It's better than sitting here," Gordon snapped, "unless you think he's coming back to Paris!"

Unfazed by his anger, she shook her head slowly as if lost in

thought. "But I know where he's going next. Or maybe I should say
. . . last."

Templehof Airport, West Berlin   07:11 ZULU

"That aircraft landed over an hour ago."

Alexander Antunov could not believe what the Soviet Liaison Officer
was telling him. "But the East German air controllers were supposed
to delay it until I could—"

"The delay was countermanded."

"Countermanded? Impossible. By who?" Antunov was growing
more baffled by the minute.

"Stavka GSFG."

The headquarters of the Group of Soviet Forces Germany! Antunov
was stunned. The military had sabotaged his mission. He ordered his
men back to the cars.

For forty minutes, Antunov struggled through rush-hour traffic
across town to the Free University where the press conference was set
for 10 A.M. Spread over a ten-block area in the suburb of Dahlin, the
Free University occupied a score of grand old houses seized from the
Nazis, who themselves had taken many of them from Berlin's Jews.
Contributions from the United States established the Free University,
but it soon reflected the contrary character of Berlin by becoming a
bastion of left-wing radicalism and anti-Americanism.

Antunov pulled up in front of one of the few buildings specifically
constructed for the campus, the Henry Ford Auditorium. It was
draped with a huge red-and-black banner, US NUKES GET OUT—NO
EUROSHIMAS.

His men reconnoitered the outside of the building while Antunov
went inside. A plain-faced young woman in surplus army fatigues and
a butch haircut manned an information desk. She did not know
Bauer's whereabouts. The session with the press was open to the
public, he could go right in.

With less than an hour to go before the conference, Antunov knew
that if he tried to stop it he would create an incident that would give

Bauer's story credibility. But he was still determined to apprehend Bauer.

While his men took up positions near the doors, he settled into an inconspicuous seat at the rear of the auditorium where he could have a good view of the proceedings. A bare table sat in the middle of the stage. Next to it, students fitted a lecturn with a microphone and connected it to a mult-box. To the left, several other students completed the installation of risers. A few camera crews were already setting up their tripods. It appeared that the news conference would be well attended by the television media.

Only a handful of press had arrived, among them a large blond man sitting in the front row. Antunov recognized him. It was the man whose name he could not remember. The man on the flight from Moscow. The Latvian.

<u>Aboard the Hohenzollern Express, near Magdeburg,</u>
<u>German Democratic Republic   07:53 ZULU</u>

Riding backward, Culver stared out the compartment window at the receding landscape. For the last twelve hours, his mind had focused on only one thing: Horst Bauer was alive. Even the thrill of hearing Graciela's voice had been eclipsed by his obsession with Bauer. And he would be in Berlin. It could not be more perfect.

Culver made an odd sight. He had strapped the SADM to his chest with its parachute harness. To cover it, he wore an oversized raincoat. The weapon filled his lap, and made it difficult to breathe.

On the bench opposite, a young German couple prepared a breakfast snack for their children. The man held a bottle for his infant son while his wife carved a slice of cheese for their four-year-old daughter. The little girl held it out for Culver.

"*Essen für Kris Kringle.*"

She broke through the spiral of his thoughts. The kid thinks I'm Santa Claus, he thought, and smiled nervously. You don't want this present.

"*Nein,*" the young woman scolded, pulling the little girl onto her lap. She then asked in English, "Would you like something also?"

Surprised, Culver accepted their hospitality. The man introduced himself as Kurt Lauk. His wife's name was Greta. The boy was Bruno, the five-year-old girl Renata. They all had just spent a week in Hannover with the children's grandparents.

Kurt rocked Bruno to sleep and Greta and Renata whispered little jokes to one another. Culver bit into her homemade sandwich of hard salami, *Braunschweiger* and *Kronkäse*. Renata started singing a familiar German nursery rhyme that first appeared during World War II after the town of Pommern in eastern Germany had been totally destroyed by Allied incendiaries.

> *Daddy is in Pommernland,*
> *It's not the baby's fault,*
> *Pommernland has all burned down,*
> *So sleep, baby, sleep.*

Culver started trembling uncontrollably. He turned to the window as his eyes filled with tears.

Aboard the Spirit of Revolution, Spitsbergen   08:12 ZULU

"We have reason to believe Culver could be headed for Berlin," Admiral McCollough said. He was standing in a small compartment near the rear stairs of Chalomchev's plane. He had never seen teak paneling in an aircraft before. It made him long for his boat.

"What reasons?" Nemchev translated as Chalomchev's eyes drilled into him.

"It's circumstantial evidence—"

"What? Tell me!" Chalomchev demanded in a voice accustomed to interrogation.

Admiral McCollough hesitated. "His girlfriend, Graciela, she claims that where he's gone so far, Venice, Vienna, Paris, Amsterdam, are all the places they went together. Berlin is the only one left." Under the Russian's withering gaze, it suddenly seemed stupid.

"This is romantic nonsense," Fyakov said.

"Maybe," Admiral McCollough allowed, "but Interpol reports that the German police found several passports in a trash bin at the Hannover railway station, near the platform for the train that goes to Berlin. Culver had been using them."

"And what's he using now?" Chalomchev asked.

"We don't know," Admiral McCollough replied.

The General Secretary hurriedly began whispering to Fyakov, holding up his hand to tell Nemchev not to translate.

"Dimitri, contact the East Germans immediately. Tell those pigs to stop all trains heading for Berlin. Give them Culver's description. If we catch him on East German territory, it will be my turn for proposals. I'll make this American President shit in his pants. We'll take care of Ogorodnik, too!"

The General Secretary turned to Admiral McCollough and smiled. "This is most important news. I suggest we postpone our next meeting to consider fully the implications."

Berlin Air Corridor   08:26 ZULU

"Say that again, Chip. I can't believe it!" Gordon was aboard his DC-9, using the scrambler phone to Spitsbergen.

"Chalomchev asked the question. I checked the alert list. Sure enough, it had all of Culver's aliases, but not his real name. He must've gotten through the inner-German border on his regular passport."

"I'll have all the train stations covered. We'll set up road blocks at the exits from the Autobahn too."

"What will the Germans say?"

"Screw 'em. We still run Berlin. How're the big boys doing?"

"Counting on you," Admiral McCollough said.

Gordon broke off, and ordered the communications chief to get the Commander of the US Berlin brigade. As he waited for the call, he strained to see an autobahn or a railroad track. From the low, ten-thousand-foot ceiling of the Berlin air corridor, farmhouses, cars, and herds of cows were clearly visible in the bright morning sunlight. He could make out what appeared to be a line of schoolchildren crossing a meadow. But no autobahn or railway. He saw a crowd in front of a small village church. In East Germany, he knew it could not be a wedding. It had to be a funeral.

<u>Aboard the Hohenzollern Express, Brandenburg,</u>
<u>German Democratic Republic   08:47 ZULU</u>

Culver had managed to fall asleep for the first time in days and did not realize the train had stopped until he heard the sliding compartment doors snap open.

"Passports!"

He looked up to see three Vopos crowded in the doorway.

As Kurt Lauk handed over his family's papers to the East German border guards, Culver fished in the inside pocket of his raincoat. He felt the two passports. Should he use his real American one, or the East German one? This was not the control point. Why had they stopped the train? His head was clearing. They were looking for him! He took out the East German document. It had helped him escape from Czechoslovakia, and he had saved it for luck.

The Vopo looked at the picture. "You've gained weight."

He pushed his chin down further onto his chest trying to make his face look fatter. "I travel in Poland and Czechoslovakia. They have nothing to eat but potatoes," Culver said.

"The damned Russians take everything," the Vopo agreed. "We send them coal, and they send us snow. Where are you going?"

"West Berlin."

"Where is your permission?"

"In the back."

"Your profession?"

"Art curator."

As this conversation continued in German, Culver could feel Kurt and Greta Lauk staring at him. They had spoken in English. He had told them he was an American.

"Where did you come from? the West?"

"No," he lied, glancing again at the Lauks. "I got on at Magdeburg." He hoped the Vopo would not ask for his ticket receipt.

Reaching through the pocket of his raincoat, he gripped the switch attached to the detonator. He knew the German compulsion to tell the truth to officials in uniform and he was beginning to sweat. But Kurt and Greta said nothing.

"What's the matter, are you sick?" the Vopo asked. "Why don't you take off that coat? Help him," he said to Kurt Lauk.

"No. It's just a little flu. I don't want to give it to anyone."

"You shouldn't be in a compartment with children," the Vopo chided him. "Here," he held out Culver's false passport, turning his head away as if to avoid contamination, and quickly backed out the door.

Culver looked at Kurt Lauk and did not know how to thank him. Kurt spoke first. *"Macht nichts,"* he said in German. "I wouldn't tell those bastards anything. They killed my uncle and my cousin at the Wall."

A few minutes later, the train started rolling. It paused at Potsdam West and then passed through the control Bahnhof, where Culver again used his East German passport. Finally, shortly after 10 A.M., the train crossed into West Berlin and stopped at the Güterbahnhof in Wannsee.

The platform exit was blocked by wooden barricades guarded by U.S. Army MPs. A sergeant was arguing with a contingent of Berlin police, while a platoon of US soldiers checked the travel documents of single arriving male passengers.

They waved the Lauk family through, including Terence Culver, who carried baby Bruno over his shoulder.

Templehof Airport, Berlin   9:10 ZULU

The pilot drove the aircraft hard onto the runway. The door was unlatched and swinging outward before the engines died and the plane came to a stop in the VIP area. Gordon was taken aback by the reception committee: three limousines, the acting CIA Chief, the head of the DOE NEST team, a representative of the US Commandant in Berlin, one representative each from Army Intelligence, Air Force Intelligence, Defense Intelligence, and even Naval Intelligence, along with the two representatives from the State Department. The only face he recognized was Billy Kelly's.

"Billy! What the hell is going on? Is this some kind of circus? Where's the TV cameras?"

"This is what you get when you file a VIP flight clearance through the State Department."

"Get everyone out of here except the CIA guy, the NEST commander, and whoever's from the Army garrison."

The State Department representatives protested as Kelly herded them into their car. "We've arranged coffee inside," said one. "We've not been informed about his purpose here," said the other. "We've not been briefed!" they complained together. Kelly slammed the door and waved.

"Sean, I've got some bad news," Kelly said as the crowd pulled away. "The train from Hannover already came in. He didn't get off at Wannsee or the Zoo Bahnhof. At least we didn't pick him up," Kelly added after a pause. "The train was pretty full, and the Berlin cops were all over us. We could've missed him."

"We haven't got time to be discouraged," Gordon replied. "He could come by car or have gone through to East Berlin and is coming back through the checkpoints. Make sure they're alert."

He spread a map of Berlin over the hood of the black Chrysler limo. "Graciela identified more than a dozen places where we might find him. You follow up on all the blue dots. The Army should cover the red ones." He pulled over the NEST team leader to take a closer look at the map. "You run a pattern starting at the Europa Center and work outward.

"Here's his picture." He handed around Culver's photo. "Make copies. I want the maximum number of patrols on the street. But don't approach the target, and keep the Berlin authorities out of it. I want all of you to report instantly any—and I mean *any*—developments. This car have a radio?"

The Station Chief nodded.

"Fine."

"Where are we going?" Kelly asked.

"Graciela thinks love brings him here. I think maybe it's hate. Let's go find Horst Bauer."

Henry Ford Auditorium,
Free University of Berlin   9:33 ZULU

Antunov was not an expert on press conferences, but this one did not appear to be going very well. It started late, and although Bauer gave a detailed statement about who stole the weapon—when, from where, even the type and serial number—the press did not seem to believe him.

Q: Where's the weapon now?
A: I don't know.
Q: Do you have it?
A: No.
Q: What proof can you give us that this story's true?
A: Check with the Americans.
Q: We have. They say they don't know what you're talking about.
Q: What's your interest in this?
A: What do you mean?
Q: How are you involved? How do you know so much about it?
A: I can't discuss my sources.
Q: We can take it on faith, buster.
Q: Did you help steal it?
A: I've nothing to say on that.
Q: Is that how you got injured?
A: No.
Q: But you don't deny being involved?
A: I never touched it.
Q: Did you ever even see it?
A: No.
Q: If you never saw it, and don't have it, and don't know where it is—how do you know it's stolen?

Bauer seemed rattled by the questioning. "You'll just have to ask the Americans," he said, his frustration obvious.

"Shit, we're just going in circles here," a US correspondent said loudly.

Antunov noticed some of the journalists fold their notebooks and the cameramen start to unplug their equipment. The press conference was winding down. He motioned to his confederates on each side of the room to be alert for Bauer's exit. Out of the corner of his eye, he noticed the Latvian stand up. He'd been keeping him in view throughout the entire session trying to remember how he knew him. It suddenly came to him. Bilgis, Colonel Ringin Bilgis, GRU, Special Center!

Antunov instinctively started down the aisle toward him. He saw Bilgis reach into his camera bag and pull out a chrome American .45 automatic. Antunov yanked out his Sauer P230 and pushed a woman out of the way. Bauer stopped in mid-sentence as he caught sight of Bilgis' gleaming weapon rising toward his face. Antunov fired first.

The bullet shattered Bilgis' right elbow, sending the .45 flying. The second shot blew open the base of his neck. Stunned, Bauer's bodyguards failed to draw their weapons. Antunov's men converged on the stage as the screaming and pushing started. Most of the reporters dove to the floor. Some tried to run for the exits. The cameramen rushed toward the stage for better pictures.

Antunov grabbed Bauer by the shirt front, twisting him off his feet, and pinning him on the table while his men disarmed the bodyguards. Seizing Bauer, they punched and kicked their way through the fire exit to a waiting car. Antunov jumped into the front seat. Bauer was jammed into the back. They pulled away, tires smoking, sliding sideways on the cobblestones as the driver tried to point toward an arched passageway to the street. Another car, big and black, suddenly loomed ahead. Both hit the brakes too late. They slammed together head-on.

Dazed, Antunov was vaguely aware of the right rear door being opened. He turned around enough to see a large fat man wearing a raincoat poke a long black object into the back seat. Then he recognized the soft rip of a silenced MAC-10, and pieces of Bauer's head began flying around the inside of the car.

Antunov passed out. When he awoke, the police and an ambulance were there. A man opened his door and tried to help him get out. It was Sean Gordon.

77

Imeni Gastello, USSR   10:03 ZULU

Work is the only satisfaction, Colonel Sadoff said to mollify himself. Supervising the alert in his buried command capsule, he was still angry from his telephone conversation with his wife. Once again, Masha refused his plea to leave her position as an engineer at the hydroelectric power station in Magnitogorsk. "What would I do on the empty steppes of southern Russia, living in a military *shtetl*?" Her use of a Yiddish word for a Jewish village to describe the base under his command deeply offended him.

He was proud of his troops at the Strategic Rocket complex and how smoothly they had implemented Vigilance II. The crews had topped off the tanks for fuel and oxidizer, recycled the programs for the fourteen separate warheads on each of the ICBMs in his battery, and spun up the gyroscopes that guided the "bus" that would dispense each weapon to an American ICBM silo. Packing the power of two million tons of TNT apiece, there were enough warheads on just his nine heavy missiles to destroy the entire United States Peacekeeper ICBM force, with weapons to spare to take out the Lo-Ads antimissile defense, NORAD, SAC, and other high priority targets. And there were thirty-three more heavy missile batteries just like his—in addition to more than 1200 other multiwarhead ICBMs scattered across Russia.

But if the Americans fire first, Colonel Sadoff thought to himself, what would be left? One or two missiles, if he was lucky. His steel and concrete command capsule was made from an ICBM silo, and could withstand two thousand times the pressure of the atmosphere. But it would probably end up inside the bomb crater. And even if he lived, what would he shoot at on the American side, empty holes?

Then he thought of Masha tending her turbines in Magnitogorsk. Maybe she was right to refuse children, he admitted. Whether there or here, she would not survive no matter who went first.

Warren Air Force Base, Wyoming 10:27 ZULU

Major General Andrew Hanson could not help wondering if the exercise had anything to do with Chip McCollough's call over the weekend. He rechecked the console: all four squadrons in his wing of M-X Peacekeeper ICBMs were on line. Two were reporting anomalies that were expected to clear up. The Lo-Ads close-in antiballistic missile defense for the silos was up and ready. "For all the good it will do," he said to himself.

As a young Air Force staff officer, Hanson had fought for the Midgetman—a small, truly mobile ICBM that could hide from any Russian attack. But the Air Force bureaucracy could not resist making it heavier and heavier. And when the costs had soared, the Congress had cut it back to only a few squadrons.

"Those of us stuck with the Peacekeeper are just sitting ducks, hoping the Army can protect us with Lo-Ads," he lectured every entering group of Squadron Commanders. "But the Army knows, and we know, and the Russians know, it can't. Lo-Ads just guarantee that the Soviets will strike first while they have plenty of warheads to overwhelm our defense."

General Hanson knew that if this were a real crisis, the vulnerability of the Peacekeeper and the Minuteman ICBMs would be putting enormous pressure on Washington to "use 'em or lose 'em." But he firmly believed that the United States would never be the first to launch a nuclear war. Nonetheless, he was nervous. The exercise had a funny smell. It was too sudden, too big, and at a strange hour of the day for a routine test. Maybe he would tell his wife to take the kids and spend the day up at the fishing cabin in the Medicine Bow mountains—just to make sure.

Arkhangelsk, USSR 10:58 ZULU

The meal would not be sumptuous but, despite the limits of a one-room apartment, Galina Makarova had done her best to make it a festive occasion. Excited that her two cousins Anatoly and Arkady

Kropotnik both were in port, she had made them a special supper. Anatoly had just become Captain of the S-421 Typhoon ballistic missile submarine, a promotion that had not been properly celebrated. Arkady, having made Captain two years earlier, was returning to Arkhangelsk from patrol in the North Atlantic in his S-217 D IV Class ballistic missile submarine.

With rumors of the crews being suddenly called back to their subs, Galina was relieved when she opened the door and found Anatoly with a jar of fresh caviar left over from an official reception. Arkady arrived moments later with two bottles of vodka. One was consumed over the caviar, and the other almost empty before they had finished the borscht. Anatoly was relating how he felt, after being sworn in as Captain, to learn that his new Typhoon submarine had defective pumps and would have to be overhauled for three months before it left on its maiden voyage. Since that already was four months ago, he described how he tried to complain to the Ministry of Heavy Industry.

"So there sits this *aparatchik* looking like a sack of potatoes, and before I can even start to protest about how far behind they are on my pumps, he starts in on me:

"'Captain Kropotnik, you are behind in your Equipment Failure Analysis Report. You're behind in your revised specifications. You're behind in obtaining Fleet Replacement Request . . .'

"And so I finally interrupt Comrade First Deputy Second Alternate Minister. I say, 'I come here to talk about your behind, not my behind!'"

His brother Arkady started laughing and coughing so hard that Galina had to hold his chair from tipping over.

There was a knock on the door. An ensign from Fleet Headquarters stated the two Captains were to report to their ships immediately.

In fifteen minutes, Arkady's S-217 was under way. As Anatoly watched him depart from his immobilized Typhoon, he deeply envied his brother. He did not know that two miles outside the harbor the US hunter-killer submarine SSN *Stingray* lay waiting on the bottom.

Like more than half of the Russian ballistic missile subs, the 217 spent most of its time at sea unknowingly in the boresight of an American hunter-killer submarine. The *Stingray* had trailed the S-217 across the North Atlantic and White Sea for three weeks, and when Arkady left port, it would pick him up again. If a US first strike order were given, the *Stingray* would launch four MK-48 torpedoes. Two minutes later the S-217 would die a muffled death two hundred fathoms down in the White Sea. If the Soviets were ordered to attack first, Arkady would only be able to launch two missiles before the *Stingray* would strike.

But while Arkady felt safe, Anatoly, stuck on the surface in port, felt extremely vulnerable. If the Americans struck first, Arkhangelsk would be a prime target. He would die standing on the bridge tied to the dock. His cousin Galina would be killed in her tiny apartment with the uneaten reindeer stew waiting in the oven.

His instructions were to be prepared to launch all twenty of the nine-warhead SS-N-23 ballistic missiles from dockside. They were targeted to destroy every port and airstrip on the Atlantic Coast and the Southern Great Lakes. He had seen the numbers. One hundred ten million Americans would die. But only if he received orders to fire first.

Aboard the USBN-733 Nevada,
Diego Garcia, the Indian ocean   11:29 ZULU

"Dive! Dive! Dive!" lieutenant Commander Jason Berkely shouted over the intercom as the three-hundred-foot Trident submarine cleared the last coral reef coming out of the lagoon. The Chief Operations Officer's voice had the extra authority of genuine anger. The *Nevada* had planned to stay in port another twenty-four hours, and Berkely was still nursing his sunburn and his hangover when the alert sounded.

"What a fucked-up patrol," Berkely said to Captain Paul Nuzzo. "First this lieutenant j.g. gets an attack of appendicitis. Then Washington gets an attack of the loonies and orders an inventory. And you get an attack of the dip shits and drag the men back from shore leave." The two had been friends since running on the same mile relay team at the Naval Academy.

"I didn't call it," Nuzzo said evenly.

"Well, when was the last time the COMPACSUB called—"

"Never, to my knowledge. Jay, it looks to me like State Orange. You'd better get to your station. If we get the authenticator, we're to go with target set Alpha."

Berkely was staggered. He made his way slowly back to his position at the missile launch console and strapped himself in. He thought of his wife, Boots, and his five-year-old son, Jay, Jr. They were at home in Charleston, no more than a mile from the likely aim point of any Soviet attack. There was no way he could warn them.

I never really got to know the kid, Berkely thought. He's just a baby. I always thought I'd have time when he was more of a person. Tears welled up in the Lieutenant Commander's eyes at the thought that there might never be a grown person named Jason Berkely, Jr.

He wiped his eyes with his sleeve and began deploying the ELF receiver and the receptors for the blue-green laser communications link from the ORICS satellite. An authenticated message from either one would send two hundred forty missile warheads arching into Russia. He had no way of knowing that the missile warhead targeted on Charleston would come from Anatoly Kropotnik, nor that the *Nevada* would be killing Galina Makarova in Arkhangelsk, Masha Sadoff at the hydro power station in Magnitogorsk, and Boris Sadoff at Imeni Gastello. But he knew it would be at least ninety million Russians.

Pechora, USSR   11:36 ZULU

For over an hour the Bear, Backfire, and Blackjack bombers and the TU 121 tankers had been arriving at the northern Arctic staging base at Pechora. Fyodor Yefimov sat on a bulldozer at the edge of the runway. His usual job was to clear the runway of snow, but on emergency alerts his task was to push crashed airplanes to one side so others could take off and land. Thus far, he only had to drag a disabled Backfire off the tarmac.

Yefimov was freezing. He took a sip of vodka. Reindeer piss, he swore. Across the runway and over a low rise, Yefimov could see the huge Hen House radar cranking up to full power. The radar was the size of a soccer field turned on its side, and at maximum power, a faint blue halo of ionized air surrounded it even in daylight. Overhead, a flock of migrating Arctic terns suddenly froze in the radar beam. A hundred birds hung in the air a moment and then plunged to earth, cooked well-done before they hit the ground.

As Yefimov sat pitying the birds, he felt a warm flash of light to his left. He turned in time to see an aging Bison tanker, its landing gear collapsed, scraping down the runway in a plume of fire. This will take some work, Yefimov thought, and took another drink.

Flight Commander Vladimir Borodin saw the crash from the cockpit of his disabled Backfire bomber. He checked the tail number. It was not his tanker, and he forced himself to give it no more thought. He also had been trying not to think of his mother and father in Moscow. But the effort itself was a way of thinking about them, and his weakness irritated him. He had more urgent matters—his crew was searching for a replacement for the connector that had caused a major electrical failure in his aircraft. He did not want to be grounded when the American missiles arrived.

As the long minutes passed, Borodin studied his attack route. It would take him over central Canada, across Montana, to the missile fields of Wyoming. Arriving long after the Russian missiles had landed, his mission was armed reconnaissance. He was to locate and attack unused or undamaged ICBM silos. His backup targets were the oil fields near Casper and the town of Cheyenne. If we go first, Borodin thought, our big missiles will take out their air and missile defenses. If not . . . That was another thing he did not want to think about.

Hudson Bay, Canada   11:44 ZULU

The strange bat-like aircraft had just finished midair refueling from a KC 10 Tanker and turned north past the "fail-safe" line. General "Tex" Whittiker was at the controls. His copilot, Colonel "Bud" Budreaux, said, "You know, we practice this so much we probably won't know when it's the real thing."

"That's the idea," Tex Whittiker responded. "But this here no-notice exercise's kinda strange. I've never, in twenty-five years, seen a no-notice exercise with no notice."

The General had three months to go before retirement and was one of the few senior officers in the Air Force entrusted to fly the Stealth bomber on its most sensitive peacetime mission—to enter Soviet airspace secretly and conduct reconnaissance against Soviet ABM sites and mobile and dispersed command and control headquarters. On receipt of orders, he was to attack and destroy them. If the US struck first, his would be the opening blows of the war.

As they approached the Russian coast, General Whittiker reached into a pocket in his flying suit and brought out a black eye patch.

"Are you really going to wear that?" Bud asked. "I thought it was just an old-timer's myth."

"Bud, my boy, I'm probably the only one still flying in the Air Force who's ever seen one of these babies crack off. I want to have at least one good eye to try and steer me home."

"But we've been told that these gold plated goggles will—"

"Listen," Tex Whittiker interrupted as the aircraft silently slipped across the invisible line into Russian airspace, "when these mommas cut loose, you'll find that everything you've ever been told is bullshit."

Trans-Siberian Railway, USSR   11:51 ZULU

From the outside, it appeared to be an ordinary freight train pulling slowly through the vast Siberian forest. Inside the false boxcars, General Staff Officers of the Railborne Alternate Stavka of the Strategic Rocket Forces monitored the status of the Vigilance II alert: Air Armies at 80 percent readiness. Nuclear Missile Submarine Forces Pacific TVD in Prime Minus One condition, Sub Forces Arctic TVD at Prime Minus Four, Atlantic TVD at Prime. Theater Rocket Forces in Western TVD assuming Dispersed Survival Posture. Intercontinental Rocket Forces ready to pre-empt.

The huge "Hen House" and early warning radars had been tied to the "Dog House" and "Cat House" battle management radars for the new antiballistic missile rings around Moscow, Leningrad, Kiev, and

Volgograd. The PVO STRANY air defense forces across the Soviet Union had reached full alert.

The double encrypted Operations Message flashed from the Train, to the Airborne Command Posts, to the Alternate STAVKA VKG, and to Stremski Fortress in Moscow.

1. VIGILANCE II IMPLEMENTED.
2. IT IS JUDGMENT OF THIS COMMAND THAT US STRATEGIC FORCES POISED FOR FIRST STRIKE. IN SUCH EVENT, NEITHER ARMED FORCES NOR PARTY CAN ASSURE MILITARY AND POLITICAL INTEGRITY OF SOVIET STATE.
3. TO LIMIT DAMAGE, RECOMMEND VKG SEEK DEFENSE COUNCIL AUTHORIZATION FOR PRE-EMPTIVE EXECUTION OPTION OMEGA AGAINST KEY AMERICAN COMMAND AND CONTROL FACILITIES.
4. AWAITING ORDERS.
Y.P. MAKSIMOV, COMMANDER IN CHIEF SRF.

Offutt AFB, Omaha, Nebraska   11:55 ZULU

CIA and Defense Department satellite systems fed a continuous stream of data to SAC headquarters on the identity and changing position of mobile targets in the USSR, on the radar "order of battle" of Russian air defenses, and on the status of Soviet strategic offensive forces. JSTPS mission planners in the underground bunker of the SAC Headquarters building used the data to continuously update the bomber attack routes and the target programs in the command data buffers at missile control centers across the western United States.

General Phillip Tinguely, Chief of the Strategic Air Command, also reviewed the data on the status of the exercise. He was pleased that his people had produced a 97.8 percent readiness rate for Peacekeeper and a near-perfect 99.3 percent rate for its ABM LOAD defense system. The subs, as usual, were in good shape, but he took personal satisfaction in the fact that his bombers managed to pull an unprecedented 63 percent availability rate. Half the B-52s, laden with bombs, nuclear-tipped SRAMs, and cruise missiles, were on airborne alert. The B-1Bs had already dispersed to civilian airports outside of Des Moines, Tulsa, Indianapolis, and a dozen other, smaller cities. The FB-111s at Pease AFB, New Hampshire, and Plattsburgh AFB, New York, were standing strip alert. His bombers alone could drop five thousand nuclear bombs on the USSR, some as large as twenty-five million tons of TNT.

However, General Tinguely grew increasingly concerned as he watched the progress of the parallel Soviet alert. He placed a conference call to the Chairman of the Joint Chiefs of Staff, the Secretary of Defense, and the White House.

"Gentlemen, I have to advise you that sometime in the next few hours the Soviet Union will be in a position to launch a small-scale attack that would completely paralyze our ability to retaliate," General Tinguely reported.

"How's that possible?" Loggerman protested. "Sure, the ICBMs are vulnerable, but we put the subs at sea, the bombers are on alert—"

"It's our command and control," General Tinguely responded. "Two hundred and fifty, maybe three hundred weapons max, and we'll lose connectivity. We won't be able to fire back. Some subs might go on their own, but that's about it."

"That's preposterous!" the Secretary of Defense exclaimed. "What've we been spending our money on?"

"Mr. Secretary, a few years ago the Russians could've put us out of business with only a dozen weapons."

"What about your airborne command post—Looking Glass?" Loggerman asked.

"The Russians can barrage it. They've got a general idea of its location, and they can put twenty two-megaton warheads in the vicinity." General Tinguely did not bother to tell them that the five-mile-long VLF antenna trailed by Looking Glass had, as usual, broken off.

"We can count on the KNEECAP, but you've got to get the President ready to move," General Tinguely concluded.

A yawning silence greeted the SAC commander, who was not privy to the fact that the NEACP was on Spitsbergen with the President.

"Any other recommendations?" Loggerman finally asked.

"Declare State Scarlet."

"What would that do?"

"Predelegate launch authority to local commanders. So if the Soviets go first, at least we wouldn't be caught with our pants down."

"I don't know . . ." Loggerman said hesitantly. "There must be other alternatives . . ."

"Yes," General Tinguely took a deep breath. "We could consider preemptive options ourselves," he said quietly, trying to keep his voice even.

"The policy of the United States is retaliation," the Defense Secretary said woodenly. "To strike second."

"We've never ruled out first use," Loggerman corrected him. "But could we really keep the Russians from striking back?"

"That's not really the question." The Chairman of the JCS spoke for the first time. "If you really think it's going to happen, that there's going to be a nuclear war, you don't compare going first to going second. If they get in the first shot, hit Washington, Omaha, NORAD, the Rock, we'd never recover. Never recover control, never recover anything . . ."

78

Spitsbergen   12:02 ZULU

They walked in silence down the road from the airstrip to the mining complex. Even with the car following them, Fyakov worried about Chalomchev walking so far in the cold. He had never seen the General Secretary so despondent. It frightened him.

Chalomchev had not spoken two words since receiving the message from the Defense Council and word that Culver was not on the train. Now Fyakov steeled himself to give him the news about Bauer. He did not know how to begin.

The mining camp consisted of only a few buildings, an office, a power station, several equipment sheds, two dormitories for workers, and a canteen. The faded yellow wooden structures were dominated by a huge ore processing facility clad in rusting corrugated iron. A web of conveyor belts rattled overhead carrying the crushed rock from the nearby mine. They turned toward the open pit, the circle of Kremlin guards shifting in their direction.

Chalomchev's thoughts had fled into the past. They were not comforting thoughts. The crimes came back to him. But he always told himself that the terror, Stalin's cruelty, even Brezhnev's injustice and corruption were all necessary to defend the motherland and build Communism. The Russian people had been made to sacrifice everything for the future, now the future was threatened as well.

"So, the Stavka VKG recommends full civil defense measures, including evacuation?" the General Secretary said.

"Yes. I sent a message warning that evacuation could provoke an American first strike."

"And their response?"

"The Stavka of the Strategic Rocket Forces is arguing that they must pre-empt the anticipated American first strike."

"I've spent my whole life strengthening our military," Chalomchev said bitterly, "so that Russia would never be attacked again. But now our very strength brings on this peril."

They had come to the edge of the pit. Only a few steam shovels and bulldozers and a handful of men were working. The quality of the ore did not justify a larger investment, since the main purpose of the mine was for the Soviet government to assert control over the island. Still, in forty years they had managed to dig a hole a mile across and almost a thousand feet deep.

"We are no longer in control of events," the General Secretary said.

"Our agent in Washington questions the President's control."

"The President has my sympathy. Our comrades in the Defense Council are all trying to distance themselves from me."

"You can still count on the Party against the military," Fyakov protested.

"Perhaps. But the message to come home means that they have decided that I made a fatal error in meeting the President. It put me at his mercy. I must get concessions or it's over for me."

They watched the digging for a few more minutes before Fyakov spoke again.

"I have more bad news. Bauer is dead. Antunov reports that the military sabotaged our plan to apprehend him in Berlin. They tried to kill him, too, after his press conference."

"I thought you said he *was* killed?"

"Yes, later, by Culver, but he got away again."

"So Culver *is* in Berlin," the General Secretary almost shouted. Color had come back to his cheeks.

"But we don't know where. I authorized Antunov to join the hunt, but—"

"That still deals me another card! We go back." Fyakov waved for the car. As they got in, Chalomchev said, "I want to talk with every member of the Politburo *not* on the Defense Council. Then arrange for a full Politburo meeting at 17:00 Moscow time."

"That's only an hour before the deadline . . ."

"Exactly!" Chalomchev pulled off his gloves to rub his hands together.

79

West Berlin   12:11 ZULU

"We used to call this 'cruisin' for burgers,'" Gordon said to Antunov and Graciela Morena. We'd drive up and down the Coast Highway listenin' to the radio, starin' at people." Gordon was trying to keep his spirits up. The army driver behind the wheel of the open jeep turned off Berlinerstrasse and into Clay Allee, making ever widening circles around the Free University.

The radio crackled, "That's a roger, oh-nine-hundred, sector Victor two is negative." The Army was running a radio check every ten minutes on each of its patrols. Culver could not be found.

"We told ourselves we were looking to pick up girls," Gordon mused, "but more often got into punchouts. Girls were more scary than fights." The young army driver nodded in agreement.

"We would drink," Antunov said, getting into it, "but no cars. In a park or, in winter, a cabaret. Then there would be fights. And not real fights, pushing fights. Vodka makes you too drunk to really fight."

They rode in silence while the radio continued a string of disheartening negatives. Gordon noticed his watch creep past one o'clock. "Where the hell is Culver?" He slammed his hand on the dash, his frustration breaking through.

"I tell you, growing up a teenager in America is a trial by violence," Gordon tried to resume the previous conversation. "Graciela, you're virtually a teenager, am I right?"

"I wasn't afraid of other kids. There were bad gangs, but they were just trying to be like grown-ups. I was afraid of my stepfather."

"Sir," the driver broke in, "I think we're being followed."

Gordon turned to look back. Their slow cruising had added to the heavy lunchtime congestion. Gordon could see a dark sedan darting back and forth in traffic, trying to gain on them.

"Alex?" Gordon demanded.

"It's not one of ours."

"We're sitting ducks in this thing. Turn the corner!"

The jeep tipped up on two wheels.

"Pull over behind the kiosk. Graciela, head for that door. Okay, now!"

The jeep leaped over the curb then slammed on its brakes. Gordon dove behind the kiosk. Antunov took cover between the line of parked cars while the driver deployed his M-16 in firing position across the hood of his jeep.

Down the street, the sedan pulled into a driveway, then up onto the sidewalk and hurtled toward them. The army driver snapped his M-16 onto full automatic.

"Don't shoot, don't shoot!" Billy Kelly was standing half out the sunroof of a Volvo waving his arms. The car slid to a stop.

"What the hell are you trying to do?" Gordon said angrily. "Why didn't you radio? We could've killed you!"

"CIA's radios can't call yours. I had to find you. The NEST team's got him localized near the Ku Damm on Sybel and Lewishamstrasse, maybe Mommenstrasse."

"That's where we took a hotel room," said Graciela, "Mommenstrasse."

"How far?" Gordon asked anxiously.

"Ten minutes, if we're lucky," Kelly said.

Culver did not feel well. He stood on the corner of Waitzstrasse looking at the hotel from across the street. It had a new name, the Teheran. The hand-lettered sign was the only freshly painted thing on the whole block. He crossed the street and entered the front door. The lobby was dark and smelled of curry and cooked goat.

Most of the furniture that he remembered had been removed. One side of the lobby was stacked with piles of carpets. Boxes and crates took up most of the rest of the room. He sat on the one remaining couch.

The clerk, a young Iranian, came out from behind the reception counter. Assessing Culver as an American, he asked in English, "Can I help you with something?"

"I stayed here once," Culver replied.

"We've no vacant rooms. We're not really a hotel anymore. We have long-term tenants."

"Can I sit here for a moment?" Culver asked.

"Yes," the clerk said dubiously.

Culver sank back into the lumpy cushions. He was spent. The food the Lauks had given him was turning to acid. Mental images of Bauer's head coming apart and the suffocating odor of cooking made him nauseous. But he felt too weak to rise and go outside.

Gordon's jeep closed in on Mommsenstrasse from the south. The CIA car carrying Billy Kelly cut through the Holtzendorffplatz and approached from the west.

Sean Gordon was on the radio to a military patrol rushing in from the east. "Stop every bus and taxi on the Ku Damm, Kantstrasse, Lewishamstrasse, and Leibnizstrasse. And get somebody into the U-Bahn station at Wilmersdorferstrasse. We just can't miss him again!"

* * *

Culver sat forward on the couch. He could feel the salami he had eaten on the train rise into his throat.

"Do you have a bathroom?" he gagged.

"To the right, in the back."

Culver stumbled down the hall and through the door into the Herrentoilette. The Western-style toilet had been yanked out. It was now only a fetid hole. He threw up all over the floor.

A US Army Hummer blocked Mommsenstrasse to the east at Wilmersdorferstrasse. Kelly's black Volvo sealed off the western end of the street at Lewishamstrasse. Gordon coasted the jeep quietly up Waitzstrasse, turned, and brought it to the curb in front of the hotel. He jumped out and stepped quickly in the door with Graciela right behind him.

The clerk instinctively knew what they wanted. "If you're looking for a large American man, I believe you'll find him in the water closet." He pointed down the hall.

Sean Gordon knocked on the door. There was no response. He carefully pushed it open. The only evidence of Terence Culver was the remains of his breakfast.

Gordon dashed into a small walkway behind the hotel leading to the Gervinusstrasse. There was no sign of Culver. Shouting into his walkie-talkie, Gordon ordered Alex to pick him up and the other cars to fan out over the next two streets. They found nothing.

"Where the hell is he?" Sean said, pulling Graciela aboard the jeep. "He can't be far. He's carrying at least forty pounds. There's no taxis or buses."

"Perhaps," said Alex, pointing upward, "he took the S-Bahn." Gordon stopped. Of course, Gordon thought, the East German elevated train. No one in West Berlin had used the S-Bahn since the Wall was built more than twenty-five years before. But the East Germans kept it running as part of their claim to all of Berlin. So it had circled the city, year after year, a ghost train, blocked from consciousness, seemingly invisible. The Charlottenburg station was only a block away.

Just as Kelly's car and Gordon's jeep converged on the S-Bahn station, two trains pulled out, moving in opposite directions. Gordon ordered Kelly to chase the train headed to Westkreuz. Gordon, Alex, and Graciela caromed through traffic trying to beat the other train to the Zavignyplatz station.

Terence Culver was not on either train.

Having run out of West German marks, Culver had been unable to buy a ticket with US dollars.

"You stupid woman, you won't take a thousand-dollar bill for a fucking railway ticket? That's Germany for you!"

In a rage, he pushed open the doors of the waiting room to hear the squeal of tires against the cobblestones below. He looked over the railing in time to see an olive drab US Army jeep and a Chevrolet do a brief minuet to get around one another and back onto the street. The car headed west, the jeep toward downtown.

Culver recognized Graciela. Where are they going? Then he glanced around at the trains disappearing in opposite directions and started laughing uncontrollably.

Still gasping for breath, he made his way heavily down the iron steps to the street. After gaining control of himself, he crossed over to the Dresdener Bank, to buy German Marks. He then hurried two blocks to Fritschestrasse, where he ducked into a post office.

Culver squeezed his bulk into the single international calls booth. Through the window, he could see a line of military patrol cars pass by. It had been close. But he felt no panic or alarm. Culver was, in fact, puzzled that the only thing he did feel was a slight sense of disappointment.

Peter Andretti, immediately patched the call to the KNEECAP.

"Mr. Culver?" said Admiral McCollough.

"This is the last call I'm going to make."

"Mr. Culver, the President of the United States wants to speak with you."

As in Paris, Terence Culver had the odd desire to stand up, but in the small booth with the weapon strapped to his middle, he could not.

"Mr. Culver."

"Yes," said Culver trying to keep a surge of panic out of his voice.

"I've been negotiating nonstop with the Soviet leaders for the last fourteen hours." The President's own voice was growing shaky. "We've been making progress. You've accomplished a great deal by bringing us together. All we ask is more time."

"What have you agreed on?" Culver asked.

"Mr. Culver, we need more time. We'd like to be able to talk to you." He paused and continued as if reading from notes. "We're reopening your case. The Czech matter. I'm sure we can get you an honorable discharge."

"But I just killed somebody. I've stolen a nuclear weapon. It's strapped to my chest."

"Of course you'd have to return it," the President went on hurriedly. "And we've talked to your mother. She's concerned about you . . ."

"Was she sober? Look, no more deals. No more betrayals. Forget me. It's over for me. Get rid of the weapons."

"It's not that damn simple!" the President finally exploded.

"I don't want to do this," Culver said quietly, "but I'm setting the timer for 15:00 ZULU. It's gonna happen some time, Mr. President. Better here than in America. Maybe it will wake people up."

The line was silent for a moment.

"Mr. Culver, why did you call?" the President asked wearily.

"I don't know, I guess I just feel sorry for everything."

80

Aboard NEACP, Spitsbergen   12:33 ZULU

That close to the North Pole, magnetic anomalies filled the secure voice system with shrieks and pops, making it a strain for the President to follow Loggerman's detailed description of the Soviet strategic alert. However, the basic message was loud and clear.

"In sum, Mr. President, the possibility of a major Soviet nuclear attack must be taken seriously," Loggerman concluded.

"Karl, I've been trying to tell *you* that for several days." The President's mind was reeling. He felt unsteady on his feet as his aircraft bounced and swayed from the fierce wind that swept Spitsbergen every afternoon. He sat down in the chair at the head of the metal conference table and tried to think systematically, but his thoughts kept being blotted out by the face of his anxious wife and then his accusing son. "Why do you want to be President?" they asked him over and over.

"Why would anyone do that? Even consider it . . ." the President sounded lost.

"If the Russians could decapitate us, they might keep their casualties below World War II," Loggerman explained.

"What ever happened to tit for tat?"

"Mr. President, you're the primary target, now," Loggerman ignored his question. "The Soviet soldiers guarding the KNEECAP can put it out of business with their AK-47s. Unless you get out of there soon, you'll be the first to go!"

The Russian alert. State Orange. Safety catches slipped on both sides. Culver setting the timer. The President felt trapped in a waking nightmare. "But I have to try to negotiate. If I leave, that's tantamount to pushing the button . . ."

"If you stay, the NSC has to declare State Scarlet. We've got to predelegate authority to fire—"

"I don't know what authority *you* think *you've* got, Karl, but I'm not predelegating anything!"

"But Mr. President, you could even tell the Russians. That would protect you and strengthen our deterrent."

The President was silent for a moment, then he spoke slowly and forcefully. "I am not predelegating my authority over nuclear weapons in any way, shape, or form. No way. If there's a nuclear war, either the Russians are going to start it, or I'm going to. We've already got one person too many running around with his finger on the trigger."

"But there's no alternative."

"Yes, there is."

"What do you mean?"

"Turn it off!"

"That's impossible!" Loggerman exclaimed.

"The alert was supposed to be a signal. It was defensive. Not the start of nuclear war!"

"Mr. President, nuclear alerts are extremely complicated." Loggerman's tone had become patronizing. "They've been planned and refined over the years. We can't just step in and try to micro-manage—"

"I don't want to manage anything!" the President shouted. "I want it stopped!"

Loggerman took a moment to respond. When he did, he spoke indulgently, as if to a backward child.

"We can't. It could be fatal. There'd be an enormous drop in readiness. You can't turn it on and off like a faucet. We'd be more vulnerable than before the alert."

"You mean there's no brakes on this goddamned machine?"

"Mr. President," Admiral McCollough broke in, "it's time for your meeting with the General Secretary."

The President turned and opened his mouth to yell at the Admiral and stopped. He fought for control. "Dr. Loggerman, I have to go. But I want you to call a meeting of the full NSC immediately. I'm going to talk to all of you myself. And in the meantime you figure out how to turn this monster off. That's an order!"

Afraid to hear Loggerman's reply, the President hung up. He sat for a moment trying to compose himself. With reluctance, Admiral McCollough spoke.

"I hope you realize, Mr. President, that you're not the only one who can release nuclear weapons."

"What are you talking about? Only the President has the authority—"

"Legally, yes. And your constitutional successors, and the NMCC, and the 'Rock', and SAC, and Looking Glass. They all can launch if you're incapacitated."

"I see." The President was starting to get the picture.

"As a practical matter, sir, they can also launch even if you're not."

81

"So! You are preparing for war!" Chalomchev declared.

"Correction, *you're* preparing for war," the President retorted. "We're responding to your actions . . ."

"And you think you can threaten to attack the Soviet Union and we will do nothing?" Chalomchev shouted.

"You've no further response to my proposals?" the President asked uncertainly.

Chalomchev looked at him as if he were mad. "Here's our considered response!" He pulled a folder out of Fyakov's hands and threw the contents at the American interpreter. "You read!"

The interpreter hurriedly looked at the message.

"It's from my Defense Council. They say your alert is a breach of good faith. It's unacceptable intimidation. It requests that I terminate the talks immediately."

The American interpreter nodded his head to confirm Chalomchev's version of the message. The President sat perfectly still, as if the slightest movement would shatter the air around them.

"We must talk under four eyes," Chalomchev finally said in English. The President looked baffled.

"He wants the two of you to talk, privately," the interpreter said.

"Don't you think that's dangerous when we don't speak the same language?"

"Mr. President, our advisors prepare for war. No help are they for peace. We are maybe only ones of our countries who speak same language."

The President gestured for the others to withdraw. But when they were finally alone, Chalomchev sat and said nothing.

"Is this some kind of a goddamned game?" the President demanded.

"Unfortunately, yes, and game we are losing both, no?" The General Secretary watched for his reaction.

It was the President's turn to say nothing.

"I do not hide fact I control little now. I know also you are not controlling American actions."

The President winced at the accuracy of Chalomchev's remark. "Then why 'four eyes'?" he asked testily.

"We are responsible men. We have interest in peace." He allowed a small and rueful smile to appear. "And we share interest in neutralizing home enemies."

"Yes, events are out of control," said the President. "But there's still time. If you could agree to a mutual—"

Chalomchev held up both hands. "No, no, no! Understand, please. If this were peace talks, Brest-Litovsk, following after weariness and horror of war, then dramatic changes would be possibilities. But instead what? Bullying by madman and threats by America. Russia full of power and pride. Ask in such circumstances yourself what would do your government? What you propose can only come *after* wars, not *before* them."

The President felt the hopelessness of that truth wash over him. "So where does that leave us?" he asked quietly.

"In Berlin!" the General Secretary exclaimed. "You have not thought meaning of bomb exploding in Berlin?"

Startled, the President waited.

"We both suffer! East! West! We both damage! Is no justification to attack us. We could threaten same attack."

"You already have. That's part of the problem." Behind the flippant reply, the President struggled to figure out where the General Secretary was heading.

"Can you not read between lines?" Exasperation came into his voice. "We are in same boat, Gaspodin, President. I you help."

The President knew that meant he was asking for help.

"What can you do for me?"

"I have secret. Powerful secret. Why I know troubles you have. How you get control."

"And in exchange?"

"You help me control, too. Maybe then, both we can deal."

"Tell me your secret first," said the President.

82

The Tiergarten, West Berlin   13:10 ZULU

Sunlight stuttered on the windshield as it filtered down through the branches of the linden trees. Spring had come suddenly to Berlin, and the park had exploded with green leaves and filled with people admiring them.

By the time Gordon, Antunov, and Graciela had arrived at the Bundespost office, Culver was long gone. They circled futilely and then decided to retrace Graciela and Culver's route through the city. That had led them to the Tiergarten and the Berlin Wall.

Alexander Antunov could not avoid the bad feelings he always felt approaching the Wall. All ideology and politics fell away in its presence. The watchtowers, the armed guards, the minefields and barbed wire, all made the human failure of the East obscenely obvious. It was a prison, and Alex knew the shame of being a warden.

Only official cars and tourist buses were allowed on the wide avenue that led up to the Wall. It had once been part of Unter den Linden, Berlin's most famous thoroughfare, filled with stylish motorcars and fashionable people. Now it was a dead-end called the Street of June 17, the date of the 1953 uprising against the East German Communist regime.

They passed the Soviet War Memorial. Ahead, the Brandenburg Gate stood in the no-man's-land between East and West. To the left rose the burned-out hulk of the Reichstag, a testament to the fire that had catapulted Hitler to ultimate power. Culver and his ultimate power were nowhere to be seen.

"I can't remember every step we took," Graciela complained. She seemed exhausted. Her bronze skin looked gray. "But I know we came down the street here," she said, "and then we went up onto the platform to look over into East Berlin."

A bus had parked near the platform and a crowd of young Africans were milling about waiting their turn to see over the Wall. The group leader said that they had just arrived and had seen no one fitting Culver's description.

As Sean Gordon turned the jeep around, Alex said, "I'm going to ask the guards at the Soviet Memorial if they have seen anything."

The two guards refused to speak. While Antunov waved his KGB identity card and cursed in Russian, they stoically stood guard over an old T55 tank. Gordon asked the British Tommies who guarded the Russians whether they had seen Culver. They had not, but they threatened to arrest Antunov. Sean had to drag him back to the jeep.

"Graciela, think!" Antunov turned on her. "Where did you hold hands? Where did you kiss? He had to relieve himself. Where did he go to the toilet? Where did he shit?"

"Hey, take it easy," Sean intervened.

Antunov slumped down in his seat. The pressure was getting to him, and he knew it. He regretted taking it out on Graciela. Was it because he was Russian, he wondered, that he found it so difficult to say, "I'm sorry."

83

Aboard NEACP, Spitsbergen   13:20 ZULU

"I can't do something like that just on the say-so of the General Secretary of the Soviet Communist Party!"

Admiral McCollough could sense the President's nerves were about to snap. He had seen it in other commanders, paralysis of decision, a form of overload. "What did he say the man's name was?"

"Weat or something."

The name struck a bell for McCollough. "Could it have been Weede?"

"I suppose." The President did not seem interested.

McCollough picked a large brown envelope off the conference table. It was marked LOGGERMAN'S BOOK.

"Reginald Weede."

"That's it."

"He's a Brit. Related somehow to MI6."

"So Chalomchev said."

"Mr. President, according to Dr. Loggerman's notes, Weede's an old personal friend."

"That doesn't make him a spy."

"How about the fact that it was Weede who convinced Loggerman that Culver was the double agent responsible for blowing the Czech operation?"

The President sat back, trying to absorb the implications.

"Culver walked into a trap. Antunov told Sean it was a setup. Culver claimed that the British agent was the double, but our people decided it was Culver, mostly on the word of an unknown British intelligence source."

"What does that prove?"

"Loggerman was our contact with the source, and the source was Weede. He talked Loggerman into killing any investigation and making Culver the mattress."

The President looked as if he'd been punched in the stomach.

"Do you think Loggerman deliberately . . ."

"I'm not saying that," McCollough said. "But you do have grounds to isolate him!"

"I think I'd better lie down for a little bit."

"You called an NSC meeting," Admiral McCollough objected. "They should be in the Sit Room now. You wanted to talk to them. You've got decisions—"

"Dammit, I've got too many decisions!" he shouted at McCollough. "Even if I can get my own people under control, what then? What should I do? Save my Administration? Save lives? Save NATO? Seize the moment and risk God knows what on the hope for a deal with these sleazy, fucking Russians? I'm sorry, Chip. I'm so tired. I need a nap. . . . Maybe Sean can still find him . . ." the President said vaguely and wandered down the corridor to his room.

Admiral McCollough was at a loss. He put through a call to Sean Gordon. As he filled him in on the President's condition, the Admiral could hear the noise of street traffic in the background.

"Put him on the line," Gordon said.

The President took the call in bed. "It's not really a deal, Sean, Chalomchev still insists we don't retaliate," he said dully.

"Turn it into one," Gordon said angrily. "Make some demands. Get something from them."

"I'm not even running our government anymore . . ."

"You can change that!" Gordon insisted.

The President shut his eyes. His mind circled endlessly on the dilemma—that an agreement with Chalomchev that would keep Culver from setting off the weapon could only be reached after the weapon explodes.

"Mr. President, the trail's gone cold here. In one hour, the bomb will go off. What happens after that is entirely up to you. We'll be dead." Gordon hung up.

The President looked at the phone for a long time and then said to Admiral McCollough, "Get me the Attorney General and the Secretary of the Treasury."

84

The Potomac Terrace Apartments, Washington D.C.
13:51 ZULU

"Why doesn't Karl answer the bloody bell?" Reginald Weede muttered to himself and burrowed deeper under the down comforter over his head.

The doorbell continued ringing insistently.

Weede sat up, remembering Loggerman had not come home the night before. Getting out of bed, he hurriedly searched in his luggage until he found his silk Turnbull and Asser robe. He paused momentarily at the door to check the knot holding the robe across his middle and to run his hands through his hair. Then he cracked the door open a few inches.

"My God!" he exclaimed, staring at the Cultural Attaché of the Soviet Embassy. "What are you doing here?" He flung open the door. "Get inside, quick!" He pulled the Russian forward by his lapels.

"I had an urgent message from Moscow Center that you had to speak to me, here!"

"What on earth—"

"The desk downstairs said you were expecting me . . ."

Panic crossed Weede's face. "You must get out of here!" He opened the door again and pushed the Russian into the hall.

"What are you doing?" The Russian resisted.

"It's a trap, you bloody fool." He kept pushing.

The elevator bell sounded and the light went on.

"No! Take the stairs!" Weede started dragging him in the opposite direction. The Russian began to run. Weede turned around to find the door had closed and locked behind him. The elevator began to open.

Weede dashed down the carpeted corridor and turned right toward the stairs. He could hear loud knocking on a door and then footsteps rushing up the stairs ahead of him. He stopped at a door marked FIRE EMERGENCY. It was open. The Russian was inside.

Weede squeezed in with him. They could hear the voices in the hall, and someone saying, "The apartment is empty." Then it became quiet. They waited in the dark for what seemed to Weede an eternity while the Russian's breath, stinking of the pickled fish he had had for break-fast, made him feel faint. He had to open the door. As Weede turned the knob, it was yanked out of his hand.

"You girls are under arrest," said the calm beefy young man with the .38 Special.

Weede held out his wrists to be cuffed. "I assure you, I intend to cooperate fully," he said.

The Situation Room, the White House, Washington D.C.
14:03 ZULU

No one made small talk. The atmosphere in the cramped conference room was anxious and grim. They waited for the Vice President to arrive. Compelled to break the silence, the Secretary of Defense began to complain that *The Washington Post* was about to blow the story.

"That's the least of our problems," Loggerman cut him off. He sat in the President's seat at the head of the table.

The Vice President came in, and hesitantly took the seat at the other end of table, usually reserved for the National Security Advisor. There was no greeting.

"We're called upon to make fateful decisions in the face of great uncertainty," Loggerman said solemnly.

"The first uncertainty is Soviet intentions. You can be sure that Chalomchev's telling the President that if the weapon detonates in Berlin there's no basis for retaliation. While that may be correct in some respects, an American weapon going off in West Berlin would still raise fundamental questions affecting the solidarity of the Alliance. Moreover, the elimination of West Berlin would be a great boon to the Soviets, since it's always been a profound embarrassment for them.

"We also can't dismiss the possibility that by some mad logic the Soviets will see a detonation in Berlin, which could affect the Soviet sector, as justifying retaliation against us. Indeed, they may seize it as a pretext for launching a pre-emptive attack—their alert makes that possible, perhaps inevitable. We must therefore consider our options, including," he paused, "pre-emption. In this connection, I believe we must promptly relocate to hardened facilities outside of Washington."

"What does the President want? Shouldn't we find out what he thinks?" the Vice President asked.

"The President is the greatest uncertainty," Loggerman replied. "He's on an island, ostensibly Norwegian, but to all intents and purposes controlled by the Soviet Union. You must all understand what this means. He may even now be a virtual prisoner of the Soviets."

"Are you suggesting," the Vice President asked, "that we invoke presidential succession? The Twenty-Fifth Amendment?"

"No, I don't think that's required. This is a military crisis, and we've procedures to deal with it. The NSC can invoke State Scarlet and release our weapons for use. We of course would retain decision authority over targeting and timing."

"Holy Mother of God," the Defense Secretary said quietly, "there's going to be a war."

"Not necessarily; the Soviets will intercept the State Scarlet messages. They will know we're relocating. I think you'll see them blink."

He looked at the others. They looked afraid and confused. "All the intelligence points to a Soviet first strike. Isn't that correct?"

Reluctantly, the Chairman of the JCS and the CIA Director nodded.

All eyes turned to Loggerman as a muffled bell began to ring. "A declaration of State Scarlet is a minimum response. If the Soviets strike first at our command and control, we may not be able to strike back. We've got to show that their strategy won't save them from retaliation. We must also—" The bell continued to ring. Loggerman paused to open a small drawer in his end of the table and picked up a concealed phone.

"Mr. Loggerman, this is the Sit Room Duty Officer. The President would like to speak to you privately on secure line two. You can use my office."

He thought of telling the President to wait, but decided against it. "Excuse me for a minute," he said. Loggerman mounted two steps and opened the door to the small sitting area where aides usually waited for their turn to brief the NSC. In a single stride, he took two more steps up to the left, crossed an open area, and entered the small office.

The first Secret Service agent pulled him inside while the second slammed the door shut. The third agent pinned Loggerman in the plush leather chair.

"Don't struggle, you're under arrest."

"By whose authority?" he demanded.

"Mine," came the voice of the President from the speaker box on the desk.

85

Hangar B, Spitsbergen   14:18 ZULU

The General Secretary reread the message a third time before letting the feeling of relief flow through him. I'm getting too old for this, he said to himself. Looking up, he saw that Dimitri Fyakov was frowning.

"You see, it is done." Chalomchev allowed himself a smile. He waved a cablegram. "Ogorodnik is under arrest." He tossed the message to Fyakov. "I never doubted that in a struggle between the Party and the military, the Party would win!"

"But you had to tell them the Americans agreed not to retaliate!"

"Dimitri Andreyevitch, everything is permitted to build the future. Without a future there's no justification for Communism. All the crimes would have been in vain."

"But the President didn't—"

"Do not worry. I know this President. He can read between the lines. The message reporting the arrests in Washington told me that we had a deal."

As if to say, "We'll find out," Fyakov raised his eyebrows and tilted his head toward the President's party entering the hangar.

Chalomchev stood to greet him. "Mr. President, and how isn't Mr. Loggerman, your advisor?" he smiled cheerfully.

The President sat down. "He's been detained for questioning because of his relationship with one of your spies. I don't consider that particularly amusing."

"You have my personal regrets in this matter." Chalomchev returned to using his interpreter, but continued smiling. "It's in the cause of peace. Now I would welcome your assurance that the Soviet Union is no longer under the threat of attack from the United States." He said this pleasantly, making it sound like a routine matter.

"I can't give you that commitment," the President said flatly.

Chalomchev looked at him sharply, then turned quickly to his interpreter, his face turning crimson as he listened to the translation. Then he started to speak rapidly in Russian, his voice rising in fury. Suddenly, he stopped. He reached out to keep the interpreter from speaking. His eyes lost focus.

"You will have to excuse us." Fyakov put his arm around the General Secretary and urgently waved to a Kremlin guard standing in the shadows.

The President withdrew from the table listening to the translation of his own interpreter while anxiously watching Chalomchev. The General Secretary's hands were shaking as he downed first an orange capsule, then a white pill. A doctor came in and spoke with him insistently, but he kept shaking his head no. After a few minutes, Chalomchev began waving at the President to rejoin the table.

"I thought we agreed to prevent nuclear war?" His voice was shaking and plaintive.

"Yes, but in a half hour, the first nuclear weapon since Nagasaki is going to kill a hundred thousand people—mostly people who've relied on the United States for their security. That won't be wiped away by arresting a Russian spy and an unwitting accomplice."

"What do you want?"

"You were right in saying that we don't have the power to agree on mutual steps to meet Culver's demands. Only the shock of the bomb going off will give us that power. I insist we use it to do some good."

"If you threaten us, I am still helpless—"

"I'm *not* threatening you. But look at the situation. Both our nuclear forces are on hair triggers. They threaten each of us regardless of what we want. Words won't make that go away. We need an agreed plan of action to break through our governments' obsession with who's going to strike first. It's not enough to get rid of a few troublemakers. If we don't have an alternative, Culver's bomb will be the signal for both sides to pre-empt."

The General Secretary glanced at Fyakov, who nodded his agreement with the President's assessment.

"You have concrete proposals?"

The President handed over a single page with no heading or date.

"It's not an American proposal. It's not a Soviet proposal. Consider it a 'nonpaper.'" The President looked at his watch. It was twenty-five minutes to the deadline. He began to read.

"When the weapon detonates, the two governments will:

"First, devote all available resources to an immediate international relief effort to assist the inhabitants of Berlin, East and West, and any others affected."

"Of course," said the General Secretary.

"Second, Berlin will be reunited. No wall will be rebuilt."

Chalomchev said nothing.

"Third, the city will be independently administered, reporting to the East and West German governments under Four-Power supervision.

"Fourth, the West German government may move its capital to Berlin."

"Wait!" said Chalomchev interrupting, "this is one-sided—"

"We recognize East Berlin," the President shot back. "Our Embassy's there. We want reciprocity for the West Germans. They're going to suffer most."

Chalomchev began to calculate rapidly. An independent administration over a nuclear wasteland? Who should care? If the West Germans want to move their capital to such a place, again who would care?

"It's possible," he said, "if that's all."

"It's not. Your huge troop deployments in East Germany have always been the greatest threat to stability in Europe. You say you want disarmament? Prove it. Cut the number in half."

"Mr. President, you go too far! What do I take home?"

"NATO will go down to your level. If you reciprocate, we'll also cut our nuclear stockpile in Europe by fifty percent."

"After your bomb goes off in Berlin, you will be lucky to keep any of your weapons in Europe."

"Finally," the President responded, "you get my point."

Both sides were silent. The President opened a bottle of Russian seltzer water, his hand trembling as he filled his glass. It bubbled over onto the table and gave off the odor of a swamp. The General Secretary rolled an unlit cigarette between his fat fingers, turning his wrist to check his watch. Twenty minutes. He weighed his options.

"We've been negotiating troop cuts in Vienna for twenty-five years."
Fyakov broke the silence.

"You mean haggling," the President snapped. "We both know how
to do it. All it takes is willpower."

"If we agreed," said Chalomchev, "it would still take time to imple-
ment. There would be details. Even your bomb might not wipe away
the inevitable objections."

He could see the President bristle.

"Don't think that if you drag your feet you can watch NATO unravel."

"You misunderstand—"

"There'll be war before I'll let the Atlantic Alliance disintegrate."

"The Soviet Union will meet its commitments!"

"If you don't, we'll be right back where we are now!"

"And what of this alert?" asked Chalomchev, his voice cracking with
strain.

"Here's a schedule of mutual steps." The President handed him a
second nonpaper. "We'll go first, as a gesture of good faith."

He saw relief sweep over the General Secretary's face.

"If you agree, the PARCs radar and Grand Forks will be turned off,"
he checked his watch, "in seven minutes. The Cat House radar at
Leningrad or Kiev must go off the air no more than five minutes later."

"My military assistant has to review this."

"Work out any changes with Admiral McCollough."

The General Secretary seemed to have difficulty keeping up. He put
his head in his hands to think. He could debate, but he could see no
alternative. "If we agree in principle, you must reciprocate immediately."

"We will," said the President. "As soon as we've got confirmation
that the weapon's detonated, I suggest we both fly to Geneva and
announce what we've agreed upon."

"Our troop withdrawal will be a gesture to ease the situation." Chalomchev was formulating his explanation to the Politburo.

"And we should stay there until all the details have been worked out
and the alerts ended," the President added.

Chalomchev balked. Remaining in Geneva could reduce his control at home and subject him to more pressure from the Americans. But it would also maintain the political initiative against the Ogorodnik clique and avoid the need to answer awkward questions. "Agreed," he finally said.

"While we're there," the President continued, "maybe we can put some life into the START negotiations. Get rid of these first-strike weapons that brought us to the brink . . ."

"Crises make history," Chalomchev declared, "but peace overnight? It's only a little bomb, after all. And you may be impeached like our only true American friend, Mr. Nixon." Chalomchev tried to smile.

"You said our highest responsibility is to avoid nuclear war. That doesn't stop with this crisis. You're proud of your revolutionary tradition. Fate has given us the opportunity to turn this disaster into an even greater revolution in the history of mankind." The President's remarks took the cadence of a speech. "If we can agree to the first steps—"

"Yes, yes, we agree on the steps," Chalomchev cut him off. "Except for the missiles. That's not so simple. We can agree in principle, and I will say so publicly, but there are important details. Revolutions are not so easy, even from the top. I am sincere. I would not make exceptions, if I were not sincere."

The President and the Chairman looked at each other in silence. They shared a feeling of relief; they knew better than to feel hope.

"And who will you blame?" Chalomchev asked. The President looked perplexed. "Take my advice," the Chairman continued, "blame the explosion on the Arabs. People think they would do anything. But you must not invade any of our friends." He laughed and began uncorking a bottle of vodka. "Better still, bomb Iran. We will do nothing. We might even help!" He laughed again.

As the two of them held the glasses of vodka up to the light, the NEACP's communications officer quietly entered the hangar and handed Admiral McCollough a note.

"*Mir e Druzhba,*" the General Secretary said.

With twelve minutes to the deadline, they clinked glasses. But before they could bring the toast to their lips, McCollough interrupted.

"They've found Culver."

86

Six minutes earlier, Sean Gordon's jeep had turned onto Stülerstrasse after exiting the park by the Hofjägerallee. He crossed the small bridge over the canal and drove onto Budapesterstrasse. At the Europa Center, the jeep rounded the ruin of the Memorial Church and turned left onto the main thoroughfare of West Berlin, the Kurfürstendamm.

Passing the Hotel Kempinski, Graciela said, "Before going over to the Mommenstrasse we tried to get a room there."

"The Kempinski's pretty rich for a lieutenant," Sean said.

"Was he showing off?" Antunov asked.

"No, it was an impulse." Graciela sounded defensive. "We'd just been sitting in a café up the street when Terry said he was afraid he loved me—"

"Where was this?" Alex demanded.

"The Europa Center across from that ruined church. There's a café—"

Sean did a U-turn through the tulips in the meridian of the Kurfürstendamm and raced through a series of red lights. He pulled the jeep up onto the sidewalk in front of the Europa Center. To the left, an open air café spilled out toward the curb. It was full of patrons absorbing the warm sun of a late spring afternoon. Culver was not among them.

"Inside," said Graciela.

At a small table near the window overlooking the street, sat a man bundled up in a raincoat. He had a Berliner Weisse in front of him. The German tabloid *Tageblatt* lay on the table with a picture of Bauer's body and the headline, ERMORDET IN ATOMKONFERENZ! on the front page.

Gordon pushed Graciela forward.

"Terry?"

He looked up at her.

"Terry, can I sit here?"

He said nothing. She sat down.

"These are friends, Terry—Sean and Alex."

Culver simply looked at them. Gordon noticed that he had his right hand around his drink, but his left held a computer joystick with wires running inside his coat. He kept the button on top pressed down. It was a dead-man switch—if he let it loose the weapon would explode.

"Mr. Culver, I want to ask you a question," Sean said quietly. "Why are you doing this?"

Culver did not respond.

"I assume you want to pull out the weapons to save lives," Gordon continued. "How will you do that by setting off the SADM? Look at the people on the terrace. Look at them, do you really want to kill them?"

Culver took a sip of Berliner Weisse. He refused to look out the window. "Maybe you only care about America," said Antunov. "I am Russian. Do you care that you have brought us to the brink of nuclear war? Americans will die in that war."

Culver turned his face to the warm sun pouring in from the terrace. He closed his eyes. The chatter from the other tables and the sounds of the afternoon traffic filled the silence. He smiled.

Gordon fought the urge to shoot him. They would never reach the dead-man switch in time.

"Terry, look at me!" said Graciela sharply. "I'm not asking anything. Blow up the world, for all I care." Her tears had started. "But this time before you kill me, I want you to know I love you."

Culver's face remained impassive. She reached out and touched his right sleeve. After a moment, he let go of the glass and took her hand. They sat quietly for a while. She pressed the back of his hand to her damp cheek.

Suddenly, he stood up and opened his raincoat. The SADM bulged out from his thin chest. He looked at Sean, then Alex, then Graciela. He yanked on a yellow tab hanging under the weapon. It pitched forward and slammed onto the table.

Glass, beer, and strawberry syrup sprayed all over them. Sean leaped on the weapon, jerking the wires out of the dead-man switch. A backhand blow from Alex sent Culver to his knees. Gordon's knife sliced through the few straps still connecting the weapon to Culver's chest.

Alex and Sean ran to the jeep with the weapon between them. "Don't worry about breaking it," Sean said as they heaved it into the rear.

Alex backed into traffic. "Head to the Tiergarten," Sean ordered. "There will be fewer casualties if it goes off there."

Spitsbergen   14:48 ZULU

"How much time do they have?" the President asked.

"About eleven or twelve minutes, we don't know exactly," Admiral McCollough replied. "The SADM's on automatic sequencing now. It has to be dismantled."

"Communications set up?"

"Yes, from the plane directly to the jeep."

"Mr. General Secretary, may I invite you aboard my aircraft?"

"Yes, Mr. President."

As they walked to the plane together, the President and the General Secretary talked urgently. Entering the conference room, the President said, "Chip, the Chairman and I would like complete privacy." He sat down in the huge chair on the inside curve of the large boomerang-shaped table. He invited the Chairman to sit across from him.

Chalomchev allowed himself to light the mashed cigarette he had been clutching.

"So, there's nothing we can salvage from our agreement?" asked the President.

"If bomb disarmed, no."

"We're back where we were before?"

"Lucky we would to be back before," Chalomchev said. "Many broken eggs, but no soufflé. Salvage I try for myself."

"And the whole story will get out," the President said, mostly to himself. NATO will be badly damaged anyway. I'll be in trouble. "I'll have to point the finger at you and Bauer."

"No blame will we accept! We tell world about your threats!"

Neither spoke. Then the President sighed. "We could've changed direction, we could've gotten off this dreadful treadmill . . ."

"Ourselves, too, we could save," the General Secretary said.

"At a great cost in human life," the President noted.

"We pay higher cost in future, no doubt."

"Yes, we came close this time to—"

"We not out of woods yet! The alerts . . ."

"I'll try to follow the nonpaper."

"I can give no guarantees," Chalomchev replied. My position . . ." He shrugged.

They stared at each other for a long time. The President thought, my God, I'm beginning to think between the lines. They both knew what they had to do.

"We'll proceed to Geneva immediately to make the announcements?" the President said.

"But in my own aircraft, please."

"Of course."

They each regarded the other in silence.

Chalomchev thought, this President is like a birch tree, more wind than wood. He bends and shakes and trembles, but stays rooted to one spot.

To the President, the General Secretary looked spent. He wondered if Chalomchev would live to make the deal work. But when the Russian leader spoke, exhaling blue cigarette smoke, his voice was strong.

"Mr. President. Do not mistake. My purpose is safe world for Socialism."

"We're not afraid of competition. We've got some advantages on our side—like the human spirit."

He punched the button to call Sean Gordon and Alexander Antunov.

West Berlin   14:53 ZULU

Gordon, in the back, desperately worked to cut the pouch away from the weapon, as Alex swung the car around the Siegessäule and onto the Strasse des 17 Juni. Above and to the right loomed the East German TV tower like a great metal golf ball. In the reflection of the afternoon sun, a golden cross appeared on the dimpled surface. In spite of being an atheist, Antunov hoped it was an omen of peace, not Armageddon.

"Pull over!" Sean shouted. They hauled the naked weapon and a tool box out onto the sidewalk, where Sean slipped a crowbar under the identification plate and popped it off, revealing a square hole with a nipple at the bottom. He pushed the head of a custom-made hydraulic extractor into the hole and began to apply gentle pressure to the handle.

The radio in the jeep started to squawk. They heard the voice of the President.

"Sean, come in. Come in, Sean. I'm here with Secretary Chalomchev. It's extremely important."

Antunov stretched the microphone cord and held it so Gordon could respond.

"There is not much time, Mr. President," he shouted, still concentrating on the weapon.

"I know, Sean, I want you to stop."

Gordon felt paralyzed. He looked up at Antunov.

"*Lexi.*" It was Chalomchev. "*Prekrati rabotat'!*"

"Comrade Chairman, *no*—" Alex began.

"*Khuatyt!*" Chalomchev cut him off.

"Mr. President, you want us to just let it go?"

"Just get away, Sean. Get away if you can," the President said softly.

87

The Wall, West Berlin   14:57 ZULU

Time seemed to have halted. Sean Gordon caught the image of an elderly man with white hair pointing with his cane up at a linden tree. Two women, arm in arm and pushing a baby carriage, were poised to step off the curb into the street. A tour bus had pulled up to the viewing platform near the Wall. The children bursting out of its confines seemed frozen in joyful liberation. Alexander Antunov stood immobile over Gordon.

Without thinking, Gordon found himself continuing to press down on the hydraulic extractor. Antunov took out his gun.

"We have our orders," he said.

"Fuck our orders."

"Sean, you must do as I ask." The President's insistent voice came from the radio. "I can't explain—"

"I'll bet you can't," Gordon said and started to push harder on the lever.

Antunov slipped off the safety. Their eyes locked together.

"Colonel Antunov, Colonel Antunov," Chalomchev called out. "Stop him!"

Antunov pulled the trigger. The radio exploded.

Gordon looked at his watch. "We've got two minutes, maybe less. I can't dismantle it. We've got to destroy it!"

"Won't it detonate?"

"Pray it's still one point safe!"

Antunov motioned Gordon to stand back and emptied the clip of his Sauer 230 at the weapon and the bullets ricocheted futilely off the titanium dome.

They stood helpless for a moment.

"The Wall!" Antunov said. Gordon nodded. They threw the weapon back onto the jeep and jumped in. Gordon put the throttle to the floor aiming at the Wall. "Alex, get out!" he shouted.

"No! No!" Antunov started to explain, but the Vopos in the tower on the other side of the Wall started blasting their bull horns, "Achtung! Achtung!" The jeep crashed through the wooden warning barricades. The Vopos opened fire. The front tires exploded. Steam and water burst from the radiator. The jeep went into a long skid. It slammed sideways into the curb in front of the Wall and flipped over.

Gordon was thrown clear. Antunov was trapped under the jeep. The SADM lay against the Wall, intact.

"Sean," Antunov was calling to him. "The Wall, *over* the Wall!"

Gordon suddenly understood. The mine fields on the other side. If he could just heave the weapon over the Wall, a mine might set off part of the high explosive. He scrambled over to the SADM. Without its pouch there was little to hold on to. He staggered back to get a run and the Vopos started firing again. He dove back for the cover of the Wall.

Crouching, he tried to use his legs and back to hurl the device straight up. It slipped from his hands.

Desperate, he tore off his jacket and wrapped it around the weapon. Like a hammer thrower, he spun around once, twice, and let fly. He heard it bounce against the top of the Wall. When he glanced up, it was gone into no-man's-land.

He waited for the blinding flash. But there was none. Then he felt the earth move. The Wall came toward him and a roaring filled his ears. He started to smile as he was swept into unconsciousness. He knew he had succeeded. If he had not, he would never have known.

. EPILOGUE

The news of a stolen US nuclear weapon was a sensation. The *London Daily Mail* screamed PINCHED YANK NUKE RISKS WAR. *Le Monde* thundered, "France will assume the thankless task of nuclear deterrence if the Americans cannot keep their nuclear weapons secure." And the prestigious West German newsmagazine *Der Spiegel* had only three words on its cover, AMERICA THREATENS US.

Parliaments railed. The governments in Italy, Denmark, and Belgium fell, only to be replaced within hours by virtually identical coalitions. The Bundestag opened a Parliamentary Inquiry, and the British established a Royal Commission. The Senate passed a resolution condemning the Spitsbergen talks. The House of Representatives threatened impeachment for a cover-up. The White House had to invoke Executive Privilege to prevent Sean Gordon from testifying. Both the US and USSR exchanged accusations and threats. Not surprisingly, the nation rallied around the President. Karl Loggerman was credited with exposing Reginald Weede as a dangerous spy, and then made Ambassador to NATO.

At the Kremlin, former Chief of the Soviet General Staff Marshal Ogorodnik was made a member of the Politburo, where he was allowed to take the lead in hurling charges at the West—in exchange for his full support of Chalomchev. The leaders of both the US and USSR survived.

The furor soon died down. Soviet propaganda proved so heavy-handed that a backlash developed. A week after most of the details had come out, including the story of Bauer and the Soviet role, conservative editorialists were writing that Europe had to run such risks for the sake of the American nuclear guarantee. Even the left-wing press turned from pillorying the United States to demanding that both Washington and Moscow resume negotiations on the "Spitsbergen Accords."

Peace groups carried out scattered demonstrations, but their single concrete accomplishment was to force the Dutch government to give sanctuary to Terence Culver and Graciela Morena. Charges against Culver for killing Bauer were ultimately dropped for lack of evidence.

After a month in a Berlin Hospital recovering from plutonium poisoning, Sean Gordon returned to his cliffside cottage in La Jolla. Laura looked after him for a while, but finally moved out, saying she could not stand the stress of the publicity. He was grateful that his son had decided to join him for the summer, and pleased when his ex-wife and her new husband paid them a visit.

By the autumn, his life had returned to the normal routine of foggy mornings jogging alone on Blackwell's Beach and sun-filled afternoons teaching tanned college students that International Relations was something other than what went on in nearby Tijuana. On weekends, he would often go fishing with Admiral McCollough, who had been hurriedly assigned to command a destroyer flotilla in San Diego. At Christmas, he received a case of Pshorrbräu from Billy Kelly, who had been forced to retire and had settled in Munich. The President never called again.

Gordon thought often of Antunov. They spent several weeks together in the hospital before the West Germans turned Antunov over to the Soviet authorities. He had refused Gordon's offer to try for political asylum.

Shortly after the New Year, Sean Gordon received a call from the Salk Institute. Someone on a visiting Soviet scientific delegation had left a letter for him. Eagerly, he drove down the cliff to the odd collection of concrete buildings facing the sea. The envelope had no stamp or address. The letter had no salutation or signature. He read it with growing happiness.

*　　*　　*

I never finished telling you what happened to the boy whose father took away the money to buy the three newspapers.

Shame-faced, the boy returned empty-handed to his mother, who demanded to know what happened.

"I met Papa in the stairwell," he explained. "He made me give him the money. He said we didn't need newspapers—we have a radio."

"I see," the mother said. She dug deeper into her purse and came out with twenty more kopecks. "Here, go out and buy a *Pravda* for me and *Komsomol Pravda* for yourself."

"And what about Papa?" the boy asked.

"Your Papa?" she replied. "He can wipe his ass on the radio."

ABOUT THE AUTHOR

Few men know as much about nuclear security and the intrigues of Washington as David Aaron. He has served on the National Security Council in both Republican and Democratic administrations: from 1972 to 1974 as Senior Staff member, and from 1977 to 1981 as Deputy Assistant to the President for National Security Affairs. From 1974 to 1976, he headed an investigative task force for the Senate Intelligence Committee. He was a member of the first SALT negotiations, directed the work of the SALT II negotiations as Chairman of the NSC Mini-Special Coordinating Committee, and participated in the Vienna Summit of 1979. He has been sent on sensitive presidential missions to Europe, Africa, China, and Latin America, and in 1981 he won the National Defense Medal, the Pentagon's highest civilian award.

David Aaron currently serves as an advisor on foreign affairs and national security matters to several New York- and Washington-based institutions and individuals, and is on the board of Oppenheimer & Company's Q.F.V. Fund. He lives in Weston, Connecticut.